THE
TAINTED JADE

THE TAINTED JADE

A Michael Garrett Mystery

Richard Blaine

To DJ and, of course, to Ilsa Lund

Chapter One

I t was late-summer sultry. The palm trees lining the downtown streets had the tired droop of soldiers after a full day's march. Every now and then, a dry breeze would slap the tops of the trees, making a brittle rustling noise among the parched leaves. The people passing in the street moved in slow motion, not talking, spending only the effort it takes to get to the next patch of shade. The afternoon sun was raising a shimmer off the pavement along Wilshire Boulevard. The dust rode on the heat pouring in from the valley, lacerating the storefronts along the street and tumbling through my window in the Patterson Building. I had the window open and the fan going, trying to keep the office a few degrees below broil.

Off in the distance, I could hear a siren bleating, announcing the start of the brush fire season. I got up and went over to the window, and looked out into the street. The traffic rolled by in a quiet trek, adding exhaust fumes and overripe rubber smells to the air. Across the street, two men were standing under an awning, talking. They had their jackets off, their collars open, and their sleeves rolled up. One pulled out a handkerchief and wiped his forehead; the other just shook his head. Lots of places get hot, but not many quite like Los Angeles.

I turned away from the window. It had been a long, hard day of counting the pages on my desk calendar, and since 1948 was a leap year, there was an extra page to turn. I had made it as far as September and decided to leave the rest until tomorrow. It was already a week since I'd gotten back from Seattle, but I was still tired from the trip. With bail-jumping cases, you always lose sleep and shoe leather. So, I had decided to rest up over a couple of Scotches at Lacy's.

I was just reaching for my jacket when I heard the rap on the outer door. I waited a minute, hoping it would go away. It didn't. The rap became a metallic tapping—harsher, more insistent. Through the pebbled glass on the outer door, I saw a shadow. It moved impatiently from side to side; then the tapping started again. Sometimes, your instincts tell you to leave things alone. Just walk away and don't look back. You don't often get in trouble listening to your instincts. I went over and opened the door. That's how much I listen to my instincts.

He was a tall, modestly built man, about thirty, and dressed as if the heat was less than a nuisance to him. He had on an ash-gray, worsted suit and vest, a faint orchid shirt with a gray tie, and gray gloves. A soft magenta display handkerchief was barely showing out of his breast pocket, and he was holding a long, rolled umbrella with a gold knob on the end. He looked at me out of blue-gray eyes set wide apart in a thin, pale face. A long, slender nose hung over his small, rounded mouth, and his pencil-thin mustache matched his light brown hair. His delicate features were woven together like the petals of an artificial flower. I couldn't help staring at him. He glanced at my name on the door, then looked back at me. "Mr. Garrett?"

"I'm closed," I said, leaning on the door. "Come back tomorrow."

"But I'm leaving town tonight."

He was standing there cool and dry and dressed like something out of *Esquire*. I could feel the sweat rolling down under my shirt collar, and the thought of Lacy's was making me impatient. I could have knocked him down the hall as easily as flicking an ash off a cigarette. But he had a frail kind of dignity, and I was too tired to argue. "Okay," I said, "Come on in."

I motioned him toward the inner office and closed the door as he brushed by me. A heavy scent of talcum with a hint of rose water around the edges trailed after him. I moved around behind the desk, sat down, and watched as he settled into the client chair with the fluid ease of a heron. He crossed his legs and idly dangled a polished shoe toward the desk. You can tell a lot about people from their shoes. Some are worn. Some are scuffed and beaten up. Some are clean, sharp, and carefully prepared. This guy had shoes that I only saw in store windows and with the kind of shine you expect to see on a new Buick.

He leaned his umbrella against the chair and carefully pulled off his gloves one finger at a time. Then he took out a gold cigarette case and extracted a long, thin thing rolled in lavender paper with a gold-colored filter. He fitted the filter between his lips, took a small gold lighter out of his vest pocket, and, with a graceful scoop, flicked it and held a restrained little flame up to his cigarette. I pulled out a Lucky and lit it, and tossed the pack on the desk.

He inhaled like an asthmatic sparrow, blew the smoke toward the window, then folded his hands in his lap. He perched his cigarette between the first two fingers of his right hand and pointed it at the ceiling. "I am Willis Canton Ordway," he said. Then he added, "The Third."

"You mean two weren't enough?"

"I beg your pardon?"

I shrugged him off and pushed the office ashtray over in front of him. "What's your story, Mr. Ordway?"

He gazed warily down at the ashtray, full of the day's remains, then slowly brought his gaze up to me and twisted his mouth as if he'd just tasted something awful. "I want to hire you ...I think."

"Well, don't think too long. I'm a busy man."

He sat back in the chair and swallowed hard. Then he took another shallow drag on his cigarette and drummed the fingers of his left hand on his knee. The smoke trailed out of his nostrils in unhurried little wisps as his eyes fastened on me, studying, questioning.

He swallowed again, reached over toward the desk, and crushed out his partially smoked cigarette in the ashtray. Then he sat back and put his hands on the arms of the chair and started to squeeze. His voice came out with a shrill insistence. "I'm sorry, Mr. Garrett. But this is very important. It's a matter that requires a great deal of trust. I hope you understand."

I took a deep drag on the Lucky, exhaled heavily, and looked at him. It always spoils my mood when people are polite.

"All right," I said, "but don't expect a lot. It's late, and I'm thirsty." Then, I reached over and crammed the end of my cigarette into the ashtray.

"I'm Michael Garrett. You saw my name on the door. I'm a private investigator, licensed by the state of California. I used to be a cop until I told somebody in the department to go to hell. It happened to be the Chief of Detectives. I work on my own, no associates and almost no overhead." I waved my hand upward across the desk, inviting him to look around the office. He did and started to cringe.

"People usually hire me," I continued, "because they don't want to go to the cops or because they already have and got the gate. I do a lot of work that the cops don't have time for, like hunting up stolen property or chasing after a bail jumper. I don't take divorce cases, and I try to stay inside the law. If I take your case, I'll stick with you for almost anything short of going in front of a grand jury. For that, I might blow the whistle. If you want more loyalty, buy a dog."

He took his hands off the chair and squeezed them together in his lap, the skin around his knuckles starting to whiten. A slow flush began creeping up the sides of his neck.

"I'm sorry," he said. "I didn't mean to offend you. I'm afraid I'm not used to this sort of thing, hiring a detective. To be entirely candid, you're the third person I've interviewed this afternoon. As I said, it's a matter involving a great deal of trust."

"Why did you come to me?"

He leaned forward in the chair. "Actually, I was referred to you by someone at the Clement Agency. You may know them? Over on Sepulveda?"

"I know they charge a lot more than I do."

The muscles around his jaw tightened about a half-turn. "Yes, well…." He reached inside his coat and pulled out an oversized brown leather wallet. From this, he took out a small white card, which he placed carefully on the desk in front of me. Then he returned the wallet, sat back in the chair, and focused an uncertain expression on me as I picked up the card. It had black embossed lettering that read, "Ordway's Antiques and Imports," and it had a Brentwood address and phone number.

I replaced the card on the desk and looked at him. "All right, Mr. Ordway. This is the last time I'm going to ask. What can I do for you?"

"It's about... Well..." He took another swallow and put his hands back on the arms of the chair. "I want you to be me." He read my stare and quickly added, "That is, I want you to represent me at an auction."

I sat there and watched a nervous pulse start to throb over his right eye. He began to blink rapidly and fidget in the silence. His eyes darted around the office and then back to me. I just kept watching him. He recrossed his legs and cleared his throat.

"The auction is being held in El Paso on Thursday, day after tomorrow. It's a private auction being conducted on behalf of Colonel Stanfield Wearing." He paused and looked at me for some sign of recognition. When I didn't give him any, he went on. "Colonel Wearing owns and operates a chain of newspapers. As you might suspect, he's a very powerful and a very wealthy man. The Colonel is also an amateur collector. He is reputed to have a very fine collection of Mexican relics and artifacts, although not many people have actually seen his collection."

Ordway paused long enough to lick his lips. "About three months ago, he began auctioning off pieces from his collection. The auctions have all been held privately, with invitations sent to selected museums and a few private collectors, but no dealers. So far, the sales have brought about seventy-five thousand dollars, quite respectable for an amateur collection, of course. But I have reason to believe that on Thursday, there will be a piece put up for sale that's worth a great deal more than that amount by itself."

He leaned forward in the chair, put both hands on the edge of the desk, and lowered his voice to a shrill whisper. "I'm not sure you understand, but I think it's part of the Marina Jade."

I didn't say anything. He wouldn't have heard it anyway. He caught his breath and lifted his left hand in front of him, the fingers probing the air, while his eyes floated off to a distant fascination.

"Just think of it, Mr. Garrett," he said. "The Marina Jade. It dates back to 1519, you know, to the Spanish conquistador Cortez." He cleared his throat and began speaking as if he were reading to me out of a history book. "When the Spaniards first landed in Mexico, they took a number of the native people into their retinue as guides and interpreters. One of them, a young Indian maid named Marina, caught the eye of Cortez. She became his courtesan and the mother of one of his sons."

He brought his palms together and began rubbing them back and forth, then went on. "As Cortez and his forces started inland toward what is now Mexico City, the great Aztec emperor Montezuma received word of their approach. He was told of demon armies laying waste to everything in their path, and he became fearful that Cortez was really the legendary Aztec god Quetaz returning to avenge some past sins. As a peace offering, Montezuma sent a pair of Jade figures, a prince and a princess, hand-carved and said to be in the likeness of Cortez and his beloved Marina. Cortez accepted the gift and then imprisoned Montezuma. From that point, the Spanish rule of Mexico became one of increasing repression until a religious uprising occurred in June 1520. At the height of the rebellion, Montezuma appeared on the steps of the great temple and tried to calm his people. But they stoned him, and he died later that evening. Not long after that, Marina died mysteriously, and the jade figures disappeared. Cortez became a lonely, embittered man. He finally died in 1547 after years of dissipation and sickness. The Aztecs believed that it was Quetaz taking his revenge."

Ordway eased slowly back into the chair, folded his hands, and focused his gaze on me again. His voice had picked up a trace of self-assurance. "There is no record of the figures for over three hundred years following the death of Marina," he went on. "Then, around 1850, a German archaeologist named Braunheit is reported to have found them in the ruins of an Aztec temple. But almost immediately after their discovery, Braunheit died for no apparent reason, and the figures were left at the Mission of Vera Cruz. They remained there until they were confiscated years later by Benito Juarez on behalf of the Republic of Mexico. But after the death of Juarez in 1872, the figures were not to be found, and the entire episode has always been disputed."

He clasped his hands together and brought them up under his chin, resting his elbows on the arms of the chair. A look of quiet certainty crept over his face. "There was a jade figure sold at the auction last month. From the description I think it may have been part of the Marina Jade...the Princess.

It went for a terribly low price, under ten thousand dollars. I really think the Colonel doesn't know what he has. If I'm right, then the Prince could be put up at the next auction. I want you to go there and see. If you can verify that it is the Prince, then I want you to buy it for me. I'll back your bidding up to, shall we say," he swallowed hard, "fifty thousand?" He looked at me expectantly, then dropped his hands sharply back into his lap. "Of course, I don't expect you to have to bid anywhere near that much. Still…" He shrugged. "There is no known source of jadeite or 'pure' jade in Mexico, so the Marina Jade must have been brought from the Orient by the earliest ancestors of the Mayans and the Aztecs. As an art treasure, the figures are very valuable, but their historical value is almost beyond estimate." He drew in a breath and let it out with the resignation of someone rolling the dice for his last buck. "Yes. If it is the Prince, I'll back you for whatever amount you need." He finally stopped talking, leaned back in the chair, and projected a look of quiet satisfaction, as if he'd just finished delivering the Gettysburg Address.

I studied him for a minute without saying anything. Then I reached over and pulled out another Lucky, lit it, and slowly blew the smoke across the desk at him.

He shifted abruptly in the chair and gave me a brittle scowl. "Well? Have you nothing to say? Doesn't any of this mean anything to you?"

I let out a sigh and shrugged. "It leaves me breathless."

His eyes widened. "I beg your pardon?"

"Oh, don't," I said, "not again. Just tell me how I'm supposed to get into this auction."

He brought his hands tight together and licked his lips. "I'm meeting someone tonight who will give me one of the printed invitations. Tomorrow evening, you come to my room in the Hotel Del Norte, and I'll pass the invitation over to you. I'll also give you a description of the Prince." He paused. "And, Mr. Garrett, I hope you can manage all this without attracting attention. My presence in El Paso must be kept secret. Any speculation that you are really representing me could push the bidding up beyond all reason."

"What about the money?"

"After the bidding is over, you'll have twenty-four hours to make payment and claim the figure. If you fail to do so in that time, the figure goes to the next highest bidder. All you have to do is call me at the hotel, tell me the amount, and I'll wire for the money. You'll have it in plenty of time. Once you have the figure, leave town immediately. There should be a late train. Just come straight back here and wait for me to contact you."

"Is that all?"

He nodded. "But I must implore you, Mr. Garrett. Keep the Prince safely hidden and speak to no one about it. And please try not to handle it unnecessarily."

"Don't worry," I said. "I'll see that the Prince gets the lower berth. And would silk pajamas be all right?"

He pushed himself against the back of the chair and scowled. "You needn't be sarcastic."

"How do you know about these auctions?"

His face turned the color of a boiled egg. He spoke almost without moving his mouth. "Through a friend."

I grinned at him. "I could have guessed that much. Does your friend have a name?"

The corners of his mouth turned a taut gray. His eyelids began to flutter. "I don't see how that makes any difference."

I chuckled. "I didn't think you would." I took another lazy drag on the cigarette and sat back, and watched the pulse over his right eye begin again. "So, all I have to do is sneak into El Paso, pretend to be an uninvited guest at an auction, and outbid everybody for a little green statue without letting on what it's really worth. Then, while nobody's looking, I just scrape up a loose fortune, tip my hat, and sneak back out of town without disturbing the Prince and without getting shot at. Is that about it?"

He opened his mouth to speak, but nothing came out.

"No good," I said. "Try again."

He swallowed hard. "I...I don't know what you mean."

"All right. Let's assume it makes sense for a dealer in Brentwood to know all about some private auctions in El Paso, including what was sold and for how much. I still want to know why you need a detective to do a job that could be done better and maybe cheaper by a lawyer or another collector. I want to know who you talked to at the Clement Agency. I want to know why you were turned down twice before coming to see me. And if it's not asking too much, I want you to tell me something that isn't just a pile of bird droppings."

His face twisted into what seemed like anger. "Now, see here! You've no right to speak to me that way."

I abruptly crushed out my cigarette and stood up, and motioned toward the door. "I can't help you, Mr. Ordway. Let's just call it a day."

He stood up stiffly, his fingers trembling. Then he grabbed his umbrella and began wringing it in his hands as if he were throttling a goose." But... But I'll pay your fee. And your expenses. Isn't that enough?"

I eyed him for a minute and then chuckled. "You're a hot one, Ordway. You come strolling in here and put me on the grill and talk about trust. Only, you haven't given me an ounce of it. And that gives me no reason to trust you. Maybe you think that a detective doesn't have to trust his client. And maybe you think that Mae West is just a skinny kid."

He stood rigid and looked at me as if I were a firing squad. I looked back at him now without really seeing him. I was picturing the cool glass of Scotch sitting on the bar at Lacy's. I walked around to the side of the desk and pointed toward the door again. "I was closing the office anyway, so I won't charge you for the time. Just beat it, and we're square."

His face fell all at once, like summer rain. For a minute, he stood and stared at me. Then he sagged and slumped back down into the client chair. He let his umbrella fall carelessly against his leg while he rested his hands limply in his lap and shook his head.

"Dammit, you're right," he murmured. "I'm just no good at this. But she won't listen to me. She just won't." He squeezed his hands together. "I simply don't know what to do."

I stood there in the heat and watched him. Somehow, you always know when it's one of those special times when you have to make a choice. You have to decide to get in or get out. When you make the right choice, you forget the moment. It's gone forever. When you make the wrong choice, it keeps coming back. Asleep or awake. You have to live with it. And the ones you remember most are the times you got in when you shouldn't have. It was none of your business, but you got in anyway. I looked down at Ordway. This was none of my business.

I went back around behind the desk and sat down. I let my breath out heavily and dragged out another Lucky. I lit it and sucked in a quarter inch of poison, and covered the top of the desk with smoke. Ordway was still sitting limply and shaking his head. I sighed again and let a fleeting picture of Lacy's drift off into nowhere.

"All right," I said. "Let's have it."

He heaved out a long sigh and looked up at me slowly. There was a firm set to his jaw. "I've told you the truth," he said. "It's just that…well, there's more."

"There always is," I said dryly.

He settled back in the chair. "I've known the Wearings for over ten years," he said. "Or at least I've known Gabrielle. She's the Colonel's daughter. I met her when I was at Yale. We've been friends for a long time. Not really close, you understand, but we've kept in touch. About two years ago, Gabrielle's mother died. Then, late last year, the Colonel remarried. Since then, I hadn't heard from Gabrielle until suddenly yesterday she called me. She seemed very upset, worried about her father. She told me about the auctions. She said her father has been sick, and his new wife is actually arranging all the sales. Gabrielle thinks that this woman may be stealing from her father by taking auction proceeds. The woman couldn't know the real value of the collection. She simply sells off a few things each month, not getting very much for any single item. But the Colonel is losing a great deal in the depleted value of his collection."

"Sorry, Mr. Ordway. The courts don't call that stealing. They call it community property."

"I know," he said. "Gabrielle asked me to see what was being sold, and if anything of real value was put up, I was to buy it for her. Of course, that was to be kept secret. That way, she could protect at least the important parts of her father's collection. You could call it Gabrielle's way of buying off a woman she believes to be a gold-digger. After enough is sold, she hopes the woman will leave."

"So, you play Good Samaritan for Gabrielle," I said. "You can do that without me."

He nodded. "I agreed to help, but then I heard about the jade. That's when I knew, when I understood the danger. I tried to explain it to Gabrielle, but she wouldn't listen. She just called me superstitious."

"Listen to what?"

A glaze crept into his eyes. His voice took on a reverence mixed with fear. "To the ancient warning. To Quetaz. According to legend, after the death of Montezuma, Quetaz became enraged and demanded that his people return the figures to his temple in central Mexico. He promised great wealth and power to anyone who served him by returning the figures. But for those who were unfaithful, who tried to possess the figures for their own gain, Quetaz vowed certain destruction for them and their families." He blinked his eyes and sucked in on his lower lip. Mr. Garrett, I'm afraid for…for Gabrielle. The figures must be returned to their rightful place. That's why I need your help."

He reached abruptly into his coat, brought out his wallet, took out a pair of C-notes, and laid them on the desk in front of me. I peered down at them. Benjamin Franklin was looking very well.

"You'll be taking a serious risk," he said. "For that, I'll pay you this now and three hundred when you return."

I sat there eating my cigarette and staring at the money, and staring at him, and staring at the money. When I didn't say anything, he leaned over, placed both hands on the front of the desk, and spoke to me from someplace far away.

"Mr. Garrett, for over four hundred years the Marina Jade has been sought after by explorers and adventurers from all over the world. It's a prize that men have fought over again and again. But the ancient Aztec writings say that the curse of Quetaz remains with the Prince and Princess, that no one shall possess them. And Mr. Garrett"—his voice fell to something barely above a whisper—"the jade is tainted. Almost everyone who has been in direct contact with the figures has mysteriously died."

Chapter Two

The Santa Fe Limited streamed into the desert morning. It cruised past the layered rock formations and cactus plants and the endless miles of sand and dust. The long shadows of dawn shortened, and the bright patches of early-morning color faded into gray-brown as the sun moved up higher in the sky. Off in the distance, some lingering currents of night breeze churned up little eddies of dust that danced across the horizon, looking close yet far away. Distances blur out here, especially at this hour. What's near seems far and what's far seems near. It's just part of the vast indifference that the desert shows every traveler. I watched it all through the coach window. There's a majestic monotony to a train ride across the Arizona desert. There's also time to think.

Ordway had insisted that we travel separately to El Paso. He took an early flight, leaving me on my own hoof and warning me not to arrive any sooner than necessary. That was all right with me. I prefer the train. He didn't exactly tell me to hide out, but under no circumstances was I to let on that I was meeting him. And, of course, I was to stay at a different hotel. When it was dark, I was to call him, get the number of his room, and go directly there. No checking in the lobby.

He had told me what he could about the Wearings, which wasn't much. They had lived in Chicago until after the war, then moved to El Paso because of the climate. The Colonel's wife had always suffered from asthma.

The Wearings had two children: Gabrielle and an older son named James. According to Ordway, James was something of a rogue. I took that to be his word for someone who likes to play in fast company and doesn't care about the cost. And Gabrielle was the family upstart. She had gone to school in the east, left for a while to travel, and then returned there to study law. She refused to live the life that her father had planned for her, avoiding all the men that he deemed acceptable. Before starting law school, she had pranced around Europe with everyone she could find who had a title and a pair of pants.

In the later years, Mrs. Wearing's asthma had gotten much worse. Even the desert hadn't helped. The Colonel flew doctors to El Paso from all over the country. But his wife declined steadily and finally died.

Since moving to El Paso, the Colonel had become interested in Mexican relics and history. When his wife died, he began spending more and more time with his collection. Ordway had speculated that her death was connected to the jade figures. The Colonel seemed to lose interest in everything else until he met and married his second wife, Monica, a woman not much older than his daughter. Beyond that, Ordway didn't have much to tell me except to repeat what he called the ancient warning. I didn't much care for his story about an angry Aztec god and a pair of jade figures. But I cared a lot for the two hundred bucks he had given me.

My train hadn't left L.A. until close to midnight. That gave me time to do a little digging on my own. I made a stop at modern man's most overlooked source of information—the public library. From there, I visited the morgue at the *L.A. Times*. This flash of detective brilliance gave me more background on Colonel Stanfield Wearing.

One way or another, Wearing had been in the newspaper business for over forty years. He grew up in Chicago and started delivering as a kid, later working after school at the *Daily Sun* as a copy boy. When he finished high school, he wrote obituaries until, around the end of the First World War, he landed a job as a reporter covering fires and chasing ambulances. His name first started appearing in print in 1923 with a series of articles linking some local bootleggers to City Hall. The stories got a lot of attention, and Wearing parlayed that into an appointment to the governor's anti-rackets commission. From there, he campaigned against the mob, built a tough law-and-order reputation, and made a lot of important contacts.

In 1925, Wearing married Victoria Clement, the daughter of a Chicago judge. He was promoted to managing editor of the *Daily Sun* in 1927 and began writing syndicated articles and making radio broadcasts exposing some dirty politicians with mob connections. By the time of the crash in 1929, Wearing had saved enough money to buy the *Daily Sun*'s rival paper. During the next ten years, he built that small paper into a chain extending from New York to LA.

Wearing ran his operation like a dictator. He used his political savvy and connections and gradually became very influential in state and national politics. His papers put a lot of muscle into supporting the New Deal and, later, the war effort. Wearing himself was given several awards, first by President Roosevelt and later by President Truman.

He was called the Colonel, yet as far as I could tell, he had no military record. But then, what else would you call somebody worth almost fifty million dollars? He was a self-made man who had built an empire by being single-minded, tough, and ruthless. He had accumulated both wealth and enemies. Somehow, they always go together.

I yawned and stretched and tried to coax the blood back into my arms and legs. The midnight run of the Limited had only a single sleeping car, and that was full, so I had spent the night dozing in my seat. By morning, I felt as if I'd gone fifteen rounds.

I leaned back in the seat and looked around the coach. It was almost empty. Behind me, toward the rear of the car, a heavy-set dark-haired woman was tending two small children, a boy, and a girl, both dark-haired. The boy was stretched out on the seat, and the girl was cradled in the woman's arms. They had been that way most of the night. A few rows in front of me, two Mexican boys in their early twenties took turns sleeping and smoking and looking out the window. They sat across the aisle from a slender man in a dark suit and hat. From what I could see, he had very pale skin and almost pure white hair. And he kept his left arm pressed close against his side, as if he had something to protect. I hadn't seen much of his face, but when he got on the train in San Bernardino, his movements had been smooth and firm, not aged. Now he just sat there in the seat, not moving, maybe asleep, maybe not.

Across the aisle from me was a man in a coffee-with-cream suit, brown shoes, brown-and-white check tie, and a coconut-colored straw hat with a wide chocolate-brown band. He was heavyset, with thick legs and an urgent paunch that strained the buttons of his salmon shirt and pushed against his belt as if he had a basketball strapped to his middle. He had boarded just behind me, prowled up and down the car looking at the seats, and then settled into the one across from me like a sultan lowering himself into his bath. He had spent most of an hour poking at a small brown notebook with a mechanical pencil and muttering to himself. Once he had finished muttering, he had leaned back, tipped the brim of his hat down over his face, and gone to sleep. He hadn't moved since.

I watched some more parched landscape roll by and wondered about Ordway and the Wearings and the jade. I tried to get interested in the paper I had bought the night before. That wasn't easy. News these days didn't amount to much except stories about the fall election. And everybody seemed sold on Governor Tom Dewey. As far as the papers were concerned, Harry Truman had nothing left to do but pack his bags and head back to Missouri. It all seemed pretty far away to me. Neither one of them knew anything about a guy named Garrett. I looked out the window again. I felt dry and humorless, just like the desert.

"How're you betting?"

I looked across the aisle at a pair of light hazel eyes stuck in the middle of a bloated, reddish face. They stared out from under the coconut straw hat. They went with a thick-lipped mouth, a double chin, and a short, wide nose that showed a mesh of tired, straining capillaries. The face was at least forty-five.

"I said, how're you betting?" he repeated. "On the election?"

I put down the paper. "Does it matter?"

He curled his mouth into a smile that wasn't really a smile. "Guess you're right at that. Looks like poor old Harry's pretty well washed up." He shook his head. "Still…"

He shook his head again and waved his pale, puffy hands around in the

16

air, as if groping for a conclusion. He didn't find any. He pushed his right hand in my direction and curled his mouth a little more. "Jack Springer," he said. "I'm a reporter for the El Paso *Sun Register.* Maybe you've heard of me?"

I took the hand and squeezed. It was moist and limp, and it had the bracing feel of cold mashed potatoes. "I don't think so," I said.

"Then you're not from El Paso?"

I dodged the question. "I don't read the paper much. I guess if I did, I'd know all about you."

He smiled like someone who wanted me to know all about him. "I was a war correspondent for one of the news services. After the war, I was offered a job with the Wearing chain. I've had a couple of stories that made the wires. One good crime story, and I figure I can break into syndication."

"There must be a lot of money in crime," I said.

He chuckled. "There sure is, friend. A lot more than you get for writing about lonely hearts." He took his hat off and put it on the seat next to him. A thin, horseshoe-shaped fringe of brown hair stretched around the back of his head and just over his ears. He was as bald as an egg.

He sat back in the seat for a minute and seemed to reflect. "You have to have a nose for it," he said. "You have to be able to sniff out the stories. And you have to be sharp; keep your eyes peeled. You can pick up a lot just from watching people."

A scowl popped onto his face, and he turned back toward me. "Take you, for instance. Now, I don't know who you are or what you do, but I'll bet I can peg you pretty close." He made an elaborate study of my suit. Then he frowned. "I'd say that you travel a lot, that you're out selling something. Right?"

"That's amazing," I said.

His eyes brightened, and a grin started. "Insurance. Right?"

"How do you do it?"

His grin sent creases up both sides of his bare skull. "It's all the years in the business, the experience." He raised his right hand and poked his nose with his index finger. And it's this, the talent." He folded his hands across his belly and looked at me with a satisfied smirk. "Okay, so who are you, and what do you do?"

I thought about not answering him again. I thought about giving him a hundred different stories just for fun. But the conductor chose that moment to come through the car and announce that breakfast was being served. Springer bounded down the aisle and into the next car as if his shorts were on fire. The other passengers got up and slowly meandered after him.

I went into one of the lavatories, washed up, shaved, and then decided to try the dining car. I sat alone by a window and ordered coffee. I sipped it, lit a cigarette, and watched the other passengers.

Farther down the car, Springer sat with his back to me across the table from the white-haired man. I couldn't hear what he was saying, but I didn't have to. His puffy hands fluttered back and forth above the table like pigeons courting a statue. The man just sat there with his hat pulled low and his arms folded. Finally, he rose abruptly and moved quickly past me, head down, and disappeared into the coach.

Springer sat there, his hands suspended in mid-flutter. He looked around at the other passengers, wondering if he ought to be embarrassed. After a minute, he shrugged and got up from the table. As he started up the aisle, he spotted me. Without asking, he poured himself into the seat across the table from me. He put his hat down next to him and watched me sip my coffee the way a cat watches a mouse hole. Finally, he got tired of waiting for me to say something.

"I told ya," he said. "I can always sniff 'em out."

I just looked at him.

He put both elbows on the table, leaned forward, and lowered his voice. "That guy with the white hair. He's into something. And I'll bet it's something big."

"Did he say anything?"

Springer shook his head. "Nope. Didn't have to. I told ya. I can peg 'em. That's my business. And with this guy, I smell a story."

"How can you tell?"

He gave me a knowing look, the kind you get from a magician when you

18

ask him how a trick works. He leaned forward a little farther. He brought his voice down a little lower. "Like I said, ya gotta be sharp. Like, for instance, from up close I could see that the guy isn't really an old man."

I sat back and looked at him. "Imagine that."

"Yeah," he said. "And I'll tell you something else." He looked around quickly to make sure no one else could hear. "I think he's carrying a gun."

Chapter Three

T he train plodded through the day. It stopped in Phoenix and then Tucson just long enough to remind me that there's more to life than sitting down. Springer spent the time napping and poking at his notebook. A couple of times, he walked up the aisle and back, each time inspecting the white-haired man. He moved with the stealth of a bowling ball rolling down an alley. But the man just sat there with his arms folded and his hat pulled down and didn't budge. He considered Springer with the same regard you give the lint caught in your cuff.

By late afternoon, we rumbled across the Texas state line, slowed, and finally crawled into the El Paso station. The terminal was a low, cinder block building with sand-caked windows. It was stretched out, tired and dusty, behind a wooden platform that ran along the track. The coach lurched and settled directly in front of a pair of screen doors in the middle of the building.

We had barely stopped when the white-haired man got up, quickly went up the aisle, and left the coach. He darted across the platform and into the terminal and didn't shoot anybody. Springer struggled to follow him, but he was ten years and forty pounds off the pace.

I took my bag off the overhead rack and watched the other passengers begin to gather on the platform and drift toward the baggage car. On my way out of the coach, I stopped to ask a porter if there was a hotel in town besides the Del Norte. He looked at my suit and told me to try the Desert View Motel. I wasn't sure if I should thank him, but I did.

I walked through the small dusty terminal, past an empty ticket counter, and out into the street. The sun was settling behind a mountain off to the left, leaving streaks of orange overhead. The air was cooling, but it still carried a parched scent of afternoon. In the desert, you can even smell the heat.

Along the curb was a parade of maybe a dozen orange taxicabs. They were mostly old and battered. They all had men standing next to them, eager men with dark hair and dark faces, all raising the chorus, "Taxi, meester? Taxi?"

Singer was there. He was leaning on the hood of the first cab and shaking his head. He puffed like someone who had run six miles.

"Did you see that?" he wheezed. "The guy disappeared faster than spit on the prairie. Had somebody waiting for him. Went off in **a** limousine." He paused and tried to catch his breath, then shook his head again. "He's up to something."

"What are you going to do?" I asked.

He just stood there, head down, stomach heaving. I could hear the breath rushing in and out of him like air through a pair of bellows. After a minute, he turned and looked up at me. "I'll find him. This isn't a big town, and that guy smells like a headline. I'll find him."

Springer ducked into the first cab in line. The door was still closing when the driver gunned the engine, and the cab bounded off down the street. As I watched it round a corner and disappear, I felt a tug on my sleeve. I turned and stared down into a dusky round face. It had thick black hair over the top and along the sides, and it smiled up at me with shiny carbon-black eyes and a mouth wide enough for three sets of teeth.

"Taxi, *senor?* You come with Hector. I geeve you good ride. I know all thee right places."

I tossed my bag into the back seat and climbed in after it. We drove down Alameda Avenue through the Lower East Side and out to the edge of a flat, browned-out section of scrub cactus, mesquite, and yucca trees called the Ysleta Valley. We turned onto Platt Street, drove a block past a gas station and a liquor store, and finally pulled up against the curb.

The Desert View Motel was a narrow, one-story brick building with a pawn shop at one end of it and a row of warehouses behind it. At the other end, the road just curved around and stopped, there being no place beyond that worth going. Next to a door at the pawn shop end of the building, a hand-written cardboard sign had been tacked up. It said, "Vacancy." I told the driver to wait, and I went into the office.

I found a sleepy-looking old man with white hair and wrinkles. He was wearing overalls and a pair of sandals, and he was sitting behind a counter tenderly nursing an almost empty bottle of mescal. I went over and slapped a ten down on the counter. He looked up at me slowly, his washed-out gray eyes only half open. Then he let his head bob back down to the bottle.

"Take any one ya want," he said. "Key's in the room."

I went into the first room, next to the office. It was small and square and decorated like the inside of an orange crate. There was a metal frame bed that was little more than a cot, a wooden night table with a key on it, and a chest of drawers. On the right was a lavatory and a closet, and on the back wall, a heavily smudged window offered a panorama of the warehouse across the back alley. There was no phone. I dropped my bag on the bed, pocketed the key, closed the door, and went outside.

I went back into the office and spotted a wall phone next to the counter. I looked behind the counter, found a dog-eared directory, looked up the number for the Del Norte, dialed it, and asked for Ordway's room. The hotel operator put me through, but there was no answer. Then I went outside and lit a cigarette, and looked out into the desert.

"Where to, *senor?*" The expanse of teeth flashed up at me from inside the cab. I flipped the cigarette into the gutter and climbed into the back seat.

The Hotel Del Norte was eight stories of tan stucco, sitting on the north side of Mesa Street just a little west of downtown. It was a modest place, no bigger than a football stadium, with a white-columned porch that stretched forward like the flight deck of an aircraft carrier. It was set on a little hill at the base of a mountain that jutted almost into the middle of El Paso and forced the city into the shape of a crescent. The entrance to the hotel faced south toward the Rio Grande.

From the front porch, you could see most of the city of Juarez sprawling below the border. It was almost dark now. Lights were flickering around the city, and the night sounds were drifting up the hill. I stood there for a minute, watching, listening, not thinking about much of anything. Then I went into the hotel.

The lobby was one of those places you see on postcards, always ready to have a picture taken—no bags on the floor, no one waiting at the counter, not even a dirty ashtray. The main section was square, covering almost half an acre, with four matching oriental rugs set in the corners. Directly in the center was a stonework fountain. It was full of ferns, and it had small stone-carved mermaids sitting next to a ledge with water running off it into a pool that never quite filled up. I walked up and stood next to the fountain and felt as inconspicuous as a panhandler at Tiffany's.

Across the back of the lobby was a long counter with the usual cadre of efficient-looking men in maroon sports jackets behind it. On either side, behind a series of channeled Doric white columns, were rectangular sitting areas with more oriental rugs and elaborate Victorian furniture. The area on the left was empty. On the right, a pair of wizened old men in dinner jackets sat smoking pipes and arguing over why the French strategy of the Maginot Line hadn't worked in 1940. Beyond them on the right, a row of elevators faced across the lobby toward a pair of double doors with a sign over the top reading "Sunset Room."

I went over and was starting through the doors when a man in a dark suit brushed by me and stalked across the lobby toward the entrance. He slapped his hat on his head, pulled it down tight, and almost covered his thick white hair. He moved with the springy purpose of a middleweight in the early rounds. I could have watched him leave if I hadn't been hit by the flabby freight train that came through the doors behind him. I reeled back enough to keep from falling, steadied myself, and looked into the fleshy, bewildered face of Jack Springer.

"Sorry, buddy," he said with a hint of recognition. "I'm onto something with this guy." He made a portly dash toward the front door. I watched him leave; then I headed through the double doors.

The Sunset Room felt a lot more like home. It was small and quiet, with a bar on the right, some circular tables with padded chairs, and padded leather booths on the left. In the back was an empty stage and a small dance floor; the lighting was something out of a Humphrey Bogart movie. I eased down to the end of the bar and ordered a Scotch. The bartender, a tall, willowy man with salt-and-pepper hair and an angular face with cocker spaniel-brown eyes, laid a glass in front of me and followed it with a question.

"You staying at the hotel, mister?"

"As long as the drink lasts," I said. "Is there a house phone around somewhere?"

He pointed toward a wall phone next to the first booth. I went over, dialed the operator, and asked for Ordway's room. Still no answer. I walked back and settled down over my Scotch. After several sips and some careful surveillance, I determined that the bartender and I were the only ones in the place. Just then, the double doors burst open, and a tall, dark man flanked by a set of shapely ornaments came in and lumbered into the booth across from me.

He was six feet and a couple inches of heartbreaker, all his brains from the neck down, and built like a silo. He had a round, ruddy face with deep creases, clear brown eyes, a square jaw, and black curly hair. He wore black trousers, a black and white herringbone tweed sport coat, and a cream-colored silk shirt open at the collar.

The two girls had dark hair, dark skin, and eyes full of dollar signs. They both wore tight-fitting, low-cut dresses, one metallic pink and one aqua, and they both looked as if they had given up breathing for the evening. Each one was clinging to an arm of the sports coat and looking up hungrily, waiting for the chance to earn her next meal.

The man slapped an open hand down on the table. "Champagne, Tommy."

The bartender reached into an ice chest and then ambled over to the booth with a magnum of something expensive and three glasses. When he came back, he slid over and leaned on the bar in front of me and grumbled, "Rudy's girls. I wish they'd stay at the Parrot."

24

I lit a cigarette, nursed my Scotch, and listened to the Mexican version of a back-street bargain being made. I didn't need a translator to know what they were saying. It sounds the same in any language. The deal was almost set when a stormy number came in and caught their attention. She was a slim blonde in a quietly tailored gray suit, about five and a half feet tall, with flushed cheeks and hard blue eyes. She wasn't the brassy kick-you-in-the-teeth blonde. She was more the cool I-can-do-it-without-you blonde. Of course, with blondes, you can't ever be sure.

She marched over to the booth and gave the curly-haired man a glare that would freeze an erupting volcano. The two girls crouched back into the booth, still clinging to the sports coat. An icy pallor fell over their faces like rain running down a slate roof. The blonde didn't even look at them.

"When I saw you this afternoon, I thought you were going home," she said. "Instead, I find you in here with these bimbos." She passed a hand angrily over the table. "Don't you care about anyone but yourself?"

The man waved his hands feebly and said something with such an alcoholic slur that I didn't get it. The blonde stepped back and twisted her face into a mask of furious contempt. Then she pulled a small purse out of her pocket, took out a couple of bills, and threw them down on the table. Finally, she spoke to the two girls. She measured out her words with an iron certainty. "I'm going to call the police. Don't be here when they arrive." Then she turned and walked out.

Instantly, there was a rustling of lame and an almost neon flash as the two grabbed the money and legged it out the door. The man just sat there, his eyelids hanging at half-mast. He shrugged and then slowly toppled over and lay on his side in the booth. His breathing filled the room, slow and heavy.

I turned back and looked at the bartender. "Nice place you've got here, Tommy. Does this happen a lot?"

Tommy grunted and shook his head. "Too damned much," he said.

He came around the bar and walked routinely over to the booth. He grabbed the man by his lapels and hoisted him upright and began shaking him." Come on, Jimmy. You know you can't sleep here."

The man groaned and made brushing movements with his hands as if he just wanted to be left alone. Tommy let go of the lapels, and the man keeled over again in the booth. Tommy stepped back and turned toward me. He stretched out his arms and his palms upward. "What I gotta put up with!"

I was about to say something when the door opened, and a tall man in a khaki uniform walked in. He had straight black hair, olive skin, and coal-black eyes with sharp points of light at the centers. Without hesitation he walked over and stood next to Tommy, and the two of them stared down at the well-dressed drunk in the booth. After a moment, the officer turned and said, "Why do you keep letting him in here?"

Tommy put his hands on his hips and hunched his shoulders toward the officer. "Goddammit, Vic. You know why. If I try to keep him out, his old man buys the place and fires me. What the hell am I supposed to do?"

The officer shrugged and sighed heavily. "All right. Help me with him."

They hauled the man up out of the booth and got him tottering on his feet. He started making gurgling noises. With quick, practiced movements, each man took an arm and draped it over his shoulders. Then, they all began lumbering toward the door like an elephant walking sideways. I heard Tommy say, "He's sure gonna have a head tomorrow."

The door closed, and I sat there alone in the bar, enjoying the silence. I thought about the old man at the motel. I thought about the chessboard and the friendly bottle of Scotch in my apartment in L.A. And I thought about Ordway and the jade and the two hundred bucks in my wallet. The bar was completely empty. I could have knocked over the register and just strolled out. Instead, I finished my drink and went over and picked up the house phone.

For the third time, Ordway didn't answer. I just waited, and finally, the hotel operator came back on the line. "I'm sorry, sir. Your party doesn't answer."

"Are you sure you're ringing the right room?" I asked. Mr. Willis Ordway?"

There was a pause and a rustling of papers. "Yes, sir. Mr. Ordway, Room 417. There is no answer."

I thanked her and hung up. People are always ready to give you information you don't ask for, if you just don't ask for it. I went across the lobby and into one of the elevators. It was one of the new push-button kind. I pushed four.

When the doors opened, I got out and walked down a thickly carpeted hallway past a series of numbered doors and potted ferns. When I got to 417, I found the door partially open. I gently pushed it aside and looked in.

I stood there in the doorway, feeling the hair on the back of my neck come to attention. There were two people in the room. They were staring at each other, not moving, not saying anything, not giving me any notice. I didn't expect any. One of them was dead.

Chapter Four

It was a large room, expensively furnished, with a little alcove entryway. Covering the floor was a mushroom-colored carpet with a pile so thick it almost needed mowing. There was a walk-in closet on the left with the door ajar, and beyond that, in the corner, another alcove with a dressing area and a bathroom. To the right, the wall was almost hidden by a chest of drawers the size of a small barge, which had an attached mirror facing out into the middle of the room. On the far wall away from the door, a pair of tall casement windows, covered by frothy white curtains and framed by moss-colored brocade drapes, stared back at me with an aristocratic reserve. They stood on either side of an extra-large double bed that looked comfortable and had a blonde standing next to it. I recognized her. She was the same blonde in the quietly tailored gray suit I had seen in the bar downstairs.

I stepped quietly into the room and eased the door shut behind me. That's when I recognized the smell. It had the familiar tang, the acrid heaviness. It was a penetrating smell, not the way you sometimes get it in hospitals or even in the morgue. It was the way I remembered it in the South Pacific. It was the smell of blood.

The blonde's mouth gaped, and her eyes stood open at least an inch. She was staring down at the bed, her hands squeezed together in front of her, knuckles white, nails digging into her flesh. I walked over and stood next to her and looked down at what was left of Mr. Willis Canton Ordway, the Third.

He was sprawled face-up on the unmade bed, his legs draped over the

28

side. He was wearing pajamas, a bathrobe, and one slipper, the pajamas and robe stained reddish brown like the sheets under him. The amount of blood in the human body may not seem like much, only a few pints. But when it's all spilled out, it can look like an ocean.

Ordway just lay there, staring up with a look of frozen astonishment, his pale eyes the color of gelatin, mouth open, tongue grayish. I reached down and turned his head over to the left. It moved easily, but I could see the dark, livid stain across the back of his neck. That meant he'd been there for a while. And on the side of his neck, I could see what had killed him. A single deep slash started just behind his left ear and ran around to the front, cutting across his windpipe. It had been a clean and certain stroke.

I stepped back and looked down at his hands. His left was curled into a tight fist. His right was wrapped around a small, blood-covered dagger. I loosened his fingers enough to get a look at the handle. It was sticky, smeared with blood. But I could see that it was thin, the blade some sort of metal alloy, long jade-green inlays on either side. On each inlay was a carving that looked like the sun setting behind a giant bird. And the bird was standing there with its wings spread wide apart, looking like a B-29 with feathers.

I was about to lift the knife out of his hand when I became aware of the girl next to me. Her breath was coming short and rapid. I turned and looked at her. She had brought her clenched hands up against her mouth in one large, tight fist, and her eyelids had started to flutter. In the corner behind her was a stuffed green chair. I grabbed her just below the shoulders and pushed her back into it. Her head bobbed back against the chair, and her eyes began to roll upward. I gave her a few light slaps.

"Come on," I said. "Stay with it. You can faint later."

She blinked a few times and sat upright. "He's dead, isn't he?"

"Just a little." I let go of her and stood up. "Are you all right?"

She continued to stare at the bed. "Could...could I have a glass of water?"

I went around through the dressing area and into the bathroom. I filled a glass with cold tap water; then I brought it out and handed it to her. She took the glass in her left hand and drank carefully. After some reassuring swallows, she looked tentatively up at me.

"Who are you?" she asked.

I jerked my thumb over my shoulder toward the bed. "Someone he hired to do a job."

I caught a hint of something in her eyes. It could have been recognition. It could have been fear. I pushed my hat back on my head and watched her. "What are you doing here?"

She brought her right hand up and began rubbing the back of her neck. She held the glass out toward me. "Could I have some more?" When I hesitated, she added, "Please?"

I went back into the bathroom and filled the glass again. This time, when I came out, I just stood there. I felt like a rube after his first sideshow scam. The chair was empty. The door was open. And I was standing there looking at a glass of water and a stiff. Maybe someday I'll learn to be a real detective.

I went over and looked out into the hall. It was as empty as a busted flush. I closed the door, took the glass back into the bathroom, and then started to look around.

The dressing area contained a counter, a wall mirror, and another sink. On the counter to the left was an assortment of grooming articles—razor, brush, comb, hair tonic, toothbrush. They were laid out with a delicate precision, like soldiers in a close-order drill. Next to them were several crusted pools of blood. I looked up at the mirror and saw a spray of crimson, where more blood had hit and then run down in streaks. Under the counter, I found the other slipper. It lay next to a trail of dark spots that led back over to the bed.

I looked in the closet and found about what I expected. There was a suitcase, a hat, a couple of suits, and several shirts. Everything was clean and freshly pressed. On the floor was a pair of expensive black shoes. They weren't new. The right heel was worn down about a quarter inch, the left a little more. But they were carefully polished and buffed.

I checked the suitcase. It was empty. There was nothing in either nightstand, but Ordway's cigarette case and lighter lay undisturbed next to one of the lamps. And in the chest of drawers, I found his underwear and another pair of pajamas, all neatly folded and stacked. Ordway had been a methodical, orderly man.

I went over to the bed and took a last look at my client. I could picture him talking to me, telling me something important. But I couldn't tell what it was. I left the room and headed back downstairs. I felt like getting very drunk.

The night clerk was a thin, pinch-faced man with gaunt features and long, bony hands and fingers. He gave me a petulant stare, as if a fly had just landed in his vichyssoise. I asked him if anyone had been around to visit Ordway earlier in the day. He explained to me how the Del Norte prides itself on respecting the privacy of its guests. I showed him a picture of Lincoln. He went down to the end of the counter and spoke quietly with another clerk. Then he came back and told me that there had been no guests. He told me that Ordway had been in his room all day, that he had called room service for breakfast and lunch, and that he hadn't had dinner. So much for privacy. I thanked him, complimented him on running a nice, respectable hotel, and told him to call the police. I even told him why.

I went over and sat in one of the plush chairs in the corner of the lobby and listened to the elevator doors open and close. I lit a cigarette and looked back over toward the desk. One of the clerks was missing. The other one just stood there fidgeting. In a minute, the phone rang. The man jerked the receiver up to his ear. He made a harsh mumbling noise and then began dialing frantically. I sat back and waited.

I had just lit my third Lucky when they came in, two of them in khaki uniforms, both large, both mean-looking. The one in front was about six feet tall with the body of a beer truck. He carried the kind of weight that looks like a sack of putty but can hit you like cast iron. He had a ruddy, pulpish face with a square chin, a large coarse-grained nose, and thick black eyebrows. He was wearing a pair of rimless spectacles, and he was chewing on the stump of a cigar that looked as if it had never been lit. He wore polished brown boots and a tan Western hat set at a rakish angle. It had a braided red and gold band and a large gold star pinned to the front of it, as if that meant something. The other man walked a pace behind. He was more plainly dressed. He looked a little taller, a little thinner, and a little meaner.

As the two men moved past me, the one in front muttered over his shoulder. "This better be something. They said come right away, so I had to fold. And me holding three queens, with a double sawbuck in the pot."

They marched over to the desk and spoke to the clerk. He shifted uneasily from side to side, waving his bony hands in the air. Finally, he motioned toward me. Then the second man disappeared into the elevator, while the big one sauntered over and stood next to my chair. He spoke to me with a voice full of smoke and booze and late nights.

"Stand up, boy," he growled.

I slowly put out my cigarette and stood up. I took my time. He didn't like that. He inhaled deliberately and set his jaw.

"I'm Sheriff J. J. Stonebreaker," he growled again. "Now, what's your name, boy?"

I looked into his filmy brown eyes. Behind the glasses, they looked like mud on a wet street. "Garrett," I said. "And I haven't been a boy for a long time."

He grunted. He didn't like that either. "You the one reported the body upstairs?"

I nodded.

He bit down on the cigar, flashing a set of brown-stained teeth, and gave me a quick up-and-down look. Then he narrowed his eyes, leaned forward, and thrust the cigar toward my chin. I got a quick whiff of bourbon.

"You got some I.D.?" he asked.

I slowly brought out my wallet. But before I could get it open, he yanked it out of my hand and began ransacking it. He slipped the I.D. out of its holder and made a show of holding it up to the light.

"Well, well. It says here, 'Michael Garrett, Private Investigator, Los Angeles.'" He leered at me. "Kind of a ways from home, ain't ya, ...boy?"

I just looked at him.

He went on exploring and found the two C-notes. Then the leer became

32

a baleful grin. "Well, would you look at this. Sure is a lotta dough for a shamus to be carryin'. I better look after this for you." He folded up my wallet and stuffed it in his shirt pocket. Then he put his hands on his hips, leaned forward, and growled at me out of the side of his mouth. "Okay, what's your story?"

I could see the setup. A little grift on the out-of-town chump. Just scare him enough to make him homesick. Lean on him a little, and he'll whimper and jump on the next bus. Please, Mr. Sheriff. I don't want any trouble. I'm just an honest citizen. You keep the money. What's two hundred bucks? Just let me go home. It was easy money, easier than holding three queens.

I glanced over toward the main desk. The two clerks were leaning on the counter. They were nothing but ears. I raised my voice just enough.

"Sheriff, if I tell you a story that you like, do I get my two hundred bucks back?"

He stood rigid. I could see his neck start to turn purple. He bit down on the cigar again and hissed at me through his teeth. "Smart guy, huh?"

He fished my wallet out of his shirt and slapped it against my chest. I barely got the wallet tucked away when he spun me around and pushed me hard against the wall. He patted me down brutally, found nothing, then wrapped a meaty hand around my arm and jerked me toward the elevator,

"All right, *Mister* Garrett. Let's go upstairs."

We rode up quietly. Stonebreaker did a slow burn in the corner of the elevator. When we got to the room, the other officer was just hanging up the phone. "I called the station, boss," he said. "Doc's on his way."

Stonebreaker snapped at him. "Don't call me boss."

Then he pushed me into a chair, took a quick look at Ordway, then came back and stood glowering over me. Without taking his eyes off me, he spoke to the other man. "Hal, this is *Mister* Garrett. He's a keyhole peeper. A flatfoot, all the way from L.A." He turned and spoke to me. "That's Officer Weems. He does what I tell him." He folded his arms and let his voice sink into the tone of an angry bulldozer. "All right, boy. We've had our introductions, nice and polite. Now start talkin'."

I took my time and told him about Ordway and about the auction. I told him about the jade and about Ordway's fear of it. I wasn't sure why, but I didn't tell him about Wearing or the girl. It didn't matter anyway. When I mentioned the jade, Stonebreaker seemed to lose interest in everything else. I was just finishing when there was a rap on the door.

It was another officer. He was followed by the usual quiet little man in the usual dark suit, dark hat, and squeaky shoes, carrying the usual black bag. He poked at the body, gathered up some blood samples, and made nervous clucking noises. The officer went to work with his chalk, his pieces of string, and his dusting powder. Stonebreaker just sat in a chair and chewed on his cigar. Weems stood in the corner, arms folded. I sat there and chewed on a couple of Luckies and tried to see the humor in the whole thing.

Finally, the little man folded up his bag and spoke to Stonebreaker. "Been dead for some time, Sheriff. I can tell you more after we get him to the morgue."

Stonebreaker grunted. "Was he bumped?"

"Can't be sure. Might be suicide. The Japs do it this way sometimes. I saw it in the war." He shrugged. "Anyway, that's your racket." He adjusted his hat nervously and left.

Stonebreaker got up out of the chair and spoke to the officer, who was then busy dusting the window latch for prints. "You wait for the boys with the wagon." Then he nodded to Weems and reached over and grabbed my arm. "Come on, boy. Let's go."

"Go where?"

He flicked out a desultory laugh. "To the station, boy. To the station."

Chapter Five

We left the hotel, got into a blue-and-white Ford patrol car, and headed down Mesa Street. Weems drove while Stonebreaker sat next to him and chewed on his cigar. I sat in the back seat. Nobody spoke. Two or three times, Stonebreaker rolled down the window and spat, then rolled up the window and grunted contentedly.

An orange taxicab followed us out of the hotel parking lot. It kept pace behind us for several minutes. But when we got down toward the center of the city, the cab slowed and turned and drifted into the back-street shadows. We drove for about ten minutes. It seemed like ten days.

We finally pulled up in front of the El Paso police station, a two-story brick building with barred windows and cement steps leading up to a set of glass-paneled double doors with globe lights on either side. Stonebreaker got out and stormed up the steps while Weems manhandled me out of the car and pushed me along after the sheriff.

We walked past a reception desk with a sandy-haired, prune-faced man in uniform sitting behind it. He nodded as we went by. We went up a short, tiled hallway and into a small, uncomfortable room with a tiled floor, an overhead light, and painted walls the color of spoiled milk. It had a wide wooden table, several straight-backed wooden chairs, and no windows. Weems pushed me into one of the chairs next to the table. Then he moved back and stood against the wall behind me.

After a few minutes, Stonebreaker came in, settled into a chair across the table, and stared at me with the comely warmth of a black widow. He took off his hat and put it on the table next *to* him. His forehead was high and shiny, in sharp contrast to his ruddy features, and his thinning black hair was swept straight back on his head. There was a small scar along his hairline, just above his left temple. It could have been made by a bullet or a knife or a bottle or an old lady's umbrella.

He folded his arms and set both elbows down on the table. He adjusted his glasses and chewed on his cigar; teeth bared in an angry grimace. When he spoke, only his lips moved. "All right, boy. Let's get down to cases. Tell me about this here jade."

I crossed one leg over the other and wondered how far he might try to push his little skin game.

"All I know is what Ordway told me," I said. "The jade figures belonged to an Aztec emperor with a yen to be liked. After he was killed, the figures seemed to inherit some kind of curse. Ordway wanted the jade, but he was afraid even to touch it."

He snorted at me. "So, he hired you to get it for him?"

I nodded.

He leaned forward. "How much is it worth?"

"He didn't say."

"Who owns the jade?"

"Look, Sheriff. I don't even know if there *is* any jade. Ordway wasn't sure of that himself. He just wanted me to go to the auction and look for it."

He pursed his lips around the cigar. "Where is this auction being held?"

"I don't know. I was meeting Ordway tonight to find out."

He made a hungry grunt. "How much were you tapping him for?"

"Nuts," I said. "I just felt like taking a little trip to the desert."

He leaned forward a little more. "Are you telling me the two hundred is your own money?"

I shrugged. "I'm independently wealthy."

He spread his hands flat on the table and let his eyes drift over me greedily. There was a glint of amusement behind his glasses.

"Could be a smartass LA dick would figure to bump off his client and sell the jade for himself," he said.

"Could be," I agreed. "If the dick didn't care about the curse. And if he thought it would be fun to stick around afterward and play button-button with the law."

He raised a leer up from somewhere under the table. "So now you're gonna tell me that this Ordway was killed by some dead Mexican emperor, or that the curse made him kill himself."

"Aztec," I said sourly, "not Mexican. And it wasn't suicide. Any newsboy could see that."

That stopped him. His eyebrows shot halfway up his forehead, and his face went blank. "What do you mean?"

I took off my hat and laid it on the table. Then I pulled out a cigarette and lit it, and sent a slow trail of smoke up into the middle of the room.

"All right," I said. "Your coroner was right. People do sometimes kill themselves by cutting their throats. But they almost never do it with a single cut. They usually make several wounds, trial cuts, looking for the right spot for the knife. There was only one wound on Ordway's neck. And a suicide victim almost always tilts his head back to give himself an easy target. That causes the knife to miss the carotid arteries, so there isn't much bleeding. Ordway was swimming in blood. Then there's the blood on the handle of the knife he was holding. It wouldn't have been there when he slashed himself. He would have had to make the cut, drop the knife, smear his hand with blood, and then pick up the knife again. And all this while he was staggering back and collapsing on the bed, with blood running out of him like water from a faucet. With the wound he had, he was already a goner. But if he really wanted to make a second try, he would have stayed there in front of the mirror to make sure of it instead of going back to the bed."

I took a casual pull on my Lucky and watched a scowl form all over Stonebreaker's face. He looked at me with what might have been a strangled kind of respect. I wasn't sure I wanted that, but it was too late to stop.

"If all that isn't enough," I said, "he was only wearing one slipper. The other one was under the sink. I never saw a suicide victim who slashed himself so neatly and then kicked off a slipper just to look untidy." I paused. "No. Ordway didn't kill himself. What you've got is a nice friendly murder."

Stonebreaker rubbed his hands together and swallowed hard. "You could be right. But it isn't very solid."

"Sure," I said. "Forget I ever mentioned it."

He reached around to his hip pocket and brought out a small metal flask. He took a couple of quick slugs of something with a smell that filled the room. I admired him for that. Then he put the flask away and leaned back in his chair, and looked at me with a new interest.

"So, you're a pretty smart boy." He nodded in my general direction. "But if what you say is true, you could almost be confessing to this murder."

"Yeah. And you could be the next prom queen."

He jumped halfway out of his chair. "Now, you can just shut your goddamn mouth, Garrett. I don't need some big city tourist coming in here and crackin' wise. Another one like that, and I'll run you in so far you won't see daylight again until you're too old to care."

"Don't be a chump," I said. "You can't turn this rap on me. The evidence won't let you. There were already signs of lividity on Ordway's neck. He'd been dead for at least three hours, maybe even five or six. Your own coroner will tell you that. And I hadn't been in town for much more than an hour when you got the call from the hotel. I came in on the late train. If you don't believe me, ask a newspaperman named Jack Springer. He was on the train with me."

Stonebreaker swallowed again and looked at me defensively. "Maybe I'll do just that."

"Fine," I said. I had the advantage now. I decided to press it. "Just stop trying to work your small-time con angle. I'm tired of it. I'm sorry about your three queens, but I didn't take the pot."

I crushed out my cigarette on my heel. He was glaring at me now, the muscles on his neck flushing purple again.

"You don't really doubt my story," I went on. "If you did, you would have had somebody checking with the LA boys even before we got to the station. I'm clean, and you know it. So, book me, or let me go. I'm tired."

He spat the cigar on the table and lurched up out of his chair, snarling like a pit bulldog. I might have pressed too hard. I'm good at that.

I started to get up when a pair of size-fourteen hands grabbed me from behind and held my arms against my sides. Stonebreaker came around the table and snarled again, and planted his fist in the side of my neck. It was a hard punch. It knocked me back down into the chair. I sat there and listened to a fire engine racing down an endless freeway somewhere between my ears. A taste of bile came up in my throat. I licked my lips carefully and looked up at him.

"Does this mean I'm pinched?"

He grabbed the lapels of my suit jacket and started shaking me. "You goddamn big-mouth flatfoot," he yelled. "I've had enough of your crap."

I was about to let him hit me again when the door opened, and another man in khaki came in. He had olive skin, black hair, and coal-black eyes. He came over quickly and whispered something to Stonebreaker.

The sheriff's mouth dropped open. He turned and shook his head. "No, damnit."

The dark man whispered to him again.

Stonebreaker clenched his teeth tight enough to crack a Brazil nut. "All right, Vic," he rasped. "It'll just be a minute."

The officer turned abruptly and left. Stonebreaker nodded to Weems, and I felt my arms being released. It was like taking off a tourniquet. There was a throbbing in my neck now, and I started rubbing it. But Stonebreaker grabbed my jacket again and pulled me upright. He brought his nose up about three inches from mine and snarled at me. He let go of the coat.

"Get the hell outta here, Garrett. You're sprung." His punctuation was about eighty proof. "And take some advice. If I were you, I'd be on the next train back to L.A."

Chapter Six

She was waiting for me at the reception desk. She had on the same quiet gray suit, a plain buff-colored blouse, open at the throat, and black open-toed shoes with modest heels. She wore a wristwatch, no other jewelry. Her clear blue eyes caught the light and reflected it back at me in little circles, like a pair of marbles. Her honey-blond hair was cut in a pageboy style, but without the usual bangs—just a few light strands arranged carelessly over her forehead. Her small nose had a slight upward turn at the end, leaving room for a full mouth, with a lower lip that stuck out just short of looking defiant. She was pretty. With a little effort, she could even be beautiful.

She held her arms folded and looked at me with a businesslike impatience. All she said was, "You look awful. Are you alright?"

"Just fine," I said. "The sheriff and I were having a cup of tea. Can I get you some? Or would you prefer a glass of water?"

She flushed and squeezed her hands together. Then she cleared her throat, picked her composure up off the floor, and stuck her right hand out in front of me. "Mr. Garrett, I'm Gabrielle Wearing."

I took her hand and shook it. It wasn't the usual woman's handshake. It was strong, confident. I said, "Uh-huh."

She raised an eyebrow. "You're not surprised?"

"I'm supposed to do handsprings?"

"Don't be impertinent," she snapped. "I'm doing you a favor."

I laughed dryly. "Lady, I wouldn't even be here if you hadn't taken the air from the hotel. I've been in town just three hours, and in that time, I've been punched, threatened, and set up as a murder suspect. I've lost a client, and I damn near lost all my money. That doesn't put me in a very good humor."

She swallowed hard, and her look softened. "I'm sorry. I..."

Before she could finish, the dark-haired officer appeared through a door by the far end of the desk. He came over and offered me a reserved smile. "Mr. Garrett, I'm Deputy Sheriff Sanchez. I'm sorry we had to detain you."

I rubbed my neck. "I'm sorry, too."

He went on as if all I'd done was rub my neck. "Miss Wearing here has vouched for you, and we have no reason to hold you. So, you're free to go. We'll need your official statement, of course. But you can come in for that tomorrow."

A polite cop. All business. No mistreating the public. I put my hat on and eyed him carefully. I just grunted, "Uh-huh."

He turned and spoke officially to the girl. "Miss Wearing, I'll call you tomorrow."

She looked at him demurely. "Thank you, Victor."

Then she turned back to me. "Mr. Garrett, my car is right outside. I'll drive you to your hotel." Without waiting, she turned on her heel and marched out the door.

Her car was a little convertible roadster with the top up. It had leather seats and a panel full of gadgets, and it smelled like money. I wedged myself in and sat with my chin, chafing my knees. Wealthy people pay a lot just to be uncomfortable.

She pulled away from the curb and spoke to me. "You are staying at the Del Norte?" It was a question that didn't sound as if it was looking for an answer. Wealthy people ask a lot of those.

"No, I'm at the Desert View Motel, out in the valley."

She looked over at me abruptly, the same eyebrow raised. "What on earth are you doing in that place?"

"Never mind," I said sourly. "Just how the hell do you know me?"

She squeezed the steering wheel tightly, her eyes fastened on the road. "Willy...Mr. Ordway told me he had hired someone, a detective. After I left the hotel, I realized that it must have been you."

41

"What were you doing in Ordway's room?"

"I went there to tell him to leave, to go home and forget the whole thing. When I met him last night, I could see how frightened he was. He kept ranting about a pair of jade figures and a curse. He said there was great danger. But he was determined to stay. He said that he would have help. That's when he told me about you."

She sent me a sideways glance that didn't quite make me feel like a worthless heel, but it tried. I didn't say anything.

"Anyway," she went on, "this morning, I decided to send him home, even if he objected. I called and told him to meet me, but he refused. He said he wouldn't leave his room. I became worried, so this evening I went to his hotel and found him…That was just before you arrived."

"How did you get in?"

"The door was unlocked."

I took out a cigarette and rolled it around in my fingers, and thought about things. I looked over at her. She looked like someone I could almost believe. "But you didn't go up to the room right away."

"No," she said bitterly. "As soon as I arrived, the clerk told me that my brother was in the lounge…again. I went in and found him with those…those women. I called Victor, and he came right away. After he took Jimmy home, I went upstairs." She paused, glancing sideways at me. "When I saw Willy, I was stunned. Then, when you came in, I guess I panicked. That's why I ran away." She shook her head and spoke quietly. "Poor Willy. He was so frightened."

I fiddled with the cigarette some more. I could still see Ordway staring up at me, trying to tell me something. "You must know the deputy pretty well."

She nodded. "Very well. We grew up together." Her jaw muscles tightened. "Victor has taken Jimmy home before—many times before. She wrung her hands on the wheel, then relaxed. "By the time I got to the house, I realized who you were. Victor was still there, so I told him. Then, the two of us went right down to the station to see that you were in no trouble."

"Yeah," I muttered. "No trouble."

We rode in silence through the sleepy downtown streets. I lit my cigarette and watched her. She wore just a trace of lipstick and almost no makeup. She didn't need any. Her skin was soft and evenly tanned, showing none of the leathery look you get from the desert sun. I guessed that she was in her late twenties, but I wouldn't make book on it. She could have been older. Some of us are born looking old. Some of us grow into it. But she had the kind of face that looks twenty-five forever.

She held both hands firmly on the wheel and squinted pensively. She gnawed on her lower lip, as if she might rather bite it off than ask the question she wanted to ask. She let a parade of minutes go by and then finally let her voice come out cool, unconcerned. "How much did Willy tell you about my family?"

"Enough."

"And your discussion with the sheriff, it was…frank?"

"Enough."

"Well, you needn't be so laconic," she snapped.

"That's very good," I said. "You must have gotten that at Vassar. Who says an expensive education doesn't pay off?"

She squeezed the wheel hard enough to crack it. "I'm trying to find out how much you told him."

"Well, your technique is lousy."

She bristled like a cat with its fur rubbed the wrong way. "Must you be so brusque?"

"I've had a pretty brusque day," I said. "But just to put your mind at rest, I didn't tell Stonebreaker anything about your father. I didn't even tell him about you. Not that it matters, since you already told the deputy."

She cleared her throat nervously. "I'm grateful that you left my father out of it. But might I ask why?"

"Damned if I know. Why is your father selling off his collection?"

"He's not," she said icily. "It's Monica, his wife. I'm not sure he even knows. I've tried talking to him, but he won't even discuss it. He won't discuss anything that involves her."

As we turned onto Platt Street, she gnawed on her lip again. "Mr. Garrett, when you give your statement to the police, will you have to tell them everything?"

"Not if they don't ask. I don't have to tell them anything except what I was doing in Ordway's room." I shrugged. "I was there because it was none of my business."

She pondered that for longer than it was worth, then decided it wasn't worth anything. "After you see the police, I think it best if you just leave," she said. "I don't believe in any curse, but..."

"But for my own safety, I'd better not risk offending the Aztecs. Is that it?"

"Don't be silly. I just think it would be better to avoid any trouble."

I laughed. "Lady, look around. All you can see is trouble. Trouble doesn't like to be avoided." I reached up and rubbed my neck and remembered Stonebreaker's advice.

"Then you're staying?"

I nodded.

"But why?"

I grinned at her nastily. "Let's just say I'm a sucker for strays, even if they do have pedigrees and painted toenails and wear tailored gray suits."

She reddened all the way to the roots of her hair. "Of all the nerve! I can't even imagine why Willy hired you."

I turned and stared out at the dark street. "Neither can I, but he did. Maybe that's why I'm staying. He hired me and gave me some money, and I haven't earned it. You don't take a case and then just walk out on your client, even if he is dead. It's bad for business." I tossed the cigarette out the window. "And speaking of that, how well did you know Ordway?"

"You mean you actually suspect me of..."

"I suspect everybody but myself. Sometimes, I'm not even sure about myself. How long did you know him?"

"Not that it's any of your business," she steamed. "I met him in college. We've been friends ever since then."

"Just friends?"

"Yes. Just friends," she barked.

"Uh-huh."

"And just what do you mean by that?"

44

"Nothing," I said. "It figures that someone like you wouldn't be too friendly with a guy who had polished nails and smoked purple cigarettes."

She almost went through the roof. "How *dare* you? You're the most crude and disrespectful man I ever met."

She pulled sharply up in front of the motel. I got out and leaned against the side of the car, and looked back in at her. "Maybe that's why you haven't shed any tears."

She stabbed at me with her eyes. Every word had ice on it. "For your information, I cared very much about Willis Ordway. His death is a terrible shock. I will go home now and have a stiff drink. Then, I will go quietly into my bedroom, where I will do my crying in private. That's something you wouldn't understand, because it involves dignity and respect. And those are things you don't have. I'm sorry I even bothered with you. Good night, Mr. Garrett."

She slammed the car into gear, did a quick U-turn, and went tearing down the block. I watched her drive away. She wasn't what I had expected, if I had expected anything. I thought I could even get to like her.

I stood in the street in front of the motel, rubbing my neck. The ride in the car had stiffened it up, and I was starting to feel as if I had an elephant sitting on my shoulder. It wasn't very late, so I decided to walk the block and a half down to the liquor store. There was a middle-aged woman with black hair and eyes behind the counter. She was holding a half-eaten burrito—a tortilla made from flour and wrapped around anything from leftover vegetables to a stray cat. She didn't understand my Spanish, but she understood my money. I bought a pint of hundred-proof Kentucky painkiller and headed back up the street.

There were no lights on in the motel, but the moonlight reflecting off the desert was bright enough for me to make out part of a grill and an orange fender poking out just past the far end of the building. I slipped into the shadows, went quietly through the back alley, and came up behind the taxi. The window was open. The driver was leaning over, arm resting on the door, his ear nestled comfortably into the palm of his hand. He might have been dozing. I slipped my left arm around his neck and held tight to his right shoulder. With my right hand, I took the pint bottle and poked the cap into his back just below the base of his neck.

"Feel this?" I said. "Move, and I feed it to you."

He let out a squeal. "Aye! *Por favor, senor.* Don't shoot. Please."

I opened the door and yanked him out, and pushed him up hard against the side of the cab. I pushed his chin back far enough to see his face in the moonlight. It was a face I recognized.

"Please, *senor*," he bleated. "It's me, Hector. Hector Armendariz." I let him go and stepped back. He brushed himself off and rubbed his chin. *"Hijo de la—Senor,* you almost frighten me out of my life."

"Why are you following me?

He hesitated. "You are *Senor* Garrett?"

"I'm Garrett. What do you want?"

His eyes brightened, and he spread out his teeth. "I have something for you, *senor.* A letter." He reached into his shirt and brought out a crumpled envelope. He handed it to me and grinned proudly. There was no writing on it.

"Where did you get this?"

"A man, *senor.* An Anglo. He geeve it to me last night. I peek him up at thee beeg hotel. He says to drive him around and then just bring him back to thee hotel. He ees very strange, senor—frightened. *Que se cagaba de susto.* He says I should come back to thee hotel tonight after sunset. He will meet me and take back thee letter. But eef he does not meet me, then I must find you and geeve you thee letter."

"Did this man have a name?"

"Si, senor. He says hees name ees Ordway."

I grabbed him by the shirt and hauled him around the corner of the building and into my room. I sat him on the bed and let him sample the pint while I opened the letter.

Dear Mr. Garrett:

My worst fears have been realized. Quetaz is here. I can feel his presence all around me. There is great danger.

I spoke with Gabrielle earlier this evening. I tried to make her understand. If

I do not survive, then she will be in great peril. She must leave at once. But she remains as stubborn as ever. I fear for her, Mr. Garrett, and for you. You must guard yourself and protect Gabrielle. Make her listen.

Tonight, I received the Bird of Death—the messenger of Quetaz. That means Quetaz is coming soon. I have until sunset tomorrow. Until then, I can only wait. I shall remain in my room and keep my door closed and locked until you arrive, hoping you never read this note.

W. C. Ordway

I looked over at Hector. He was sitting on the bed, coaxing some more hooch out of the bottle. He grinned back at me. "Thees ees good stuff, *senor. Muy bien. Gracias.*"

"How did you know this letter was for me?"

"*Senor* Ordway describe you. He say you are coming on thee train. When I see you at thee station, I theenk it ees you, but I am not sure. And it ees not yet sunset. So, I wait at thee hotel. When *Senor* Ordway does not come out, I start to look for you. Then I see you with thee *policia*. I don't know what to do, so I come here and wait." He frowned and angled his head to one side. "There ees trouble, *senor?*"

"Yeah," I said. "You might say that. Take me back to the hotel."

It was about ten when we pulled up to the Del Norte. I told Hector to wait. He grinned and patted the bottle on the seat next to him. I went into the lobby and found the same clerk behind the front desk. He wasn't anxious to talk to me until I reintroduced him to Mr. Lincoln. He told me that Ordway had checked in early the previous evening, that he had come down later for dinner, and that he had met Miss Wearing in the lobby. They talked for a while, then Ordway went back up to his room. I asked if anyone could have gotten into the room without having a key. He didn't think so. There was a fire escape, but all the windows were painted shut. I thanked him again and walked into the Sunset Room.

If you want to know what really goes on in a strange town, talk to a bartender. A good one knows how to listen. He can talk to you like a father or a brother or even a maiden aunt. He can be a judge settling disputes or a priest hearing confession. He's always got a willing ear. And you can ask him for anything, except money.

I found Tommy leaning over the end of the bar, talking with a plump middle-aged woman. She had hair the color of an old broom and a face like an unmade bed. "So, they don't know," Tommy said to her. "He mighta gashed himself."

She shuddered and lifted a double-shot glass full of something that might remove nail polish. "Not me," she said huskily. "I'd rather do it with this."

Tommy spotted me and strolled casually down the bar to where I was sitting. "What'll it be, Mister?"

Before I could answer, he frowned and then stepped back and tried to reach the ceiling with his eyebrows. "Say, isn't your name Garrett?"

I nodded and said my name was Garrett.

He hollered at the woman. "Hey, Mable. This is the guy I was tellin' ya about."

She looked over at me and grunted, then put her nose back in the glass. Tommy gave her an I-told-you-so wave with his hand and turned back to me. "What can I get ya, Mr. Garrett?"

"Scotch," I said. "And some company."

"Sure thing." He reached under the bar and brought up a glass and a bottle of Vat 69, something I seldom see up close. "Hal Weems was in a little while ago," he said. "He tells me how you got old Stonebreaker ta back down."

He poured a couple of inches into the glass and then pushed it over in front of me. I started to reach for my wallet, but he held up his hand and shook his head.

"Uh-uh," he said. "This one's on me. Anybody that stands up to that old bastard is an okay guy in my book."

I pulled out a bill and laid it on the bar. "In that case, have one yourself."

He grinned, grabbed a glass, and poured himself some of the Scotch. Then he took a long swallow, licked his lips, and leaned on the bar. "So, about this guy upstairs. Any idea who mighta croaked him?"

"I was hoping you might have the ideas," I said.

"Naw. He was a stranger. Don't know anybody woulda had it in for him.

48

Must be big stuff, though. Cops told all the hotel people ta keep mum. Wouldn't even say where it happened. They're keepin' it all hushed up."

"I can see that."

He lowered his voice and let a tone of conspiracy settle into it. "Is it true what Hal said, about a curse?"

I let it go by. "Did you see Ordway?"

He nodded. "Came in here early last night. Had one drink. Quiet sorta guy, didn't talk much. Said he was waitin' for someone. It was that Wearing dame." He leaned toward me and lowered his voice a little more. "Now there's one for ya. A real spitfire. Her old man is loaded, see? Only she won't touch a nickel of it. I figure with her looks and his dough, she can have anything she wants. So, what does she do? She gets herself educated and sets up her own law practice. Can ya picture that? A lady lawyer?"

"Why not? I've seen lady wrestlers."

He laughed. "Yeah. I guess so. But somehow, it just don't figure. A sweet-lookin' dame like that."

"What about her brother?"

"Jimmy?" He shook his head, the corners of his mouth almost reaching the bar. "That's a sad story, brother. He was shot up pretty bad in the war. Hasn't spent a sober day since that I can see. Wounds healed all right, but..." He tapped a finger up against his temple. "Know what I mean?"

I nodded. A lot of guys came back with scars that no one could ever see. Even if they hadn't been shot, they were wounded just the same.

"Jimmy sees some doctor up in the hills," he went on, "but I don't think it does him any good. He's in here all the time, a coupla times tonight even. He comes in early and gets tanked up, buyin' drinks for everybody. Then he disappears and comes back later with them two broads. You saw them. Guess he went down to Rudy's place."

"Rudy?"

"Yeah." His face hardened. A gathering of fear showed in his eyes, like early frost. "Rudy Delmar. He's got a joint over in Juarez." He inhaled and let his breath out slowly. "Now, there's a guy who is tough like you don't want to know. You want some action? Rudy's got it. But I wouldn't mix it up with him, brother. You could be lookin' up at daisies from the roots."

"Hey, Tommy. Quit jawin' and pour." It was the woman at the end of the bar.

Tommy went down, filled her glass, and came back just as I was finishing my drink. "You stayin' in town long, Mr. Garrett?"

"Can't say, Tommy. Can't say."

"Sure is too bad about that Ordway fella." He stopped and scratched his cheek. His eyebrows fretted, and he pursed his lips. He was remembering something. "You know? There was another guy in here tonight askin' about him. Didn't even stay for a drink. Just comes in and asks me to describe Ordway, and then he leaves."

I felt my stomach tighten. "Did you know him?"

"Never saw him before. And he's somebody you'd remember. Strange-lookin' guy, real pale with reddish eyes. And his hair was white. I mean really white, the color of chalk."

I dropped another bill on the bar and went outside. I lit a cigarette and listened to my neck and shoulder tell me how glad they were to be part of me. I walked out through a knot of yucca trees in front of the hotel and stood on the sandy edge of the parking lot. The lights below the border were flickering in the waves of heat still rolling off the desert, inviting, promising.

I took out Ordway's note and reread it. I thought about an Aztec emperor and about birds. I thought about a white-haired man on a train. I thought about Gabrielle Wearing and about Ordway, holding the dagger. I stopped thinking and walked over to the cab. My head was getting as sore as my neck.

I climbed into the cab and listened to Hector explain how he hadn't really meant to finish off the pint. I didn't care. On the way back to the motel, we stopped at the same liquor store, and I bought another cheap bottle. Then I took it back to my room and worked myself into a cheap drunk.

Chapter Seven

The fist hit my door about the same time the razor nicked my chin. It's funny how they call them safety razors. I grabbed some tissue and swabbed my face, tightened the belt around my terry cloth robe, tramped over, and stood next to the door. I wasn't ready for visitors. My head felt as if someone had built a parking lot on it. Not knowing what else to do, I just stood there and listened. There was no sound.

I knew it wasn't Stonebreaker. He'd have been knocking on my face instead of the door. And it wasn't Hector. He'd be nursing a hangover bigger than mine. I thought about the Luger buried somewhere in my suitcase. The fist hit the door again, and a harsh, wheezing voice followed it.

"Hey, Garrett. Open up. It's me, Springer." I opened the door.

He shuffled in and collapsed into a sitting position on the end of the bed. He wrestled a soiled handkerchief out of his hip pocket and began mopping his forehead. I closed the door and watched him. He was wearing a lightweight gray suit, no belt, and a tired white shirt open at the collar. He wasn't wearing a tie. His black-and-white shoes were scuffed and streaked gray-green as if he had been kicking sagebrush. He lifted his straw hat and mopped the top of his head. Then he put a few damp folds in his handkerchief and stuffed it back in his pocket. Nobody ever sweats in the desert—almost nobody.

"Boy, I sure read you wrong," he said. "Vic Sanchez called me in this morning—wanted to know all about how I met you on the train. I had to go over it three times. He told me about that guy being bumped at the hotel, too. And he said you had a run-in with Sheriff Stonebreaker. Guess you needed an alibi, huh?" He cocked his head and looked at me out of the corner of his eye, waiting for a reaction. When I didn't give him any, he went on. "So, you're a gumshoe. Boy, did I read you wrong."

"How did you know where to find me?"

"Vic told me." He smiled quickly, tightly, flashing a row of yellow teeth. "He's a smooth customer for a Mex, does his homework."

I walked over to the sink and toweled off my face. My legs were a little steadier, and my head was almost getting to be something I could live with. A quick look at my chin in the mirror told me I didn't need a transfusion. I reached into the closet, pulled out my suitcase, and tossed it on the bed.

Springer hitched himself around on the bed, his belly quivering like a plate of aspic. He peered at me carefully over his shoulder. "So, what are you doing in El Paso?"

I stepped back and folded my arms. "If you're the big news hawk, you already know that."

"Yeah." He grinned again. "Vic said that this guy Ordway hired you. He said you came here to go to some kind of auction. What were you supposed to do there?"

"Behave myself."

He chuckled uneasily. "You sure got off on the wrong foot." He pulled out his handkerchief and mopped some more sweat off his forehead. Then he put the handkerchief away and made a sharp sucking noise, drawing air through his teeth, and shook his head. "And I thought you were selling insurance."

"How do you read the other man on the train?" He gave me a foxy look. "You mean ole Whitey?"

He reached into his coat pocket and brought out a pack of Camels. He stuck one between his teeth, lit it, and kept looking foxy. "I have names for all of 'em, ya know—everyone I go after for a story." He paused and took a deep drag. Then he drew his lower lip in under his teeth and chewed on it while he measured me with his eyes. "I think I'll call you Whisper on account of you haven't given me the first whisper of who you are or what you're up to."

I just let it go by without saying anything.

A rose-colored flush began to stand out at his temples. Something uncertain, almost fearful, flitted in and out of his expression, and I could see small jewels of sweat forming just below his hatband. He held his eyes on me while he crossed one leg over the other.

"You wanna know what I think about Whitey?" he said, projecting an air of confidence. "Well, I still think I've got him spotted. I think he's out-of-town talent, a trigger. I don't have a name yet, but I will."

"What makes you so sure?"

"I told ya. It's my business to spot people. And this guy shows all the signs."

"Uh-huh."

He swallowed carefully, took another drag, and let the smoke flow out of his mouth while he talked. "I thought I'd lost him. But then I spotted him in the bar at the hotel. Tried to get him to talk to me, but he wouldn't. He just put his hat on and left. I don't know how long he was there." He took another short drag. "You think he might've killed Ordway?"

"Could be."

"But why?"

"If you're right, then somebody hired him."

"All right," he said. "Who?"

I opened my suitcase and pulled out a clean shirt. "Maybe I did. Or maybe he hired himself. Or maybe it was two other guys."

The color at Springer's temples deepened. The corners of his mouth twitched into a grimace. He tried to pretend it was a smile. He shrugged and reached for his handkerchief again and wiped it over his face. Then he held his cigarette out and flicked the ash onto the floor. He ground it under his heel and turned and looked back at me. "So, tell me about this auction."

"Tell you what? You already know as much as I do... "

"Cut the crap," he wheezed. "I didn't drive down to this dump just to be waltzed around. Remember, you'd be counting the bars in the caboose if it wasn't for me. Now, what would old man Wearing be collecting besides money?"

"When I see him, I'll ask him."

He shook his head and snorted quietly. "You're a close-mouthed bastard, Garrett. With the kind of cooperation I'm getting from you, I might as well be interviewing a parking meter."

"The Colonel must really have you on the string," I said.

"Wearing? Naw. He doesn't even run the paper anymore. He's retired. The city editor runs it—a guy named Bartels."

"Then you don't know the Wearings?"

"Hey, look." He struggled up off the bed and gave me an indignant scowl. "I came here to get information, and you're the one asking all the questions."

I reached into the closet and pulled out my other suit, the one I hadn't slept in. "What good is a Pulitzer Prize if you don't sweat a little to get it?"

He drew his head back and laughed, rippling his extra chin. He sounded like an ox grunting.

"All right," he said, "have it your own way. But I'm sticking to you like glue on a stamp. There's a story here, and you're part of it."

I grinned at him. "Then you won't mind driving me to an appointment."

"Oh, yeah?" He pushed his hat back on his head. "Where to?"

"To the police station."

It was close to ten when Springer turned his brown Studebaker onto Alameda Avenue and headed into the city. The morning sun was rising high and hot, blistering everything it could reach. The streets were still and quiet, marking time under a spread of dust. We drove past rows of stores and office buildings, separated by unpaved side streets. The windows and the corners of the buildings all had a vague look of erosion, abraded by daily visits of blowing sand. There was little traffic. And the few people on the street moved along slowly, heads down, avoiding the sun.

We reached the center of the city, swung around a traffic circle, and came up in front of the police station. As I was getting out, Springer scribbled something in his notebook. Then he tore out the page and handed it to me, saying it was the number of the city desk and that I should call him if I came across something that might help him out. I stuffed the number in my pocket and watched him drive away. The glare of the sun came up off the pavement and wrapped itself around me. It was like standing in a medium oven. I figured I was the one who needed help. I went up the steps and ducked into the police station.

The same wrinkled old man in uniform was waiting behind the desk. I asked for Deputy Sheriff Sanchez. He reached for a phone and mumbled something I couldn't hear into the receiver. Then he hung up and motioned me over to a bench by the door and told me to wait. It works that way in every police station. If they pick you up and bring you in for something, half the force is on you like a bad smell. But just try coming in on your own, and you wind up cooling your heels.

I sat down on the bench and chewed on a Lucky. The minutes trudged by in single file. Finally, Sanchez came through the door to the left of the desk. He had on a freshly pressed khaki uniform with creases as sharp as the edge of a razor blade. He came over to me and held out his hand. "Mr. Garrett. I'm glad you're here."

I stood up and shook his hand. We went down another tiled hallway to the back of the building. At the end of the hall, Sanchez opened a door and ushered me into his office. It was the usual cop's office, bare walls, wooden chairs, and a metal desk sitting in front of a barred window with a shade, cracked and yellowed by the sun, pulled halfway down. Through the window, I could see a sandy open yard behind the station and a line of arid houses and apartment buildings along the street beyond. Behind them, the stark, uneasy line of a bare, rock-strewn mountain pushed up abruptly and seemed to crowd out everything around it.

Sanchez went over and raised the shade. He looked out admiringly for a minute, then turned back to me. He waved a hand toward the window. "Ranger Peak," he said. "Impressive, isn't it?"

His voice came out with an informed precision. "We are standing in the middle of a major break in the Rocky Mountain chain, Mr. Garrett. Not much more than fifty years ago, the Ysleta Indians were still making their spring and fall migrations through this area. They called it 'El Paso Del Norte.' That's how the city got its name."

I pulled out a cigarette and twirled it around in my fingers. "I know," I said. "The pass to the north. But I didn't come here for a history lesson."

He frowned—not angry, just curious. "Are you ready to make your statement?"

"Yeah," I said.

"Have a seat, please."

Without waiting, he turned and went out. I took off my hat and dropped it from habit over a telephone that was parked on the side of the desk. I sat in one of the wooden chairs, pulled a large glass ashtray over to the edge of the desk, and lit my cigarette. I blew a lungful of smoke toward the window and studied the mountain. I wondered if the Indians knew anything about jade.

Sanchez came back with a stenographer. She was a mousey-looking woman, with brown hair and horn-rimmed glasses. She looked youngish but careworn. She sat down took out a steno pad, and steadied it in her lap. I dictated my statement. I went over all the details I knew the police would want to hear. I left out the ones I knew they wouldn't think to ask for.

When I finished, the girl folded up her pad and left. Sanchez had been standing with his back to me, looking out the window. Now he turned and sat down behind the desk. He used his thumb and forefinger and gingerly lifted my hat off the phone. He dropped it like a piece of spoiled meat on the front of the desk. Then he folded his hands in front of him carefully and gave me the cool, steady stare of a blackjack dealer.

"I called Los Angeles," he said. "I spoke with Detective Ed Rawls. I think you know him?"

I nodded.

"He tells me that you used to be a cop, a good one. He didn't exactly say so, but I get the idea that he trusts you." He paused, as if searching for the right words. "And he said that you can be...difficult to get along with."

I crossed one leg over the other, just to be difficult.

Sanchez went on. "Rawls also tells me that you do things your own way, that you work on your own—alone." He rubbed his hands together. "I can't have that. I'm willing to give you some elbow room, but I have to know

56

what you're doing."

I lit another cigarette and looked at him. "Just what makes you so willing all of a sudden?"

"Look," he said. "I have a murder to investigate, and I need your cooperation. If I wanted to, I could just bundle you up on the next train back to Los Angeles."

"If you were any other cop," I said, "you'd be doing exactly that. You see, the LA cops and I have an understanding. I stay out of their way, and they don't punch my face in or throw me in the tank too often just for breathing their air."

"I'm sorry about last night," he said.

"Sure," I replied. "Any minute now, you'll just break down and cry all over your desk. Why the hell should you be sorry? Who's pulling your strings, Sanchez? Is it Stonebreaker? Or is it someone else?"

He let out a long, slow sigh, turning down the corners of his mouth. His eyes darkened. "I'm in a difficult position, Mr. Garrett. And I need your help."

He leaned back in his chair and folded his hands in his lap. He was young, maybe in his early thirties. But there were already lines around his eyes and across his forehead—the lines that a cop gets from hearing too many lies, from seeing too many desperate faces. When you're young, you think about changing things. When you get older, you think about how things are changing you. Sanchez was getting older in a hurry.

He cleared his throat and smoothed out his features with some effort. "I spoke with Gab…Miss Wearing. I take it that you and she didn't quite hit it off?"

"No? I thought she was impressed with my charm and good manners."

"Actually, the word she used was 'insufferable,'" he said. "She used it quite a lot." He cleared his throat again. "She told me about the auctions and about how she contacted this man, Ordway. She also said that the auctions are a private matter and that she wants them kept private. She's very concerned about her father, Mr. Garrett. And she's quite suspicious of Mrs. Wearing."

I nodded.

"I know that Ordway hired you to represent him at the next auction. Can you tell me why?"

"You've heard the story," I said. "Ordway wanted me to look for a jade figure. If I found it, I was to buy it for him."

"Yes," he said. "But why you?"

"I guess because I don't look like a dealer," I shrugged. "And I guess because my rates were the lowest he could find on a hot afternoon."

"I see," he said. "And what do you know about him?"

"Only that his business was antiques and imports, that he knew the Wearings, and that he was very afraid of some ancient Aztec curse involving the jade. He told me that he and Miss Wearing were in great danger."

"Why Miss Wearing?"

"Better ask her."

He inhaled and let his breath out slowly. He held his eyes on me. They were dark and deep now, like the ocean at night, full of strong currents. "Any theories on why Ordway was killed?"

"Not yet," I said.

"You think he could have been mistaken for someone else?" He looked down at the desk, then up again quickly. "You, perhaps?"

I chuckled. "Sure. I deal in antiques on the side, and I'm an expert on Mexican jade." I crushed my cigarette out in the ashtray. "Whoever killed Ordway went to some trouble. The room was locked, and he didn't leave it all day. I verified that at the hotel. As far as I know, I'm a stranger in El Paso. Any number of people in LA might want me dead, but none of them would come here and kill Ordway thinking it was me."

He pursed his lips. "Jack Springer said something about a white-haired man on the train with you. He said he saw the man at the hotel and that he saw you there too. Could this man have been following you?"

"No," I said. "He left the train before I did. He couldn't have known where I'd be staying. And he was already at the hotel when I got there. He was too busy shaking Springer off his tail to be interested in me."

"Jack thinks the man is a hired killer."

"Could be." I nodded. "I'm certain Ordway wasn't killed by an amateur.

But who would be looking for outside talent around here? And what would he have against Ordway?"

Sanchez shook his head. "I don't know. The only one with enough long-range influence to import a specialist would be a man named Delmar."'

I tried not to look interested. "Who?"

He tightened his jaw and drew his mouth into a sardonic twist. He leaned forward and put his elbows on the desk, squeezing his hands together. "Rudy Delmar. He operates a nightclub down in Juarez, not much of a spot for someone with his background."

"What is his background?"

He raised an eyebrow. "You mean you've never heard of Rudy Delmar? That's hard to believe."

I shrugged. "I've led a sheltered life."

He stretched the corners of his mouth into something just this side of a smile. "All right," he said. "Delmar grew up in Kansas City, ran a small-time numbers racket there. In 1933, he moved to Chicago with a handful of his street troops. He bought himself an expensive limousine and began muscling in on Big Ray Floren's territory. There was talk of a war. But then Colonel Wearing's paper started printing some anti-mob editorials, and they put the spotlight right on Delmar. He couldn't even sneeze without reading about it the next morning. So Floren just sat still and waited.

"In 1938, a Chicago policeman was found dead in the backseat of Delmar's limousine. There was a scandal that reached all the way to Denver. Delmar claimed he was set up by Floren. But the police found a witness, a young girl who was a waitress at the club that Delmar used for a headquarters. So, they arrested him and charged him with murder. It looked like a closed case. But just as the trial was starting, the witness disappeared. The D.A. was left empty-handed, and the case against Delmar was dismissed for lack of evidence."

He paused, lifted one leg over the other, and let the corners of his mouth curl upward. I just sat there and tried to look like someone just sitting there.

"That made the Colonel furious," he said, "and so he put every inch of coverage he could on Delmar. Day after day, he ran editorials about corruption and miscarriage of justice. He couldn't change the court decision, of course. Delmar couldn't be tried again. But the Colonel kept the heat on anyway, and after a while, the Internal Revenue Service got interested. Then, the picture changed.

"Early in 1939, the heads of the Chicago families held a meeting. They didn't like the idea of having federal agents around. Once an investigation was started, it might not stop with Delmar. After the meeting, they informed Delmar that it was time for him to leave the country—one way or another. He had no choice, so he left and hid out in Mexico City. After a while, he surfaced over in Juarez. He's been there ever since, always just out of our reach." He paused, as if to reflect. "They say that he's still bitter, that he never forgot what the Colonel did to him. I know Colonel Wearing. He hasn't forgotten either."

I lit up another Lucky and stared across the desk. The smoke chafed the back of my throat like a wood rasp. "Springer was right," I said. "You do your homework."

"I try."

I got up and walked over next to him, and stood looking out the window. "So, what do you want from me?"

"If there's any possible connection between Delmar and this killing," he said, "I want it."

"Are you telling me to find a connection?"

"Absolutely not. But I want you to show me anything you uncover before you act on it."

I remembered Ordway's note. "What makes you think I'd do anything else?"

"I'm just not taking any chances," he said. "I think Delmar may be involved in this somehow. If there's a way to smoke him out, I don't want to lose it."

"And what are the police doing while I'm out being the cat's-paw?"

The first real smile I'd seen on him edged up the sides of his face. "Investigating a murder, of course."

"What about Stonebreaker?" I reached up and rubbed the side of my neck. "He suggested that I leave town. He might try to turn me into hamburger."

"Just don't break any laws," he said, "and I'll try to run interference for you."

"Uh-huh. What about the white-haired man?"

He kept smiling. "I've got some people looking for him. And I already asked Detective Rawls to find out what he can."

I reached down, grabbed my hat, and pulled it on tight. The desert air was drying up my brain. I let my breath out heavily and shook my head. "I ought to walk away from this whole mess, Sanchez. It's like a dead fish under my nose."

He was about to say something when the phone rang. He leaned on the desk and lifted the receiver. He spoke with a cool, professional tone.

"Deputy Sheriff Sanchez... Yes, sir... Yes, sir. He's right here. We've just finished... Yes, I think so... Yes, sir. I will." He hung up.

Sanchez straightened slowly and looked back at me. A few traces of the smile were still clinging to the corners of his mouth. But there was a peremptory set to his jaw. "I hope you didn't make any plans for lunch, Mr. Garrett. Colonel Wearing wants to see you."

Chapter Eight

T he sun was directly overhead, leaving almost no shadows, baking the car and the pavement and the tops of the buildings in a stone-dry heat as we drove out Mesa Street heading west. Before leaving the station, I had read and signed my statement. Then Sanchez had hustled me into a patrol car and jumped into the driver's seat. As we drove, he explained that Colonel Wearing didn't like to be kept waiting. He said it was most unusual for the Colonel to invite a stranger to his house. I said it felt like an invitation from my draft board. Sanchez stopped talking, and I sat back and watched the landscape roll by and wondered why I hadn't just put myself on the LA train.

The road curled around the base of the mountain, past a diner, a library, and some scattered office buildings. Some distance to the left in a shallow ravine, I could see the Rio Grande, a thin trickle of mud and brackish water you could wade across without wetting your cuffs. We crossed Sunland Park Drive and kept going west a few more miles. The buildings fell away, leaving an open stretch of rock and sand and mesquite and scrub cactus. Finally, the road bent around to the northwest, and we came to an intersection. Sanchez turned right, and we headed back up toward the mountain, past a sign that read "Sunset Hills."

The road snaked back and forth in a series of S-turns, going past homes that would bring a stare from most of the residents of West Hollywood, each yard a landscaper's masterpiece. We drove about two hundred feet up the side of the mountain and then turned onto a street marked "Coronado Crescent." The street went another fifty feet and dead-ended at a pair of eight-foot stone pillars standing on either side of a wrought-iron gate. There was a sign on the gate, painted in black lacquer with shiny gold numbers: "2422." Sanchez pulled up and honked twice, and a dark face peered through the gate at the patrol car. There was a nod. The gate slowly swung open, and Sanchez nudged the car up the drive.

The two-lane blacktop driveway was as smooth as a billiard table. It ran up a gentle slope, slicing through half a dozen sets of stonework terraces, each filled with crushed lava and limestone poured into swirling patterns like an oriental tapestry. Set into the terraces were rows of low palms and flowering cactus plants standing erect and unapproachable. At the upper end of the drive, a paved semicircular parking area, bordered by foot-high blocks of sandstone, was laid out like a tablecloth in front of a wall of stone and poured cement. The wall had shiny black wrought-iron spikings across the top and a black chest-high wooden gate in the center with a small plaque on it that said simply, "The Manor." Sanchez pulled up and parked next to a familiar little convertible roadster. We got out and went through the gate.

Inside the wall was a flat, square yard. It was a little smaller than the infield at Yankee Stadium, and it was covered with lush sod as thick and green as an English park. The corners of the yard were accented by small jacaranda trees, freshly watered and giving off a heavy smell. Along the wall, a line of mimosa bushes was interrupted here and there by manzanita and Mexican cactus, exploding with red, yellow, and purple flowers.

Through the center of the yard, a hand-laid red brick walkway ran up to the front of a two-story tan stucco house the size of an airplane hangar, covered by a burnt-carmine pantile roof. The second floor was fronted by a balcony with louvered doors in the center, standing directly above a brick-lined porch that stretched the entire width of the house. Sanchez strode briskly up the walk. I straightened my tie and followed him.

The front door looked massive. It was made of expensive-looking paneled oak, well polished, with an aristocratic look and a button next to it on the right. Sanchez pushed the button, and there was a sound of chimes from inside the house, followed by heavy footsteps. The door opened. I stood there and tried to catch my jaw before it fell on the porch.

The man in the doorway was an Indian. He had a couple of inches on me in height, and he outweighed me by a good thirty pounds, most of it in his neck and shoulders. He had shiny black eyes nestled under heavy lids. They angled together over the bridge of a nose that looked more carved than grown. His mouth was almost without lips, just a flat crack in the lower part of his face. And he had long black hair fastened behind his neck and held in place by a yellow and white beaded headband.

He was dressed like an undertaker—black shoes, black suit with knife-edge creases, black tie, and a white shirt with a collar big enough to bridle a horse. I could almost hear the seams of his suit jacket straining against his bulging upper arms and shoulders. He stood motionless in the doorway, slowly rolling his black eyes from side to side. He looked at me, then at Sanchez, then back at me. He had about as much expression as the wall around the front yard.

Sanchez spoke to him routinely. "I've brought Mr. Garrett, Randolph. The Colonel wants to see him."

The Indian stepped back, holding the door open. Sanchez moved quickly inside without even looking in my direction. I took off my hat and followed him.

We stood in a wide, brightly lit entrance hall. The door was a polished brown parquetry that matched the dark wood moldings and the crossbeams on the ceiling. The buff-colored walls were almost entirely covered with Mexican tapestries and paintings, strong earth colors, chosen by someone who wasn't afraid of red or orange.

To the right was a walk-in closet the size of the hat check room at Lacy's. Sanchez handed his hat to the Indian. I did the same, and then followed Sanchez up the hall.

On the left, almost at the end of the hallway, a large desk sat facing the front door. There was a PBX unit on the wall next to it, and there was a prim brunette on a swivel chair just behind it. She wore a charcoal-gray skirt and the obligatory white blouse. And she had extra-long fingernails polished in a coral varnish that glowed like tossed cigarette butts as they darted over the plugs on the PBX. She answered each call with a smooth efficiency: "Wearing Manor. I'm sorry, the Colonel is not receiving calls. Let me have your name and number, please." She would listen, jot something down on a notepad, and quickly move to the next light on her board. After all, people would be calling all the time. People have a lot to say to you when you have forty or fifty million dollars.

As we approached the desk, the girl looked up and spotted Sanchez. She immediately pushed a button on her unit and spoke into the headset. "Deputy Sheriff Sanchez is here, sir. He has someone with him... Yes, sir." She looked up at Sanchez. "You are to go right up. The other gentleman is to wait."

Sanchez nodded and moved around the desk toward an open doorway. I was starting after him when the girl took off her headset and flashed a smile that was supposed to make me roll over on my back and purr. "You must be someone important."

I put my hand on the desk, leaned close to her, and nodded. "The other gentleman."

I started after Sanchez, my stance showing her that I preferred to wait inside.

We walked through the doorway into the main hall. It wasn't so impressive, only about forty feet from front to back and half again that wide. The ceiling was two stories high. The back wall was tessellated cement and mortar, checkered with six-inch rose-tinted glass inlays, a pair of partitioned doors in the center.

Through the doors, I could see part of a stone patio and a swimming pool. On either side of the hall, a rounded archway was carved into the rough brown stucco wall, showing another hallway to the left and what looked like a sitting room on the right. Past the archways, twin wooden staircases led up to a balcony that ran around the entire upper floor. The walls above the balcony were covered with paintings, all western scenes and landscapes. From where I stood, each painting looked about a hundred feet high and priced just as steep.

The Indian glided up behind us with the quiet certainty of a floorwalker. He put one hand on my arm, and with the other, he motioned toward a cluster of showroom furniture in the corner by the right-hand staircase. I went over and lowered myself almost waist-deep into an overstuffed chair and watched the Indian and Sanchez go upstairs. They walked around the balcony to the front side of the building. They stopped in front of a single wood-paneled door. The Indian knocked twice and opened the door, and they went inside.

I took out a Lucky and lit it, and tossed the match into a glazed terra cotta receptacle next to the chair. This was sitting beside a wooden stand with a tall brass reading lamp on it hovering over a copy of the El Paso *Sun-Register*. I picked up the paper and began thumbing through it. The front page had another piece about all the changes Dewey was going to make when he became President. The sports writers were saying it would be the Yankees and the Dodgers in the series.

Just inside the back page, I spotted a short article.

DEAD MAN FOUND IN HOTEL

Willis C. Ordway of Los Angeles was found dead in a fourth-floor room of the Del Norte Hotel Wednesday evening. Foul play is suspected. According to Sheriff Jesse Stonebreaker, Ordway may have been the victim of a burglary attempt. The police are investigating.

I folded up the paper and threw it into the receptacle.

My stomach was just reminding me that I hadn't eaten in almost twenty-four hours when I heard the music coming from the sitting room. Someone was playing the piano. I put out the cigarette, got up, and started toward the music. I didn't quite get there.

Above me, loud voices started coming from the front room. I looked up in time to see Gabrielle Wearing come through the single door. She paused and hollered back into the room, loud enough to be heard in Tacoma. "You don't own me. You don't run my life. I'll do as I please!" Then she gave the door a slam that sent shock waves into my molars.

She stalked around the balcony and down the stairs, her narrow heels making staccato reports on the wood. She was wearing a businesslike red dress that was a few shades lighter than her face, and she carried a crimson leather purse hung on a shoulder strap. She was squeezing the purse in both hands, digging her fingers in almost up to the first knuckle. Her jaw was clamped as tight as a steam press. As she came off the stairs, she turned and looked in my direction.

"Remember me?" I asked. "Insufferable?"

There was a quick flash in her eyes, like chain lightning. Then just as quickly, the flash was gone, and a practiced composure settled in.

"Oh, Mr. Garrett," she said. "I'm glad you're here." She dug deep into her purse and came up with a small white card, and handed it to me. "Please come to my office this afternoon. Three o'clock. I have business to discuss."

I took the card. I was still stuffing it into the pocket of my suit jacket when she stamped through the entrance hall and out the front door.

I turned around and fumbled for another Lucky. As I pulled out the pack, I happened to glance toward the sitting room. That's when I saw the other woman. She was leaning against the archway, smiling. I had all I could do to get the cigarette out of the pack and not drop it on the floor.

Tall and slender, she had enough curves to pitch nine innings. A flood of chestnut red hair, parted above her left eye, spilled over her shoulders and down the front of a pale-yellow halter held together in front by a set of drawstrings that wouldn't last through a stiff breeze. Between the halter and the floor, a pair of brief white shorts clung to her like adhesive tape. Then, the long sweep of her legs ran down to a pair of bone-white sandals, showing off a full set of scarlet toenails. She kept smiling as I gave her the once-over. She seemed to like my looking at her. There was plenty to look at—plenty of trouble. She turned slowly and ambled back into the sitting room, waving enough sex appeal my way to make Lana Turner look like a Girl Scout. I thought about going back and sitting in the corner and minding my own business. Then, I followed her through the archway.

The room was ordinary size and decorated in a lot of shades of blue. It was crowded with thick padded furniture and plants, mostly tall and leafy. At each window, a pair of shallow dishes hung from a set of brass armatures angled to catch the light. Several Mexican orchids, white with faint indigo throats, lounged disdainfully in each dish, just waiting to be pampered. I walked in and stood on a carpet that was thicker than the air in a poolroom after midnight.

In the far corner by the window was a concert grand piano, a Steinway. The redhead was sitting behind it, playing softly and paying no attention to me. A serving cart next to her carried an assortment of decanters and glasses and an ice bucket. She had a tall drink sitting on the piano in front of her, and next to it, a large ceramic ashtray with a cork-tipped cigarette burning in it. I walked over next to the piano and lit my Lucky. Then I dropped the match in the ashtray and stood there and let her go on ignoring me.

She was on the high side of thirty-five. Her creamy white skin had a few lines in it, but none deep enough to be called a wrinkle. And she wore just enough makeup to cover a hint of shadow under her sea-green eyes. Her nose was long and straight, but somehow soft. It rested easily above a full red mouth, with a sulky curl to the lower lip. I studied the graceful line of her neck as it ran down past her throat. It was the kind of neck that old men like to buy trinkets for, hoping not to be treated like old men.

She modulated into an old wartime number, playing it with the smoky style of a torch song. She swayed easily with the music, leaning forward slightly and letting the front of the halter fall open just enough to invite a stare. I accepted the invitation.

She looked up at me slowly, not missing a note, her long, delicate lashes moving up and down indifferently, like the wings of a butterfly idling in the sun. She sent a doubtful glance over the front of my suit, then looked back down at the keys and kept on playing. "You're not from around here," she said. Her low, silky voice flowed like syrup from a bottle.

"Somebody told you."

"I heard her call you Mr. Garrett," she said.

"And I didn't hear her call you anything."

The corners of her mouth took a whimsical turn upward. "You wouldn't want to. Gabrielle doesn't approve of me. She thinks I'm a fortune hunter."

"Are you?"

"Of course. Aren't you?"

"Sure," I said. "I get up every day at noon and comb my hair and polish my nails and spend an hour in front of the mirror practicing my smile. Then I go out in the afternoon and camp on the doorsteps of rich old ladies."

She stopped playing and looked up. "Aren't you here to see Stanfield?"

"He sent for me."

She angled her head to one side and gently raised an eyebrow. "You don't look like one of them. I'll say that for you. Most of them are nervous little men—glad-handers with shifty eyes and greasy handshakes."

"We're not all like that," I said. "Some of us wash our hands first."

A playful cunning sidled into her expression.

"What do you do?" she asked.

I took an easy drag and let the smoke drift out over the piano.

"I'm a pilgrim in the dark. I go in places people don't want searched, looking for things they don't want found. I play footsie with bums and hypes and chippies and grifters, and sometimes the law. I'm a redeemer of lost souls. And I beat the bricks for time and expenses."

This time she lifted both eyebrows. "You're a detective? A private dick?"

I crushed out my cigarette and didn't say anything.

She stood up and moved over to the serving cart. "Would you like a drink?"

"I'd rather have something to eat."

"Don't be silly." She smiled. "Detectives always drink."

I shrugged. "Then give me something to hold in my hand."

"Scotch?"

I nodded.

She dropped a couple of ice cubes into a tall glass and filled it halfway out of one of the decanters. She handed it to me and picked up the drink she had left on the piano. Then she paraded her body over in front of a puffy-looking sofa in the middle of the room. She sat down and motioned for me to sit next to her.

There was a wooden captain's chair with a padded plush seat next to the sofa. I pulled it around, sat in it, and watched her. She frowned. I sipped the Scotch. It was smooth enough to make me think I was half-sober.

She sprawled out and stretched her arms across the back of the sofa, and lifted one knee over the other.

"Now what?" I asked.

"I thought private detectives were all dirty little men with flat feet who smelled of garlic."

"That's me."

She let a deep chuckle roll out of her throat. "I don't think so."

She adjusted the halter enough to give me another invitation. Then she took a healthy gulp from her glass, leaving a red smear on the rim, and eyed me tentatively. "Do you have a first name?"

"It says Michael on the license. In the Army, it was Mickey."

"Mmm," she murmured. "I like that. My name is Monica."

"I know, Mrs. Wearing."

She frowned again. "I see. Why do you want to see my husband?"

"Better ask him," I said. "As I told you, he sent for me."

"So you did." She brought up a fresh smile. "How is it that you know Gabrielle?"

"We have a mutual acquaintance."

"And who is that?"

"Better ask her."

Her eyes widened, and her jaw muscles tightened. "Aren't you being rather coy? Or do you just not like to talk?"

"Talking's fine," I said, "if it doesn't mean giving away secrets."

"Then, what shall we talk about?"

"Let's talk about your auctions."

She drew her mouth into a tight smile. "I'm afraid that's a private matter too."

"Not so private if I know about them."

She snorted. "Through Gabrielle, I imagine." Then, a trace of suspicion edged into her eyes. "Are you interested in Mexican relics?"

"Not much. But a man named Ordway was. He's dead."

She stiffened. "Are you always so abrupt?"

"Sorry. Murder makes me a little testy."

Her expression didn't change, but her fingers tightened around her glass. "I heard about that business at the hotel," she said quietly. "Did you know him?"

"He was a client. He hired me to do a job, and I haven't done it. It isn't much, but I like to make good on a sale."

She stared at the floor. "I don't see what that has to do with me."

"Maybe nothing," I said. "But Ordway was after something—something you might be putting up for sale. Only he didn't live long enough to find out."

She tried to look surprised. "But we're not offering anything of great value. Just some historical pieces."

"Is there any jade in your collection?"

"I'm sure I don't know," she said breezily. "You'd have to talk with Mr. Dentin."

"Who's he?"

"'Eugene Dentin," she said. "He's the curator of our local museum. He is the custodian of the collection, and he actually runs the auctions."

"Who attends these auctions?"

"Some local collectors and a few personal friends."

"Does that include Rudy Delmar?" It was a wild swing, but it connected.

"Mr. Garrett..." Her words came out like bullets. Then she caught herself, and her voice softened. "I mean, Mickey. Can't we talk about something more pleasant?"

I took some more of the Scotch. "All right. Let's talk about you, Mrs. Wearing."

She stood up abruptly, went over to the cart, and came back with a decanter. My glass wasn't empty, but she bent over in front of me and slowly poured in about three more fingers of Scotch. Then she went back to the sofa and filled her own glass. She set the decanter on the floor and took a long swallow.

"Polite drinking bores me," she said.

She crossed her legs again, rested the glass on her knee, and slowly waved

71

her lashes at me. "There isn't much to talk about. Where shall we start?"

I leaned forward and cradled my glass in both hands. "I like the way you play the piano."

"Oh, that. "She grinned. "My father used to work in a speakeasy. He taught me how to play."

"What else did he teach you?"

She cocked the corner of her mouth almost into a leer. "Not as much as I've taught myself."

I yanked in another mouthful of the Scotch and felt the warmth from it flow all the way down to my feet. I looked at her. "Uh-huh."

She chuckled again. "Now, Mickey. I've had to work hard. And it hasn't been easy for me. Stanfield understands."

"That's convenient."

She fretted her eyebrows and pursed her lips playfully. Little dimples formed along the corners of her mouth. "Oh, don't be so snide," she said. "What can he expect? I'm still young. And I like men."

"I'll bet they like you too."

She shrugged. "I drum up some interest." She raised her eyebrow again. The cunning crawled back into her face. "You must understand that." She paused just long enough. "Gabrielle looked interested."

It didn't take much to see where she was heading. I decided to go along just for fun. "I don't kiss and tell, Mrs. Wearing. I wouldn't be in business long if I did."

She spread out a brand-new smile and looked at me as if I'd just blabbed a deep secret. She leaned forward, resting her elbows on her knees. The drawstring at the top of the halter was holding its breath.

"Is that what it is? But she's so young and headstrong. Wouldn't you rather have someone who can be more...discreet?"

"I might," I said. "Can it be arranged?"

She sat back and laughed. "You're a cold-blooded bastard, aren't you? I'm not sure I like you very much."

"People don't usually like me at all. It isn't part of the job."

She started to say something and then stopped. Her eyes darted up over my left shoulder. I looked around and saw Sanchez standing in the archway.

"Mr. Garrett," he said. "The Colonel is waiting."

Chapter Nine

S anchez ushered me upstairs and around to the front room. Before he could knock, the door opened, and a thin, grating voice like a thresher cutting wheat crawled out. "Come in, Mr. Garrett."

I walked past the Indian, stood in the middle of the room, and started to look around. Sanchez nodded and left, and the Indian shut the door behind me.

It looked like the office of a Castilian general. The walls were decorated with knives and broadswords and pikes, all polished and freshly sharpened. On either side of the room were glassed-in trophy cases filled with metal shields, helmets, and gauntlets—enough hardware to outfit a cavalry troop. And across the back wall were floor-to-ceiling bookcases, crammed with journals and folders and leatherbound volumes, mostly on Spanish military history. Four straight, high-backed chairs sat in the middle of a brown-and-flax-colored Indian rug that looked hand-woven. They were lined up crisply in front of several thousand dollars' worth of desk. Colonel Stanfield Wearing was standing behind the desk.

He was a little more than six feet tall and built like a drainpipe, a tailor's nightmare. His suit must have cost as much as my car, and it hung on him like a parachute caught in a tree. A thin, knotty neck poked up out of the suit and struggled under the weight of a head that looked too large. His brittle gray hair was brushed back flush to his skull. Despite a dark complexion, the papery skin had a gray-brown pallor to it, stretching uneasily over his gaunt features. The strain of age was trying to show in his face, but he held it back with a ruthless defiance. He stood with his arms folded and stared at me out of slate-gray eyes with pupils as dark and deep as gun barrels. I had nothing else to do, so I stared back at him.

Wearing looked down at a panel full of buttons and switches perched on the left side of the desk. He reached out with a claw-like nicotine-stained finger, prodded one of the buttons, and spoke into a microphone contained in the unit. "We'll have lunch now."

He folded his arms and stared at me again. Something like a smile creased the lower part of his face. "I am told that detectives are often armed. Are you carrying a gun, Mr. Garrett?"

"No," I said. "I almost never need one for lunch."

He grunted and motioned toward the Indian. "I gather you've met Randolph," he said. "I'd like him to make sure you are not carrying a weapon."

"Am I supposed to stand for a frisk?"

Wearing's smile widened, and he nodded toward one of the chairs.

The Indian went over and bent down next to the chair and wrapped a hand around the base of one of the legs. Then he stood up and held the chair out in front of him with one hand, as if it were a popsicle stick. His face was full of nothing. He just stood there holding the chair while the Colonel spoke to me.

"Randolph's been in my employ for some time, Mr. Garrett. He is a full-blooded Cherokee. His tribal name is Two Trees. I didn't much care for that, so I changed his name to Randolph and sent him to Princeton."

I looked at Randolph, then back at Wearing. "And they say we've mistreated the Indians."

The Colonel nodded again. Randolph put the chair down and turned toward me. He looked as worried as a fencepost. I decided to let him frisk me. He patted me down with the delicate grip of a pipe wrench, then stepped back and motioned me toward the chair. I decided to sit down.

Wearing took a cigarette out of a small pewter box to his right. He offered one to me. I refused. He pulled a wooden match out of his coat pocket, lit it with his thumbnail, and guided it up to the end of his cigarette. I fished out a Lucky and helped him pollute the air.

"I heard about your encounter with Jesse Stonebreaker," he said. "You're not easily intimidated. I like that."

He reached into the middle drawer of the desk, took out a single typed sheet of paper, then laid it out in front of him and began reading from it.

"Michael Garrett. Born in Los Angeles, parents deceased. You attended college but didn't graduate. You joined the police force in 1932 and built up an impressive arrest record. Then, in 1935, you were asked to leave the force." He looked up. "The reasons are a little vague."

I didn't say anything.

He looked down at the paper again. "You became a private detective, making a rather unspectacular living. In 1942, you joined the Army. Served in the Pacific, twice decorated. Then you returned to Los Angeles, where you resumed your detective business."

He stopped reading and looked up at me. "The rest is also quite vague. No one seems to know much about you, Mr. Garrett."

I sucked in on my Lucky and aimed a lazy cloud at the front of the desk. "There's not much to know. I smoke. I swear. I like good music, chess, and baseball. And when I'm hungry, I like to eat. I can still speak English if anyone wants to hear it. I've also been known to take a drink. And I like to wear shorts with little red hearts on them."

"Very droll," he said. "You never married?"

"I've had a few narrow escapes. Why?"

He waved his cigarette at me. "Since you're still a private investigator, I take it that means you're for hire.

"I can always listen to something with a dollar sign next to it."

He turned sideways in his chair and looked away. "What do you know about me?"

"Not much," I said. "You run a string of newspapers, and you probably have more money than I can write zeros. At a guess, I'd say you've got most of the town in your pocket. And that goes for the police, or at least a deputy sheriff. You have a son who drinks, a daughter who yells, and you're married for the second time.

He tried to smile. "You're a perceptive man, Mr. Garrett. I take it you've met my wife."

I nodded. "She gave me a piano recital with a Scotch chaser."

"What do you think of her?"

"She looks healthy."

"She is," he croaked. He turned back and looked at me. "I have a certain fondness for Victor Sanchez. He works hard. I sent him to Stanford, and he graduated with honors. As a result, he feels obliged to show me certain... courtesies. I'd say he's done rather well...for a Mexican."

"You're just a walking scholarship fund," I said. "You even sent your daughter to law school. Did you change her name too?"

He almost let out a cackle. "No. And she paid her own way." A quiet mirth played in his eyes. "You made rather a strong impression on my daughter, Mr. Garrett. She was, shall we say, ...incensed."

"That's fine," I said. "I'm everybody's favorite." There was a glass ashtray on the desk. I crushed out my cigarette. "Look, Colonel. Just what the hell do you want with me?"

Before he could respond, there was a knock. Randolph opened the door, and a young, dark-haired maid came in and laid a tray on the desk. Then, she retreated and Wearing motioned to me.

"*Huevos rancheros,* Mr. Garrett—a Mexican omlette. I hope you like it."

There was a single plate and a silver service for one. I thought about being polite, but I couldn't convince my stomach. The plate was warm and covered with a greenish sauce that peeled back the roof of my mouth on the first bite. I didn't care. I was hungry enough to eat the desk.

Wearing leaned back in his chair, puffed on his cigarette, and eyed me, smiling. "I'm not able to eat much anymore," he said. "But I enjoy watching others enjoy good food."

I cleaned the plate with a few scrapes. Then I sat back and tried not to look as if my mouth had just been cauterized.

"All right," I said. "Now, why am I here?"

He ignored the question. "You were wrong about one thing, Mr. Garrett. I don't run the papers anymore, not even the local one."

I decided it was worth trying again. "So, you got tired of trying to square off with Rudy Delmar?"

The closest he could get to a flush crawled up the sides of his face. He bared his teeth and snarled at me. "That son of a bitch! That scum! People like that don't deserve to walk on this earth, fouling the air that we breathe. History will deal with such people."

He took a violent drag on his cigarette, drawing the ash almost up to his nose. He shook his head and let the smoke run out his mouth and nostrils. Then, the anger slowly washed back down under his shirt collar.

"When you reach my age, Mr. Garrett, day-to-day matters become less important, and you begin to see things on a larger scale. It's called perspective, vision. After Victoria, my first wife, died, I decided to look to other things. I gave up active control of my newspapers. Now I have larger concerns."

I gave him my nastiest smile. "Well, somebody's running your local paper tight enough to put a hush on a killing."

His face clouded over, and he spoke slowly. "Yes, that man, Ordway. An insignificant little man, really. But there was no need for him to die. I'm afraid that was Gabrielle's fault for bringing him here. I told her not to interfere. I demand loyalty from my people, Mr. Garrett. And I've tried to teach my daughter obedience. But as you've found out, she's hard to control."

"Interfere with what?"

"With things that don't concern her."

"Like the auctions?"

"They don't concern you either."

"They concerned somebody enough for a man to be murdered," I said. "Why are you selling off your collection?"

He sat back and folded his arms, and gave me a perfunctory smirk. "Mr. Garrett, I've turned the collection over to my wife. What she does with it is her affair. I don't care to discuss it any further."

I stared at him. He had the sensitivity of an elephant. "What do you know about a pair of jade figures?"

He looked at me for a long moment. "Do you do much reading, Mr. Garrett?"

I shrugged. "I look at a racing form now and then."

His eyes drifted off over my head. They held the same fascination I'd seen In Ordway's the day before.

"There is something mystical about jade, Mr. Garrett. Legend has it that once you've seen a piece of jade, you can't resist touching it, holding it, possessing it—much like a woman. It was first found and revered by the ancient Chinese dynasties over five thousand years ago. They believed that the jade was a gift from their God of the Sun. They carved idols from it and worshiped the idols. Centuries later, jade containers were used by pirates and slave traders to smuggle opium into Central America. The jade became a great prize among the Mayans and the early Aztecs." He smiled. "It's ironic. The Indians didn't care about the opium. They used it for fertilizer."

I lit another Lucky. "Tell me about the Bird of Death."

He inhaled slowly and let out a heavy sigh. "Quetaz, the god of the Aztecs, was said to be jealous and vengeful. He demanded strict obedience. When a member of the community broke tribal law, he would find a dagger on his blanket. It was a ceremonial object, always with a jade handle and always with a carving of a large bird standing before the setting sun. The Indians called it the Bird of Thunder—the Bird of Death. Any man finding it had until the next sunset to use the dagger on himself. When the sun set, Quetaz would appear. If the man was still alive, his death would be...horrible."

I crossed my legs and looked at him. "And you think that's what happened to Ordway? An Aztec god doing a ceremonial rubout?"

He lowered his eyes and looked down at the desk. "I've lived a long time, Mr. Garrett. I've seen a great many things, and I've studied history. Man has always been faced with things he couldn't explain, with mysteries. Being afraid of the unknown, he even invented science to solve the mysteries and take away the fear. But science couldn't do that." He shrugged. "The mysteries remain, and so does the fear."

I reached over and squashed my cigarette in the ashtray. "People don't get killed by mysteries. They get killed by greed, revenge, and all the other forms of human corruption. They get killed for jealousy. For money. Sometimes, they get killed just for the fun of it. And there are all kinds of killers. It might be a clerk, a mailman, or a cab driver. Or it might be an expensive hood with an army of hired gunsels. But it's never a mystery."

He folded his hands and scowled. "There is a certain order in things, Mr. Garrett. The Aztecs understood that. I had hoped that you could see it, that you might be a man of vision. Perhaps I was wrong. Perhaps you're *not* the man I want to hire."

"I have enough vision to see when I'm getting the royal runaround."

His scowl turned into an angry grimace. "Young man, my people don't speak to me that way."

I stood up. "For your information, Colonel Wearing, I'm not a young man, yours or anyone else's. And I don't much care if you want to hire me or not. I've already got a client, a dead one. I've also got a sore neck from talking to your sheriff. I've been hauled into jail and then told to leave town. I've been set up for a patsy for some hood I don't even know. Your daughter thinks I'm insufferable. Your wife tried to play footsie with me before I'd had lunch. And except for Sanchez, nobody really seems to give a damn about finding out who killed Ordway."

He glowered across the desk. "I didn't bring you here to listen to this."

"Then why *did* you bring me here?"

He frowned and pursed his lips and didn't say anything.

I turned and started for the door. "Then, I'll just be running along."·

I had my hand on the knob when he spoke. "Mr. Garrett, wait…please."

I turned and looked at him. He cast a quick glance at Randolph, then looked back at me. He exhaled heavily. "I'm being blackmailed."

I felt like throwing one of the chairs at him. Instead, I went back and sat in it. "All right, Colonel. I'll play your game a little longer. What gives?"

He reached into a drawer and came up with a large, unmarked tan envelope and tossed it across the desk. I picked it up and pulled out a black and white photograph and a sheet of paper. The picture showed a large, curly-haired man in his underwear stretched out on an extra-large bed. His eyes were closed. He was being attended by two dark-haired, dark-skinned girls. They both wore smiles, nothing else. The picture reminded me of something I'd seen at the Del Norte the night before.

I looked at the sheet of paper. It was covered with words clipped from a newspaper and pasted in place. They said, "If you don't want the wire services to get this, put $10,000 in unmarked bills in locker 100 at the train station by midnight Friday."

I laid the paper down on the desk and put the photograph on top of it. "This isn't you."

He shook his head, and his tone was grim. "No. It's my son, James. From the look, I'd say he was on one of his escapades. Even though it doesn't involve me directly, it wouldn't do James any good if that picture appeared in public. And it would be…an embarrassment to me."

"So, you haven't been to the cops."

"That's what blackmail is all about, isn't it? Avoiding the police?"

"Sometimes," I nodded. "Just what do you want me to do?"

He put his elbows on the desk and sent me a steely-eyed stare. "I want you to find the person responsible and obtain the negative and all the prints. And if possible, I want you to impress upon James that this must not happen again."

I shook my head. "Sorry. I can't help you."

He sat back and lifted his eyebrows. "Why not? What would you do if you were in my shoes?'

"I'd pay."

He glared at me. "But this is a matter of pride and honor."

"Somebody's banking on that," I said. I pointed at the photograph. "When did you get this?"

"It was delivered by messenger last night. Some Mexican boy brought it to the door."

"Uh-huh." I lit up another Lucky. "Look, Colonel. Chances are the negative is in Topeka by now. Ten grand means nothing to you. And since they asked for so little, this is probably just a small-time caper. You may never hear from them again. As for your son, I'm not in the babysitting business."

He rubbed his hands together and shook his head. Then he let a tight smile play at the corners of his mouth. He reached into the desk once more and brought out a small envelope, and dropped it in front of me. I picked up the envelope and looked inside. It was Benjamin Franklin again, three times.

"Let's call that a retainer," Wearing said tonelessly. I tried to think of all the reasons I shouldn't take it. Then I put the envelope in my pocket. "Let's," I said.

"And I'll put a car at your disposal." He reached over, poked a button, and spoke into the intercom.

"James, bring the car around for Mr. Garret."

"What about the ten grand?" I asked. "In case I need it for a dodge."

He waved his hand and snorted. "That can be arranged."

I picked up the photograph and the sheet of paper and stuffed them into my coat pocket. "I'll need these."

He hesitated, then nodded slowly. "I am relying on your discretion, of course."

I got up and left.

He was just a friendly old man, a student of history. He was a public-spirited citizen, spending his money to educate the underprivileged. He was a father protecting his son. He was a man of pride and honor. I could believe every word he said. The same way I could almost put a broken egg back together.

I went downstairs with Randolph at my heels. He ducked into the closet off the entryway and came out with my hat. I dropped it on my head and said, "Thanks, chief."

His black eyes flashed. His voice came up out of his shoes. "Mr. Garrett, I don't care for your provocative attitude."

I stared at him. "I can't say I'm fond of it either, Randolph. But in my business, provocative is all I can afford."

Then I left.

Chapter Ten

The car was a late-model Buick Special, black with spotless whitewalls. It was waiting in the parking area by the front gate. The man leaning against it, his foot on the running board, was dressed like an Easter egg. He wore white shoes, a pale avocado suit, and a lavender shirt; the collar folded stylishly outside his jacket. He was tall and husky, he had a thick crop of curly black hair, and he hid part of a deep tan behind a pair of Hollywood sunglasses.

"So, you're Garrett," he said. Before I could answer, he flipped a set of keys to me. "Let's go, hot shot."

I slid in under the wheel, and he climbed in next to me. I turned the ignition and listened to an expensive roar jump up out of the engine. Then I meshed the gears and cruised down the drive and out the gate. He sat watching me as I eased down the mountain, but he didn't speak until I turned onto Mesa Street.

"Where are we going?"

"I need some company," I said.

He kept hiding behind his sunglasses while I drove back toward town. After a few miles, I found a small liquor store, pulled over, went in, and bought a cheap bottle of Scotch. I tried it out in the car. It wouldn't win any prizes. I offered some to my passenger.

He put up his hand and shook his head. "Too early."

I helped myself again, then put the bottle in the glove compartment.

"What do I call you?" I asked.

"Jimmy," he said. He angled his head to one side. "Are you going to lecture me, reason with me, or try to buy me off?"

"I'm going to drop you at the nearest bus stop."

He laughed. "That's not the way it's done. You're supposed to wise me up, get me to be proud and responsible—like my father."

"Nuts," I said. "Not when you're having so much fun being an embarrassment to him."

He leaned back in the seat. "So that's your strategy: honesty." He turned and looked out through the windshield. "Well, why not? It's never been tried."

I started the car and continued toward town. He sat and brooded behind his sunglasses. We headed into the center of the city. Under the afternoon sun, the pavement was like a roasting pan, glistening and radiating the heat. Even the steering wheel was getting hot. I rolled down the window and loosened my tie. At an almost busy intersection, I pulled over to the curb and parked next to a mailbox.

"You can catch a lift here," I said.

He just kept on brooding.

I took out the envelope with the three C-notes and sealed it. I used my fountain pen and addressed it: "Michael Garrett, c/o Col. Stanfield Wearing. 2422 Coronado Crescent, El Paso. Then I put a stamp on It and got out and dropped the envelope in the mailbox.

When I got back to the car, Jimmy Wearing had taken off his sunglasses. Doubt lines creased his face. "That was some real dough," he said. "I know. I've seen those envelopes before. What the hell did you do with it?"

"I put it in the bank."

He frowned. "But you are still working for my father?"

"Until I tell him to open the envelope."

He grinned and shook his head. "You're not like the others. They all bowed and scraped—anything to please the old man. But you're different. You really don't care about his money, do you?"

I looked out into the street. "You can get out here."

He put his sunglasses back on and dropped his arm over the back of the seat. "Drive."

84

So, I drove. We headed down into the valley. There wasn't much traffic, just a few cars, an occasional bus, and a half-dozen orange cabs racing to and from the border. Down along Alameda, a long black limousine whirled out of a side street behind us. It kept pace for several blocks, then turned right and headed off into the lower valley.

By now, Jimmy Wearing was ready to talk. "No sir," he clucked. "You're not like the rest of them. There's been almost one a month for the last six months. I don't know where he gets them. Doctors, lawyers, even professors." He turned and looked at me. "But you're the first private dick."

"Lucky me."

"What's it like, being a sleuth?"

"Like having a boil where you sit," I said. "What do you do to keep off the streets?"

He stared straight ahead. "The streets aren't so bad. I spend a lot of time at the club...on the golf course, and in the gym. Sometimes I try to write. I've been doing more of that lately. Got an apartment down on Piedras where I can be alone. Helps me think, ya know? The old man says if I get good at it, he might get me a job on the paper." He spoke half to himself, his voice lowered. "Fat chance.

"I thought you lived at the house."

He shifted uneasily in the seat. "I've got a room there—first floor in the back. I wake up there a lot. The old man's left orders all over town. When somebody finds me tanked up, bring me to the house."

"And you don't make yourself hard to find."

He clenched his teeth. "You don't know how he really is, how hard. He sits on top of the world and looks down at everybody. I could never do anything to please him. Not in school, not working. I even thought a stretch in the Army might be something he'd respect." He snorted. "But not him. After a while, I just stopped trying."

"What are you trying now?"

His mouth twisted halfway into a grin. "Finding myself. Isn't that what they call it?"

"Is that why you were handling those two at the hotel last night?"

He chuckled. "Rosetta and Lupe? They're just out for a good time. They're harmless."

"Their boss isn't."

I felt the seat stiffen. "You mean Rudy? I don't have much to do with him."

"But you know him."

"Everybody knows Rudy."

I turned off Alameda and pulled up, and parked in front of the motel. There was a note fastened to my door with a thumbtack. It read, "Call Jack Springer." I unlocked the door, and we went inside.

I dug into my suitcase, fished out the holster, and strapped it on. I fitted the Luger under my arm and tucked the suitcase back into the closet. Jimmy Wearing leaned against the chest of drawers, watching.

"'Whew," he breathed. "I guess you really mean business."

"I told you I needed some company."

We locked up and went into the office next door. It was empty. I dropped a nickel into the wall phone and dialed the number Springer had given me for the city desk. I got a thick voice that told me he wasn't there.

"This is Garrett," I said. "Any message?"

"Oh, yeah. He wants you to meet him at the racetrack, Sunland Park."

"Did he say when?"

"Right away, I guess. Sounded important."

I hung up and went outside and asked Jimmy Wearing how to get to Sunland Park. He pointed the way, and we drove farther down Alameda and turned right on Rio Dominges. The road curled left along the river and stretched into the lower valley, past a few adobe houses, and then into nothing. After another mile, Jimmy motioned to a dirt road off to the left.

The Buick bounced along for about a quarter mile, and we came to a chain-link fence. A gate at the entrance was closed and locked. I got out and stood in the afternoon sun. An uneasy wind had started coming in off the desert. It was dry and hot, and it chewed at my face like sandpaper. Through the fence, I could see an open parking lot and a grandstand, stark and empty, as inviting as a mausoleum.

I got back into the Buick, and we went to the right along an access road around the grandstand. On the far side, I spotted a brown Studebaker nosed up against the fence. I parked next to it, and we got out. I opened the passenger-side door and peered inside. It was clean. I checked the glove compartment and under the seats. Nothing. I got out and went around to the back. The trunk was open, keys in the lock, the spare and the jack untouched. I stepped back and stood scraping my thumbnail over my front teeth, wondering what I was doing out here in the middle of a deserted piece of real estate.

Jimmy Wearing walked past me to the other side of the Studebaker. I heard him stop. He made a sudden noise, sucking in air through his teeth." Oh, my God," he breathed. As I went around the car and stood next to him, I had that bad news feeling.

Chapter Eleven

There would be no Pulitzer Prize for Jack Springer. He was stretched out face down next to a clump of mesquite in that disconnected position that always looks the same. Blood had spotted his suit and dried on the ground. The back of his head was broken open like a cracked watermelon. His jacket was twisted to the right partway under him, and I could see a bumpy red stain on his shirt. I knelt down, poked gently, and felt part of a rib broken by something hard and tapered like the point of a shoe. I lifted his shoulder enough to get a look at his battered, pulpy face and shook my head.

I started through his pockets. It was a nasty job, and I found nothing. I was still looking when I heard Jimmy shuffling in the gravel off to the left. I turned and saw him standing there, his shoulders trembling. As I watched, he suddenly dropped to all fours, hitched once, and dumped his insides on the landscape while I finished searching Springer's pockets.

After a few minutes, Jimmy stood up and stumbled back over to the car. His tan had turned to a sickly green tint. "Sorry," he said. "I saw guys get shot in the Army, but nothing like this. I guess I'm not used to it like you."

"Nobody gets used to it," I said. I stood up and walked over to him. "Are you alright?"

"I guess so."

"Then go find a phone and call Sanchez. Tell him to bring the coroner."

I watched him get into the Buick and drive off down the access road. Then I went back and started to look around.

Along the outer edge of the access road, thick knots of mesquite stood like a cordon of soldiers protecting the desert. The ground was littered with beer bottles and paper cups, remnants from a busy night. Beyond the mesquite, the desert basin spread out low into the distance. Across the horizon to the east, the harsh lines of the Guadalupe Mountains loomed, remote and unconcerned. I listened to the stirring quiet of the desert. As I stood there, a quick-heated gust came up and covered my suit with sand. The wind whipped around and pushed against me, as if it was telling me to stay away. I've had worse advice. I started toward the desert.

About ten yards past the mesquite, I found Springer's hat and, just beyond that, a tire iron. One end was smeared with red, still glistening wet in the afternoon sun. A squad of black ants explored the iron, gathering around and over the sticky surface like assault troops on a captured island. The desert was already staking its claim.

Nothing succeeds like dumb luck; the wallet must have been right between my feet. I was just turning back toward the car when I stepped on it. It was lying half-buried in the sand next to a crumpled piece of paper. I used my handkerchief, picked up the wallet, and poked through it. It still held Springer's license and press pass and about forty bucks cash. Tucked into a plastic case behind the license was a folded-up dollar bill, still crisp and new. In one corner, somebody had written a date: 3-14-45, near the end of the war. People save the damnedest things.

I wrapped the wallet in my handkerchief and put it carefully in my coat pocket. Then I picked up the crumpled paper. It was a prescription for sleeping pills made out for Springer, and it had been written in the usual medico scrawl by "Dr. Morris Kintner, 174 Blackstone Terrace." On the back, another hand had written, "Garrett, Desert View Motel." Even in the dusty heat, I felt a chill walk down my spine. I tucked the form in with the handkerchief and went back to the Studebaker.

The wind was picking up, steady and hard. I watched a ball of tumbleweed bobbing lazily across the basin on its way to nowhere. The last twenty-four hours drifted through my head the same way. All I could see were a train, a jade figure, an angry bird, and two dead men. They were all saying something, but I couldn't make out the words.

It was then I noticed a set of tire tracks. They were on the desert side of the Studebaker, opposite where I had parked. The markings were faint in the blowing dust, but the edges were still sharp. They had been made by something with a wide, solid tread, something heavy, something I had seen before. I could almost feel proud of myself. Brilliant detective work, Garrett. Nothing succeeds like dumb luck.

A parade of cars came up the access road behind me, rumbling and growling like Patton's tanks. There were two squad cars and the Buick. Stonebreaker and Weems bolted out of the first car, with Sanchez and Jimmy and the coroner trailing not far behind. The little man with the bag went over and knelt down next to Springer. He began his ritual of squeezing and scraping. Sanchez and Weems stood beside him and watched, looking properly sober. Jimmy moved over next to me and leaned against the Studebaker.

Stonebreaker sauntered over and looked down at the body, and then grunted. Then he strutted back and forth a few times, chewing on his cigar and kicking up dust with his boots. Finally, he stopped in front of me, leaned forward, and stuck his cigar under my nose. His face was covered with a dark red sneer.

"I thought I told you to drift," he said.

"I wanted to see some of the sights first."

"What the hell are you doin' out here?"

I motioned toward Springer. "I got a message that he wanted to see me."

"What for?"

I shrugged. "I guess he wanted to give me his views on classic desert paintings."

His eyes narrowed to slits, and he bared his teeth around the cigar. "Still crackin' wise, huh? Well, I'll show you, you smart-assed son of a bitch."

He grabbed a handful of my lapel and cocked a meaty fist up by his right ear. Before he could throw it, Sanchez grabbed him and pulled him back. He spoke quietly while Stonebreaker just stood and speared me with his eyes.

"Jesse, the Colonel wants us to leave him alone."

Stonebreaker's face turned the color of an enraged eggplant. His words hissed out through his teeth. "Well, tell this punk to keep his goddamn lip buttoned around me, or by Christ, I'll burn him." He wheeled around and stalked over next to the body.

Sanchez turned and looked at me, his eyes pleading. "Take it easy, will ya? He's got a short fuse."

"But not much of a charge," I said.

He frowned. "You were supposed to keep me informed."

"I'm informing you now." I pointed out past the mesquite. "There's a tire iron out there. Your man will want to examine it." I reached into my coat pocket and brought out the wallet and crumpled paper. And I found these."

He looked carefully through the wallet and then at the prescription. He pushed his hat back on his head. "So, he wasn't robbed." He tugged at his lower lip. "Wonder why he was taking sleeping pills."

"Maybe he had trouble going to sleep."

"Very funny." He turned the prescription over and found my name. "You think this means anything?"

"It means that somebody knows where to find me."

"Who?"

I shook my head. "Maybe that's what Springer wanted to tell me."

Sanchez folded his arms and turned his back toward Stonebreaker and the others. "What about that guy he was bird-dogging, the one with the white hair?"

I shook my head again. "Don't know."

He knitted his eyebrows. "You sure? Haven't you got any ideas at all?"

"Just one," I said. "You know anybody who drives a limousine?"

He looked as if he'd just been jabbed in the gut. His mouth was still hanging open when the coroner came over, followed by Weems and Stonebreaker. Sanchez gave me a sharp look, then turned and spoke. "What do you think, doc?"

The little man rubbed his hands together nervously. "Still warm," he said. "Must've happened recently." He shook his head. "Damnedest thing I ever saw. Both his arms and legs are broken. Whoever or whatever killed him

91

must have been awfully strong."

Weems shuffled his feet and looked sideways at me. "Maybe there was more than one of 'em."

"Sure," I said. "Me and the Marines."

He shot an angry look at Sanchez. "Well, he coulda had help."

"I did," I said. "I was with Jimmy Wearing. Why don't you take the both of us in?"

I looked over at Jimmy. He slipped on his sunglasses and grinned. "That's right, Hal. We came out here together."

Weems' face fell down to his belt. "Well, I didn't exactly mean it that way," he mumbled. "Coulda been some of them beaners. You know, wetbacks lookin' to skin some Anglo and take his dough."

Sanchez glared at him. "Listen, Hal. Garrett found this." He opened the handkerchief enough to show Weems the wallet. "It still has Springer's identification and money in it. So, you can take your wetback idea and stuff it in your hat." He folded up the handkerchief and handed the bundle to the coroner. "Better check this for prints, doc."

"Sure, Vic." The little man gingerly tucked the handkerchief in his coat pocket. Then he turned and walked quickly over to the first squad car.

Sanchez turned back to Weems, his face as stony as the mountains on the horizon. "Garrett says there's a tire iron out there." He motioned toward the mesquite. "Go and get it. And be careful with it. It's evidence."

Weems ducked his head and hurried off toward the desert.

Stonebreaker was still standing there; fists dug into his hips, his eyes trained on me like artillery. "I don't care," he growled. "Colonel or no Colonel. Don't get in my way, flatfoot." He turned and strode over by the mesquite.

I turned to Sanchez. "How long has he been sheriff?"

"A long time. Why?"

"It must not be an elective office," I said.

Sanchez snickered and shook his head. "Jesse's all right. He just hasn't kept up with the times. He still thinks a cop works best with his fists and a rubber hose."

The wind laced through the mesquite, kicking up more dust and filling the cuffs of my trousers. I pulled my hat down and turned up my coat collar. "Don't things ever stay still out here?"

"It's that West Texas wind," he said. "They say that during the day, Texas blows into New Mexico, and at night, New Mexico blows back again." For a minute, he just squinted into the teeth of the wind. Finally, he turned back to me. "I guess you're working for the Colonel now."

"I guess."

"Our deal still stands. Anything you get, you bring to me."

Now I looked toward the desert. "I haven't gotten anything yet but a pain in the neck."

He stretched his lips into a tight smile. "You said something about a limousine. You think Delmar did this?"

"Don't ask me," I said. "I don't even know the guy."

"You talked with Springer. Any Idea why he was killed?"

I shrugged. "Maybe somebody didn't like the way he was digging up his stories."

"You think there's a connection between these two killings?"

"I don't think anything yet. Thinking hurts." I put my back to the wind and looked at him. "What about the knife in Ordway's hand? Can you trace it?"

"Not a chance," he said. "You can pick one up on any corner in Juarez—four, maybe six bits. Handle's made of onyx painted green to look like jade. It's a tourist gimmick. Probably break if you tried to use it."

"Anything from the boys in LA.?"

"You mean about the white-haired guy? Not yet. Why?"

"He was asking for Ordway at the hotel last night."

His eyes grew an inch. "Listen, Garrett. If there's something I should know..."

"Give Jimmy a ride home," I said. "If you don't know the way, stop and ask a bartender." I started for the Buick.

"Where the hell are you going?"

"To see my lawyer."

Chapter Twelve

On the way downtown, I stopped at a drugstore and bought a couple of packs of Luckies. While I was there, I ducked into a phone booth in the back of the store, dialed the Operator, and placed a long-distance call to Los Angeles. Then I dropped in a bunch of change and waited. Finally, the desk sergeant at the Eighth Precinct in LA told me that Detective Rawls was out on an investigation. I could see him investigating the bottom of a beer glass. I left a message and hung up.

As I approached the front of the store, a black limousine rolled slowly up to the curb and stopped. There were two men in the front seat. The one on the passenger side wore a dark gray hat pulled down over the front of his face. He inspected the Buick and then turned and said something to the driver. I caught a glimpse of white hair.

I yanked the door open and ran out toward the street—not the smartest thing to do. I was just in time to hear the roar of an engine and watch the limousine cruise around the corner. I scrambled into the Buick and hit the ignition. By the time I turned the corner, the side street was empty. I pulled over and idled the engine, and thought about it. Two men in a limousine. Not so tough to catch. I could do it. Then what? I circled the block and headed back into the center of town.

The card Gabrielle Wearing had given me listed her office as Suite Six in the Kenwood Building on Montana Street. She had said she wanted to talk business. I had done business with lawyers before, only none of them had had long blond hair and nice legs.

I eased the Buick up in front of the Kenwood and got out. It was eight stories of postwar building, all steel and tinted glass, fronted by a row of knee-high shrubs browning in the sun. A royal blue awning ushered the way through a set of revolving doors and into a lobby full of blue tiles and afternoon glare. Between the two elevators at the back was a building directory. Suite Six was on the second floor.

The elevator doors opened onto a quiet corridor, a pale gray carpet stretching in both directions past pale-grained wooden doors with black stenciling. Number Six was across the hall from the elevator. I went through the door marked "G. Wearing, Attorney" and found a small reception room lit by harsh fluorescent bulbs recessed into the ceiling. To the left, a low burnt-orange couch, flanked by polished chrome chairs with black seats, faced a glass-top coffee table covered with the usual worn-out magazines. On the right, a young brunette with a scarlet mouth and dark eyes surrounded by too much mascara sat behind a desk, pounding a typewriter with the urgency of someone trying to set a new record for the Minute Waltz. She looked up at me and canvassed my suit the way a butcher looks at a side of beef, deciding where to make the first cut.

She stopped typing and put a wry tilt to her mouth. "Can I help you?"

"Sure." I grinned at her. "I need lots of help. The name's Garrett. I have an appointment."

She sat up straight, disappointment falling down over her face like a theater curtain. She leaned over and peered at an open notebook next to the typewriter.

"Oh, yes," she said. "Three o'clock. You're late."

"I was held up."

"Were you?" Irritation clawed at her voice. She motioned toward the couch. "Have a seat."

Before I could get to the couch, the door to the inner office opened, and an old, worn-looking Mexican woman stepped out, followed by Gabrielle Wearing. The woman ambled over to the outer door, with Gabrielle keeping a reassuring hand on her arm.

"Don't worry, Mrs. Gonzales," she said. "They can't foreclose without due process. We'll fight them."

The woman turned and looked back uncertainly, then went out into the hall. Gabrielle stood staring at the door. She let out a heavy sigh. Then abruptly, she turned and looked at me.

"Mr. Garrett, thank you for coming."

I nodded.

She turned and spoke to the brunette. "Angela, no calls, please." She looked back at me. "This way, Mr. Garrett."

She marched past the desk and into the office. I followed her and paused in the doorway long enough to watch Angela attack the typewriter again.

The office was a smaller version of the Colonel's, but without the armaments. Rows or shelves on the left were crammed with sets of well-worn law books, and three dark green metal filing cabinets stood against the wall on the right, towering over a spindly potted fern in the corner. Just to the left of the fern on the back wall was the usual array of framed diplomas. You can't be a bona fide lawyer without having a dozen certificates on the wall.

Gabrielle sat down behind a plain wooden desk stacked with folders, books, and loose papers. She motioned toward a chair in front of the desk.

"For someone with money, you don't put up much of a front," I said as I sat down.

"I don't have a lot of money, Mr. Garrett. My father does."

"Could have fooled me." I took off my hat, reached for a cigarette, and looked around for an ashtray. I didn't find one.

She leaned forward against the desk and looked at me evenly, her eyes bright blue and hard. "Mr. Garrett, I came here a little over two years ago, right out of law school. My father had arranged a position for me with a local firm, but I turned it down. I wanted to help people who need help the most. Not the businessmen or the corporations—not my father's people. I wanted to help the merchants, the laborers…the Mexicans struggling for a living in this country. People who have no one to stand up for them. I've worked hard to start this practice. And I haven't taken a cent from my father. Many of my clients can't pay, and I haven't made much money. But sometimes it's worth it just the same."

"So, you're a hardworking, solid citizen. But you still have your father's money to fall back on."

She squeezed her hands together and measured out her words like a bank teller counting change. "Mr. Garrett, my father thinks I'm wasting my time—that what I'm doing is unnatural. He says I'm out of step with the order of history. He thinks women should be docile and doting, like my mother. Or they should be show ornaments like…" She clamped her jaw and made a sound of distaste through her teeth. "Don't misunderstand. I love my father very much. But I'd rather die than give in to him."

"I guess Ordway wouldn't give in either."

Her eyes flashed. "He didn't have anything to do with… Must you always be so…so…"

"Insensitive?"

She smiled disdainfully. Her voice dripped irony. "The big-shot private eye. Hard-drinking, hard-living, hard on everybody. I should have known. I suppose you still suspect me of having something to do with Willis Ordway's death."

"No. I was just trying it on to see how it fit. You didn't kill him."

Her eyebrows shot up, and her voice softened. "How do you know that?"

"The same way I know Ordway didn't commit suicide, even though it was made to look that way. He was cut on the left side of his neck, and there was blood all over the mirror. If the killer had stood in front of him, the mirror would have been clean."

I leaned back in the chair and crossed one leg over the other. "Whoever did it stood behind him, reached around from the right, and slashed his neck. That gave the most leverage. That's why he could do it with a single stroke. Anything else would have looked like a butcher job. A left-handed man would have reached around from the left, and the wound would have been on the right. So, the killer was righthanded. That's why he planted the knife in Ordway's right hand." I paused. "Only Ordway was left-handed."

She sat still. All the anger had run out. "How do you know?"

"I saw his shoes. The left heel was worn down more than the right. And when he came to my office, he held his cigarette in his right hand. A smoker habitually uses his weak hand, leaving his strong hand free in case somebody offers him a drink. When I brought you the glass of water yesterday, you took it in your left hand. If I'm any good at guessing, you're left-handed too." I stopped looking for the ashtray and put the cigarette away. "Ordway didn't commit suicide. And you didn't kill him."

She sat without moving. The room was loud with silence. She swallowed and spoke quietly. "You're very perceptive."

I shrugged. "'That power which erring men call chance.'"

Her mouth fell open. "You…that's Milton!"

"He won't mind. He's dead, too."

She leaned forward and looked straight at me. "I've misjudged you, Mr. Garrett. And I owe you an apology. I was very cross with you last night. Willy's death was a terrible shock. Please forgive me."

I sat there feeling like leftovers. "Just why did you want to see me, Miss Wearing?"

A scarlet flush came up from her neck and into her cheeks. She looked away for a moment, then looked back. "I want you to help me save my father."

"From what?"

"From that…." She clenched her teeth. "From his wife. I'm convinced that she's cheating on him. At the very least, she's stealing his money."

"I don't take divorce cases, Miss Wearing. Besides, as you know, I've met the Colonel. Your father doesn't act like a man who needs to be saved."

She waved her hands over the desk. "It isn't that. She has some power over him. I think she may be blackmailing him."

"What makes you think so?"

"Well, just look at them," she said. "She's much younger than he is, and they have nothing in common. They even sleep in separate rooms."

"That's no crime," I said. "And lots of older men marry young, attractive women. It's their way of trying to be young again. Maybe it doesn't make sense. But what has sense got to do with vanity?"

She shook her head. "No. I'm sure there's more to it than that. Look at what she's doing with these auctions."

"Just what is she doing?"

"That's the point. I don't know, and I can't seem to find out. I've asked Father, but he simply refuses to discuss it."

"What do you want me to do?"

"I want you to find out what she's up to and help me expose her."

I let my breath whistle out through my teeth. "So, I cuddle up to Monica, and, being the big-shot detective, get her to spill the beans. Your father doesn't mind. She doesn't suspect. And I just pass the word on to you." I shook my head. "Take my advice, Miss Wearing. Drop it."

She folded her hands on the desk and fastened her eyes on me, her face at full flush. "I can't, Mr. Garrett. I love my father."

I looked back across the desk. "All right," I said. "Tell me how they met."

"It was in Kansas City. My father was there at a newspaper convention. He retired after my mother died, but he's kept active in the national news associations. Monica was working at the hotel. She must have seen how lonely he was and latched on to him. They were married right away and came back to El Paso together. At first, all she did was spend his money, buying things—clothes, jewelry, a car. Father was completely wrapped up in her. He simply had no time for anything else, not even Jimmy and me."

"And you both resented it."

She snorted. "Why shouldn't we?" Then she let out a slow sigh. "I know Jimmy's suffered from what happened to him in the war. His drinking and his running around. But who knows?"

"Let's go back to your father and Monica," I said.

"Things seemed to settle down after a while. Monica stayed at home, and father became involved with his collection. But then, after several months, Monica seemed to grow restless, bored. She began going out alone at night, to the club and to that...that place in Juarez. Then, about three months ago, she began putting my father's collection up for sale. And, as if that weren't enough, she began taking up with men, horrible men—gangsters, even that disgusting man from the newspaper, Jack Springer. She didn't even try to hide it."

I felt as if I'd just been smacked in the teeth. "So, then you hired Ordway."

99

"Yes. But as soon as I saw him the other night, I changed my mind. He was terribly frightened of something, and I just knew he couldn't help." She shook her head. "Poor Willy."

"Did he say why he was frightened?"

"Nothing I could understand. He just kept talking about those jade figures and a curse. And he said there was terrible danger."

"Did he say how he heard about the figures?"

"No."

I exhaled heavily. "How do I get into the auction tonight?"

She looked up at me sharply, eyes wide. "Then you'll take the case?"

"No. But I'll let you know if I find out anything."

"But why should you—"

"I told you. I'm a sucker for strays."

She hesitated. Then she reached for a pad on the desk, scribbled something on it, tore off the page, and handed it to me.

"That's my home address and phone number," she said. "If you find out anything at all, please let me know. I don't care what time it is."

I folded up the paper and stuffed it in the pocket of my jacket. "I usually have to work a lot harder for a girl's address and phone number."

She flushed enough to light up a darkroom. She started to say something but never got it out. The door opened, and Angela poked her head in past it.

"There's a phone call, Miss Wearing."

"Gabrielle fumbled with some loose papers. "I said no calls, Angela."

"But it's Deputy Sheriff Sanchez. He wants to talk to Mr. Garrett."

Angela retreated, and Gabrielle motioned toward the phone on her desk. I picked it up and growled into the mouthpiece.

"Garrett."

"Thought I'd find you there."

"Nice work."

"Yeah. Well, we searched Springer's apartment. Didn't find anything suspicious."

"So, the house wins again," I said.

"Maybe. But I got something for you. Detective Rawls just phoned.

He may have a line on our friend with the white hair. The guy's name is Voss—Norman Voss. Used to be a leg-breaker for a loan shark. Business went sour, and he became a contract killer. One of the best and one of the dirtiest. He's been in Joliet. The yardbirds there hung a tag on him—Schitzy. A real nut case. He just finished doing some hard time in Folsom. Got out about six weeks ago and just disappeared. The street talk has it that he's doing contracts again."

"Thanks," I said. "Stay with it. You might get to be a good cop."

"Sure," he said. "One thing more. Rawls said to be careful. The guy does things with knives."

I hung up.

Gabrielle was standing behind the desk. Her face was an anxious mask. "What is it?"

"He's after me for double parking," I said. "What about the auction?"

She reached into the top drawer of the desk and brought out a large white invitation card with gold embossed lettering. "Eight o'clock tonight, at the museum. This will get you in. But..." She clutched the card in both hands and pursed her lips. "I just don't know. I hope I'm doing the right thing."

"You've got no choice now," I said. "There are two men dead, murdered. There may be a connection. And it may have something to do with that auction."

"Two men?"

Now I stood up, slowly, deliberately, hoping it might take a few hours. "Look, Miss Wearing. I'm sorry, but there's no way to break it gently. Jack Springer was killed this afternoon. He was beaten to death, carefully, systematically. Whoever did it may have killed Ordway. And whoever it is may be after me."

She fell back into the chair, the color draining out of her face like water running down a gutter. "My God, how awful. I never imagined..."

"Nobody ever does."

She looked down at the card, still stuck between her fingers. "I don't know," she said. "I'm not sure..."

I reached across the desk, grabbed the invitation out of her hands, and slid it into my pocket. "Yes, you are."

Chapter Thirteen

Blackstone Terrace curled off Mesa Street on the near side of the mountain. It wound through one of those new neighborhoods that had started springing up after the war. The builders would grab off some cheap tract of land, level it, and throw up rows of cracker box houses. Not too big. Not too fancy. Just four walls and a roof. With the housing shortage, most people didn't care.

Number 174 was on the far side of a cul-de-sac at the end of the drive. It was a one-story white cottage with a black shingle roof and black trim. A row of quiet shrubs nestled across the front, trying not to be noticed. They were parted by a short flagstone walk and a couple of brick steps that led to the entrance. At the end of the walk by the street, a sign hung from a wooden post. It said, "Morris Kintner, M.D." I parked the Buick behind a cream-colored Packard convertible and got out.

As I started up the walk, the door to the house opened, and Jimmy Wearing came out. For just an instant, he stood and eyed me suspiciously. Then he quickly slipped on his sunglasses and grinned.

"Okay, hot shot," he said. "You found me. Guess you want to tell the old man you've been keeping tabs. Huh?"

"I didn't come here after you," I said. "But what are you doing here?"

He cleared his throat and spoke softly, as if the shrubs might overhear. "I'm a regular. I come a couple times a week for treatment. Have since I got out of the army hospital over at Fort Bliss."

"Treatment for what?"

He shuffled his feet. "Doc Kintner calls it a nervous disorder. In the army, they called it battle fatigue."

"Sorry," I said. "Where did you serve?"

"In the Pacific." He rubbed his oversized hands together nervously. "Look, I gotta run. I'll see you later."

"Where can I find you later?"

"Try the hotel." He grinned. "I got friends there. Know what I mean?"

He climbed into the Packard, gunned the engine, and drove off. I watched him swing around a curve and head out of sight. I knew what he meant. I went up the steps and into the house.

The front of the house had been made into an office. To the right of the main hall, what used to be a parlor was now a waiting room, with Mediterranean furniture sparsely placed around a thick oriental rug and several Degas prints resting against azure walls. To the left and back of the hall were closed doors with an olive-green metal desk between them that looked as easy to step around as a tank. A mule-faced woman in a white uniform sat behind the desk. She had a white nurse's cap pinned in the middle of a helmet of iron-gray hair, and she stared at me through a pair of rimless spectacles that made her watery brown eyes look as big as chestnuts.

As I entered, she was talking on the phone. "I'm sorry, Mrs. Worsham, but you know that the doctor has just returned from his trip to California, so he is very busy. And he is not in the office on Fridays... That's right. He can give you your vitamin shot on Monday... I know you're tense. You just take those sleeping tablets that Dr. Kintner prescribed and get plenty of rest.... Yes. Good-bye." She hung up.

I walked over and stood in front of the desk. The woman sat stiffly and gave me a careful going over from behind her glasses. She looked at me as if I'd just dropped a dead bird in her lap.

"Yes?"

"My name is Garrett. I'm here to see Dr. Kintner."

She leaned over and looked conspicuously at an appointment book to her right. Then she straightened and folded her hands on the desk and looked at me smugly. "You have no appointment."

"He'll see me," I said. "Tell him it's official business."

"I beg your pardon?"

I put both hands on the desk and leaned toward her. "I said official. You know—licensed, sovereign. That means with authority."

She stood up and clamped her jaw defiantly. She marched around the desk and then around me and knocked on the door to my left. There was a sharp thump against the wall, and then the door opened abruptly. She leaned inside and mumbled something I couldn't quite make out. There was a pause, and then she stepped back, pushed the door open, and motioned to me. "This way, please."

I stepped past her into a polished white room with an antiseptic smell. Along the wall on the left was an examining table with a metal stool in front of it. Next to it on the back wall was a long white table with a row of glass containers showing neatly arranged cotton swabs, Band-Aids, and tongue depressors. A desk stuck out from the wall on the right, and next to it, a tall, glass-fronted cabinet with a heavy metal latch and a Yale lock held neat rows of bottles and vials, all carefully labeled. A bubbling sound came from the corner next to the cabinet. I looked over and saw a little white stand with a heating unit on it full of boiling water and enough syringes to inoculate a platoon.

Dr. Kintner stood in the middle of the room. He was a soft-looking man in his late forties, not quite my height, with fleshy jowls and pouches under his eyes. The eyes were small and dark and set deep into his head, and they darted around and over me like water bugs skipping over a pond. His brown hair was layered into thick waves. He wore a white office duster over black trousers and a white shirt with a sporty bow tie. His delicate-looking fingers sported the nicest manicure I'd seen east of Hollywood Boulevard.

"Mr. Garrett," he said. "How may I help you?"

I turned and looked sideways at the nurse. "It's a private matter."

Kintner spoke to her. "That will be all, Margaret. I won't need you until Monday."

She gave me a frosty look, then went out and shut the door. Kintner went around and sat behind the desk and began playing with a handful of pencils lying on top of a large green blotter. Without being asked, I pulled up a wooden chair from the far corner of the room. I sat down, took off my hat, and watched Kintner carefully arrange the pencils in a neat row exactly parallel to the edge of the blotter. When he finished, he looked slowly up at me. I glanced casually around the room. The walls were lined with more Degas prints.

"I guess you're a fan of Impressionism," I said. He brightened like a wino with a fresh drink. "Oh, you know painting?" He leaned back in his chair and looked admiringly around the room. "Degas. My very favorite."

His eyes fell on a picture by the door hanging slightly askew. He almost bolted out of his chair and then tenderly straightened the print with the careful machinations of a diamond cutter. He returned to his chair, eyes still on the print. Finally, he turned and looked at me; his stare focused somewhere between my chin and my tie.

"I'm sorry," he said. "You were saying?"

"How do you feel about jade?"

He barely moved. Maybe there was a slight shortening of breath. Maybe there was an edge to his expression. Maybe I was seeing things.

He cleared his throat. "Just what is it that you want?"

"I'm interested in one of your patients—Jack Springer."

He began blinking rapidly. "I believe you said this was official business. May I see some identification, please?"

I pulled my I.D. out of the wallet and flipped it across the desk to him. He took it and carefully read both sides twice. Then he handed it back to me and looked at my tie again.

"This says that you're a private investigator...from Los Angeles. You haven't any authority here."

"I have authority enough. Just pick up the phone and call Deputy Sheriff Sanchez. He'll vouch for me."

He pressed his lips together thoughtfully. "And just why are you here?"

"Because Jack Springer was murdered this afternoon."

His mouth fell open. His chin disappeared into his neck. "My God. Why... How...

"With a tire iron, out by the racetrack. I don't know why. I thought you might be able to tell me."

He clutched at the edge of the desk, the skin around his fingers pressed white. His eyelids fluttered, and a restless sadness mixed with fear swam in his eyes. "I...I... But surely, I don't know. He... He was just a patient."

"What were you treating him for?"

He hesitated. "That's privileged information. It would be unethical for me to divulge...

"Listen, doctor," I said. I dropped my hat on the desk. "I can have someone come here and make it official if you want. The man is dead."

He swallowed hard. He began playing with the pencils again, shifting them into horizontal rows across the top of the blotter. "He has...had a very difficult job at the newspaper. Looking around for stories and having to meet deadlines. He was under a great deal of pressure. He was very tense. I prescribed tranquilizers and sleeping pills."

"What would you say was wrong with him?"

"I'd call it a nervous disorder."

"Uh-huh," I said. "You must get a lot of that around here."

He looked up sharply. His eyes met mine for the first time since I'd entered the room. "What do you mean?"

I shrugged. "This town, this country. It's hard on everybody. Migrants looking for work, widows on pensions, and young wives with their husbands out trying to earn a living. They must all get pretty tense.

His eyelids stopped fluttering. "I don't think..."

"What about James Wearing? Aren't you treating him too?"

"Well, yes. But..."

"I saw him passed out in a bar last night. I'll bet it was from a nervous disorder."

He stood up. His face began turning the color of raw liver. His voice had the harsh ring of resentment or fear or both. "You've no right to come in here and talk to me this way. I'm a professional man. I'll not stand for it. You can just get out."

I stood up. "Thanks for your time," I said. I picked up my hat and put it on, and headed for the door. "I'll find my own way out. You make me nervous."

He was about to say something when the phone on his desk started ringing. He grabbed it and spoke sharply. "What is it?" There was a pause. His face caved in like a fallen souffle. "Yes, yes. Tonight. I understand. But... Just a minute." He looked up at me and put his hand over the mouthpiece. "Will you please get out?"

I left.

The Sunset Room was almost empty, just Tommy and his friend Mable. As I slid up to the bar, Tommy waved and poured a couple of fingers of the Vat 69 into a glass and put it in front of me.

"Here ya go, Mr. Garrett. The good stuff."

"Thanks, Tommy," I said. "Has Jimmy Wearing been in?"

He shook his head. "Naw. Ain't seen him."

"He said he'd be here."

Tommy scratched his chin. "Well, it's early yet. He's probably gone south. Know what I mean?" He winked. "Two to one, he'll come in later."

He put both hands on the bar and raised his eyebrows. "Hey, how 'bout that Jack Springer? Guess he finally stuck his nose where it didn't belong, huh?"

"I guess. How did you hear about it?"

"Hal Weems came by. Said you found him out by the track. Said his brains was spread all over the ground. Pretty bad, huh?"

"Yeah," I said. "Pretty bad."

He looked quickly over at Mable. She was staring down into her glass, lost in the ripples of memory and alcohol. Tommy leaned forward and spoke quietly. "Hey, Mr. Garrett. You think it's that curse Hal was talkin' about?"

"What do you think?"

"I don't know 'bout curses," he said. He put his elbows on the bar and leaned even closer. He spoke just above a whisper. "But I know about killin'. I ain't one ta be sayin' this real loud. Could be bad for a guy's health. Know what I mean? But I'll lay odds, if there's killin' bein' done, Rudy knows about it."

"What makes you think so?"

"Stands to reason. Two guys bumped in two days? Doesn't happen around here." He shook his head, his mouth twisted in a disdainful grin. "Mexicans, maybe, but not Anglos. You take my word. Rudy doesn't just run things in Juarez. He's top dog, even up here. Talk is he's aimin' to move north again. And brother, when he does, I wouldn't wanna be in his way."

"I'll try to remember."

He clucked his teeth. "Do that, Mr. Garrett. Watch yourself."

"How about that white-haired guy?" I asked. "Have you seen him again?"

He straightened up and shook his head. "Nope. Him, I'd remember. Ain't been around."

"Thanks, Tommy," I said. "When you see Jimmy, tell him to look me up."

I drank the rest of my dinner, left a fin on the bar, and headed for the door. Tommy called after me. "Where ya gonna be?"

"At the museum," I said.

Tommy gave me a funny look. I probably deserved it.

Outside, the sun was sliding down over the ragged edge of the desert, streaking the sky with orange and purple. The wind had died down, and the tufted leaves of the yucca trees in front of the hotel were hanging limp. As I crossed the parking lot toward the Buick, a battered orange cab with a yard of teeth showing above the steering wheel came slowly up the drive and struggled over next to me. A laughing little voice came out of the front seat.

"*Senor* Garrett. *Amigo. Qui pasa?*"

I shrugged. "*Nada,* Hector."

"We go for a ride, *si?*"

"We go for a ride, no." I leaned into the cab. "You know two *senoritas* who hang around here? Rosetta and Lupe?"

He opened up his grin even wider. His lips were stretched out like rubber bands. "Oh, *si. Ellas estan canijas.*"

"I know," I said. "Very hot stuff. Can you find them for me?"

"*Si.*" He nodded. "Climb in. We go."

I shook my head. "No. Find out where they are, and then come and pick me up."

"Si. Muy pronto."

"Not pronto," I said. "Later. I'll be at the motel."

He nodded and gunned his engine. The cab spun around in the lot and churned down the drive, spitting gravel from under the wheels and leaving a trail of blue smoke as thick as meringue. I got into the Buick and headed down Mesa Street toward the city, looking for the address on the invitation Gabrielle had given me.

I drove about a mile, past a couple of lights and some dark side streets. I kept one eye glued to the mirror. No limousine. After a few blocks, I noticed a blue Ford coupe cruising through the shadows about half a block back. I drove another mile through three more lights. The Ford was still there. At the next intersection, I swung into a side street, circled the block, and came back out onto Mesa. The Ford stayed with me all the way. I felt a cold front move through my legs and up into my stomach.

After one more light, I turned into another side street and put the pedal on the floor. Near the end of the block, I pulled sharply into an alley, drove all the way to the back, and got out. I stood flat against the building in the shadow of a fire escape and a row of trash cans. The Luger jumped up into my hand. I looked down the alley toward the street and held my breath. The skin on the back of my neck was prickling. My hands were wet.

The Ford pulled slowly up to the front of the alley and stopped. The spark from a cigarette poked through the shadows. I licked my lips, squeezed the grip of the Luger, and waited. The spark glowed, then jumped out of the dark of the car and fluttered to the pavement. The Ford growled and quickly moved past the alley out of sight. I waited and listened to the drumming of my pulse. Nothing moved. A pair of feet started slowly up the alley. They crept lightly, gingerly, held by stone legs, moving without trying to move. They were my feet. I reached the end of the alley and peered out into the street. No cars. No people. No sound. I decided it was all right to breathe again.

Chapter Fourteen

I t was a little before eight when I pulled up in front of the museum. I parked across the street, went inside, and walked through a marble-tiled lobby lined with tall ferns and *ficus benjamina* plants standing like sentries. I followed the signs down a long corridor and knocked on a door marked "Curator."

A shrill voice said, "Come in, please."

I opened the door and edged my way into the office. It was about as easy to get into as a milk bottle. It was small and cramped, just a desk and a couple of chairs and three walls lined with overcrowded bookcases. The desk was piled with books and folders, with a small space cleared in the center lit by a tarnished old lamp that had passed retirement.

The man behind the desk was short and round and almost bald, a careless fringe of white hair shooting sprigs down over his ears. His bright blue eyes sat in the middle of a generation of wrinkles and squinted over cherubic cheeks. The eyes smiled with enough light to brighten the room even without the desk lamp. He wore a tired gray suit and vest with the middle button missing and a gold watch chain dangling out of the pocket. He nodded and smiled at me. He seemed glad to have someone open the door.

He held his hand out to me and shook mine as if he were trying to pump water from a well. "Dentin's the name. Eugene Dentin. Are you here to make a contribution? Every little bit is appreciated, you know. Yes indeed."

"Not exactly," I said. "My name's Garrett. I'm here for the auction." I showed him the invitation.

He looked mildly disappointed, but he kept smiling. "Well, yes. Of course.

111

I see. Please sit down. What can I do for you?"

I took off my hat and sat down. "I understand you're in charge of selling the Wearing collection."

He nodded vigorously. "Yes, sir. That I am. I'm in charge."

"Well, I'm very interested in a pair of jade figures. They're carved in the likeness of an Aztec prince and princess. Is there anything like that in the collection?"

He scratched his nose the way someone scratches something that doesn't itch. "There was a jade piece sold at our last auction just over a month ago. It could have been one of the figures you describe. Possibly the Princess."

"What about the Prince? Is that here?"

His eyes drifted over the desk, and he sucked his upper lip in between his teeth. He thought for a minute. "No, sir. Not that I'm aware." He pulled on his ear. "Funny you should ask, though. There's been quite a lot of interest in that jade piece. A young man came in to inquire about it last week." He chuckled and folded his hands over his vest. "Of course, to me, they all look young. He let out a chuckle and then went on. "And another gentleman was in just this afternoon. He asked me the same question about the Prince."

I drew a breath silently. "Did he tell you his name?"

He scratched his chin. "No, sir. I don't believe he did, now that you mention it."

"What did he look like?"

"Well, sir. I wouldn't call him ordinary-looking. No, sir, I wouldn't. He was tall, and he had very plain features. But he had the most striking white hair."

I shifted in the chair and tried not to scream at him. "Did he have an invitation?"

"Why, yes, of course. Otherwise, I should not have discussed the auction with him. I'm not permitted to do that, you know."

"Of course. Was this man interested in anything besides the jade?"

He nodded. "Well, yes. He asked me if anyone else had inquired about it."

"And you told him?"

He nodded again, and his face began to cloud over. "May I ask, do you know this man? Is he perhaps a broker or a dealer?"

"Not the way you mean."

He leaned forward on the desk. "And you, sir. Just whom do you represent?"

I reached into my wallet and handed him one of my business cards. "You could say I'm looking out for the Wearings' interests."

"I see." He leaned back in his chair and pondered the card. Then he looked up at me cautiously. "Mr. Garrett, I hope there won't be any difficulty. Mrs. Wearing has been quite explicit. There are to be no brokers or dealers. And the auctions are strictly private, not to be discussed. Only the people receiving invitations are to know about them."

"Who gives out the invitations?"

"Mrs. Wearing, naturally."

"Naturally. What do you do with the proceeds?"

"They are retained by the museum," he said. "Mrs. Wearing has stipulated that we keep all the proceeds from the auctions, just so long as they are held according to her terms."

"That's very generous," I said. "And what are the terms?'"

"That the auctions remain private, as I said. And that no more than a dozen pieces be put up at any one time." He knitted his brows into another nest of wrinkles. "But surely, if you're working for the Wearings, you must know that already."

"Mrs. Wearing neglected to mention it. I guess she's been pretty busy."

His face brightened, and he nodded again. "Yes, sir. She has, indeed. A delightful lady—most generous. And quite charming, I might add."

"Yeah." I nodded. "Charming."

He hesitated. "Mr. Garrett, the museum depends on such contributions. We haven't much money. I shouldn't want anything to jeopardize…"

I stood up. "Your museum is in no danger from me, Mr. Dentin. Thanks for your help."

He gave me a wide grin. "Quite all right, sir. Quite all right." He struggled up out of the chair and looked at his watch. "It's almost time. Shall we go?"

We dug ourselves out of the office, and I followed him back up the corridor and through a pair of double doors into a large meeting room lined with heavy crimson drapes, fronted by pedestals holding busts of Texas patriots and politicians. Long rows of folding chairs, about two hundred in all, filled the room.

The crowd was already gathering. Plump middle-aged men in suits stood in groups smoking pipes and mumbling to each other. In the back, a red-faced man in a Stetson sat with his arms folded and ten gallons of boredom all over his face. I could appreciate his point of view. Around the room, several over-rouged women sat trying to fight off age with heavy coats of cosmetics and feathered hats. Dentin excused himself and began wandering through the crowd, smiling, nodding, and shaking every hand he could reach.

I drifted toward the back row and sat down out of the way just in time to see Dr. Morris Kintner enter the room. He moved up to the front, looking straight ahead, speaking to no one, and sat in the first row directly in front of a tall wooden podium.

At exactly eight o'clock, a young, dark-haired attendant wheeled in a cart carrying an assortment of pottery, blankets, and stone relics. Dentin stepped to the podium, gavel in hand, and began the auction, his voice an insistent whine. One by one, the attendant held up each piece. Dentin fluttered around the podium, raving about the historical significance, and the bidding started.

I looked around the room. There was a quiet choreography of eye blinking, nose twitching, and ear pulling. When it slowed down, Dentin would nod in the direction of the last blinker, then nod again, pound his gavel, and the piece was sold. I sat without moving and did my best to stifle a sneeze. It could have cost me my whole bankroll.

It went that way for almost forty minutes. I watched Dr. Kintner. He just sat quietly and raised his hand to make his bids. He bought about half the items, spending in the neighborhood of three grand.

It wasn't a neighborhood I could live in. But if Ordway was right about the collection, Kintner was making a killing.

I counted twelve items being sold—and still no jade. The last was a piece of pottery. Dentin called it a ceremonial urn. To me, it looked like an Aztec cocktail shaker. Kintner bought it anyway. I got up and went outside. I felt like tailing somebody myself for a change.

Jimmy Wearing was leaning against the Buick, dressed as before. It was dark now, but he still wore his sunglasses. As I approached, he laid out a casual smile.

"Okay, hot shot," he said. "What's up?"

I nodded back at him. "Never mind. I'm giving you the night off."

"How come? Tommy said you wanted to see me."

"Not now. I'm busy."

His voice took on a sly tone. "So, the shamus is working, huh? What is it, a tail job? Who're you after?"

"The Duchess of Kent," I said. "Now blow."

"Sounds like fun," he said. "I think I'll tag along. I've never shadowed anybody before."

I shook my head. "Uh-uh. This is a one-man job. And in that outfit, you'd stand out like a wino at an A.A. meeting. Just make tracks, and I'll catch up with you later."

He stopped leaning against the Buick and stood up. "Look. I passed up a night with the girls just to find you. You're supposed to be straightening me out. How're you gonna do that if we don't stick together?"

I could hear the door to the museum opening behind me. People were starting down the walk. "Listen," I said. "This isn't some goddamn game we're playing. Two men are dead. You saw one of them. It made you sick. Now get the hell out of the way and drift out of sight."

He clamped his hands on his hips and bellowed at me. "Jesus Christ. You sound just like the old man. If you think..."

He never got to finish. His voice was lost in the screech of tires. The black limousine leaped out of the alley on the far side of the museum. In a frozen instant, it wheeled past the corner and was bearing down on us. My mind was full of everything and nothing. I grabbed Jimmy and flattened him to the pavement. A stampede of tires and grinding gears sounded above me. A rush of air and the smell of hot rubber hammered at us as the wheels whistled past my head. I looked up and saw long fingers of flame reaching out the rear window of the limousine. The Buick shuddered, and broken glass fell all around me.

I lay still and wondered if I was still alive.

Chapter Fifteen

Nothing gets your attention like being shot at. It takes your mind off things like earning a living or remembering your name. This wasn't the first time. I'd been shot at before. It happens. After all, every business has risks. Bankers get cramps in their fingers from counting money. Showgirls get sore behinds from being pinched. Salesmen get doors slammed in their faces. In my business you get shot at.

I stood up and brushed off what was left of my suit. The right sleeve was torn, and there were spots of blood on the front of my shirt. I looked at my right hand and saw that part of the skin had been scraped off the knuckles. I wrapped my handkerchief around the hand, then picked up my hat and dusted it off. I fitted the hat on my head, slowly, carefully, taking time to adjust it. The little things are important. They bring you back. After somebody's been shooting at you, tie your shoes, light a cigarette. Otherwise, you'll be screaming like a banshee. I straightened my tie.

Several people from the museum clustered around us, their mouths gaping dumbly with unspoken questions. I looked off down the street. The limousine had been swallowed by the night, leaving only a roar of silence. I could still hear the squealing tires and the breaking glass. I'd be hearing them for days.

Jimmy got up slowly and leaned on the hood of the Buick. His sunglasses were just fragments scattered on the pavement. He turned slowly and looked at me, a stony pallor spreading over his face like syrup on a pancake. "They were trying to kill us."

I looked at the Buick. The driver's window was smashed. Below it, two holes stared out like empty eye sockets where the slugs had punched into the door. "Or the car."

"But why?"

"Maybe it's the way you're dressed."

He balled his large hands into fists and held them in front of him. "Christ, Garrett. Can't you—"

"Steady," I said. "Are you alright?"

He exhaled heavily. "I think so." He brushed a pair of shaky hands down the front of his suit, then looked back at me uneasily. I don't know if I wanna hang around with you. You're trouble."

"Tell that to your old man," I said.

The crowd had begun buzzing like flies around a piece of meat. A short fat man in a Panama hat stepped up next to me. "Jeez," he said. "I never seen anything like it. You guys okay?" He didn't wait for an answer. "I mean, shouldn't we call the cops or somethin'?"

"Nix," I said. "Just call us a cab." He started to protest, but I stopped him. "You want to spend the rest of the night at the station answering questions?"

The man clamped his jaw shut and scuttled off through the crowd toward the museum. As he approached the entrance, Dr. Kintner came out and brushed by him, a large parcel wrapped in brown paper tucked under his arm. He came briskly down the walk, turned, and headed up the street without even glancing toward the Buick. The milling crowd meant as much to him as Mozart means to a deaf-mute.

I turned back to Jimmy. "When the cab gets here, get in it and go out to your old man's place. Spend the night. He'll be delighted."

A sharp frown creased his features. "Why the hell should I go out there? If I'm goin' anywhere, it's home."

"Listen," I said. "We don't know which one of us those pokes in the limousine were gunning for. If you go home now, you could wind up on a slab."

"You mean...?" He lifted his hands and then let them fall in exasperation. "I don't get it."

"Never mind," I said. "Just get out of sight."

He looked up sharply. "Aren't you coming too?"

"I told you. I've got work to do."

"Are you going after that limousine?"

I let my breath out heavily and thought about it. I was tempted. "No. I'm going to see a doctor. Zinging bullets give me a headache."

I climbed into the Buick and watched Kintner get into a white DeSoto parked halfway up the next block. He pulled out slowly, then cruised back past the front of the museum, heading downtown. I waited until he had enough of a start. Then I nosed the Buick out through the crowd, did a quick U-turn, and aimed the car at Kintner's taillights.

The DeSoto moved leisurely down Mesa Street toward the lower part of the city, then crossed over onto Montana and, after a few blocks, turned north on Piedras. There was little traffic, and the intermittent streetlights threw a pale yellowish glow over the road. I stayed about a block behind, timing each light so that I wouldn't get too close.

I followed the DeSoto about two miles up Piedras into a tired-looking residential section that was full of brick-front apartment buildings and pre-war houses. Most of the houses sat back from the street, reclining in the shadows of gnarled, blistered trees and withered shrubs. They looked like the women at the auction, trying to hide the passing years behind heavy coats of paint.

Kintner pulled up to the curb in front of a set of rowhouse apartments fronted by a tall hedge with a rusted iron gate at one end. I drove past him, parked up the block, and watched in the mirror as he lugged the package through the gate and let himself into the first apartment.

I lit a cigarette, sat back, and tried to listen to the quiet of the desert night. The tart scent of mesquite hung in the air. The street seemed peaceful. Nothing was moving. The only sound was in my head—a shrill confusion of grinding metal and pounding feet and whining bullets. That's the way it is when there's shooting, whether it's on a mud-covered island in the Pacific or a dark street in west Texas. It's all confusion and noise. You don't get to see much. You just keep your head down and listen. And you remember the noise.

119

I settled into the seat and unwrapped my hand, and let the pain take my mind off remembering. A radio started playing across the street, a lilting Harry James number, broken by a rock-hard voice like a shovel scraping over asphalt. "Hey, babe. How's about another beer?" I blew smoke over the inside of the windshield and remembered hearing the same tune just a week earlier. It was in Lacy's, in a nice quiet corner, over a nice quiet drink. It seemed years away.

I tossed the rest of the Lucky out into the street and looked up just as Kintner came back out through the gate, this time without the package. He walked casually over to the DeSoto, glanced around quickly, and climbed in. He started the car, did an intricate turn in the middle of the street, and then rolled easily back down the hill toward Montana Street. I waited a minute, then did another U-turn and headed after him.

This time, I let him get several blocks ahead, almost out of sight. I didn't need to get close. He moved along slowly, leisurely, back around toward the mountain. He stuck to the main roads, stopping at almost every light. He gave no sign of knowing that someone was following him. After all, he was a smooth citizen, a professional man. Why should anyone be following him?

When I pulled up on Blackstone Terrace, the DeSoto was already parked in front of Kintner's house. A light was on over the front door, and another was showing from a window on the left. I parked about thirty yards up from the cul-de-sac, cut the engine, and waited. I didn't know what I was waiting for. Somehow, it was just my night to wait. I reached into the glove compartment and found the bottle I had put there for emergencies. You never know with emergencies. I felt one coming on.

I returned the bottle and snapped the compartment shut just as a badly tuned engine came chugging up the road behind me. A faded orange cab rolled past and pulled up behind the DeSoto. The cab idled while a young woman got out and walked quickly up to the house. She had dark hair and dark skin, and she wore a shimmering aqua dress that clung to her like flypaper. Even from that distance, I recognized her as one of the girls I'd seen in the hotel with Jimmy.

The front door opened before she could ring the bell. She went inside, then came back out in less than a minute, with Kintner mincing along behind her. They got into the cab, and the girl motioned to the driver. The cab grunted and belched a cloud of blue smoke and then slowly started off down the street, grinding along like a cement mixer.

I sat there for a minute and thought about the Good Samaritan doctor being summoned in the night by a poor young girl. He was a professional man. He was needed. Please come quickly, doctor. It's an emergency. Mother has a nervous disorder. Once again, I swung the Buick around in the cul-de-sac and headed after them.

The cab wound back through the city, then south across Alameda and down a dark, narrow street called Verdes Place. I cut the lights and trailed along for three blocks, past boarded-up storefronts and run-down warehouses dotted with broken windows. The doorways stared out at the street, gaunt and empty. The frames around the windows and doors were mostly bare wood, dried and twisted by the sun, a few splinters of paint still fighting to hold on. Here and there, streaks of red and yellow paint spread grotesque calligraphy on the empty brick walls, back-alley literature warning any intruding Anglo that he was in the wrong part of town. At the end of the last block, a small cafe sat behind a grimy glass front. The promise of "Cervesa" hung behind the glass in flickering red neon letters.

The cab slowed in front of the cafe and turned off the street into a dusty parking area on the far side of the building. I stopped and quietly backed the Buick into a side street on the near side of the café. Then, I got out and eased my way around, tipped-over trash cans and spilled garbage, and went toward the parking area around the back. The smell of raw sewage hit me in the face like a Joe Louis, right? In the darkened doorways, I could hear the scratching sounds of rats scurrying in the shadows, their nightly scavenging interrupted.

I came to the far corner of the building and leaned around it just enough to see across the parking lot. Kintner and the girl were standing beside the cab, not talking, not looking at each other. She was carelessly smoking a cigarette while he just stood and fidgeted. Occasionally, one of them would glance off down a dirt road that ran in the back of the lot and wound past the shadowy outline of an oil refinery. Beyond and to the right of the refinery, an arch of yellow lights outlined one of the bridges that spanned the Rio Grande and emptied into downtown Juarez. There wasn't much traffic on the bridge. There never was at this hour. And the customs boys weren't paying much attention.

I leaned back against the building and thought about reaching for a Lucky. Then I thought about not reaching for it. I licked my lips and waited.

An uneasy breeze had come up, carrying the heavy, clinging odor of the refinery. It smelled better than the alley. I peered around the building again. A harsh purring sound came out of the distance. Kintner and the girl turned and stared down the dirt road as a long, dark shape grew out of the shadows. The limousine, running without lights, pulled slowly into the lot and stopped next to the cab.

The doors at the rear of the limousine opened, and two men got out. One was tall and dressed in a dark suit and hat. In the red-orange glow from the cafe, he seemed to have a shock of very light hair. The other man was shorter, but he walked with the assurance of someone eight feet tall. He wore a lighter suit, but his hair and features were dark. From the neck up, he was just a shape in the night. He moved over and stood in front of the girl and lifted his hand up toward his face. The end of a cigar glowed quickly like an orange beacon, then died. The man jerked his arm and sparks scattered over the ground next to him.

The girl began speaking quickly, and I thought angrily. I wasn't close enough to hear what she was saying, but the pitch of her voice seemed to carry an accusation. She waved an arm in the direction of Kintner, and he started hopping from foot to foot. He put his hands up like a boxer, backed into a corner, and began a whining protest. The man with the cigar put up his hand, and the talking stopped the way water stops flowing when a faucet is snapped shut. He pointed toward the limousine, and the girl moved over to it quickly and climbed in.

Then I could almost feel Kintner shaking as the two men moved over next to him and crowded him against the cab. The tall man grabbed him and seemed to lift him off the ground. Kintner's head rolled back onto the roof of the cab. The other man puffed deliberately on his cigar, then held the orange end of it up under Kintner's chin. There was a whimpering sound, and then a sharp scream and the two men stepped back. Kintner stood with one hand clasping his neck, the other waving desperately in the air. He made soft mewling noises while the two men just stood and watched him. I licked my lips again.

For a moment, there was a menacing silence, then a quiet sound, like a raspy whisper. The two men turned abruptly and went back to the limousine. A door slammed. And another. The big engine began purring insistently, and the long, dark car moved easily off into the shadows. Kintner stood limply for a minute, then stumbled into the back seat of the cab. The driver started the engine, and the cab chugged around the corner into the street. I heard it grind past the front of the building, the engine sending a baleful rumble up the street behind me. I waited.

I stood there and wondered which one to go after. I had a score to settle with someone in the limousine, but by now, it was on its way back over the bridge into Juarez. And you don't go down there without knowing your way around, at least not alone at night.

I turned and went back through the alley and started up the side street toward the Buick just as a pair of headlights flashed from the alley across Verdes Place. They pierced the dark and lit up the side street like a stage. I hugged the side of the building and waited. The headlights moved, and a blue Ford coupe sprung out of the alley and roared up the street toward Alameda Avenue. I scrambled into the Buick, ground up half the gears, and reached Alameda in time to see an empty street. The yucca trees waved gently, and the streetlights winked behind the drifting motes of dust. Nice going, Garrett. Late again.

I sighed heavily and cruised up Alameda back into the city and pulled up in front of a little diner directly across the traffic circle in front of the police station. I opened the glove compartment and bought myself a drink. Then I replaced the bottle, reached for a cigarette, and thought about going across the street.

Chapter Sixteen

"Wa hat the hell happened to you?"

Sanchez was sitting alone in his darkened office, the only light coming from a small desk lamp. The contents of a manila folder were spread out in front of him like the pieces of a jigsaw puzzle. As he leaned forward over the desk, the thin rays from the lamp angled upward and raised sharp arching shadows above his eyebrows, giving him something of a satanic look. It made me stop and think twice about where I was.

"What happened?" he repeated.

I sat down in front of the desk, dropped my hat over his phone, and lit up a Lucky. "Since I saw you this afternoon, I've been dodging cars and dodging bullets. I think somebody in this town doesn't like me."

His mouth dropped open. "What the..."

I held up my hand. "In case you haven't figured it out, the tire tracks out by the racetrack where we found Springer were made by something big and heavy—like a limousine. Maybe it was the same limousine I saw cruising in that direction when I was driving downtown with Jimmy Wearing. Or maybe it was the same one that followed me and got close enough to sniff out my car while I was on my way to see Gabrielle. Or just maybe it was the same one that whistled by Jimmy and me in front of the museum tonight—close enough to count the buttons on my shirt and put a couple of slugs in the car." I took a deep drag and sent a cloud across the desk. "You sure know how to set up a target, Sanchez. I might as well be wearing a sign saying, "Kill me."

He stood up and slammed a fist down onto the desk. "Delmar—that son of a bitch! He got onto you faster than I thought." He glared down at me, his eyes full of boiling anger. "Why didn't you tell me about the limousine? Goddammit, Garrett. I told you not to hold out on me." He began shaking his fist. "I ought to throw your ass all the way back to LA."

I stood up slowly and took a careful drag on the Lucky. Then I picked up my hat and put it back on. "Everybody I've met in this town is holding out on something—doctors, lawyers, reporters, cops. They're all working an angle. Even Colonel Money Bags and his Ivy League totem pole. I trust him as far as I can throw my car. Right now, I'm wondering just how far I can trust you, Sanchez. You want to send me home? Fine. I can get shot at in Los Angeles, and not by strangers—by people I know, people with reasons I can understand. At least there, I won't be attracting attention like a stripper at a Sunday school picnic. And the cops won't be inviting the local hood to take a shot at me."

He kept glaring for a minute, then slowly started to smile. "Rawls was right. You are a hard case." He looked at the blood on my shirt, and his tone softened. "Are you alright? Did you get hit?"

I raised my hand so he could see the scraped knuckles. "Don't worry," I grunted. "It's just the price of my agility."

"What about Jimmy?"

"He may have worried off a few pounds, but he's okay. I sent him home."

Sanchez let a soft whistle out through his teeth. He leaned over and opened the bottom drawer of the desk, and brought out a large bottle of rye and two glasses. He put a good slug in each glass and handed one to me. "Here's to trust," he said and drained his glass.

"Confusion," I responded and gulped the rye, feeling it burn a trail down my gullet.

Sanchez motioned toward the chair. I sat down and took off my hat again while he poured out some more of his elixir. Then he sat back, cradled his glass in both hands, and studied me over the rim. "I guess you were lucky. Know who it was?"

"Somebody who's taken a real interest in the places I go and the people I talk to. Maybe there's something about the auctions I'm not supposed to know, something I'm not supposed to see."

"So, you think it was a warning?"

"Either that, or somebody was making sure he *didn't* hit one of us. From that range, a guy like Voss doesn't miss unless he wants to. If he had wanted us both, we'd be dead."

He sat up sharply. "You saw him!'

I let out a soft cloud of smoke that covered my hat. "I saw nothing but a faceful of pavement. But a guy who fits his description was at the museum this afternoon asking about a jade figure and about anybody who might be interested in it."

He stared down into the rye. "So, Delmar knows about the auctions. That isn't good."

"There's more," I said. "You know anything about a Dr. Morris Kintner?"

He cocked an eyebrow. "You mean the guy who wrote that prescription for Springer? Not much. Why?"

"Just this," I said. "Kintner was at the auction tonight. He bought enough stuff to open his own museum. I got curious, so I followed him. He drove to an apartment in town and then went home and met one of the girls that Jimmy was sparking at the hotel."

I could see the muscles knotting in Sanchez's neck. I crushed out my cigarette, took another pull on the rye, and went on.

"From there, the two of them took a cab down to a dive on Verdes Place. They waited in a lot across from the oil refinery. I watched them from an alley. Kintner and the girl met two men in a limousine. One of them might have been Voss. The other…" I just let it hang.

Sanchez bolted upright in his chair. "Was it Delmar?"

I emptied my glass. "How the hell would I know? It was dark. And I don't even know what Delmar looks like. The man had a cigar. Maybe it was Edward G. Robinson."

He finished his drink. "Then what happened?"

"Then they put the girl in the limousine, roughed up Kintner, and sent him home. I might have followed, but you told me I should check in with you."

He smiled grimly. "I'm sorry. I didn't expect things to happen so fast. I'll have someone keep an eye on Kintner, and I'll get some protection for you."

I waved my hand at him. "Never mind that. Cops make me nervous, and you may need them somewhere else. Just tell me what you know about Kintner."

Sanchez rubbed his hands together and brought out his words one at a time, as if each one had a bad taste. "Kintner is what you'd call a society doctor. He came to El Paso just last year from up in the Midwest. He worked up a practice out in the hills treating wealthy families, people who have very little wrong with them except for having too much time and too much money. They invite him to dinner and to parties, and he flits around, clucking and prescribing sleeping pills. Then he gives them a bill, and they pay. He makes a good living."

I snorted and lit another cigarette. "I thought so. In another town, they'd call him a quack."

He shrugged. "Maybe. But nobody's complained. And it's not against the law for a doctor to humor a few hypochondriacs."

"How do you happen to know so much about him?"

A pained expression slid over his face. He stood up and turned, and stared out the window. After a long moment, he turned back toward me, his features drawn and tired. "I started to investigate Kintner just after Jimmy began going to him for treatments; only the Colonel made me drop it. I've known Jimmy for a long time, and I'd like to see him get some help. It's just that..." He folded his arms, leaned on the windowsill, and shook his head. "The Colonel's been good to me, and I owe him a lot."

He looked out the window and sighed, then looked back. "But he's been awfully hard on Jimmy. I guess he wanted his son to take over the papers when he retired, so he kept pushing harder and harder. It wasn't enough for Jimmy to be good. He had to be the best—at everything. And the more Jimmy tried, the more he failed. Finally, he just quit trying. Since the war, he's bounced from one thing to another, getting into scrapes and just letting his father bail him out. Gambling and women mostly. Then, last year, when he started seeing Kintner, he began to settle down a little, at least for a while. The Colonel seemed satisfied, and so I let things ride. Maybe I shouldn't have. I don't know. Anyway, Jimmy managed to stay out of trouble—until lately."

His eyes narrowed. The heavy lines of a frown creased his forehead. "But if Kintner is mixed up with Delmar, then by God, I'll punch his ticket whether he's helping Jimmy or not."

I reached into my pocket and pulled out the picture and the blackmail note Wearing had given me. I laid them on the desk. "What do you make of these?" He sat down and read the note. Then he picked up the picture and stared at it, and shook his head.

"This is why the Colonel wanted to see you?" he asked

"Uh-huh."

He kept shaking his head. "I'm surprised it hasn't happened before."

"Maybe it has."

His face went blank. He sat back and looked at me. "What do you mean?"

"It wouldn't make much sense otherwise. Why would anybody who knows that Wearing is worth enough to blackmail ask for a measly ten grand?"'

"Maybe it isn't measly to him."

I shook my head. "The girl I saw tonight with Kintner is one of the girls in this picture. And the bartender at the hotel told me they both work for Rudy Delmar."

His jaw almost fell on the desk. "You think Delmar is blackmailing Colonel Wearing?"

"I don't know. But I heard something else. There's talk around town that Delmar is getting ready to move north again."

Sanchez put his hands flat on the desk. His eyes widened. "That's why Voss is here—to flatten the opposition!"

"What opposition? Ordway and Springer?"

He shuffled through the papers on his desk. "Look. Except for your prints, the hotel room was clean. And there were no prints on Springer's car or the tire iron. They were both professional jobs. Springer was right. It had to be Voss."

"What about motive?"

His eyes narrowed again. He lowered his voice and brought out his words with a quiet precision. "The only thing Ordway and Springer had in common was you. Maybe that's why Voss is so interested."

I let my breath out slowly. "Maybe. But that doesn't explain enough." I picked up the picture and the blackmail note and put them back in my pocket. Then I brought out Ordway's note and handed it to him.

Sanchez read the note slowly. Even in the darkened room, his features looked pale. He swallowed hard. "Bird of Death?"

"It has something to do with the jade. Wearing knows about it. He explained it to me, at least some of it."

"But how does Voss figure in this?"

"Through Delmar," I said. "If Delmar knows about the auctions, it's a good bet he knows about the jade." He folded up the note and handed it to me. He squeezed his hands together and bit his lip. "It says Gabrielle is in danger. If she's..." He bit his lip again.

"Yeah." I stood up and put on my hat, and started for the door.

Sanchez called after me. "I hope you're not going after Delmar."

I turned and looked back at him. "I won't have to. He knows where to find me. By the way, you know anybody who drives a blue Ford coupe?"

He frowned quickly and shook his head. "No. Why?"

"I saw it around town. Thought it might be for sale." I turned and left the office.

His voice followed me up the hall. "You're not still holding something back, are you? Garrett?"

I didn't answer. I didn't want to lie to him.

I drove back down into the valley and pulled up in front of the motel. It was still a little short of midnight, but everything was dark. The liquor store, the pawn shop, the warehouses—all quiet, waiting under a pale moon, waiting for the desert to gather up and drift and then settle itself for morning. I reached into the car, took the bottle out of the glove compartment, and went inside.

I opened the window, peeled off my jacket and my shirt, and dropped them on the bed. I pulled a chair up beside the window and sat there in my undershirt, staring at nothing. I turned out the light, picked up the bottle, and took a long drink—nice, friendly Scotch. I reached over to the bed and pulled the Luger out of the holster. I held it in my lap and felt the reassuring weight of it resting on my thigh—nice, friendly gun. It gets lonely sometimes, being a sleuth. But I had two friends I could count on—a bottle and a gun.

I waited and listened to the wind travel past the window. I remembered lying on the pavement, hearing the deathly whirr of the tires, smelling the fetid fumes. I waited. I thought about the Wearings, about Jimmy's pale, shaken face, about Gabrielle's wide-eyed fear, about Monica's.... Stop it, Garrett. I still waited.

I waited for almost an hour. It was time enough to read the paper, to listen to part of a symphony, to prepare and eat a three-course dinner, to get good and drunk. It was time enough to see a shadow rise slowly over the ledge of the window like a dark moon on the horizon. I had time to watch the shadow climb slowly up into the window and take shape—the shape of a man. I watched the shape ease over the ledge and into the room and then slowly straighten. I could see another shape, long and pointed, like the barrel of a gun. I held my breath. Nothing moved. Even the wind was waiting. I turned the butt end of the Luger around in my hand and swung.

There was a muffled crack followed by a strained rush of air and a sound like a tent collapsing as the Luger sank into something fleshy. Something heavy clattered on the floor. I stepped back, righted the Luger in my hand, and snapped on the light. I reached down and picked up a .45 automatic with a silencer attachment. It felt as heavy as an anvil. Then I pulled the chair around and sat in it. I balanced both guns in my lap and watched the man on the floor.

He was an albino. His pasty-white skin stretched like a surgical glove over a square forehead and hard, prominent cheekbones. His nose was short and flared, and it rode too far above a thin, crooked mouth that looked wider than it was. A faint purple scar ran from the left corner of the mouth back along the jaw and then partway down the man's neck. It gave his face a permanent sneer. He gazed at me out of deep-set, reddish eyes as empty as a vacant lot.

He had an angular build, and he had that wiry look of someone as tough as telephone cable. His black suit was badly creased and covered with dust from meeting the floor. He was perched on his knees, his right arm draped on the bed, and his left hand clamped over his left ear. A trickle of blood seeped through his fingers and matted his sickish-white hair. While I watched, he slowly brought his hand down, looked at it, and disdainfully licked the blood off his fingers. Then he picked up his hat and put it on, and sat there on his haunches, keeping his eyes pinned on me. I grinned at him.

"So, you're Voss," I said. "You get that tan in prison?" He bared his teeth, made a growling noise like a treed cat, and started to move toward me. I waved the Luger in his face. "Don't bother to get up. I only have one chair."

He eased back slowly and went on staring at me. "Smart guy. Maybe too smart." He had a thin, reedy voice that was cell-block hollow.

"Yeah," I said. "Maybe Delmar should have hired me instead of you. How much do you get for assassinating a Buick?"

He threw me a couple of words I didn't like.

I kept on grinning. "And here I thought you wanted to see me. You've been following me all over town. Well, now you can go tell your boss you saw me. You can say we had a nice talk." I held up the .45. "I won't even tell him I took your gun away. That'll be our secret."

He growled again out of the side of his mouth. "Go ahead, Garrett. Go on bein' smart. See where it gets ya."

"You think it'll get me what it got Jack Springer? Why did you bop him? Was he being smart, too?"

He leaned back and looked smug. "Fish for it, big shot."

"That's a line to remember," I chuckled. "Why did you work Springer over before you killed him? Were you after something, or do you just enjoy your work?" A slow smile crept up from the corners of his mouth. "Maybe that's why they call you Schizy."

"Go to hell."

"All right," I said. "I know a big ugly sheriff who would roll his eyes and lick his lips if he found an ex-con packing heat."

The smile evaporated. Pale gray hate filled his face. He clamped his jaw, and the purple in the scar started to deepen.

I chuckled again. "Delmar sure got you out of the top drawer. What does he want from me?"

"Could be he wants you dead, Shamus," he blurted.

"Could be," I said. "But that doesn't make you look too good, does it?"

He sat and ground his teeth and squeezed his hands together into a large pale knob.

"Did he send you to the hotel after Ordway?"

"Whadda you think?"

"I think he wants something, and he's hired you to make sure somebody else doesn't get it first. What made him think Kintner might have it?"

He snorted. "I don't know what you're talkin' about."

"No? Then why did you and Delmar want to throw a scare into him?"· I saw recognition flash in his eyes. His jaw clamped shut again. "That's right," I said. "I was there."

He spread his mouth into a leer, showing a broken line of yellow-gray teeth. "I'll give ya this, bigshot. It cost Rudy some dough ta get me here." He leaned forward. "But you, I'll do for free."

"Tsk, tsk." I shook my head. "Two misses in one night. Rudy's going to be disappointed. You might wind up out of a job, Voss. You might not work again...ever."

He gave me the same two words.

"All right," I said. "Let's talk about the jade." His eyes narrowed, but he didn't speak. "How much is Rudy willing to fork over?"

He licked his lips. "You got it?"

"I might know where it is," I said, pausing, "for the right price."

"If you..."

The knock interrupted him. He turned and looked at the door. It wasn't much of a knock, just a polite little noise with an excuse-me kind of rap. It wasn't the kind of noise to make a mistake over, but I've had some experience making mistakes. I made one then. I looked at the door.

Voss snaked a handout and grabbed a leg of my chair. He yanked hard, and I went over backwards. The .45 decided to go off. It made a sharp pinging noise, and the slug shook the ceiling. I rolled over and made it to my knees in time to see Voss dive over the chair. A knife had grown out of his right sleeve. He was on me in a blur of arms and legs. I pushed the .45 in his face and leaned heavily against his knife arm. But he dipped his shoulder and grunted, and I felt a stinging jab against my ribs. I brought the Luger down hard on the top of his head. He yelped and scrambled back, and stood up. The knocking came again, this time like thunder rolling in from the desert. Voss stood there hesitating. Then, without a word, he bolted through the window and went off up the alley.

With more than a little effort, I got my feet under me and stood up. I stumbled over to the window and peered out into the darkness, not expecting to see anything and not seeing it. The dry wind raked at my face. I turned back slowly into the room and looked down. I was still wearing a gun in each hand. I might as well have been wearing mittens. A trail of dark, wet spots followed me across the room and settled next to my feet. The idea that I was leaking was just reaching me when the knocking came once more.

I dropped the .45 on the bed, moved quickly over, and stood next to the door. Then I yanked it open and poked the Luger into the startled face of Hector Armendariz. His eyes grew as big as billiard balls.

"Aye, *Senor* Garrett. *Por favor,* not again."

I lowered the gun and sighed heavily. "Hector, what the hell do you want?"

His mouth moved several times before he could say anything. *"Senor,* I hear thee noise…" He shut his mouth, swallowed, and started again. "You say to come. I find *las senoritas,* Rosetta and Lupe."

I shrugged and stepped aside, and motioned for him to come in. He scurried by me, and I closed the door and leaned against it.

Hector went over and looked down at the .45. Then he gingerly perched himself on the edge of the bed as far away from the gun as he could. He turned and looked back at me and lowered his eyes to the blood on my shirt.

"Senor, que pasa?" he murmured.

"Never mind," I said. "Where are they?"

"In Juarez, *senor*. At thee Parrot."

"Are they with anyone?"

He flashed a quick smile. Sly creases surrounded his dark eyes. *"Senor,* they are always weeth someone. *Senor* Delmar, he sees to that."

I grunted and put the Luger on top of the chest of drawers. Then I peeled off my undershirt and inspected my side. The knife had bounced off the left side of my rib cage, slicing the skin but not penetrating. It left an angry-looking gash, sore but not dangerous. Hector caught his breath when he saw it.

"Aye, *Senior.* Who did thees?"

"One of *Senior* Delmar's playmates."

His eyes widened, and he clucked his teeth. He kept clucking while I cleaned myself up and fished some gauze and adhesive tape out of my bag. I covered the wound, put on a clean shirt, and got into my other suit. Finally, I turned and looked at Hector.

"Okay," I said. "Let's go."

"Senor?"

"Take me to Juarez."

He hesitated and bit his lip. *"Senor* Garrett, you going down there after they do thees to you? I theenk you *muy loco."*

"Maybe," I said. "But I don't want to disappoint *Senor* Delmar. He'll be expecting me. Besides, I've taken out some insurance.

Chapter Seventeen

The traffic was light as we drove down the bridge to Juarez Avenue. I could see the lights of the city spreading south into the foothills, glowing lazily like embers in the desert breeze. I rode in the back and tried not to cry out as the cab bounced onto the crumbling pavement. My ribs were throbbing like a plucked violin.

We went about a half mile, turned east onto Escondido Boulevard, then, after just two blocks, turned south again into the central part of the city. Hector nosed the cab roughly back and forth through the narrow, winding streets. Suddenly, they became as crowded as a New York subway at rush hour. We drove past rows of tightly bunched buildings, low square blocks of brightly painted adobe and stucco, some not more than an arm's length from the curb. Garish signs jutted out into the street announcing *"Farmacia,"* *"Mercado,"* and even *"Dentista."* Every now and then, the line of buildings was broken by a small esplanade with a row of open-air markets and shops, where strings of pinatas and paper lanterns hung under baked-out canvas awnings. One carried a sign reading, *"Arte Y Artesanfas"*—arts and crafts for the *turistas.*

We passed more shops and some dingy night spots with mariachi music blaring, and even an occasional cafe where a heavy smell of corn and frying fat hung over the street. A hot steady breeze rocked the strings of lanterns, and the moving light on the colored walls made a kaleidoscope effect in the closed-in streets.

The hot breeze wandered up and down past shadowed alleys and doorways where people stood and mingled and looked out with hungry eyes.

135

During the day, these streets were choked with merchants and peddlers hawking trinkets to the crowds of tourists. But at night, the faces changed, and the streets were crowded with well-dressed, well-fed Anglos—people with money who came south looking for a different kind of trade. The girls were out then, preening and strutting and smiling at everyone who could rub a couple of dollar bills together, and the men convened on the street corners. They were the grifters and pimps and dope pushers—skinny dark men with flashy clothes and polished smiles. It was a place for every down-at-the-heels mug with a line out for some fast action.

We moved slowly for at least a mile until the traffic and the scattering of run-down houses thinned out into a dismal stretch of desert. Then, after only a quarter of a mile, we came to a row of cars parked along the street, not the usual Juarez hacks. There was a Chrysler, several Buicks, a Cadillac, and even a shiny green Packard Clipper parked just behind a long black limousine.

The cab pulled up and stopped in front of a purplish stucco building with dark wooden casement doors standing under a sign with blue neon lettering. The sign said, "El Cotorra Azul." The Blue Parrot.

I told Hector to wait, and I headed up the walk, giving my suit a quick brush-off, then went through the door.

I stepped into a dimly lit anteroom and into the coldly professional gaze of two large men in tuxedos. Each one had a bulge near his left arm, spoiling the cut of his jacket. The first one was built like a stump. He was balding, with narrow squinting eyes and brilliant patches of scar tissue covering his cheeks and forehead, the remembrance of a bad burn. The other man was taller. He had sandy hair and lightly mottled skin, and he spoke to me in the clear tones of South Side Chicago.

"Sorry, friend. This here's a private club. I'll have ta ask ya ta leave."

"I'm expected," I said. "The name's Garrett."

Without cracking his expression, he turned and picked up a wall phone by the door. The other man just stood and tried to frisk me with his stare. I started to reach for a cigarette, but he quickly held up his hand and shook his head.

I looked at him. "You're probably right. They might stunt my growth."

The sandy-haired man looked at me while he spoke my name into the mouthpiece. He listened for a long moment. Then he hung up and flashed me the welcoming grin of a used-car salesman.

"Okay, friend. The boss is busy, but he says ta show ya around and make ya comfortable." He hesitated, a look of mock embarrassment on his face. "Of course, I'll have ta ask Slade here ta pat ya down first. It's customary with strangers. Can't be too careful, ya know."

Slade stepped forward and made a greedy pass over my clothes, pummeling my ribs. I hadn't brought my gun. Down here, it would only start an argument. Slade stepped back, folded his arms, and grunted. "Clean."

The tall man stepped toward the inner door. "This way, friend." He turned to Slade. "The boss says ta stay put. I'll see ta Mr. Garrett here." He opened the door, and I followed him inside.

We walked into a wide room that had the smoky ambience of a speakeasy. It was full of tinny laughter, clinking glasses, and loud music. Rows of cushioned booths, separated by stone pillars and covered with thin masonry arches, lined the front and back walls. Most of them were occupied by well-dressed couples, some drinking, some nuzzling, some just sitting with dissipated stares, ignoring each other. The row in back was broken by a beaded curtain covering a single door. And on the left wall was a long bar behind which three young men in white serving jackets kept busy shaking and pouring.

The room was barely lit by small amber bulbs set into thin metal fixtures hung on the walls, and overhead, a pair of wide wooden fans slowly stirred the rising pea-soup smoke. Against the right-hand wall, a Mexican quartet was standing behind a crowded dance floor, doing everything it could to trample the memory of the old Chicago jazz groups.

To the right of the door was a hat check booth with a bored-looking brunette behind the counter. She took my hat and gave me a tentative smile. The man next to me put his hand on my arm and motioned across the room.

"The boss says ta show ya around. Let's start in back."

We waded through the tables and ducked behind the beaded curtain. The room behind was outfitted like one of the Reno road joints. There were half a dozen green felt-covered tables offering blackjack, faro, and roulette. In the front corner to the left, several fat men sat around a large table smoking cigars and playing poker. And in back, a good-sized crowd was huddled around a crap table, intently watching a chestnut-haired woman. I could see why. Monica Wearing was decked out for the evening.

She had on a tight-fitting vermilion dress with some kind of underwire arrangement that made breathing look like recreation. I got an eyeful of her, but she was too busy to notice me. As I watched, she leaned generously over the table and rolled the dice. There was a squeal, and she raked in a large stack of chips.

I followed my host over into the corner to the right, next to another door. "What's in there?" I asked.

He leaned toward me and spoke out of the side of his mouth. "The boss's office, a coupla dressing rooms, and some rooms we save for special guests."

Before I could ask the obvious question, the door opened, and a heavyset middle-aged man came out. He adjusted his tie and looked pleased with himself. He was followed by a faint odor of ether mixed with burning leaves and, behind that by a dark-haired girl in a shimmering aqua dress. I didn't recognize the man, but I had seen the girl earlier in the evening. We had visited the same doctor. She walked curtly over to the first door and went out into the main room.

The sandy-haired man closed the door and then said, "The boss said ta see that ya get anything ya want." He motioned toward the tables. "Interested in one of the games?"

I shook my head.

He pointed his thumb at the door. "Maybe somethin' in a private room?"

"No," I said. "I think I'll just go back and try out the bar."

"Okay. But if ya change yer mind, just ask for Monte." He aimed his thumb at his chest. "That's me."

I went back out front and sat on a stool at the end of the bar. I ordered a Scotch sipped it, and watched several people try to go through the beaded curtain into the back room, only to be stopped at the door. I was just considering how lucky I was to be a favored customer when the girl in aqua came back through the front entrance and sat down at a table near my end of the bar. I gathered up my Scotch, walked casually over next to her, and sat down.

"Which one are you," I asked, "Rosetta or Lupe?"

She looked up and eyed me carefully from behind a businesslike smile. She had smooth, even features, a wide nose with flared nostrils, and a full mouth covered with too much lip rouge.

"Rosetta," she said. "Deed Monte send you, *senor...?*"

"Garrett," I said. "And no, Monte didn't send me. Jimmy Wearing told me to look you up."

She flashed a quick smile. "Oh, Jeemy. You know heem?"

"We just met."

She giggled. "I like heem."

"Has he been in tonight?"

She shook her head. "Not yet. But I theenk he weel. He comes here all thee time, always to see me and Lupe. Sometimes he even take us places."

"Yeah," I said. "Like to the hotel. He says you know how to show a guy a good time, you and your friend."

Her eyes clouded, and she drew in on her lower lip. "What do you mean, *senor?*"

I gave her a nasty snicker. "Don't be cute. You know what I'm after." I put my hand on her arm and leered at her. "Jimmy says you're a real hot number." She wrenched her arm away and bared her teeth. "Jeemy didn't tell you that. We never do that weeth heem. He wouldn't. He never..."

"Never what?"

Her eyes narrowed. "Who are you?"

"Just a friend of someone who's being blackmailed." I brought the picture out of my pocket, flashed it to her, and put it away again.

She let out a little gasp, and her eyes widened, showing white under the lids. "Where you get thees?"

"Never mind that," I said. "Who took this picture?"

She sat and stared at me, fear trickling down into her features.

"Listen, sister," I said. "You're already in trouble. Don't make it worse. If I blow the whistle, you girls won't be able to step across the border without getting pinched. And that won't make your boss very happy."

She held up her hand. "Please, *senor*. I thought eet was a joke. Thees man tell us to come to thee hotel. He say we play a treek on Jeemy. Night before last we go to thee room weeth Jeemy, and he pass out—*borracho*. Thee man, he take the peectures. Then we go outside and he pay us and we leave." She wrung her hands together. "Please, *senor*. That ees all."

"Who was the man?"

"I don't know heem. But he ees a very beeg man—and dark, *muy moreno*, weeth long black hair."

"My stomach muscles started to tighten. "How was he dressed?'

She frowned. "Mmm...dark suit, *muy costoso*. And he wore sometheeng around hees head, a band like...like *el piel roja*."

My stomach fell down around my knees. "An Indian?"

Her face brightened with recognition. "*Si*. An Indian."

"Did he tell you what he planned to do with the pictures?"

Before she could answer, the door in the back of the room opened, the beads parted, and two men stepped through. They looked around the room until they spotted Rosetta and me. Then they just stood and watched us like a pair of taxidermists studying a specimen. One of them was Norman Voss.

Rosetta let out another gasp and started to get up, but I grabbed her arm. "You talk to me, or I talk to your boss," I said.

She squeezed her hands on the edge of the table. "Please, *Senor*. Not here. Tomorrow night at the Del Norte."

"How will I find you?"

"I weel find you. Ask for Charlie the bellhop. Geeve heem your room number and tell heem you are waiting for Rosetta Saens. He weel understand." She got up quickly and hurried over to the bar.

Voss was standing next to a moon-faced man with swarthy skin and black hair slicked back and shining like patent leather. His torrid black eyes were as black as any eyes could be. He wore crisp black trousers, a white shantung dinner jacket, and the smile of a hungry alligator. He pulled out a chair and sat down next to me.

"Mr. Garrett, I've been looking forward to meeting you." His voice was a raspy whisper, as if someone had stepped on his windpipe. "I'm Rudy Delmar."

I took my time lighting a cigarette. "I never would have guessed."

Voss sat down opposite me. He folded his arms and stared blankly across the table. A thick bandage was covering part of his left ear. I nodded in his direction and said, "Have an accident?"

Delmar snickered. "I hear you've been tough tonight."

I kept looking at Voss. "It's no trick rousting an empty-eyed gunny who can barely hit a parked car."

Voss ground his teeth, the purple stripe along his jaw showing like an open wound.

"Don't sell Schizy short," Delmar said. "If he can see it, he can hit it."

I chuckled. "So, he's not just a pretty face."

Delmar ran his eyes down the front of my suit. "I've been hearing a lot about you, Mr. Garrett. Frankly, you're not what I expected."

I turned and looked at him. "But you are."

He put his elbows on the table and rubbed his palms together, meaning business. "I'm told you may have a certain item that I'm interested in buying."

"Could be," I said. "What's it worth to you?"

"Turn it over to me, and I'll give you ten thousand and no questions."

I laughed. "I know someone who was willing to pay fifty. And it's already cost two lives. For ten grand you can't even get in the game."

He folded his hands and leaned toward me. "You got nobody breathing who's gonna pay that much. I'm offering you a solid deal, no strings."

"The same kind of deal you offered Jack Springer?" He leaned back in his chair and threw a smirk at Voss. "Sometimes Norman gets carried away." He looked back at me. "This time, I'll see that he doesn't."

"So, that fixes everything." I rocked my chair back and took an easy drag, sending the smoke up into the overhead fan. "Since when have you become an art lover? What would some jade statues mean to you?"

He folded his hands and gave me a shiny black stare. "More than money—power, influence. With my connections, I can use those figures to promote some serious dough, enough to build the biggest operation in the whole Southwest." He looked away, an almost wistful glint showing in his eyes. "Enough to go home in style."

"What connections?"

He turned and showed me a face full of scorn. "Don't get any big ideas, Garrett. That jade is too hot for you. I'm talking about powerful people—people you couldn't touch in a lifetime of trying."

"People like Colonel Wearing?"

I could hear his hands squeezing together. White creases showed at the corners of his mouth. "That goddamn smart-mouthed bastard; thinks he's won, thinks he's got it all. Well, nobody puts the scram on Rudy Delmar. I'll show him, the son of a bitch."

"Funny," I said. "He said the same about you."

He put a cold stare on me. "I don't think I like you, Garrett."

"I'm devastated."

He held the stare for a long moment, then abruptly started to laugh. "You're a real smart-ass, aren't you? Maybe I could use you after all. String along with me, and I'll set you up in something soft. Just play ball, and you'll have more dough than you'll ever see by peeking over transoms."

"Sounds tempting." I blew a curtain of smoke across the table at Voss and crushed out the remains of my Lucky. "But I'm used to transoms. Who killed Ordway? Was it tall-dark-and-ugly here, or did you hire someone with brains?"

Voss lurched up from his chair, leaned on the table, and hissed at me through his teeth. "Just keep it up, big shot. You're gonna be cold meat."

Delmar turned and gave him a frosty eye. "Sit down."

Without a word, Voss eased back into his chair and sat, crawling all over me with his stare.

"I'm playing for big stakes," Delmar said. "That means people can get hurt, even you." He rubbed his hands together again. ·But we're wasting time. What about the jade?"

I leaned back in the chair and toyed with another Lucky. "There's supposed to be a curse on it. Aren't you afraid of the Bird of Death?"

"What curse?" he sneered. "Quit the stall. I'm offering you ten grand."

I rolled the Lucky around in my fingers. "Maybe I'll just hang on to the jade. Green's my favorite color."

"Don't be a sap. Those figures can't mean anything to you."

"Just a million bucks worth of murder."

Delmar put both elbows on the table and glared at me. His mouth hardly moved. "I tried to be nice. I tried to do it easy. Remember that." He lifted his hand and snapped his fingers.

Voss stood up. It was the first time I'd seen him smile. I sensed a presence behind me. I looked around and saw Monte, arms folded, his face all business. I felt like the odd man at a hanging.

"Mr. Garrett!"

It was Monica Wearing. She was standing in front of the beaded curtain, waving at me. Everyone at the table froze as she moved through the crowd like an olive headed for the bottom of a martini. She stood next to my chair and spoke to Delmar.

"Why, Rudy. What a gentleman, looking after my guest while I'm busy winning your money. But you don't have to worry anymore, darling. I'm here now." She looked down at me and put a hand on my arm. "Mr. Garrett, you must dance with me."

I followed her onto the dance floor while the men at the table looked at each other. Delmar motioned to the other two, and they faded into the crowd while he went into the back room.

Monica watched me watching them and chuckled. "Having fun, darling?"

"Do you call everybody that?"

"Now, now, darling." She curled her fingers around the back of my neck and slid her leg tight between my thighs. I hadn't danced in years, but she made it seem like yesterday. We cruised into the middle of the crowd, and I felt her body rubbing against me. Her scent wafted up, and I began to forget about Delmar.

She leaned back and gave me an up-from-the-pillow look. "Do you like my perfume? It's called After Midnight."

"I knew it was after something."

She laughed. "My dear Mickey. Are you always so coy?"

"Only with practice," I said. "What are you doing here?"

"Just having fun."

"You play with a rough crowd."

She giggled. "Oh, Rudy would never bother me." She made a quick frown. "But do be careful, Mickey darling." She nestled her cheek against the side of my face and breathed into my ear. "I wouldn't like it if something bad happened to you."

We stayed in a clinch until the music stopped. Monica took my hand and led me back to the table. She flagged down a young waitress in a skimpy costume and ordered a Manhattan. I stayed with Scotch. The girl brought the drinks and left, and I took my time watching her retreating legs.

"I wish you'd look at me that way." I turned and looked at Monica. She had pulled her chair around next to me and was leaning on the table, offering enough cleavage to make a sphinx blush. "Or maybe you're just a leg man."

"Right now, I'm a hired man, Mrs. Wearing." I put down a good swig of Scotch. I had a feeling I might need it.

She fretted her lips playfully. "I told you, it's Monica. And I didn't hire you."

"No, but your husband did. And there are rules about taking up with clients' wives."

She sighed wistfully and traced a finger along the edge of my ear. "There's always a first time, isn't there?"

I brushed her hand away and took another long drink of the Scotch. "It might be a first time to get killed."

She fiddled with her glass and pretended to pout. I could see the amber lights reflected in her chestnut hair, flickering like dark fire. "You might at least say thank you," she said.

"For what?"

She gave me a mocking grin. "Oh, I see. You and Rudy were just getting acquainted. Is that it?" She folded her hands and inhaled deeply while I took another drink and almost bit through the glass. "You're not an easy man to know, Mickey," she said.

I watched the light dancing in her hair. "I didn't know you were trying."

She put her hand on my shoulder. "But I want to know all about you."

I swallowed hard. "I think you already know plenty. What are you doing down here, and how did you get into Delmar's private gambling room?"

"I told you. I was just having fun." She shook her head. Her shimmering hair seemed to spill light onto the table.

"How well do you know Delmar?"

She shrugged, and more fiery ripples spread around her. "Oh, I hardly know him at all."

"But you were in there." I waved a hand toward the back of the room. "And when I mentioned his name at your house, you jumped like a scalded cat." I dropped my hand back on the table. It felt like lead.

Monica reached for my ear again, moving close so that I could smell her perfume. The highlights from her hair danced in front of my eyes. "Well," she drawled, "he does have a reputation..."

"So do you," I said thickly. I wanted to ask about her reputation. I wanted to ask why two men were dead. I wanted to ask how she could look and smell like one of my better dreams. I didn't ask. I sat and watched the reflected lights. They were moving now, circling her face. And her face moved with them. It drifted above the table, luminescent, blotting out the rest of the room. Her fingers were stroking my neck and face. They were long, soft, warming fingers attached to beautiful hands and graceful arms—long arms, miles long. And at the end of them, her face floated, surrounded by her shimmering hair—soft and fresh, smelling like something to lie down in.

"Mickey? Are you alright?"

I pushed myself up from the table, then fell back over the chair and watched the floor rush toward me. I rolled over against a pair of legs rooted like oak trees. There was laughter, and someone said, *"borracho."* A few hundred hands covered me, poking, prodding, rooting in my pockets. They lifted me off the floor, then paraded me across the room, through the door, and into the street.

The flagstone walk in front of the club greeted me like an old friend, and

I drifted in an ocean of noise and street smells. Something hard hit me in the neck and then in the shoulder. I felt myself rolling over, and I heard laughter. I lay there and watched a scorpion saunter up onto the flagstones in front of me. I contemplated it the way you look at a ship on the horizon, something remote, far away. It leered at me, then stood back and carefully shook a long mane of chestnut red hair.

I blinked and tried to shake my head, but it was no use. I was off to a place where they fill your mouth with cotton and cover you with pink haze. There was music and flashing lights and long groping shadows. There were faces in the shadows, passing in a blur of laughter. The shadows became hands, with long gnarled fingers. And the fingers grew long, shiny claws, scraping and tearing at me. I tried to lift my arms, but they wouldn't move. I felt streams of sweat coming down my face, burning into my eyes. I opened my mouth to scream, but nothing came out. There was only silence, then growing darkness, and somewhere in it an Indian.

Chapter Eighteen

T he first thing I saw was the lamp. It was standing on a table right next to my head, a squat, blue-and-white porcelain affair with a wide-sloping shade. It seemed to be leaning over, studying me the way someone examines a snail crawling up the side of an aquarium. I shut my eyes and rolled my head to the side. That wasn't a good idea. A heavy throbbing caught me in each temple, and I heard myself groan. I lay there, slowly feeling exquisite sensations of pain from my neck to my ankles. I blinked several times and tried to swallow. My mouth felt like the inside of a catcher's mitt. I tried sitting up, but a sharp pain in my side brought me back down.

"Don't try to get up."

I opened my eyes and looked up into the quiet golden face and clear blue eyes of Gabrielle Wearing. All I could say was, "What the hell…?"

"Never mind," she said. "Drink this."

"What is it?"

"Orange juice. Randolph said you'd need it."

"Randolph said? What was he…?"

She slid a hand behind my head, propped me up, and shoved a glass up to my mouth. "No questions yet. Just drink it."

I drank it. It tasted better than the finest Scotch, better than the most expensive champagne. I drank it all. She took the glass away, and I winced and propped myself up and looked around. I was lying under a blanket on a couch in the middle of a small feminine living room. It was a nice room, comfortable, uncluttered, a room you could stretch out on a couch in.

"Where am I?" I mumbled. "How did I get here?"

"Randolph brought you. He cleaned you up and dressed your wound. You're in my apartment." She leaned forward a little, a look of deep concern on her face. "What happened to you? How did you get hurt?"

"Just a little argument with one of Rudy Delmar's goons. He made his point with a knife."

She breathed in sharply. "That's awful."

"It's all right. I gave him a good talking to."

"How can you joke about it?"

"What else is there for me to do?" I reached down and felt the bandage and the tenderness underneath. A thick gauze pad and several yards of adhesive tape were covering most of my left side. As I gingerly fingered the bandage, I realized that nothing was covering the rest of me but my shorts. "What happened to my clothes?"

"They were a mess," she said. "Randolph got rid of them. He came around this morning and left you those." She motioned toward a chair in the corner. On it was a neatly folded suit, a clean shirt and tie, even a new hat. She turned back to me. "I guess you had a pretty bad time."

"I've had worse. What was Randolph doing down at Delmar's club?"

"He didn't say. What were you doing there?"

I grunted. "Looking for a girl."

She smiled. "That's right. You told me you have to work hard with girls. Did you have any luck?"

"I found her—surrounded by a bunch of apes in tuxedos."

"What happened?"

"I was charming them to pieces when somebody dropped a goofball in my drink." I watched the concern gather on her face again. "Speaking of drinks, how about a real one?"

She made a small, resigned kind of smile. "Randolph said you might need that too." She reached down and brought up a decanter and a glass that had been sitting on the floor beside the couch. She poured out a generous portion and handed it to me.

"'What would I do without Randolph?" I said.

I took it in a single gulp. It was brandy, silky smooth and soft. It warmed its way down and began coaxing the blood back into my wooden arms and legs. I leaned back against the arm of the couch. "Have you got a cigarette?"

She grinned a little, brought her hands together, and bowed in mock servitude. "Yes, sir. At your service."

She got up and went over to the chair. I watched as she took a fresh pack of Luckies out of the suit jacket. She didn't look anything like a dedicated young attorney. She was wearing creamy white slacks and sandals and a light blue shirt, pulled and knotted around her middle, exposing a smooth, tanned stretch of midriff. Her hair hung in loose, honeyed waves and rippled gently as she opened the pack, pulled out a cigarette, and lit it. She took a deep drag, then came over, crouched next to me, and put the cigarette in my mouth. "There we are, sir. Will that be all?"

I drew in some of the welcome bitterness and let it trail out slowly. "Have you ever been to one of Monica's auctions?"

The smile faded. "No. And I'm sorry I gave you that invitation." She bit her lip and shook her head. "I knew I shouldn't have let you go."

"I wouldn't have missed it," I said. "Until last night, I hadn't been shot at in almost a week."

Her hands flew up to her mouth as her eyes filled with cold blue horror. "But…

"Never mind," I said. "How did you get that invitation?"

She swallowed hard. "Randolph got it for me…from Monica, of course. Why?"

"Because the character who roughed me up had an invitation. He flashed it at the museum yesterday afternoon."

She brought her hands up in front of her, fists clenched. "I knew it! That woman is mixed up with Rudy Delmar, and the two of them are stealing from my father."

"Not so fast," I said. "I talked with the museum curator. He told me that Monica is donating all the proceeds to the museum. If she and Delmar are making money, it's not from the auctions."

Her eyes widened. "I can't believe it. Are you sure?"

"As sure as I can be about anything around here. You said she was also involved with Jack Springer. How do you know?"

"I saw him at the house just last week. I thought he was there to see Father, but he never went upstairs. He and Monica talked alone by the pool for almost fifteen minutes. Then he left. Later, I heard from Victor that he'd seen the two of them at the hotel that same evening."

"Any idea what they were talking about?"

She shook her head. "But I never trusted that man, Springer. And I certainly don't trust Monica, even if she is giving the money to the museum." She looked at me earnestly. "You've met her, talked to her. Surely, you can't believe she isn't up to something."

"Who knows? Maybe she's got an angle. She was at Delmar's club last night."

Her eyes grew as big as half-dollars. "What?"

"Yeah," I said. "Just when I was about to let Delmar and his boys beat me to a pulp, she showed up and gave me a dance lesson."

"You see," she gloated. "That proves it."

I shook my head. "Sorry, counselor. All it proves is that Monica likes to gamble and have a good time and that she doesn't much care about the surroundings. I haven't seen her break any laws."

Gabrielle dropped her hands on the couch. "It all seems so hopeless and confused." She motioned in the direction of my battered ribs. "What is going on?"

I wasn't sure how much I ought to tell her. But there wasn't a lot I could tell anybody. "What's going on is a war between Rudy Delmar and your father. They're like two aging generals trying to settle an old grudge. All they have left is their hate for each other. And in the middle of it all is some very old jade. One of them wants it badly enough to kill people for it. The other doesn't know or doesn't care about the jade, but he's willing to let people be killed for it just the same.·

Gabrielle shuddered. There was a grim set to her jaw. "I can't believe my father would have anything to do with murder."

"Maybe not directly," I said. "But he's in a business that makes enemies.

Whenever his papers print something about greed and corruption, he's stepping on the toes of powerful people. I've talked to your father. He seems willing to step on some toes. And I've talked to Delmar. He seems upset."

She eyed me with a certain fascination. "Do you think Delmar killed Willy?"

I shrugged. "Not by himself. But he could have had it done, if he thought Ordway might get to the jade before he did. He's brought in a gunsel from the Coast. And he practically admitted that the guy squibbed Springer. Are you sure you can't tell me anything about those jade figures?"

She looked back at me and shook her head. "Nothing I haven't already. Willy just called me and raved about the figures and a curse. Nothing that made sense—just superstitious nonsense. And Father never mentioned them. But I can't imagine that he would give away anything like that, even to Monica."

"When did you tell Ordway about the auction arrangements?"

"I didn't. When I saw how frightened he was, I simply told him to go home." She pressed her lips tight together and shook her head. "I wish I'd never agreed to let him come here."

"I guess he meant a lot to you."

She gave me a cool-eyed stare. "He did, but not the way you mean." Her gaze softened a couple of notches. "Willy was...that way. You know? Something Father could never tolerate. I didn't care what Father thought, but still, there could never be anything between Willy and me except friendship." She put both hands on my arm and gave me a reassuring squeeze. "But he *was* my friend."

"Uh-huh," I said. "And he *was* my client."

She didn't move. "That's important to you, isn't it?"

I reached up and crushed out my Lucky in a small porcelain ashtray next to the lamp. Then I took the decanter, poured some more brandy into the glass, and emptied the glass.

"How long have you known Randolph?'

Her brows came together in a slight frown. "He's been with the family for years. He's devoted to Father. And I trust him implicitly. Why?"

"Why did he bring me here?"

She bit her lip and looked down. I felt her hands squeezing the couch next to me. "I expect that was Father's idea. You see, he thinks that we... that you and I... Well, you know."

"Why would he think that?"

She sighed and looked up again. "He's been doing that ever since I came back to El Paso. All the men he's hired to take care of Jimmy...he's really been pushing them at me. He thinks I should be married. But he never approves of anyone I might be interested in. Even though there's someone I might really care for, Father won't hear of it. He's biased and stubborn. He thinks it's his place to pick out the right man for me, someone who will respect his fortune and appreciate history the way he does."

"Biased and stubborn, huh." I grunted again. "He must be thrilled with me."

A playful gleam came into her eyes. "He's not. Maybe that's why I..." She left it hanging there between us.

I kept looking into her blue eyes. There was none of the hardness I'd seen the day before. They had that soft innocent look that makes a guy forget about all the years, all the miles, and all the cheap hotel rooms. She caught herself, and the moment ended. "Well, Mr. Garrett—"

"Stop calling me that," I said. "I've already spent the night in your apartment with my pants on a chair."

She laughed. "All right, then, Michael. Would you like something to eat?"

"What time is it?"

"Three o'clock," she said. "I was afraid you might sleep all day."

I propped myself up on one elbow and tenderly went about discovering the soft spots on my head. "I guess I could take a little breakfast."

"Fine," she beamed. "How do you like your eggs?"

"Broken."

She pointed to a doorway past the far end of the couch. "The bedroom's in there, and the bathroom. I wouldn't try taking a shower with that bandage, but I guess a bath wouldn't hurt.· She grinned playfully. "I promise not to peek."

"Just promise not to laugh."

She laughed. Then she got up and disappeared into a kitchen off to my right. I struggled up off the couch, picked up the clothes, and went into the bathroom. I filled the tub with warm water and got in it. Gabrielle was right. It didn't hurt.

I steeped for about ten minutes, then attempted a shave with a dwarfish razor I found in the medicine chest. Next, I put on the ensemble Randolph had laid out. The shirt was finely woven cotton, and the suit was a rich gray gabardine. I looked at myself in the mirror. I was wearing a month's worth of cases. I checked the pockets. The notes and photograph had been put there, my wallet, and my change. There was even that fresh pack of Luckies. Whatever else the Indian might be, he was thorough.

My head was still objecting to being held up when I walked into the kitchen and took in the mouth-watering smell of frying bacon and fresh coffee. Gabrielle was busy at the stove, a small frilly apron tied around her waist.

Without looking up, she said, "Despite what Father thinks, I do have a domestic side." She poked at the bacon with a fork, then looked over at me. "Well, you look a lot better."

"Than what?"

She chuckled and shook her head, then pointed to a table and chairs against the wall. "Just sit down."

I complied.

She laid a plate full of bacon, eggs, and fresh toast in front of me and followed it with an oversized mug full of coffee. Then she took off the apron, sat down opposite me, and watched as I tried to eat everything but the table. I cleaned the plate in a handful of bites, then picked up the mug and spotted Gabrielle eyeing me.

"I like watching men eat," she said.

"So does your father."

She nodded, the corners of her mouth stretching into a tight smile. "It's one of his ways of making people feel uncomfortable."

"I guess he's done that to you before."

"Some," she said. "But mostly, he just seems to tolerate me, almost like an obligation. He's never really made me feel that I was needed." She flushed a little and shook her head. "But it's nothing like the way he's been with my brother. Father's ridden him constantly for as long as I can remember. I've tried to get Jimmy to leave El Paso, but he just won't. Now I think Father has simply broken his spirit."

"What do you know about the doctor he's been seeing?"

"Nothing, except that Victor doesn't like him." She thought for a minute. "I don't think he's done much good. Jimmy's been a lot worse lately, especially during the past week. I think he's been drunk every night." A deep sadness crept into her eyes. "I just can't seem to reach him anymore. I saw him at the hotel, day before yesterday, drunk as usual. I chased him out and told him to go home, but he just came back later with those two girlfriends of his."

"What were you doing there?"

"I went there to have lunch with Willy and get him to leave, to go back home." She shrugged. "But he wouldn't even come out of his room. She looked down at the table. "Poor Willy."

I slowly drank my coffee, and we sat. I leaned back casually, listening to the silence and watching Gabrielle. She traced her finger back and forth across the top of the table and pursed her lips. After a few minutes, she looked up at me.

"I've been thinking about what you said about Father and that man Delmar. Assuming you're right, then why is it happening now? Why, after all these years? Father's always hated Delmar. He's made no secret of that. But for years, they left each other alone. Now, all of a sudden,... Why?" She clenched her fist. Her eyes glistened like the surface of a frozen lake. "Unless Monica is working with Delmar somehow to hurt Father, to destroy him, maybe even to..."

Even without words, the threat hung there in the air. I put down the coffee and took a painful breath. "It's possible. It could explain how Delmar knew about the jade, why he would want to get rid of Ordway, and how his trigger man got one of the invitations. And it could explain why Monica has been playing so cozy with me. But I'm not so sure it explains why Jack Springer was killed, or what happened to the first piece of jade—the one that was sold last month.·

"'You mean Delmar doesn't have it?"

"I don't think so. Not from the way he was talking last night."

"What's so important about the jade? Why does he want it?"

I shrugged. "It means money, big money. Somehow, Delmar knows the value of the Jade, and I think he's planning to use it to arrange a move back to the States."

"But why go to all this trouble? He must have other ways of raising money."

"Money alone may not do it," I said. "And it's obvious the jade means more than just money to Delmar. At the very least, it means taking something important from your father. It means beating him, embarrassing him. Taking your father's jade would be a form of revenge, one that would hit the Colonel where he's most vulnerable—in his pride." I started to go on, but I saw her wince. I spread my hands on the table. "I'm just guessing, of course."

She squeezed her hands together and searched my face for the answer to a question I didn't want her to ask. "You think there's more to it, don't you?"

I got up and went over and leaned against the counter next to the stove. "Yeah. There's more. There's blackmail. There's a doctor with a houseful of Degas prints who's treating half the town for nervous disorders. And there's a sheriff who wants to beat my face in and pocket the jade for himself."

She got up and walked over in front of me. "There's something you're not telling me, isn't there?"

I studied her face and thought for a minute. She was more of a lawyer than she looked. I took out Ordway's note and handed it to her.

She read it over slowly, then looked up. Her voice came out soft, even-toned. But it had an edge of fear. "What does it mean, 'Bird of Death'?"

"It's part of the curse Ordway talked about. It's what he was so afraid of."

Her eyes grew wide. "But how can…? This can't be real."

"Ordway and Springer are dead. That's plenty real."

"What will you do?"

I took the note and stuffed it back in my pocket while I tried to think of an answer. "If I had any brains at all, I'd get on the next train back to LA. All I've gotten here is being beaten up, drugged, stabbed, and shot at. I've got the sheriff and one of his stooges and a gang of hoods and your father all looking at me as if I were a spot on the wall. I've got a cab driver drinking my booze, a rich woman trying to seduce me, and an Indian undressing me and burying my clothes. And I haven't done anything for anybody. Back in L.A. I can be useful. I can sit in my office and watch the dust settle and listen to the phone not ringing."

She gave me a smile full of recognition. "You're not leaving, are you?" It was more of a statement than a question.

I just looked away.

She put her hand on my arm. "Michael, I want to help."

I looked at her again. "Fine. Then you get on the train and get the hell out of here."

"But I feel responsible for Willy's death. Can you understand that?"

"Look, lady," I growled. "We both know you didn't kill him. And whoever did has a lot at stake, enough to keep on killing. I've already got enough people breathing down my neck without having to worry about you. I haven't got time to be babysitting some lady lawyer so she won't get her sweet little throat cut."

Her face reddened. "Why, you…gumshoe!"

"That's me," I said. "I'm looking for a killer, and I'm doing it alone. So, pack a bag and take a hike."

She put her hands on her hips and glared at me. "You don't fool me, Michael Garrett. You might be hard as nails now, but you came in here last night looking worse than dead." She glared some more. "Besides, I can do what I want. I don't need your permission any more than I need my father's."

It probably wasn't a smart thing to do, but I did it anyway. I reached out and drew her up against me and kissed her lightly. She looked surprised, but she didn't pull away. "Why did you do that?"

I shook my head. "I don't know. I do a lot of things without knowing why. One day I'll drop dead and not know the reason."

She looked up at me for a minute, blinking her eyes uncertainly. "What is it about you? You talk tough, but…You're not what I expected a detective to be."

"Nobody is," I said.

Suddenly, she wrapped her arms around me and pressed her head against my chest. I could feel her trembling. "Willy's note said he was afraid for me. Is that why you want me to leave?"

I held on to her and kept my mouth shut.

"I don't mind telling you," she said, "I am frightened."

I thought about Ordway's note and felt a familiar chill down low in my stomach. I was about to answer when the phone rang on the wall next to me. Gabrielle stepped over and picked up the receiver.

"Yes? Yes, he is… All right, I'll tell him." She hung up.

She turned and looked at me, the muscles along her jaw standing in knots. "That was Father. He wants to see you right away. I'll drive." She turned quickly and started out of the kitchen, then stopped in the doorway and looked back. There was an almost puzzled expression on her face.

"By the way," she said. "I liked it."

Chapter Nineteen

Gabrielle's apartment was part of a modern complex of brick and new mortar, surrounded by manzanita and desert palms. It sat just off the northern end of Alabama Avenue, partway up the east side of Ranger Peak, looking out across West Texas. It was in a nice area, quiet and well-tended, full of blue serge suits and late-model DeSotos. It wasn't the kind of neighborhood where you'd expect to see a local Juarez taxi.

As we climbed down the long row of cement steps leading to the sidewalk, the cab started up and nosed slowly out of a driveway down the block. It idled at the curb for a minute, then turned and sped off down the hill. I climbed into Gabrielle's roadster and listened to a familiar grinding noise fading into the distance. It had the uneasy sound of a cement mixer I had heard the night before.

The drive out to Wearing Manor took almost half an hour. The sun was turning into late afternoon, leaving the streets simmering under a crusted lamination of dust and sand. An uncomfortable breeze was swirling in off the desert. It curled and twisted the yucca leaves, and it made the skin on the back of my neck start to curl with them. Overhead, several clouds were gathering into plump columns, like churned cream, the undersides darkening purple-gray. Anywhere else, I would have expected rain.

I sat and smoked and stared out the window. There was something in the back of my mind, one of those unsettling things you know is there but can't quite reach. The more you try to focus on it, the more it bobs and weaves and darts away. I smoked and stared and tried to fight my way into that corner in my mind. It was empty. Even in my head, I was late.

Gabrielle sat stiffly behind the wheel, her eyes fixed straight ahead. She kept silent most of the way, occasionally squeezing the wheel and chewing on her lower lip. Finally, as we entered Sunset Hills, she said, "He sounded upset."

I tossed the remains of my Lucky out the window and watched the mountain loom in front of the car. "Not as upset as he's going to be."

"Michael." Her voice was calm but strained. "Maybe you should leave. I really am frightened. If what you said is true, then other people may be hurt—people I care about."

"That's reason enough for me to stay."

She shot a quick look at me, then turned back to the road. "Do you think Willy was right about the curse?"·

I didn't say anything.

The front gate opened as we pulled up, and Gabrielle went straight through and up the hill. She parked, got out, and headed up the front walk almost at a trot. I moved along behind her, every joint in my body wanting me to stop and sit down. As we climbed the steps to the porch, the front door opened. Randolph stood there and stared at me. He made me feel as welcome as a case of cholera.

Gabrielle went inside quickly, but I stopped in the doorway and looked at the Indian. "Thanks again, chief."

He snorted and held out his hand to take my hat.

"It's still new," I said. "I'll just keep it."

We went through the entrance hall into the main area and started for the stairs. On the way, I glanced through the glass doors at the back and out toward the swimming pool. That's when I saw the legs. I grabbed Gabrielle's arm and said, "Wait here."

I walked quickly out through the doors, went over, and stood next to a chaise lounge. Monica Wearing was stretched out in what little was left of the sun, hiding almost nothing behind a black two-piece bathing suit and a pair of sunglasses. As I approached, she yawned and stretched like a cat waking in the morning. She peered at me over the top of the glasses, then casually adjusted them back in place.

"You need to learn to control your liquor, Mickey darling."

"Not when someone else is controlling it for me."

She made an amused little smirk. "Oh?"

"Yeah," I said. "You might almost think someone didn't want us to finish our talk."

"Do we have something to talk about, Mickey darling?" She flipped over as she asked the question, spreading herself on a terry cloth towel and arranging her butt in the dwindling sunlight.

"We might." I tried to keep my eyes level on the horizon. "I'm still curious about your auctions. If you're going to turn over the take, why not just donate the collection to the museum? It's worth more than what you're getting for it."

She smiled and made a coy movement with her hands. "Really? I guess I just don't have a head for money matters."

"'You did all right at Rudy Delmar's crap table. How do you know him so well?"

"I don't really. I'm just one of his regular customers."

"How regular?"

"Now, now, Mickey dear." Her face was now buried in the thick terrycloth towel, and her voice was muffled. "A girl has to have some secrets."

"And I'll bet it's a secret how Delmar got one of your invitations. Is that what you were doing down there last night, collecting a payoff?"

She reached out and squeezed the arms of the chaise enough to make them squeak.

I kept pressing. "'Tell me about your relationship with Jack Springer."

She looked up at me and twisted her mouth disdainfully. "With that slob? Don't be ridiculous."

"I'm good at ridiculous," I said. "I do it very well. But since it involves murder, maybe you'd rather talk to the police."

She rose to her knees and stood up slowly, taking off her sunglasses. She had the deadpan look of a good poker player. "I've already spoken to the police. But if you must know, I'll tell you what I told them. Jack Springer wanted me to help him improve his position at the paper. He wanted his column to be syndicated, but he was afraid to talk with Stanfield about it directly. He asked me to put in a good word for him, and I refused. I told him that I don't involve myself in my husband's business affairs. Then he left, and the matter was ended."

"Then why did you meet him at the hotel?"

She sighed impatiently, her tone suddenly formal. "Really, Mr. Garrett. This is pointless." She sidestepped past me and started for the door.

"Sorry about your nervous disorder," I said.

She stopped and looked back, her face suddenly blank. "My what?"

"I assume, since Dr. Kintner is one of the regulars at your auctions, that you must be seeing him." I shrugged. "Maybe you and he have been taking each other's temperature."

The muscles in her face tensed, but her eyes didn't waver. "You're disgusting."

"Yeah," I said. "I get that way when I eat radishes, or when I'm being lied to."

She made a quick move, as if to swing at me, then stopped. She clenched her fists, and her voice came out low and harsh. "You're finished here. And I'll thank you not to bother me again, or I'll have Randolph throw you out."

"'These violent delights have violent ends,'" I said.

Her face became quizzical. "What's that?"

"Just something from an old playwright. You probably never heard of him."

She looked at me for a long moment, then cracked a knowing smile. "It might have been fun at that. But you're leaving town."

She turned abruptly and went through the doors into the house. I followed her inside and watched the inviting sway of her hips as she crossed the main hall and disappeared into the corridor on the far side.

I walked over to the foot of the stairs where Gabrielle and Randolph were waiting. Gabrielle was watching me, smoldering behind an indignant scowl. "Must you?"

"It's in the line of duty," I said.

She made a contemptuous sound and started briskly up the stairs. I started after her, then stopped. Randolph had left us and was walking back toward the front entrance.

"Hold it, chief," I called to him. He stopped and looked at me, one massive eyebrow raised. I motioned him back toward the stairs. "Come on. You don't want to miss the fun."

Chapter Twenty

The yelling started before we reached the top of the stairs. It had the shrill tone of a hacksaw cutting metal, and it was punctuated by the thump of a fist hammering on wood. Gabrielle knocked, then, without waiting, opened the door and walked into the office. I followed her inside, and Randolph followed me.

The late afternoon sun poured through a set of half-open Venetian blinds hanging over the window behind the desk. Amber streaks ran along the corner of the desk, across the floor, and up into a trophy case on the left. Several came to rest on the polished blade of an old cutlass whose ravenous sheen made it seem anxious to find somebody's vital organs.

I walked into the middle of the office and looked at Jimmy Wearing. He was standing to one side of the desk, staring at the floor, hands folded in front of him. He looked like a whipped animal. The Colonel was standing behind the desk, pointing a long, knotty finger at Jimmy. He went on yelling as if nobody had entered.

"Look at you. Nothing to show for all the years I've invested. I've wasted a fortune on you, and what have you done? Have you built anything? Have you accomplished anything? All you've done is throw away money on gambling and liquor and women—Mexican women at that. You've destroyed everything I've given you. And now you want me to give you a job writing for the paper?"

The Colonel slammed his fist down on the desk. Jimmy was a big man, but he seemed small and defenseless now as he cringed.

"If you want a job, then go down there and tell Bartels I said he could put you on as a copyboy with our Denver paper."

Jimmy began a feeble protest. "But…"

The fist hit the desk again. "I didn't tell you to speak! Just get out of here before I change my mind and send you all the way to New Jersey." He waved a hand at the door. "Go on. Get out!"

Jimmy turned, moved across the room, and opened the door almost in one motion. He hurried out, closing the door quietly and leaving an oppressive silence behind him.

Gabrielle moved over to the left of the desk where Jimmy had been. She stood, folded her hands, and looked back at me apprehensively. Randolph took up a position behind me. I just waited in the silence and watched the old man behind the desk.

The Colonel followed Jimmy's retreat, a disgusted smirk stamped into his flinty face. Then he placed both palms on the desk, leaned forward, and covered me with a slow, baleful stare.

"Well, Mr. Garrett. At least now you're properly dressed."

"Yeah." I pushed my hat back on my head and brushed the lapels of my jacket. "Gray matches my complexion."

He sneered contemptuously. "I daresay that suit is the only thing about you that's worth any notice."

I reached for a Lucky and lit it, and dropped the match into a gaping ashtray on the front of the desk. "I've gotten noticed without it."

"So I've heard." He leaned forward a little more and scowled. Suddenly, he raised a hand and slapped it down hard on the desk. "How dare you involve my son in a shooting?"

"He involved himself."

He went on as if I hadn't said anything. "And you took him with you to find Jack Springer. You exposed him to a brutal murder."

I shrugged. "Sorry. Springer neglected to tell me he was going to be dead."

He shook his head and spoke slowly. "You've been a disappointment to me, Mr. Garrett. I expect more from my people. I hired you to look after James to keep him out of trouble."

"You said you were hiring me to settle some blackmail," I said. "And as I recall, I told you I'm no babysitter."

He started to say something and stopped. He stood up, folded his arms, and glared. "James is a weakling. He couldn't stay in school, couldn't hold a job. Even the military wouldn't keep him.". He shook his head. "And now, he thinks he can write. Hah? The boy has no concept of his place in history, no respect for it. And as for you—"

Gabrielle broke in. "Father, please."

The Colonel wheeled and glared at her. "And just what are you doing here? I didn't send for you."

She inhaled, stretched herself up a couple of inches, and aimed her chin at him. "I came with Mr. Garrett. We're together."

It wasn't what I would have said, but it seemed to slow him down. He turned back and put a sour eye on me. "What right have you, bringing my daughter into this?"

I took an easy puff and let the smoke roll across the top of the desk. "Why not? She appreciates history."

An angry squall moved across the Colonel's face. I shot a quick look at Gabrielle. The corners of her mouth edged into a slight upward curl. She brought her hand up quickly to cover her mouth while she looked down at the floor. I looked back at the Colonel.

"You have no more appreciation for history than my son," he snapped. "History will bury James."

"It'll bury all of us," I said.

He waved a hand in Gabrielle's direction and spoke to her, aggravation clawing at his voice. "This man is nothing. I don't care what you think. I don't care what your interest in him is. He's nothing."

Gabrielle flushed and threw up her hands. "Oh, Father!" She turned and folded her arms tightly around her and looked out the window, her neck and face turning scarlet.

The Colonel ground his teeth. He reached into his desk, took out an envelope, and threw it down in front of him. I looked at it. It was addressed to me, in care of Colonel Stanfield Wearing. The handwriting was mine.

"Just what does this mean?" he snapped.

"It means that I haven't decided to take your case. I'm not even sure there is a case."

He angled his head and offered me an ironic sneer. "I suppose you want more money."

"I like money," I said. "Money and I get along fine. But I don't always like what goes with it."

He folded his arms and looked down his nose at me. "How very noble. And all for nothing. I only sought to employ you because Gabrielle interceded." He reached into another drawer and brought out a ticket. He dropped it next to the envelope. "I don't want you to remain here any longer. I find your services valueless and your manner obtrusive. You may take the money and get on the next train."

"Since you aren't paying for my services," I said, "you can't complain about them. As for my manner, I can understand your not liking it. A lot of people don't. That pains me and makes me depressed. But you can lay off ritzing me, Colonel. I'm not going anywhere. You and Sanchez have set me up as a target for Delmar, and now he's drawing a bead on me."

Gabrielle turned sharply and stared at me. The Colonel's eyes narrowed until they were just dark slashes in his wrinkled face. "What do you mean?"

"I mean, it's one thing to take an occasional beating, even get slapped around a little. It's part of the job. It's why people hire me. Cops, mugs, even old ladies—they all figure detectives are paid to get beaten up. But you see, I don't like it when people try to kill me. It makes me think I ought to raise my rates. And it's bad for business."

The Colonel scowled; his tone was tentative now, even suspicious. "What has all this to do with me?"

"Look," I said. "I know you and Sanchez each have a score to settle with Delmar. Sanchez even admitted that he wanted to use me as bait to bring Delmar out in the open. Only the way I figure it, he couldn't do that without your say-so."

I looked quickly over at Gabrielle. Her mouth was hanging open in disbelief. The Colonel just stood glaring, arms folded. So, I went on.

"What I can't figure is why you'd want to pick me out to do your dirty work. Why not just send Randolph? And then there's the blackmail angle."

I brought out the picture of Jimmy and the girls and laid it on the desk. Gabrielle stared at it. She looked stunned.

"When did you say this came in the mail?"

The Colonel looked impatiently down at the desk. "Why, day before yesterday."

"Uh-uh," I said. "You told me it came by messenger, a Mexican boy, not in the mail." I reached over and crushed out my cigarette. "But maybe you just got confused. That can happen with blackmail. That's why I talked with a girl named Rosetta Saens last night. She knows about that picture. She's in it. She told me that a man hired her and her friend to pose for the picture after he'd gotten Jimmy drunk. Then he paid them to keep quiet."

I turned and looked at Randolph. His eyes were full of bad intentions, but his face was as still as granite. "I guess he didn't pay them enough."

I looked back at the Colonel. "And I guess that's how you got confused. That man brought the picture here. He was following your orders. Rosetta called him *el piel roja,* the redskin." I shook my head. "You must have known that I'd find the girl. What were you trying to do, dangle me in front of Delmar?"

Gabrielle leaned on the desk with both hands, her face a mixture of shock and anger. "Father, how could you?"

The old man held up his hand and motioned for her to be quiet. He looked at me and spoke in a low growl laced with a grudging admiration. "Possibly, I've misjudged you, Mr. Garrett. You are somewhat resourceful. Just what do you want?"

"It's quite simple," I said. "I want a straight story about Monica's auctions."

He hesitated. "She's simply…disposing of some property."

"What property?"

He shrugged. "Just some old relics—pottery, stonework, mostly worthless."

"And the jade? If the stuff is so worthless, why did it bring an antique dealer all the way here from California? Why did the sheriff practically wet himself when he heard about it? Why was Delmar's hired killer stalking around the museum, and why was he so worried about my being there?"

The Colonel folded his arms and stood rigid. His breathing became shallow, almost forced, but his eyes glistened like polished ball bearings. Gabrielle stepped around to the front of the desk and stood next to me. I moved forward until I was pressing against the desk.

"Tell me about the Marina Jade, Colonel. I want to know why Delmar and Ordway and the sheriff and maybe even a fat reporter and a pansy doctor have all been in a lather trying to get it, and why you won't even admit to having it."

He began stammering and making noises that were barely audible. He made a short choking sound, clearing his throat. "I warn you, young man. Don't interfere with history."

"Did you warn Jack Springer too?" A sallow color began washing down over his face. I felt Gabrielle move closer.

"Listen, old man," I went on, "You stuck me in the middle of something. You can't just order me out of it."

"Just take my daughter and get away from here," he wheezed. "Get out of El Paso, both of you."

"What?" Gabrielle could only stare at him.

"No good," I said. "There's something between you and Delmar—something you're lining up. I want to know what it is."

Even without moving, he seemed to shrivel and grow old behind the desk. His breath shortened, and he dragged out his words as if each one weighed a hundred pounds. "You must not interfere with history…"

"History doesn't give a damn about you or your money," I said. "But it might have something to say about Ordway and Springer."

He took an unsteady step back from the desk. His jaw clamped shut, and his eyes widened. He looked as if he'd just swallowed a hornet.

Gabrielle grabbed hold of my arm. "Michael, please. That's enough."

"It's not enough," I snarled. "There's more than a curse threatening this family. Your father has started something that's already killed two people. If it doesn't stop now, more are going to die." I looked back at the old man. "What about it, Colonel? Are you going to sit still for murder? If you don't come clean, then you're no better than Delmar."

The old man caught his breath and began tugging at his collar. His eyes bulged, and his face went pale. A bluish cast started forming at the corners of his mouth. He staggered back and collapsed in a heap in his chair.

Randolph bolted around me and went toward the desk. He pushed a button on the Colonel's intercom unit, then began loosening the old man's shirt. Gabrielle and I hardly had time to react before Monica burst through the door behind me. She had changed into a yellow satin robe, and she had the determined look of a lifeguard going after a floundering swimmer. In one hand, she carried a glass of water, and in the other, a large white capsule. She hurried around the desk and leaned over her husband.

"It's all right, honey," she said to him. "Just take this."

The Colonel thrust the pill into his mouth and gulped down the water so fast that he started choking. He fell back in the chair, coughing and making rattling stertorous noises. Monica stood up and looked at Gabrielle and me. There was frost in her voice. "Please go."

I started to leave, but the Colonel held up his hand. "Wait," he rasped. He coughed again, then looked at me. There was desperation behind his eyes now.

"Mr. Garrett, I regret that people have died over this affair. They got too close. But the outcome is inevitable. Quetaz will have his revenge. You must not interfere. Take Gabrielle and go. And don't say a word to Victor Sanchez. He knows nothing of this." He fell back in the chair, coughing.

Gabrielle started to say something, but I took her arm and led her downstairs to the main hall. I chewed up a couple of Luckies, while Gabrielle paced back and forth, her flushed features stretched tight. Her thin heels beat the floor like small jackhammers. After about ten minutes, she stopped pacing. She walked over and stood in front of me and spoke with barely restrained anger.

"I could almost hate you," she said.

"That's been done before. But it doesn't change anything."

"Why were you so brutal with my father? I know what he did was terrible. But certainly, you can see that he's old and sick."

"He's hiding something," I said.

"And for that, you bully him into collapse?" Her voice jumped up an octave.

"Listen, sister. He brought it on himself. Maybe his age and his money entitle him to throw his weight around a little. But he's holding the key to two murders, and he set me up. In my book, when somebody does that, he doesn't rate much sympathy."

She just stood and stared. Her eyes were icy-hard, her voice something I hadn't heard before. "You really are quite ruthless."

"'Yeah. Me and Quetaz.'"

She started to say something, but Randolph appeared on the stairs. Gabrielle darted over to him.

"How is he? Is he all right?"

The Indian nodded. "He's resting comfortably, miss."

"What's wrong? He looked terribly ill."

"Perhaps he's overtired, miss."

"Shouldn't we call a doctor?"

The Indian folded his arms. "The Colonel has instructed me to call no one. However, he wishes you to be assured that he will be fine. Mrs. Wearing is attending him now."

"But..."

Before she could finish, Randolph turned to me. "Mr. Garrett, the Colonel was quite sincere about wishing you to leave and about seeing that Miss Wearing leaves as well." He reached into his pocket, brought out the envelope and the ticket, and held them out to me. "There is enough money so you can take Miss Wearing with you to Los Angeles. The Colonel said he thought you would understand."

Gabrielle stared in disbelief. "What is this? Randolph, what are you doing?"

"Following the Colonel's instructions, miss," he said nonchalantly.

"Well, I'm not going anywhere," she thundered. "I have my home here and my practice. No one's ordering me to leave." She stepped back, folded her arms, and glared defiantly.

Randolph calmly turned back to me. "Mr. Garrett?"

"First," I said, "I want to know what you and the Colonel have been cooking up. Why the phony blackmail? And why pick on Jimmy?"

He stuck his hand out toward me again. "I have been instructed to give you these, nothing more."

I looked down at the envelope and the ticket. I shook my head. "No dice. I can be had, but not that way."

He stepped back and spoke tonelessly. "Then I shall tell Colonel Wearing that you refused his request."

"Do you always do everything he tells you?"

"Everything." The word was strung out in a deadpan drawl.

"What if he told you to kill someone—me, for instance?"

"He eyed me with the sympathetic expression of a fire hydrant. "You'd be dead."

Gabrielle drove me back out to the valley. She said nothing, but from the way she chewed on her lower lip, I knew she was thinking plenty. The Buick was still there, parked in front of the motel. Gabrielle eased the roadster around and pulled up across the street. She sat for a minute and just stared out the windshield, idly wringing her hands on the wheel.

"I'm sure Monica is behind this," she said grimly. "She's turned Father against Jimmy and me. I don't think she'll be satisfied until she's removed us from his life altogether." She turned sharply toward me. "And you certainly weren't any help."

I didn't look at her. I was too busy staring across the street. "Lady, this isn't a case of some fat landlord out to chisel a few migrant workers."

She let out a heavy sigh. I just don't know what to think."

"Think about that." I motioned toward the Buick. The late rays of sun were spraying over the bullet holes in the door. "Those holes could have been in me, or in your brother."

She put her fist to her mouth and choked a breath in convulsively. "My God."

The smart lady lawyer had disappeared. Now, she looked childlike, vulnerable. I started to wish I had taken the Colonel's ticket.

"Listen," I said. "The only chance I've got of finding the jade and putting Delmar out of business is by squeezing the old man. It might be your father's only chance of staying alive. Maybe even yours or Jimmy's."

Her eyes were wide. Her voice had the hollow ring of fear. "What do you mean?"

"It was the heat from your father's paper that ran Delmar out of the country and has kept him in Mexico all this time. But now, for some reason, he thinks the Colonel is losing his grip. Maybe he thinks he can hold the jade for ransom and keep the old man quiet while he comes back to the States and sets up his play. Whatever it is, Delmar's making plans. And my guess is his plans include revenge. If he gets the wind up, he doesn't have to go directly for your father. He can go after Jimmy...or after you.·

She just sat and stared at me. I could almost feel the car seat quivering.

"Oh, hell," I said. "This whole goddamn thing is nuts. Maybe there isn't any jade. Nobody's actually seen it. Maybe Ordway was nipping peyote. And maybe I'm just goofy."

It came out all at once—the anger, the fear, and the tears. She buried her face in my sleeve and clutched the front of my jacket. I sat and held her until it all ran out. Finally, she sat up, fished a Kleenex out of her purse, and blew her nose.

"Father makes me so angry sometimes. But I love him, and I'm afraid. Do you really think he's in danger?"

I shook my head. "Not as long as he stays holed up on his mountain with Randolph to protect him."

"Did Randolph really do what you said?"

"He didn't deny it. Neither did your father."

"But why?"

I shook my head again. "I don't know. Maybe the old man wanted to throw a scare into Jimmy. Maybe he was testing me. Or maybe he really did want Delmar to take a pop at me. All I'm sure of is that your father is afraid of something, and he wants you and Jimmy out of town."

She chewed on her lip for a minute and then looked back at me. "What

172

happens now?"

I inhaled deeply and let my breath slowly hiss through my teeth while I looked out over the hood of the roadster. The sun had finally ducked behind the mountain, and long purple shadows were eating up the street and half of the buildings.

"Delmar thinks I've got the jade, but he won't do anything until he's sure. That ought to buy me some time."

She put her hand on my arm and gave an insistent squeeze. "He'll try to kill you."

"It's been tried before."

She reached up to my chin and turned my face around until I was looking at her. Her blue eyes were dewy and deep. "Why are you doing this? It can't be for the money. Father must have offered you a lot, but you didn't take it."

I shrugged. "Maybe I'm just a sucker for Mexican relics."

She chuckled softly. "Why can't I ever get a straight answer from you?"

This time, when I kissed her, she wasn't surprised. She slipped her hand behind my neck and curled her fingers in my hair. Her mouth was something wonderful, warm, moist, and reassuring. She pressed against me, and the scent of her skin and her hair danced in my nostrils, fresh and inviting, like an ocean breeze. I held her and forgot about time passing, about where I was.

We separated, and she sat back and looked at me. "What I said about hating you... I didn't mean it."

"Maybe you should have. What did you tell your father about me?"

She flashed a coy smile. "I told him I thought you were different from the others. You made me angry, but..." She reached up and placed her hand against my cheek. "I've never met anyone like you."

"You've been lucky," I said. "Did you tell anyone besides Sanchez that you knew Ordway?"

She thought for a minute and shook her head. "No, only Victor." She pursed her lips and brought her hand down to my chest. "Michael, I still want to help."

I stared out the window again. "All right. Then go find Jimmy, and the two of you get the hell out of here. Take him to Denver. Help him find a job. Just get out of Delmar's reach."

She clamped her jaw defiantly. "All right. I'll find him. But what about Monica?"

I opened the door and lifted one foot out onto the curb. "Leave Monica to me. Just beat it."

"Where are you going?"

I snickered without quite knowing why. "I'm moving into a better hotel."

She put her hand on my arm again. "Michael..."

I looked at her for longer than I should have. I got out of the car and slammed the door shut. Gabrielle gunned the engine, and the car tore off down the street. I watched her go. I felt as alone as a wino with an empty bottle.

I walked across the street and took a quick look at the Buick. The glove compartment was open, and the trunk had been jimmied. I went into my room and found more of the same. The window was smashed, and what there was in my suitcase was spread on the floor. Somebody had been unfriendly with the furniture, but my Luger and even the gun Voss had dropped were laid out neatly on the bed. It was an old gangland message. Delmar wanted me to know that he could get to me. It didn't matter if I was packing heat. He could still get to me. It was a sign that I'd better play ball. And it was a sign that he wanted something. After all, I was still walking around.

The desk clerk at the Del Norte eyed me tentatively. Every other time he'd seen me I'd shown him a president. When I said I wanted to check in, he huffed a little and told me all the rooms were occupied. I told him the sheriff was sure that a room on the fourth floor would be open. He gave me a somewhat depleted frown, reached under the counter, and handed over the key to 417. I signed the register, took the key, and headed upstairs. It pays to know the right people.

The room had been cleaned up and the bed made, but there were still traces of dusting powder on the windows and along the sink. I tossed my bag in the closet, hung my jacket over a chair, and called down to the front desk. A syrupy voice answered, and I asked for Charlie the bellhop and a bottle of Scotch. There was a pause and a short cough, and the voice said that Charlie would be right up. I went into the bathroom and unwrapped a couple of glasses. Then I stretched out on the bed and tried not to think about Gabrielle Wearing.

It couldn't have been five minutes before I heard the rap on the door. I opened it and found a skinny kid in his early twenties with a crew cut and a hotel uniform that had never seen the underside of an iron. I guessed him to be a little under five feet ten. He had a soft, pallid face with a steep bony forehead and ears that rounded down into oversized lobes. He had brown hair and brown eyes that studied me uncertainly as he held out the bottle. "You the one ordered the jug?"

I stepped back and motioned him into the room. "Come on in and help me crack it."

He shut the door and followed me over to the dresser. I opened the bottle and poured a couple of fingers into each glass. I handed him one and began sipping from the other. He held the glass up in front of him, examined it knowingly, then drained it in one quick swig. His eyes brightened, and he licked his lips.

"Some stuff. Thanks, mac." He looked at me with a hint of suspicion. "Hey, you won't tell nobody, will ya? I ain't supposed ta be tippin' the jug with no guests."

"Relax," I said. "Have another one."

He grinned while I poured some more into his glass. "Sure thing, mac. Hey, you're all right."

"That's what Rosetta said about you."

His eyes narrowed. "You know Rosie?"

I nodded. "She's meeting me here tonight." I reached into my pocket and pulled out a sawbuck. I folded it lengthwise and waved it in front of him. "She'll need to know where I am."

"Oh, yeah." He grinned again, this time like someone who knew more than he'd been told. He held up his hand. "I'll take care of it. Only I ain't got change for a ten-spot."

I slipped the bill into his outer pocket. "Get it changed downstairs. And don't bother coming back. Rosie's worth it."

He kept grinning. "She sure is. Thanks, mac."

"I looked for her here a couple of nights ago," I said, "but I guess she and her friend Lupe were tying one on."

He nodded. "I'll say. They was with some big guy. Looked like an Injun." He motioned toward the door. "In a room just down the hall, in fact."

"When was that?"

He sipped the Scotch and scratched his head. "Lessee. It was two...no, three nights ago. Yeah, Tuesday. I know 'cause I hadda work special that night on accounta the regular hop was sick."

"'Did you see anybody else?'"

He shook his head. "Nope. Nobody."

"What about the guy in here? You see him?"

He opened his mouth to say something. then stopped before the words came out. He started again, slowly. "Say, you're sure askin' a lotta questions, mac. What are you, a copper?"

"Not me." I pulled out another bill and stuffed it in his pocket. "I'm just a guy looking for some information."

He gulped down the rest of the Scotch and put the glass on the dresser. He eyed me again, then shook his head. "Naw, I didn't see him. Heard him, though. It was later, after the girls had left. He was in here arguin' with somebody. I dunno who. Sounded pretty upset. Kept yellin' about how he couldn't leave, how he hadda protect some dame."

"How do you know it was the same guy?"

"On accounta I heard him again next day when I brought up his breakfast. Had a real squeaky voice. Just peeked around the door and told me ta leave the tray in the hall." He clucked his teeth. "Damn deadbeat. Didn't gimme no tip. When I brought up lunch, he didn't even look at me. Just reached out and shoved me away from the door. Damn strong for a little guy. Almost broke a rib." He rubbed his side and smiled grimly. "I get all the deadbeats."

"What about dinner?"

He shrugged. "Never ordered it. Nobody heard a peep from him after lunch."

I emptied my glass and set it down. "Anything else? Maybe somebody hanging around here?"

He stiffened. "Look, mac. I don't want no trouble."

"You won't get it from me."

He rubbed his hands together, and his mouth began twitching. He looked at me and let out a soft sigh. "Well, you seem like a right guy. But if anybody asks, you don't know me." He swallowed·hard. "There was this guy, see? He comes outta this room while I'm makin a delivery up the hall. He doesn't see me. He just makes for the elevator almost on the dead run. That's how come I got a little suspicious. I knocked on the door afterwards, but I didn't get no answer."

"Was it the Indian?"

"Uh-uh." He shook his head again. "Tough-lookin' guy in a dark suit and hat. And he had real white hair." He shrugged again. "That's all there is, mac. Next thing I know, the johns are prowlin' all around the hotel talkin' about a guy gettin' starched."

"Yeah," I muttered. "Next thing. You talk to them?"

"Me? Hell no," he said,. "I don t talk ta no cops."

I tried to smile at him. "Okay, Charlie. Thanks. Go buy your own jug."

He went over and opened the door, then looked back. "There won't be no trouble. Huh, mac?"

I shook my head. "Just tell Rosetta where to find me."

He turned and shut the door behind him. I listened to his footsteps padding softly up the hall. I listened until they faded into nothing.

I went back to the dresser and poured out enough toddy to stir up my brain. Then I sat on the bed and tried adding things up on my fingers. I had come to town to attend an auction, and a deputy sheriff had made me a clay pigeon for an ambitious hood. Ordway had come here to get a hunk of jade that had him scared enough to hide in his room until somebody came and killed him. And he had been in the hotel when Randolph and the girls were giving Jimmy a screen test. Colonel Wearing wouldn't admit to having the jade, but he seemed just as afraid of it as Ordway.

Rudy Delmar wasn't afraid of anything but daylight. He wanted the jade, and he had imported a hungry-eyed button man to help him get it. The two of them had put the squeeze on a nervous doctor, and now they were after me. Jack Springer had been following a killer and a hot story until something turned him very cold. The same killer he was following had gone to visit Ordway, had broken into my room, and would gladly wipe me off for the price of a nickel cigar.

I tried putting it all together, but it was like doing a jigsaw puzzle in the dark. I was almost glad when the phone rang.

I picked it up and listened to Sanchez booming on the other end. "Garrett? What the hell are you doing there?"

"Drinking," I said. "How did you find me?"

"Gabrielle told me," he said. "Look, I'm in an alley below the intersection of Alameda and Rivera Drive, near the oil refinery. We got trouble. Better meet me."

I felt my hand go wet on the receiver. "What is it?"

"Dammit, get down here," he barked. "Now."

Chapter Twenty-One

The alley was about three blocks from Verdes Place in a section of town I remembered. I got there in just under ten minutes, pulled up behind a black-and-white patrol car, and stepped out into the empty street. It was a clear night. A round, luminous moon defined deep shadows along the dark storefronts and entryways. A dry breeze was scratching against the buildings, carrying with it the heavy fumes from the refinery. I stood for a minute, patted my tender ribs, and tried to fight off the searing smell.

Another patrol car was nosed into the entrance to the alley. The headlamps were on, cutting through the darkness like a Hollywood spotlight. They lit up the back wall of the alley and silhouetted a handful of men gathered in the far corner. I took a deep breath and walked past a row of trash cans and some empty packing crates and into the light. I kept walking until one of the men turned and stopped me. He was a tall man in a uniform and Stetson, with a gaunt face set as tight and hard as an icebreaker. It was Officer Weems.

He held out his hand in a pushing motion aimed at my chest and droned at me out of the side of his mouth. "That's far enough, Garrett. We got a police investigation goin' on here, so just turn around and beat the bricks."

"It's all right, Hal. I phoned him." It was Sanchez, calling from the back of the alley. He waved a hand and motioned me toward him. "Come on over here, Garrett."

Weems followed me as I walked over, stepped between two more officers, and stood next to the familiar little man with the black bag and squeaky shoes. They were all staring down at a sheet spread over something that resembled a bag of dirty laundry. Sanchez looked at me grimly. Then, without a word, he bent down, took a corner of the sheet, and pulled it back far enough to uncover the lifeless form of Rosetta Saens.

She was lying on her side, hands tied behind her back. A long cord had been looped around her neck and stretched down her back to her ankles, tying them up tight behind her in a position that someone had meant to be very painful. The more her legs had ached, the more her tired muscles had cried out to be straightened, the more the cord would have tightened around her neck.

I looked at her face. Her lips and tongue were thick and bluish. Traces of blood had dried around her nostrils. Her eyes were bulging, frozen in a desperate fear of death. I had seen that look before. It was never easy to take. It's that empty-eyed mixing of fear and bewilderment that comes from sensing death and from being face-to-face with a killer. Strangling victims usually die quickly. But somebody had gone to a lot of trouble to see that Rosetta went slowly and in agony. I felt an icy rush move down my back and into my legs.

The little man next to me clucked his teeth. He spoke half in a whisper. "Never saw anything like it. The hyoid bone isn't broken the way it would be by a hanging or if somebody used his hands." He shook his head and muttered. "Must've taken a damn long time to die."

Sanchez looked at him. "How long dead, Doc?"

The man rubbed his chin. "Can't tell until I get her under the lights." He looked up sharply. "I'll tell you this, though. She wasn't killed here. I counted at least half a dozen stab wounds, only there's hardly any blood. And that isn't even what killed her. The rope did that. But if she'd been tied up here, she would have made some noise, called for help." He shook his head again. "She's been dead for quite a while. And whoever did it took his time—he wanted her to suffer. He brought her here after he'd had his fun."

I turned away and walked partway back up the alley. Sanchez covered the girl, said something to Weems, then walked over and stood next to me. He breathed heavily. "Hell of a way to go. She mean anything to you?"

180

"You know she did," I said. "Who found her?"

"Don't know. Somebody called the station and told us to come down here and pick up a package for you. He didn't give a name." He folded his arms. His voice was low, but urgent. "So, now I want to know what's going on."

I fished out a Lucky and lit it, and tossed the match into the darkness. "Her name's Rosetta Saens. She's one of the girls in that picture I showed you." I felt him nod. "She was coming to see me at the Del Norte. I saw her yesterday and got her to spill something about the picture. She was going to give me the rest tonight."

"Exactly what did she tell you?"

"She said she and her friend Lupe were hired to play a trick on Jimmy, to fake that picture after he'd passed out. And she said the man who hired them was an Indian."

His mouth dropped open. "What?"

"I did some checking at the hotel. On the night before Ordway was killed, the girls were there with a big guy who looked like an Indian."

His black eyes narrowed. "What are you suggesting?"

"I'm not suggesting anything," I said. "I'm giving you what you asked for. Last night, after I left the station, Voss came to my room looking for the jade that Ordway was after. I told him politely to go fry himself, and then I went down to Delmar's club in Juarez. That's where I met Rosetta. And while we were talking. Delmar was nice enough to introduce himself. He seems to think I've got the jade. He even offered to buy it from me, and when I said no sale, he threatened to have his boys turn me into hash. Then, right on cue, Monica Wearing showed up. She claimed to be one of Delmar's regular customers, and from what I could see, she knows her way around a crap table. She kept me busy while Delmar arranged to slip me a mickey that almost put me into next week. But before the lights went out, I spotted someone else. It was an Indian—Randolph."

Sanchez shuffled his feet and eyed me impatiently. "So, you went to Juarez and got roughed up. And, you saw Randolph there. So what? He was probably chauffeuring Mrs. Wearing. What does that have to do with this?" He flung his shoulder back toward the corner of the alley and what was left of Rosetta.

I took a heavy drag on the Lucky and then dropped the butt and ground it under my heel. "Nothing," I said. "Forget I mentioned it."

He started to say something, but I held my hand up and stopped him. His angular features settled into a stone-faced stare, and I started to think about the pint I'd left in the glove compartment of the Buick.

I was about to tell him the bar was open when another set of headlights flashed into the alley. A pair of doors slammed, and a burly figure in boots and another Stetson loomed in front of the car and threatened to blot out the light. I pulled my hat down, stuck my hands in my pockets, and watched Sheriff Stonebreaker march into the back of the alley.

A plumpish Mexican man in a dark blue suit and tie kept pace at Stonebreaker's heels. He was clean-shaven and clear-eyed, hair neatly trimmed and combed. He had a pleasant, almost affable face, one that could have been selling real estate. He was a pleasant-looking man out taking a pleasant stroll on a pleasant evening. He followed the sheriff past the officers and the coroner and stopped next to the sheet. He looked pleasantly down as Stonebreaker lifted the sheet. Then he started to get pleasantly sick.

The man scurried back up the alley, his eyes bulging open, stopped near the entrance, loosened his tie, and mopped his face with a handkerchief. Stonebreaker lowered the sheet, slowly walked over, and stood in front of Sanchez. His jaw was set tight, and he spoke in a low, hungry purr, like a tiger just before dinner.

"What's this about, Vic?"

"Can't tell yet, Jesse," Sanchez replied. "She may have been mixed up in some blackmail. Maybe with Rudy Delmar. Garrett talked with her last night down at the Parrot."

"If it's blackmail, who was the mark?"

Sanchez looked uneasily at me, then back at the sheriff. "Jimmy Wearing."

"You talk to the Colonel?"

Sanchez shook his head. "Not yet."

Stonebreaker turned and looked at me. His muddy-brown eyes were as easy to read as Etruscan shorthand. "Delmar see you with her?"

I nodded.

He sniffed. "Probably why she's dead."

He turned on his heel and walked over next to the Mexican. The man turned loose a torrent of anxious whispers that only the sheriff was meant to hear. His hands fluttered wildly in the air like hysterical butterflies, and the color of his face deepened into a livid shade of reddish brown. Stonebreaker simply stood, arms folded, and looked at him. When the whispering finally stopped, he growled half a dozen words and pointed toward the car. The man nodded curtly and scampered off out of sight.

Stonebreaker ambled back over in front of Sanchez again. "You take care of things here," he said. "I'll go talk to the Colonel."

Sanchez nodded.

Stonebreaker turned and gave me another slow stare. After we'd looked at each other for a long moment, he turned without saying anything and walked off. I pulled out another Lucky and listened to the patrol car start up and drive away.

Sanchez inhaled deeply and stuck his hands in his pockets. "Jesse didn't have to make that crack about why the girl died."

"Maybe he was right," I said. "What do you think he's going to tell Colonel Wearing?"

"What do you mean?"

I blew smoke toward the front of the alley. "He didn't ask many questions."

Sanchez looked down at his feet. "Well, that's Jesse. He'll just go through the motions the way he always does."

"Who was that character with him?"

He tried to smile. "His name's Julian Benitez. He works in the mayor's office over in Juarez. He's up here visiting, and Jesse's been showing him around all day." He looked toward the back of the alley where the coroner was now scribbling in a small notebook. "So, you think Delmar's behind this?"

"Don't you?"

His smile drew tight, almost into a snarl. "Yeah." Suddenly, he slammed a fist into his palm. "That bastard. I'd give a month's pay to pin this on him." He turned toward me abruptly. "But you can't really think Randolph had anything to do with it."

I took a long puff on the Lucky and shrugged. "Suppose that Delmar has somehow gotten his hooks into Randolph. What better line could he have to the old man? He could find out when the jade was being put up for auction. He could easily get an invitation and put a man inside, just the way Gabrielle had Randolph get an invitation for me. And he'd know if someone was hanging around the Wearings who might somehow get to the jade first—someone like Ordway, or me.

"That doesn't explain Springer."

"Maybe Springer found out and tried to put the bite on Delmar. It wouldn't be the first time a reporter tried dipping his hands in."

"And Mrs. Wearing?"

I shrugged again. "Maybe she's been helping Delmar shake down Randolph. Or maybe she is just a good customer."

He shook his head impatiently. "But you don't have any proof. It's all just theory."

"Got anything better?"

"What about Rosetta?"

I rubbed my neck. "Delmar did see us together. He could have sent Voss. Or he could have sent someone else, someone she wouldn't suspect. I told you Randolph was at the club."

"Now, wait a minute…"

"Either way," I said, "Delmar wants that jade. Right now, he isn't sure if I've got it, but he isn't taking any chances. He's going to make sure I don't do business with anyone else, and he wants me to know it." I motioned back toward the corner of the alley. "This is his way of telling me."

He shuddered. "Look, if you're right, then you could be next. I've had three bodies in two days. I don't need any more."

"Relax," I said. "If Delmar thinks I might have what he wants, he won't do anything now but keep me under glass. He'll wait for me to make the next move."

He let out a long, slow sigh. "Okay. So, what is next?"

"It wouldn't hurt for you to take a closer look at Randolph and at Monica Wearing. Only you'd better do it on the q.t."

"That's a tall order," he said. "What are you going to do?"

I took a lingering pull on the Lucky. "Looks like I'd better find the jade. Maybe I can turn the curse on Delmar."

He rolled his eyes. "Oh, great. Don't tell me you believe in that stuff."

"Ordway believed it. And maybe Colonel Wearing believes it, too. At least something's got him scared enough to make him try and chase me and his son and daughter out of town."

"Yeah, I heard," he muttered. "Gabrielle phoned and asked me to help find Jimmy. She told me about your meeting with the old man." He gave me a grim chuckle. "You know, Garrett, you sure have a way of making yourself popular."

I didn't say anything.

"Anyway," he said, "I'm glad Gabrielle is leaving."

"Yeah." I turned and began walking out of the alley. "Too bad, too. She's got a nice apartment."

"What?" he called after me. "What do you know about her apartment? Where are you going? Garrett?"

I just kept walking.

I pulled the Buick up in front of the El Paso *Sun-Register*. It was a gray place, four stories on the south side of town, with the name of the paper in Gothic letters over the entrance and a light on in every window. Just inside the front door, I ran into a young newsy. I asked for the editor, and he directed me upstairs.

The city room was an open area covering half the second floor. Men in shirt sleeves puffing cigars sat behind gray metal desks that were lined up in rows like a regiment standing inspection. Most of them were stabbing noisily at typewriters, using only the reporter's index fingers and staring at the growing copy as if nothing else existed in the world. At the back of the room on the left, a glassed-in cubicle surrounded another desk, a filing cabinet, and a coat rack. And in the middle of the outer partition, a glass paneled door held a metal nameplate that read, "Frank Bartels, Editor." I didn't bother to knock.

Behind the desk, a middle-aged man sat with a phone in his ear. He looked paunchy but hard. He had thick brown hair, eyebrows like wire brushes, and a florid face with enough nicks and welts to make him look like one of Jack Dempsey's sparring partners. As I walked in, he slammed down the phone and barked at me. "Yeah?"

"I'm representing Colonel Stanfield Wearing," I said.

"Not another one." He slumped in his chair and gave me a look that held more pain than authority. "Shut the door."

I followed his instructions, then went over and sat in one of the two metal chairs in front of his desk. He watched me carefully while I lit a cigarette and tossed the match into a wastebasket next to the desk. "My name is Garrett. I'm investigating the death of Jack Springer."

His right eye dropped into a squint, and he put both elbows on the desk. "How do I know you're from the Colonel?"

"Just call and ask him." I made a show of looking at my watch. "That is, if you want to disturb him at this hour."

He looked at me sourly, then snorted and folded his hands. "Aw, hell. I gotta put the paper to bed in a little while. What do you want?"

"I want to know about Jack Springer, what he was working on, and why somebody might want to kill him."

He snorted disdainfully. "He was the last guy I'd ever expect anybody to bump off." He stretched out his hands, palms up, like a moocher looking for a handout, then let them drop on the desk.

"Who'd have a reason? Ya see, he was what we call a journeyman, a hack. He put in his time, covered the local stuff, even wrote his copy so the average guy could read it. But he never wrote anything that would sell papers. All he did was talk the game. He snickered. "But he sure could do that. Thought he was great stuff. He even insisted on having the number-one desk." He waved a hand toward the city room. "Right here by my door. Of course, he only did that after the Colonel stopped coming in." He tucked the corners of his mouth into a grim smile and shook his head. "We sold a lot of papers yesterday with him bleeding all over the front page." He shrugged. "Ask me, and I'll say Jack Springer did us more good dead than alive."

"I met him on the train a couple of days ago," I said. "He said he was onto a big story."

Bartels chuckled. "Yeah. That's what he told me." He reached into his desk and pulled out a cigar the size of a salami. He bit the end off and spat in the direction of the wastebasket, then lit a match and played the flame against the end of the cigar. He pulled eagerly and filled the room with a cloud that smelled like the exhaust from a sick elephant. Finally, he sat back in his chair and went on talking as if all he'd done was scratch his ear.

"He said he had a line on something big—mob stuff. I didn't believe him, but I figured, what the hell? He said he wanted to go to LA to check out a lead, and he wanted the paper to foot the bill. I told him no soap, but he went anyway on his own scratch. That was about a week ago, and I didn't see him until he came in yesterday morning, all lathered up and jumpy as a barefoot babe on a hotplate. He didn't tell me what he had, and I didn't ask." He shrugged again. "I figured with him, what the hell?"

"Uh-huh." I crushed out my cigarette and waved a hand through the cigar smoke, trying to make a hole in it I could see through. "When I came in, you said something about another one. Has the Colonel sent someone else down here?"

He nodded. "He's always sending somebody to tell me what to do, maybe give me something for the next edition, maybe even have me put something on the wire to the other papers. Usually, he sends his Indian, Randolph."

"I thought the Colonel was retired."

He chuckled again. "Yeah. He's retired, just like I might be president. Oh, he stays up there in his mansion, all right. Doesn't come into the office. But he sends Randolph in every week, regular as clockwork. The Indian comes in and tells me what the Colonel wants done. He calls it 'giving advice.' Well, ya know, that's advice I'm damn well gonna take."

He stuck the cigar back in his teeth and moved his mouth around it. "Yeah. He said he was retiring, but he still runs everything—here and everywhere else. I get the paper out every day, but he tells me how."

"When did you last see Randolph?"

He folded his hands behind his head and leaned back in the chair. He chewed on the cigar and thought it over. "Couple days ago," he said. "Tuesday, I think. Didn't say much. Just came in, poked around in Springer's desk a little, and left."

"Has the Colonel talked to you about putting his son at the paper?"

He snorted, and a rancid gray-brown fog rolled across the desk. "Called me today. Wants me to send the kid up north—right away. Maybe put him on as a cub reporter." He smiled sourly and shook his head. "Don't know if the kid can write, but with his connections, what the hell?"

I stood up. "Where's your file room?"

"You mean the morgue? Down in the basement. Just ask for Sally."

I started for the door, and he grunted and called after me. "Hey, wait a minute. You got somethin' on Jack's killing?"

I stopped at the door and looked back at him. "Only what I read in the papers."

He chomped down on the cigar and grunted. "I get it. Hush-hush stuff. So how does the Colonel want me to handle it?"

"Hold the front page," I said, "and call Deputy Sheriff Sanchez."

"What for?"

I grinned at him as I started to close the door. "What the hell?"

Just beyond the door, a metal desk was sitting under the usual office debris—a typewriter and a plate with Springer's name. I looked through the drawers and found more paper and pencils and some file folders containing mostly obituaries. In the middle drawer was the stub of a train ticket and a Brentwood motel receipt dated just two days before. There was a handwritten note on the back of the receipt that said simply, "OK—antiques." I closed the drawer and went downstairs.

The morgue of the *Sun-Register* had the musty smell of a deserted locker room. It was a large area with cinder-block walls, no windows, and pale-green painted pipes running along the ceiling from front to back. A row of naked bulbs in overhead fixtures threw down enough light for me to see several rows of olive-green filing cabinets surrounded by miles of shelving stacked with old newspapers. There were a few tables, some chairs, and a large wooden desk. As I came in, Sally got up from behind the desk.

She was plenty of woman, extending about five feet in every direction. Her soft, suety face was almost perfectly round and layered with chins. She had green eyes, and her almost-blond hair was wound into wire-tight ringlets.

"Help ya?" she asked, offering an extra-wide smile.

I asked her for the files from 1945. She pointed me to a stack of papers on a shelf in the rear with a cabinet in front of it. I went to the cabinet and looked up March 14, 1945—the date in Springer's wallet. I found nothing. I eased the paper with that date out of one of the stacks and looked through it. The front-page story had the Marines mopping up in the Pacific and some speculation about an invasion of the Japanese mainland sometime in the fall. I combed through every section, every story, every classified. Still nothing.

I put the paper back in the stack, closed the cabinet, and went back to the desk. I asked Sally about a Chicago cop killing in 1938.

She scratched her chins. "Yeah. I remember that one."

She walked past several rows of cabinets on the right and into the far corner of the room, where she pulled out a drawer and then handed me a folder full of clippings.

I sat down and rooted in the folder while she ambled away. The clippings were all from Wearing's Chicago paper, the *Evening Chronicle.* I read the first one. It told me that a patrolman named Ed Wallis, rumored to be on the take, had been found dead in the trunk of a limousine owned by a gambler and reported racketeer named Rudy Delmar. The car had been found outside the Tamany Club, a cafe and gambling joint operated by Delmar. Wallis had been tied up, with lead fishing weights wrapped around his legs. He had apparently died from a single gunshot wound in the throat. The police called it a gangland execution and said that Wallis would have been dumped into Lake Michigan later that night. Delmar claimed the body was part of a frame-up by Big Ray Floren and the boys at City Hall. Floren was vacationing in Miami and had an alibi as tight as a new corset. The car had been wiped clean of prints, there were no witnesses, and the D.A. was caught in the middle.

Another article reported that the investigation had been going nowhere until the police turned up a witness, a young waitress in Delmar's South Side cafe. She had hidden in a closet—the article didn't say why—and watched Delmar gun down the cop. With this in hand, the grand jury returned an indictment, and Delmar was tied up like a Christmas turkey.

Next was a series of editorials praising the Chicago police and the D.A.'s office for quick and decisive action. And one long piece, written as the trial opened, said that the conviction of Delmar would send a message to the mob and would be a triumph for history. The byline was simply S.W.

Then there was a headline saying that Delmar was free. The witness and a piano player from the cafe had both disappeared, presumably so they couldn't testify. The rest of the evidence was only circumstantial, and Delmar had been acquitted.

The last clipping in the folder was written by someone named Sidney Wallis. It was an account of the coroner's inquest. It revealed that Officer Edward Wallis, killed by person or persons unknown, had been working undercover for the FBI and had died in the line of duty. The reporter noted that the death was both a public and a personal loss. One last item on the inquest caught my eye. The attending physician was Dr. M. Kintner.

I closed the folder and went over and dropped it on Sally's desk. "How is it that you remember this?"

She cocked her head and gave me a porcine cackle. "Don't get many visitors down here, mister. When I do, I remember 'em." She tapped the end of a bulbous finger down on the folder. "A guy come in just a coupla weeks ago and asked for this."

"You know him?"

She shook her head. "Don't want to, neither. He was a big guy, and tough lookin'...even for an Indian."

I went outside and stood on the front steps of the paper, and looked up into the dark desert sky. The breeze was coming down from the north now, putting an edge on the night. A bright star just above the horizon winked at me coldly. I turned up my collar and lit a cigarette. My hunch about Springer hadn't panned out, but the idea of his folded-up dollar bill kept coming back to me.

You're a smart guy, Garrett, I said to myself. You've even been to college. So what if you've been knocked around a little? Your head still works. I looked up at the winking star. It didn't believe me either.

I was just starting down the steps when the thought hit me. It happens that way sometimes. There's no sense to it, no reason. You don't expect it. It just happens. It hit me just that way, like a thump on a wall. I laughed at myself and got into the Buick.

The house on Blackstone Terrace was dark. A sheet of moonlight lay over the front yard and most of the street. It blended with a thin yellow glow from the few streetlights lining the drive, leaving most of the houses and the handful of cars on the street dappled in shadows. I eased the Buick up against the curb, got out, and looked at the darkened house. If Dr. Kintner was home, he wasn't expecting callers.

I started up the walk toward the front door, then stopped about halfway. A point of light slid across the front window on my left. Even with the shade drawn, the beam of a pocket flash was unmistakable. I moved quietly up to the house and tried the door. It was locked. I gave the knob a convincing twist and leaned heavily against the door, but it decided to stay locked. Detectives are supposed to be good at getting through locked doors. Any dime-novel gumshoe can pick a lock in nothing flat. I stared at the door for a minute, then turned and started for the side of the house.

I moved to the left, toward the corner away from the mountain and into the moonlight. Something made me stop when I reached the corner—something on the air, like the cloying smell of a cemetery. I managed to pull out the Luger without shooting myself and then hold it in front of me. I was ready for an argument. I pulled my feet up out of the ground and took a slow step forward.

I couldn't tell where the shot came from, only that the corner of the house exploded about a foot above my head. I bought a face full of gravel and sprawled out flat on my stomach and listened to the roar of the shot careen through the foothills, then roll off into the desert. Somewhere behind it I heard footsteps pounding over rock and gravel, moving away. Someone was in a hurry. I gingerly worked my way up on all fours, still holding the Luger, crawled over, and peered around the corner of the house.

A shallow ravine ran toward the back, around the neighboring house, and pitched down a hill behind that to another street. A lanky figure in a gray hat darted out of the ravine and across the street. I stood up and started running down the hill. I yelled something at him, but he didn't stop. He scrambled into a black sedan, gunned the engine, and tore off up the street without lights.

I turned and started back up the hill and heard another car. It leaped out of a driveway half a block away. There was a quick locking of gears and a screech of tires, and I was left watching the fading glow of taillights. I stood scratching my ear with the barrel of the Luger and thinking there was something familiar about the second car. I would have bet my last Lucky it was a blue Ford coupe.

Lights were flashing on around the neighborhood now, and I could hear voices coming from both sides of the street. I walked quickly up the hill and around to the back of Kintner's house. The backyard was littered with trash and covered with something coarse and wiry that wrapped itself around my ankles. I stopped at the back door, tucked the Luger away, and pulled several tendrils of mesquite off my shoes. I listened at the door for a minute, heard nothing, and tried the knob. The door opened. I went inside.

The room was as dark as the inside of a vault. I groped along the wall to my left until I bumped into what seemed to be a sink. A string brushed against my face, and I pulled it and turned on an overhead fixture. I stood and looked at a small tidy kitchen, a small Formica-topped table and two chairs in the center, and doors to the right and straight ahead. I guessed that the far door would lead to the waiting room. Since I'd already seen that part of the house, I turned and opened the door on the right.

Just inside, I found a wall switch. I flipped it and watched the soft amber light from a shaded lamp in the corner flood into a small womanish bedroom.

The room had been decorated by someone with a flair for intricate self-indulgence. The walls were papered with a textured peach blossom print, full of crafty-looking little cupids. Around the room were several Matisse prints and sketches, mostly nudes. I stepped inside and was hit by a dank, musky smell, like incense gone bad.

An ornately carved four-poster bed stood in the middle of a handwoven Indian rug. The bed was covered by a quilted magenta spread with white lace trim and accented by several corded lavender pillows with flounced edges. A dresser on the right held what looked like a silver jewelry box with a rich filigree design.

Someone had gone to a lot of trouble to put this room together. Someone else had gone to some trouble to pull it apart. The bedspread was rumpled and pulled partway off the bed, as if the mattress had been lifted. Most of the pictures were hanging cockeyed against the wall. The chairs had been tipped back against the wall, cushions removed. The dresser drawers had been pulled out, clothes tossed on the floor. And in the open closet in the corner, a good-sized investment in pastel finery had been assaulted and left for dead.

In one of the dresser drawers I spotted a plain leather-bound book. For no reason at all, I picked it up and began thumbing through it. Somehow, I wasn't surprised. It was full of pictures, arty photos—all men. I dropped the book, pulled out my handkerchief, and wiped my hands.

The smell of the incense drew me around to the far side of the bed and to a dainty little nightstand holding a small reading lamp and an oriental water pipe. I had seen pipes like that in the Pacific. The natives called them hookahs, and they used them to smoke hashish and stinkweed. I inspected the bowl. It was cold. The burnt remains of something that would part your hair were still packed inside. I stood back, rubbed my thumbnail over my forehead, and looked at the room. Somewhere in the distance, I heard myself let out a soft whistle. I had a whole new picture of the good doctor.

There was a door behind me that would lead to the front of the house and the examining room where I had met Dr. Kintner. Whoever had run out the back and down the hill had been in that room when I arrived. That made it the next place to look.

I opened the door and stepped through it into the familiar smell of sterile instruments and antiseptic. Putting on the room lights might attract attention from outside, so I decided to make my way around in the dark. I took a couple of steps, and my shin found the sharp corner of the desk. I swore and felt around on top of the desk with both hands. One hand found a small lamp. The other landed in something sticky. I turned on the lamp and froze.

Chapter Twenty-Two

He was slumped over in his chair, his head on the desk, wearing nothing but his underwear and a pair of bedroom slippers. His left hand was stretched out in front of him, the fingers seemingly poised above a carefully arranged row of pencils. From the way he looked, he might have been working late. After all, he was a professional man looking after the welfare of his patients. He might have paused long enough to rearrange his pencils along the edge of his nice green blotter. Then he might simply have dozed off. Only the blotter wasn't green anymore. And he would never wake up. Dr. Morris Kintner had treated his last nervous disorder.

An ugly brownish-crimson stain had spread over the blotter and down the front of his undershirt and shorts. It had come pouring out of an angry gash that started below his left ear and ran all the way across his throat. I felt the back of his neck. It was cold and stiff. He must have been dead a good twenty-four hours. Now, the coroner would need a crowbar to pry him out of the chair.

Something shiny on the desk caught my eye, and I went around and looked at it. In his right hand, Kintner was clutching a small knife, with a cleanly polished blade and a green handle. I pried his fingers apart enough to see the carving of a large bird on the handle, just like the one Ordway had been holding. I stepped back and looked at him and thought about Ordway and about the Colonel. They would say that the Bird of Death had come to Dr. Kintner.

I looked quickly around the room. Nothing had been disturbed. The rows of bandages and swabs still stood neatly in the receptacle jars, and the glass-fronted cabinet, showing the same bottles and vials, was still locked. Whoever had torn up the bedroom hadn't had time to search the examining room. Apparently, I had interrupted him, and he had gotten the idea to take a powder out the back. Considering the circumstances, it was an idea that made sense.

I looked around some more and spotted the Degas print hanging by the door; the one Kintner had been so careful to straighten. I used my handkerchief and took the picture down, and leaned it against the wall. The safe, a rectangular affair with a recessed dial, was where I thought it would be. I stood there for a minute. It was a long shot. I had no reason to think it would work. I turned the dial to 3, then 14, then 45—the numbers on Jack Springer's dollar bill. The tumblers clicked, and I opened the door.

In the front of the darkened compartment was a stack of envelopes and loose papers. On top was a packet of photographs, each with a negative clipped to it. I took the pictures out and began carefully thumbing through about a dozen personal portraits of what I guessed would be some of El Paso's wealthiest women. They were all stretched out on Kintner's examining table. One appeared to be asleep. The others were wearing glassy-eyed expressions. They weren't wearing anything else.

The pictures didn't do much for me until I got to the bottom of the stack. The last one made me stop and admire the view. It was Monica Wearing, and except for a pair of high heels, she was as naked as a peeled onion. I slipped the photo and the negative into my pocket and went through the rest of the papers. They were mostly receipts showing acknowledgment of payment, and they were all from women. Toward the back of the safe was a coarsely bound notebook, a little larger than a wallet, with narrow ruled pages like a ledger. It was almost half-filled, with entries dating back about a year. Each entry showed a woman's name and an art object. There were paintings and sculptures, even an oriental rug. Next to each entry was a date and an amount paid for purchase, nothing over a few grand. It looked like an amateur art collector's journal, but it showed enough merchandise to fill Ebbets Field. On the last page, a pair of entries, spaced about a month apart, caught my eye. They said simply, "Monica Wearing—auction," with amounts totaling a little over six thousand.

I put the book in my pocket and took another look in the safe. Against the back wall, I saw a large manila envelope that had been lying under the ledger. I took it out, opened it, and pulled out a fistful of newspaper clippings from a Kansas City paper dated November 12, 1941. They gave the details on the killing of a local piano player. Randy Norris, a six-year resident of the city, had been found in an alley behind a South Side cafe at about four in the morning. He had been stabbed six times. The police had no leads, but they speculated that the motive was robbery. The owner of the cafe described Norris as a good employee who kept to himself. He had no friends and no known next of kin.

I folded the clippings into my pocket with the ledger and pushed the envelopes and papers back into the safe. As I brought my hand out, my fingers brushed against something on the side near the corner, something hard and uneven and covered with cloth. I grabbed it and brought out a gray felt sack with an elaborately corded drawstring. I opened the sack and lifted out a carved figure, about ten inches high, green, and worth a stare. Strangely compelling, it was an exquisitely carved figure of a girl in long robes and a flowered headdress. The Jade Princess was everything Ordway and Colonel Wearing had said.

I brought my chin back up from around my belt buckle and put the figure back in the sack, then set it down on the desk. I used my handkerchief, wiped off anything that might have my prints, and closed the safe. Finally, I went back to the desk and went through the drawers, using my fountain pen to open them.

In one drawer, I found the camera that Kintner must have used to take the pictures. In the center drawer, I found a box of familiar-looking French cigarettes wrapped in lavender paper with gold-colored filters. Next to it was a sheet of paper with handwriting on it showing a list of phone numbers and the names of several cities. At the bottom of the list was a number in Brentwood. I fished into my wallet and took out Ordway's card. I looked at it. Then I looked again at the phone number on the list. The numbers matched. I closed the desk.

I used my handkerchief again and dialed the phone. I waited until a maid with a voice like sandpaper answered. When I asked for Monica Wearing, there was a pause and a shuffling of feet, then silence. Finally, after I'd waited long enough to be put in my place, Monica came on the line.

"Yes?"

"This is Garrett. I think it's time we had a talk."

Her voice almost frosted the receiver. "We have nothing to talk about, Mr. Garrett."

Then maybe you'd like to listen," I said.

"To what?"

"To a story—a story about blackmail and murder, about a four-flushing doctor with a hot camera, and about some missing jade."

There was a catching of breath and another pause. She spoke just above a whisper. "When?"

"An hour. My hotel room. I'm at the Del Norte—417."

"Very well." She hung up.

I cradled the receiver and hesitated. Then I picked it up again and dialed the cops. Sanchez was out, so I left a message with a desk sergeant who sounded as old and tired as something lost in an attic. I told him to tell Sanchez that a prescription had been filled at 174 Blackstone Terrace. I told him not to hurry. Then I hung up. I tucked the Princess under my arm, turned off the lights, and went out through the back of the house, wiping off everything I had touched.

The moon had shifted in the sky, and the wind had eased, leaving the night to the desert. I walked quickly to the car, looking up and down the street, half expecting something to fall on me. Every building, every tree, every blade of grass seemed to have eyes. I got into the car and kept one hand on the figure while I drove back to the hotel. I stuck to the main roads, checking each alley and side street and glancing into the mirror enough to get a good shave. Nobody followed.

The lobby of the Del Norte felt like a sad memory. The chairs in the sitting areas were empty, the front desk was deserted, and the water in the fountain running past the stone mermaids had the wistful sound of rain in the mountains. The sound of my shoes on the carpet echoed around me as I crossed the lobby and went into the Sunset Room.

Except for Tommy, the place was empty. He was standing behind the bar, yawning and idly polishing an empty glass. When he saw me, his eyebrows shot up, and he greeted me with a smile and a jigger of Scotch. "There ya go, Mr. Garrett. Looks like ya can use it."

I nodded and emptied the jigger, and motioned for him to fill it again. He did, then leaned on the bar and watched while I buried another couple of ounces.

"I heard there was another killing tonight," he said. "One of them girls from Rudy's place." He pursed his lips and shook his head ruefully. "I'm tellin' ya, Mr. Garrett, it ain't good, three people bumped off in just a coupla days. Gives a guy the jitters. Hal Weems says Delmar's up ta somethin'. What d'ya think?"

"I try not to," I said. "It's a habit that just gets me in trouble."

He gave a quick smirk, then snapped his fingers.

"By the way, Hector was in here tonight lookin' for ya. I told him ta wait and that you'd likely be in, but he said he couldn't stick around."

"What did he want?"

"Dunno. But he said it was important."

"Not important enough to keep me up." I put the sack with the figure on the bar in front of him. "I want you to keep this for me. Put it somewhere safe and then forget you've got it."

He looked down at the sack and frowned. "The hotel's got a safe, ya know."

"I know." I dropped a fin on the bar. "That's why I want you to keep it."

He grinned and stuffed the bill in his pocket. "Okay by me." He took the figure, bent over, and put it in a cabinet under the bar behind a row of bottles. Then he stood up and started to say something, but I was already on my way upstairs.

There was a quiet chill in the room, like in a morgue after hours. I peeled off my jacket and hung it on a chair, then shook my head. A brand-new suit and the jacket was already torn and covered with dust. It looked like all the rest of my suits. I took off my hat and looked at it. It was checkered with wood splinters and flecks of paint, fallout from Kintner's exploding house. Whoever shot at me must have been packing enough cartridge to stop a rhino. I shook my head again. For a small-time crook, Delmar had big-time guns.

I brushed off the hat and dropped it on the chair, then went over to the sink and ran water in the bowl. I splashed some on my face and stood looking in the mirror. What I saw looked as bad as my suit. I reached down and prodded my torn ribs and winced. I might have kept on wincing, but my stomach reminded me that, except for the late breakfast at Gabrielle's apartment, I hadn't eaten anything in twenty-four hours. The bottle of Scotch was still on the dresser where Charlie had left it, so I poured a couple of fingers into a glass and downed it. I could feel it being greeted by the two shots I'd had downstairs. It wasn't lunch, but I felt better.

I emptied the pockets of my jacket and put Monica's picture and the clipping in the drawer of the nightstand. Then I unstrapped the Luger and put it on top of the clippings, and closed the drawer. From there, the bed looked like a good place to spend the next few weeks, so I stretched out and lit a cigarette. I picked up Kintner's notebook and was just starting through it when the phone rang.

There was a deep, crusty voice on the other end. "Hold the line, shamus."

I waited. After a few seconds, I heard another voice, harsh and raspy, like a broken steam pipe. "You know who this is?"

"Yeah," I said. "A real lady killer."

There was a baleful snicker. "So, you got the message."

"Yeah, I got it. You've been busy tonight. First Rosetta, then Kintner. Don't you want me to meet people?"

"Some joker," he said. "You shouldn't have been so hard on the doc."

"What do you care?"

"Business," he said. "It's all business. A guy does business with me, and I like things to go nice and easy. No surprises. I don't like it when he comes up dead. Bad for business."

"Business must be in a slump," I said. "What happened to the limousine? The finance company repossess it?"

He paused. "What?"

"You don't look like such a big shot in that Ford."

He snickered again. "You got a strange sense of humor, Garrett."

"Not strange," I said, "just taking a break. What the hell do you want?"

"You know what I want. And it's six feet of dirt for you if I don't get it."

"Imagine my pulse racing."

"Never mind the wise mouth," he snapped. "I want that jade, and I'm giving you just twenty-four hours to cough it up. If you don't, Schizy's got another necktie."

I didn't answer that one. "What makes you "think I've got the jade?"

He laughed again, scornfully this time. "Don't try to pull my leg. The town's running out of people who might have it. The museum hasn't got it. And Wearing hasn't got it, or else he wouldn't have hired you." His voice turned crafty. "But maybe you figured to pull a fast one on him and make a deal for yourself."

"Maybe I did."

There was another pause. "Okay, Shamus. I'm game. The offer's still good—ten G's. Just turn over both figures by tomorrow, and no funny stuff."

"No dice," I said. "I need more time."

"What the hell for?"

"Could be another buyer," I said. "After all, I've got to get something out of this deal. Like you said, it's business. I'm tired of peeking over transoms to make a living."

His voice grew icicles. "Be grateful you still got a living to make. You *try* dealing with anybody else, and you can forget about having to wind your watch every day. And don't think about running out. I can get you before you even take the first step."

I didn't say anything. We listened to each other, not talking for most of a minute.

"Both figures in twenty-four hours," he said. "Or you're out of business…

permanent." The line went dead.

I hung up and looked at the cigarette in my hand. It had burned down to the nub, and I hadn't even noticed. I crushed it out in the ashtray on the nightstand and watched my hand shaking. Something Delmar had said bothered me, and I didn't know what. And that really bothered me. I was about to light another cigarette when I heard the knock on the door.

I took the Luger out of the nightstand, tiptoed over, and stood beside the door frame. If it was a sucker play, at least I wouldn't get shot through the door. I'd make them come in and get me. If Delmar had sent his tough boys. I was a dead pigeon. But they'd meet the Luger first. I almost laughed at my own foolishness. I reached over and carefully turned the knob. Then I yanked the door open and poked the Luger in the face of Monica Wearing.

She flinched and took a step back, then settled into a cynical smirk. "You certainly know how to welcome a lady."

I lowered the gun and stepped aside. "Sorry. I've been keeping bad company lately. Come on in."

She brushed past, leaving me in a wash of that same perfume. She had on a beige skirt that looked as tight as a downtown parking space, a zircon-studded leather belt, and a soft azure blouse with the top button unfastened. Her hair had that tumbledown look that women work at all day, hoping not to look as if they've worked at it all day.

I shut the door and walked over, and motioned toward the chair. "Have a seat."

She cast a dubious glance in the direction of my suit jacket, then turned and stared at me. Her arms were stretched stiffly down in front of her, and she was holding a small clutch purse that she kneaded nervously.

"No, thank you," she said. "I'll stand. I don't expect to be here long."

I shrugged. "Suit yourself."

Suddenly, she jerked up her right hand and aimed the purse at me as if she had a fistful of gun. "Mr. Garrett, I've gone to some trouble to get here at this hour. You made some scarcely veiled threats over the phone. Now, what exactly do you want?"

"Exactly?" I thought about giving it to her exactly. I went over to the nightstand, dropped the Luger in the drawer, and pulled out the picture. I unclipped the negative and slipped it into my shirt pocket, then handed the photograph to her. "Exactly this."

She looked at it slowly, then looked up at me. "What does this mean?"

"What do *you* think It means?"

A sour recognition ran down over her face. "So that's it. I should have known. Well…" She casually slipped the picture into her purse and quickly brought her hand out. This time, it was full, a small bone-handled automatic, pint-sized but businesslike. She pointed it at my stomach. "If you think I'm going to pay you…"

"Oh, put it away," I said. "I've been shot at by bigger guns than that tonight. And they all had the safety catches off." It was a simple trick, one that should almost never work. But it almost always does. She took an obliging look at the automatic. While she did, I reached out and jerked it out of her hand. She stood frozen and watched as I popped the clip and laid the little gun on the dresser. Then I picked up the Scotch and took a drink from the bottle.

"Relax," I said. "I don't want your money."

"Then what…?" The recognition slid back into her face, along with a resigned smile. "I get it. You've seen the picture. Now you want the real thing."

Her hands were almost steady as she reached up and slowly ran her fingers through her hair. My breath shortened as she reached down and slowly dragged her hands up over the curves of her hips and brought them together at her belt buckle. She unfastened the belt and then began inching the blouse up over the top of her skirt. She had everything a woman needs, and none of it wasted. It was something to see. I felt my stomach muscles tighten as the last bit of fabric slipped out and hung loose around her. She shook out her hair again, reached up with both hands, and slowly began unbuttoning the blouse. Her voice had the sultry sound of locusts on an August afternoon.

"Almost there, lover."

Somebody said, "I can wait." It might have been me.

Her fingers made a slow, practiced move around the last button. She stepped toward me and slid one hand behind my neck. With the other, she kept playing with the button, taunting me with it, almost daring me not to look. She moved even closer and leaned against me, the warmth from her body making me feel like kindling. She brought her face up to mine until we were only a breath apart. I was close enough to count the beads of sweat above her upper lip. She smiled, and I felt her hand slip off my neck and down my back. "So, this is what it's about. You are just like the rest of them, after all."

"That's where you're wrong, sugar." I leered at her. "You'll remember me."

I didn't have to look to know the Scotch bottle was in her hand. Her eyes flew open, and she stepped back and swung at me like DiMaggio going after a fastball. I crouched quickly and heard the bottle cut through the air just inches above my hairline. I leaned forward and jammed my shoulder into her gut, and brought her up in a fireman's lift. Then I stepped toward the bed and threw her down on it. She landed on her back—yelping, arms flailing. The bottle dropped to the floor and rolled over against the far wall.

I walked over and picked it up, then went back and stood looking down at her. "Fun's over," I said. "What else did Kintner have on you?"

She propped herself up on her elbows and growled like a cornered alley cat. "You bastard."

I opened the Scotch and took another slug. "That's me, angel," I said affably as I watched her struggle upright and begin buttoning her blouse. "You put on a great act," I said. "But I've seen enough. It's time for the real thing."

As she finished buttoning, her eyes were the color of Wearing's jade. "I don't know what you mean."

"Like hell, you don't. You've been stringing me along since I first went to see the old man. You've worked hard at looking easy, like a dame out for trouble. But I peg you for one who's already found it. Only it isn't the kind of trouble that pours some hooch into you and then takes you home. It isn't the kind you can get dressed and walk away from in the morning. It's got bodies in it—lots of them." I watched her jaws clench hard enough to grind the enamel off her teeth. "Maybe I can help. But only if you come clean. What did Kintner have on you?"

She looked down at the floor. "I don't know what you..." Her head shot up. *"Did?"*

"That's right, angel," I purred. "He's dead. Murdered. So, you're off the hook with him. But not with me."

The color fell out of her face. "I...I..."

"All right," I said. "I'll make it easy for you. Kintner was a blackmailer of women. He cultivated the rich ones. Brought them into his office, gave them a little sweet talk, then took their pictures—that is, after he'd doped them up and then stripped them down for action. When the dust cleared, he'd offer to exchange the pictures in return for the purchase of some art object. He'd get a receipt with every transaction, showing what he was buying and for how much. That way, the law couldn't touch him. How could they accuse him of blackmail when he was paying money to his victims and when he had the receipts to prove it? He'd buy each item for peanuts, then sell it later and make a bundle. Your auctions were just a setup so you could pay him off."

She looked down at the floor again. When she finally glanced up, she looked innocent, even frightened. "How did you know?"

I shrugged. "What difference does it make?"

"What...what do you want?"

I slipped the negative out of my pocket and tossed it to her. "I don't want this."

For a minute, her mouth just hung open, and she stared at me. Finally, she tucked the negative away in her purse. "I still don't see..."

"How did you get mixed up with Kintner?"

She shuffled her feet and looked down again. "Stanfield sent me to him."

"Uh-huh."

She sat up indignantly. "What do you mean, 'Uhhuh'? Stanfield wanted me to get a checkup, that's all. He didn't know what Kintner was doing. He couldn't."

"Yes, he did." She started to say something, but I stopped her. "I figure it this way. After Kintner tried to put the bite on you with the nude picture, you went to your husband. Maybe not at first, but you went. The Colonel surprised you by being very understanding and forgiving. He even offered to throw in the Jade Princess for one of your auctions. He told you it was to sweeten the pot, maybe get Kintner out of your hair for good."

She stared at me for a long time. "My God, that's right. But how did you know?"

I waved my hand at her, went over, pulled the clipping out of the nightstand, and handed it to her. She took it and held it gingerly, as if it burned her fingers. She barely looked at it.

"I also figure you knew this guy Norris," I said. "But not just from Kansas City. You knew him because you took the scram with him from Chicago. The two of you beat it out of town there and went into hiding, not from the cops but from an army of gunsels. Because you had seen something. And if it came out, that meant curtains for a certain party. I'm guessing you're the missing witness from Rudy Delmar's murder trial."

Her features hardened. Her voice turned to concrete. "Randall Norris was my father. That son of a bitch had him killed." She clenched both fists, then slowly opened them and exhaled. She stood up and eyed me with an element of curiosity. "You know, you're smarter than you look."

"Tell me about Chicago."

She hesitated, then shrugged. "Why not? I was working in Rudy's club. A cocktail waitress. Rudy took an interest in me. Said we could go places, the big time. I was young. I thought..." She paused and shook her head. "I didn't know he was in the rackets. But he was. He even had a cop on the string, a guy named Wallis. One night Wallis came to Rudy's office and demanded money, big money. He said he'd blow the whistle if Rudy didn't pay." She rubbed her hands together. "Rudy just went wild. I'd never seen him like that. He pulled a gun from his desk drawer and shot the cop. Right there in the office."

"You saw him?"

She nodded. "I was in the closet."

I couldn't help grinning. "What were you doing there?"

"Rudy let me keep a change of clothes there while I was working. I..."

I kept grinning.

She put her hands on her hips and barked at me. "Goddammit, it wasn't like that! Not with him." She stood that way for a minute, then relaxed. "Anyway, I was scared. I stayed in the closet until Rudy left. Then I got out of there and went home. I just stayed there and pretended to be sick. I didn't go to work. I didn't go anywhere. I didn't even talk to anybody."

She turned and walked over and parted the drapes by the bed. She stood and stared at the glass, not seeing, just remembering. "Somehow, the cops found me. Don't ask me how. They took me in and made me admit that I'd seen the killing. Then they said they'd put me in jail if I didn't testify. They even promised to hide me, keep Rudy away from me until the trial."

She laughed. It wasn't a nice laugh. It was the dry, futile laugh of someone who had given up. "I think they even believed they could. They really thought Rudy wouldn't find me." She paused. "So, I agreed."

She turned and faced me, arms folded, her eyes as cold and deep as high tide. "They kept me in a hotel until the trial. Then, on the first day, I got this note." She held out her hands and made a pleading motion. "Do you believe it? The bailiff gave it to me. It said if I talked, I'd never see my father again. That night, I snuck out of the hotel and met my father in the alley in back. We just left everything there in Chicago and drove all the way to Kansas City. I went to work in a hotel, and my father did odd jobs around town. We were safe there for almost six years. Then he started playing the piano in clubs again. He said he missed it." Her lips stretched into a tight smile, but her voice was thick and throaty. "A month later, he was dead."

"You think Delmar did it?"

She nodded. "The bartender said a man with a Chicago accent had been asking questions. That could only be one of Rudy's gunmen."

I didn't say anything.

All at once, she grabbed my shirt and began shaking. Her eyes were burning with unshed tears. "But why? The trial was over. Rudy was free. He'd been in Mexico for years. Why should he have my father killed? Why?"

I put my arms around her and held her and felt her sobs against my chest. It was getting to be a habit, having women cry on me. I stood and started to wonder whose shirt I could cry on. When she finally stopped, I led her over and sat her on the bed again. She fished a handkerchief out of her purse. I went over to the dresser and poured out the last of the Scotch. I handed it to her, then lit a cigarette.

"Delmar wasn't free," I said. "He'd beaten the murder rap. But you could still put the finger on him for bribing a cop. He couldn't come back to the country until you and your father were out of the way. Even then, he still had the Colonel to worry about. Maybe that's why you're still alive. How did you meet your husband?"

She emptied the glass and put it on the nightstand. "It was at a convention in Kansas City. He came there and stayed at the hotel shortly after my father was killed. As soon as he saw me, he just decided I was for him. He sent me flowers, candy. He bought me expensive things. I didn't know what to think. Then he insisted that I marry him. He said it would break his heart if I didn't. So, we were married by a justice of the peace, and I came back with him to El Paso." She crossed her arms tightly and let out a heavy sigh. "It's true I didn't love him. But I respected him. And I felt safe with him. I still do."

"But not safe enough to go strolling into El Cotorra Azul. Not unless you thought you and the Colonel had an edge."

She began wringing the handkerchief around in her fingers. "When I told Stanfield about Kintner, he gave me the Jade statue and told me not to worry. He said something about history and that he believed Rudy was behind Kintner's blackmail. Then he said he had a plan to trap them, put them both away so that they couldn't bother me anymore. I was bitter and confused, and I felt I owed it to my father. So, I went along."

"What was his plan?"

"I don't know exactly. He just told me to go ahead with the auctions. And he said I should be seen around town at night, even at the Parrot. He wanted me to make everyone, especially Rudy, think that I was, you know...fooling around." She looked up and smiled. "And it's a good thing for you that I did. Otherwise, I wouldn't have been there last night to get you out of trouble." Her smile turned sheepish. "I'm afraid I drugged your drink. You see, I knew you wouldn't leave with me just because I asked you. When you collapsed and Delmar's boys started to rough you up, I signaled Randolph. He got you out of there."

"What did you tell Delmar?"

"I told him you'd had too much to drink and that I needed to get you into bed…mine. I said I like men who're tall." She giggled. "I think he was jealous."

I reached over and stubbed my cigarette in the ashtray." All right. So, you and your husband were conning Delmar, using the jade to draw him out. But there's more to it. Jack Springer got wise and started horning in."

Her smile fell away. "Yes. Somehow, he became suspicious and started asking questions. I told Stanfield, and he said that it was all right. He told me to meet with Springer and just drop a few hints that Dr. Kintner was involved in something shady. I did, but nothing happened. Even after the Princess was sold, things stayed quiet. After a while, Stanfield became convinced that Kintner had hidden the jade and that Rudy didn't know about it. So, he gave me the combination to Kintner's safe." She shrugged. "He said Randolph had gotten it somehow. He told me to give it to Springer and to tell him about the jade." She looked down and spoke quietly into the handkerchief. "So, I did. That was just a few days ago. The rest, you know."

"Yeah," I said. "Lights out for Springer."

I walked to the window and stared out at the lights stretching below the border. They flickered and dimmed in the night, almost like waves breaking on a reef. I turned back away from the window.

"There's still more," I said. "Jack Springer was no ace. But he was more of a reporter than most people thought. He figured out that Kintner wasn't just a rogue doctor. So, instead of sneaking into the house right away, he followed Kintner to Los Angeles. He probably thought he could get a line on Kintner's connections and then expose the whole blackmail operation. On the way back, he even put an eye on a hired killer. And that told him he was onto a big story. Later, he did go to Kintner's house, but he didn't get as far as the safe. Because somebody spotted him. Maybe Kintner, maybe someone else, like Delmar's button man, Voss. So, Springer just got out of there as fast as he could."

Monica was staring at me now; her features a mixture of dread and fascination. "How do you know that?"

I looked down at my shoes. They were covered with gray-green scuff marks. "I got these tripping through the mesquite behind Kintner's house tonight. There were similar marks on Springer's shoes when he came to see me yesterday morning. By then, he must have put two and two together and realized that Delmar was the one behind Kintner. And that shook him. He was sweating pitchforks, like a guy afraid for his life. I think he may even have wanted me to help him. Only he couldn't quite bring himself to talk to me. Not many people do. Maybe he just needed more time to think it over. He was probably still thinking about it when Voss killed him."

I shoved my hands in my pockets and grunted. "You can tell your husband he doesn't have to worry anymore. Delmar knows about the jade now."

Monica stood up and twisted the handkerchief almost into knots. Her knuckles were white. Suddenly, she looked drawn and tired.

"I know what you're thinking," she said. "But you don't know Stanfield, not really. When he heard that Springer and that man Ordway had been killed."

"Then why go on with it? Why not just call in the law?"

She swallowed hard. "Somehow, he's become obsessed with history. And he's convinced that something is going to happen soon, something terrible. I don't know what it is, but it has to do with the jade."

I grunted again. "Why the hell is that jade so damned important to everybody?"

She shook her head. "I don't know. But whenever I ask Stanfield about it, he becomes very agitated. He says things I don't understand, things about a curse. He's afraid for his family. He says anyone who has the jade will be in danger until the figures are united again, and then only in the right hands. And he says matters are beyond his control now. He just wants James and Gabrielle out of town, and he wants me protected." She stopped wringing the handkerchief and looked at me. Her eyes became calm and steady. "I want Rudy Delmar to pay for what he did to my father. But I'm afraid. Not for myself—for Stanfield. I'm afraid because he's afraid."

I inhaled deeply and let my breath out slowly, and stepped close to her.

"What was in those pills you gave him tonight?"

She blinked several times. Wetness swelled along her lower lids. "Nitro-glycerin."

"What is it, angina?"

She looked at the floor and nodded reluctantly. "It was diagnosed earlier this year. I'm afraid he hasn't much longer."

I picked up the automatic and the clip and handed them to her. Then I turned and walked over to the door. "Can you get home all right?"

"Yes. But what are you going to do?"

"Go to bed," I said. "Now beat it, and don't say anything about this to your husband. He's got enough on his mind."

She came over and stood next to me. "You shouldn't stay here. You shouldn't be involved in this."

"I shouldn't do a lot of things. I shouldn't drink and wake up hungover. I shouldn't wear cheap suits and get shot at. And I shouldn't have a dead client." I opened the door.

"And maybe you shouldn't be so stubborn." She put her hand on my chest. "Be careful." She stepped into the hall and then turned and looked at me. There was something quiet in her eyes now, something soft. "I'm glad I met you, Mickey."

She leaned forward and kissed me on the cheek, then quickly walked down the hall to the elevator. I watched her go. Just as she got there, the elevator door opened, and two men in dark suits started to get out. They stopped in the doorway, looked at me, looked at Monica, then stepped back into the elevator. Monica got in, and the door closed.

I stood there in the hall for a minute, feeling vaguely uneasy. Something about the two men reminded me of a bad dream I'd had somewhere south of the border. I had just decided to go after them when a voice stopped me.

"You son of a bitch!"

Chapter Twenty-Three

Gabrielle stepped from behind a tall leafy potted fern partway up the hall. She stalked over and stood in front of me, nostrils flaring, scowling like a loan shark holding bad paper. I barely had time to turn around before her hand shot out and cracked across my cheek. It was a good slap, flush and hard. The sound echoed off the walls and was still echoing when she started yelling at me.

"So, this is why you came to the hotel—to make time with Monica. After you said... After we... When I..." She was sputtering like a floundering swimmer. She stopped, clenched her fists, and caught her breath. "Well, Mr. Big Shot Private Eye. You can just go to hell."

She started another swing, but I caught her arm before she could bring it up. "That's enough," I said. "You hit too hard for a girl."

She yanked her arm loose and glared at me. "Was she worth it?"

"I've had worse."

"You bastard."

I grinned. "That's me." She didn't get the joke. So, I pushed the door open, stepped into the room, and motioned to her. "Come on."

She stood in the hall hesitating, her face painted with anger and confusion. I motioned with my hand, and she finally came in. I shut the door and stood in front of her. She stared at me. I stared at her.

"Now what?" I asked.

"I trusted you."

"It's about time somebody did."

"But you..." She shook her head. "I don't think I'll ever trust men again.

Not after knowing you."

"Fair enough," I said. "I don't trust them either."

"You bastard," she repeated.

I looked into her eyes. They were wide and blue and very deep. I figured I had a choice. I could kiss her or knock her block off. I opted for the former. She put her hands against my chest and tried to push me away. I pressed my hand against the small of her back and drew her up against me. All at once, she stopped resisting and wrapped her arms up around my neck, clinging to me like a mustard plaster and just as warm. We stood that way, molded together, just touching and breathing. And the world stopped.

When we parted, she put her head against my chest, hung on to me, and talked into my shirt. "You've got some nerve, buster."

I chuckled. "What were you doing hiding behind the bush?"

I felt her tensing in my arms. "When I came to the door, I heard voices. I was afraid..."

I just stood and listened to the sound of her breathing.

"Michael, don't tell me. Whatever it is with you and Monica, just don't tell me. Please."

I grabbed her by the arms and held her out in front of me. "That's a hell of a note. Just what is it I'm not supposed to tell you about?"

Her face brightened like a new penny. "You mean you...? I mean, you and she...? You mean you didn't..."

"If I did, it wouldn't be here, and it wouldn't be now."

"Then why was she here?"

"Maybe I just like to stir up trouble."

She bit her lip and looked down at the floor. "I'm sorry. I thought..."

"That's what thinking does to people." I turned and walked over to the dresser, and lit a cigarette. I pulled in a heavy drag and then stood and watched the smoke crawl across the floor.

She kept on looking down and kept on biting her lip. She was thinking again. After I'd fed myself half the cigarette, she walked over and stood in front of me and gave me one of those demure up-from-under looks.

"'Have you ever been married?" she asked. It stuck me like the point of a knife.

"Detectives don't have wives."

She angled her head and lifted an eyebrow. A foxy smile tiptoed around the corners of her mouth. "But you won't be a detective forever. Wouldn't you like something more from life?"

"If liking made a difference, we'd all be as rich as your father."

"What do you mean?"

"I mean, kissing you is nice. I like it fine. But it's not what I came to town for."

"You could try," she went on. "Father would help. I think secretly he really likes you."

She was going on as if I hadn't said anything. Sometimes, I wonder what women's ears are for.

"Have you found Jimmy?" I asked her.

She caught her breath and threw her hands up in the air, as if she'd just remembered the name of her long-lost third cousin. "Yes. That's really why I'm here. He's downstairs in the bar with Randolph. They'll be up in a few minutes." Then her eyebrows came together in a sisterly frown. "He's not in very good shape. He's been drinking…a lot. But at least he's not with those women."

"'How did he get involved with them?"

She looked at me and let out a long, loud sigh. "I'm sure it's because of my father. He's introduced Jimmy to at least a dozen girls, mostly daughters of friends and business associates. I once heard him tell Jimmy it was important to have the right wife and that he had an obligation to history to preserve the line." She made a quick, almost embarrassed chuckle. "You can imagine what that meant to Jimmy."

"About as much as it has to you," I said.

"You're right. I know how Jimmy must feel. Father has tried much the same thing with me. He says that before he dies, he wants to see us properly placed." She shook her head. "He says the Wearings have an obligation to history."

"That's what I like about this family. You're all just plain folks." I took a longing look at the empty Scotch bottle. "But why Rosetta and Lupe?"

She sighed again. "I don't know. Maybe it's Jimmy's way of getting even with Father, of hurting him. He knows how much Father hates Rudy Delmar. So, he goes down there and drinks and then goes whoring around with those two."

I pulled in a lungful of smoke and sailed it toward the ceiling. "Well, the old man's line is safe for a while. Rosetta is dead."

Her arms dropped in the direction of the floor, and her chin dropped with them. "What?"

I took a last drag and ground out the stub of my cigarette. "Do I have to say it again?"

"How?"

"A Mexican hanging. Slow and painful and not pretty."

"But...But why?"

I stuck my hands in my pockets and grunted. "She made the mistake of talking to me. People who do that around here don't seem to live very long. I talked to Dr. Kintner yesterday. Now he's dead, too." Her hands flew up and covered her mouth. The skin around her nostrils turned white. Her eyes were as wide as the tops of milk bottles. "Oh, my God. No."

"Yeah," I said. "He cashed in sometime last night, the same way as your friend Ordway."

We stared at each other for a long time. Her mouth moved several times before the words came out. "Do you think...".

"What I think is that Kintner was dabbling in blackmail and using Ordway to fence art objects he collected from wealthy women like Monica. That's how Ordway knew about the jade."

"Monica? Do you think she...?"

"No."

She folded her arms again and thought for a minute. "Do you suppose that Dr. Kintner killed Willy?"

I shook my head. "Blackmailers don't kill people. They get killed. Especially when they're working for Rudy Delmar. I think most of Kintner's dirty money was laundered on its way south."

She shuddered and rubbed her hands over her upper arms as if a chill had crept into the room. "Then who could it be?"

"Somebody who smells money and appreciates history." I shrugged. "Or maybe your father's just afraid history is gaining on him."

She squeezed her hands together hard enough to crack a walnut. "Not Father. You can't think that."

I shook my head again. "No. But he's got the right idea. You and Jimmy better get out of town tonight. Delmar's got his people on the prowl, and the sooner you get scarce, the better."

She hesitated. "I don't know. I think I should call Victor."

"Uh-uh," I said. "You tell nobody. You trust nobody. And nobody knows where you're going. Not even me. Just take your brother and make tracks."

She looked down at the floor again. "I guess if you say so."

I was about to say so when a fist almost came through the door. With all the traffic I was getting. I don't know why I even bothered to shut it. I thought about the Luger in the nightstand, then shrugged and pulled the door open. Randolph was standing there, looking as if somebody had just poured ice water in his shorts. He was wearing his usual black suit, with his shirt collar open and his tie loose. And he was wearing Gabrielle's brother over one shoulder.

Jimmy was hanging off him like a buffalo carcass, arms limp, head drooping, his feet splayed at an unnatural angle. Randolph leaned forward, and Jimmy's head bobbed up. He spotted me, then wrenched himself free and stumbled into the room. He leaned against me, flopped an arm on my shoulder, and let out a belch that could have curled the wallpaper. His breath wasn't too bad, but his clothes smelled of enough whiskey to make a bishop sing the Marine's Hymn.

"Howzit goin', hosshot?" he slurred. His eyes rolled around in his head like marbles in a roulette wheel. He looked around the room, studying it with the slow, exaggerated care that drunks take so they can fool themselves into thinking they're sober.

I felt his arm weighing on my shoulder like a sack of gravel. "C'mon. Be nice," I said. "I just checked in here."

216

He laughed. "Whacha doin' stayina dead man's room?"

"Reminiscing," I said.

He laughed again. "You wou' be, hosshot. You wou' be."

I reached around him, got my arm under his other shoulder, and turned him toward the bed. He looked up, then made a dive for it. He landed face-first in the middle of the bed and lay there, grunting and making slow snuffling noises. I looked at Randolph. He looked at Gabrielle. She looked at me. Finally, we all looked at the bed. Jimmy grunted again, then heaved gently. His slow and deep breathing filled the room.

I looked over at Randolph. "Nice work, chief."

The Indian inhaled, stretched himself up tall enough to dust the ceiling, and gave me an indignant scowl. "Mr. Garrett, I am not in the habit of provoking people to intoxication."

"Of course not," I said. "He was ambushed by a marauding shot glass."

Randolph snorted and folded his arms.

Gabrielle looked at me, trying to hide the remnants of a stifled grin. "I guess we're not leaving tonight."

"I guess you're not," I said. "But he can't stay here. Too many people know where I am. I can't entertain Delmar with a drunk on the bed."

"Then, we'll take him home," she said.

I looked over at Randolph. Suddenly, he had the pained expression of a kid facing a smallpox vaccination. "No. It's too far," I said. "He's got an apartment near here. Know where it is, chief?"

He looked at me with as much relief as a man with his face could show. "Yes, sir."

"All right. We'll take him there." I turned back to Gabrielle. "You can come along. It'll be a good place to hide. Tomorrow, we'll all meet the train together."

She hesitated. "But…but I'll have to go home and pack first."

"Nix," I said. "Don't go near your place. It might be staked out."

She inhaled and nodded. "Well, then. I'll spend the night in my office. Maybe it's just as well. That way, I can leave a note for Angela."

I shook my head.

She came over and put her hand on my arm. "Michael, I have to. I have to leave instructions for Angela. It's important. People are depending on me."

I snorted. "I've seen Angela. She doesn't need instructions."

She squeezed my arm. Her eyes clutched at my insides. "Please, Michael. I won't tell her where we're going."

I was a fool for looking at her. I was a fool for listening. "All right," I said.

The night clerk looked quietly amused as Randolph and I hauled Jimmy across the lobby and out the front door of the hotel. I didn't think it was funny. Even with Randolph helping, Jimmy was heavier than a guilty conscience. We shoveled him into the back seat of the Buick, and I watched Gabrielle get into her roadster and drive off. I stood there and felt something clawing at the back of my mind the way a stray dog scratches on a door, wanting to be let in out of the rain. It was something Delmar had said. Or something he hadn't.

I slid in under the wheel. Randolph got in next to me, and I eased the Buick down the drive. The Indian gave me directions, but I didn't follow them. Instead, I turned west on Mesa Street, drove conspicuously out to the Westside Highway, and headed north toward Las Cruces. I drove for about ten minutes until there were no lights in the mirror and nothing straight ahead. A shallow wash stretched out along the side of the road for about forty feet. I turned into it, cut the engine, and doused the lights. Randolph folded his arms and spoke in a flat, matter-of-fact tone. "I take it this is your way of avoiding detection."

"Sorry, chief," I said. "Best I could do on short notice. Maybe I should have tied some brush onto the rear bumper to wipe out our tracks. Is that the way your people would have done it?"

He turned toward me and worked his mouth into a smile that was about as wide as a keyhole. Maybe I just thought it was a smile.

"You're right to be cautious," he said.

"Thanks." I sat and watched him. His leathery face held something I couldn't quite make out. "How long have you been with the Wearings?"

"Most of my life."

"And you're devoted to the Colonel?"

A steely flicker showed in his black eyes. "To the entire family."

I nodded. "And you'd do anything to protect them?"

"You needn't mince words, Mr. Garrett. If anyone threatened the Colonel or his family, I would...do what was necessary." He turned and looked out the window and yawned quietly.

I didn't ask him anything more. I just sat there, not mincing words, and listened to the dust settling on the hood of the car. We waited through ten minutes of nothing. No cars. No lights. No noise. The night just stood still. If someone meant to follow us, he'd have to be damn good.

I was about as convinced as I could get that we hadn't been followed, so I started the car again and headed back down the highway toward El Paso. Just short of town, I got off and cruised south on Montoya Drive. The road made a quiet dusty curve along the river, and I followed it down into the warehouse district. From there, I took every side street and alley I could find, working my way back into the city. At last, we came out on lower Alameda. Randolph directed me across Montana and up the hill on Piedras. I put an eye in every direction. I still saw no one.

We made a couple of easy miles up the hill and into a reticent neighborhood full of worn-out homes and apartments. Randolph pointed, and I pulled over and stopped in front of a set of rowhouse apartments that couldn't quite stay hidden behind a tall hedge and a rusted iron gate. I sat looking beyond the gate at the first apartment door. There was a reason the place looked familiar. I'd seen it before. I'd been there when Dr. Kintner made a house call.

Randolph got out—didn't look at me, didn't say anything. He pulled Jimmy out of the back seat, got a shoulder under him, and hauled him through the gate like a lumberman carrying a length of timber to the mill. I closed up the car and followed, rubbing my shoulder and thinking I should have Randolph with me every time I pass out. At the door, he stopped and fished through Jimmy's pockets. He brought out a set of keys and opened the door. We went inside.

It was about as close to Wearing Manor as Carnegie Hall is to a two-bit music hall: two rooms and a kitchenette, with furniture that the Salvation Army wouldn't take. The walls were not quite covered with a sallow greenish paper that was torn and peeling and full of little printed begonias and spotted with things that had been thrown at it. A tired desk had a tired Underwood typewriter on it surrounded with crumpled paper. I pushed my hat back on my head and looked around. For the first time, I was glad Gabrielle had gone to the office.

Randolph carted Jimmy through the doorway on the right and began making bedroom noises. I opened a closet by the front door and found a month's pay in clothes, wire hangers holding sports shirts, jackets, slacks, a blue serge suit, and on the end, a white office duster like the one I'd seen the day before. On the floor in the corner behind a pair of heavy black brogans was a large parcel wrapped in brown paper and tied with string. I took my pocket knife, cut a small slit in the paper, and peeked inside. I knew what it was, of course. Kintner had stashed the relics he'd taken from the auction, probably so he could look them over in daylight and decide which ones to keep and which ones to sell for Delmar. The ones he kept, he could fence for himself later. It was a nice racket until Delmar got wise. I almost laughed out loud. Crooks can't even do business with each other nowadays.

I shut the closet door and strolled into the kitchenette. Whatever else Jimmy might have been, he wasn't a housekeeper. Unwashed pots and dishes and cups and glasses and knives and forks littered the counter and filled the sink. They were crusted with half-eaten meals and piled up like chips in an all-night poker game. I opened the refrigerator. There was nothing but a loaf of bread, a few jars and cans, and a half-empty bottle of milk that was starting to smell like the inside of a tannery. I closed the door quickly and happened to glance on top of the refrigerator. A large glass ashtray sat there holding the gold-stubbed ends of at least a dozen lavender cigarettes. I shook my head. Somehow, pastels were becoming popular.

I looked quickly through the cabinets. I figured a guy like Jimmy would have a bottle here. I needn't have bothered. I walked back into the living room. It seemed like none of my business, so I began looking through the desk. In the deep drawer, I found Jimmy's war souvenirs. There was the familiar khaki garrison cap folded over a pair of corporal's chevrons, a Japanese jungle cap with captain's markings, and a ceremonial dagger with a finely curved blade dappled with what might have been rust spots and an inlaid picture of a dragon on the handle. A lot of guys brought things back from the Pacific, all kinds of things. I wondered if the captain had used the dagger on himself. Near the end, a lot of Jap soldiers chose *seppuku* over capture.

In the back of the drawer, a Colt .45 automatic service pistol lay rusting in a standard-issue Army holster. Behind that, a small leather case was resting on a sheaf of papers. I took the papers out and looked through them. I found a set of orders assigning Corporal James Wearing to the post supply unit of the Army Quartermaster Corps at Fort Ord, California, in June 1944. Next was a report from a military hospital, dated in December of that year. Corporal Wearing had been admitted, suffering from severe emotional trauma and melancholia leading to disability. That was an Army doctor's way of saying he had beaten up a couple of MPs and landed in the brig and that while he was there, he collapsed. Attached to the report was a positive test for diabetes. And finally, there were separation papers issued to Corporal Wearing in March 1945, showing him unfit for service. I put the papers back in the drawer and opened the case. It held a glass tube with a syringe in it, several hypodermic needles, and a vial of insulin. I sucked air through my teeth and shook my head again. Severe emotional trauma and melancholia leading to disability. That's just the way I felt.

I closed the desk, walked over, and looked into the bedroom. Somehow, Randolph had gotten Jimmy's trousers off, and now he was trying to wrestle him out of his shirt. Jimmy was grunting and flopping around on the bed like a live tuna on the deck of a fishing boat. Randolph kept working at the shirt, his jaw clamped tight, neck muscles bulging, and his eyes flashing with distaste. I smiled at the Indian and turned away. Undressing a drunk is almost as easy as shoving toothpaste back into a tube.

Jimmy's typewriter caught my eye, and I walked back over to the desk. There were crumpled sheets of half-written manuscript strewn over the top; a sheet with a few lines was still in the typewriter. I turned the roller and propped up the paper so I could read it:

It's night. It's always night. Maybe that's why you can't see me, why I can't see myself. Yet we're so much alike. While the father of greed hides in the curses of history, the son of shame wanders faceless through all the loving corruptions. Both seeking. Both screaming in silence. Can we ever live through these words? It's lonely in the night. But don't push me. I've shared my soul with one you couldn't know, only to find another tender betrayal. And now the bittersweetness of love is done. Now, there is no caring. Only the night.

I read it over again. Maybe Jimmy really could be a writer. It wasn't Somerset Maugham, but it made a point.

I heard a noise behind me. Randolph stepped through the bedroom door, shutting off the light behind him. He slipped on his suit jacket, straightened his tie, and stood eyeing me with a tired, almost doleful expression.

"How is he?" I asked.

"He will sleep now."

The Indian reached into an inside pocket and drew out an envelope that could barely hide a familiar bulge. I didn't have to look at it to know what was in it. He held it out to me.

"This is for you," he said. "Five thousand dollars. The Colonel wants you to see to the safety of his son and daughter."

"Put it away," I said. "That much money would spoil the cut of my suit."

He hesitated, looking for a word with enough ammunition. "The Colonel...insisted."

"Well, that makes all the difference," I said. "When the Colonel insists, things happen. The presses roll. Old women tremble, and street punks hide in the shadows. The cops look the other way. And private detectives find people shooting at them."

He just stood and stared at me, as expressionless as a flatiron.

"Listen, chief," I went on. "I'm feeling old and tired and not very nice tonight. I haven't beaten anybody up in at least a week. You try forcing that money on me, and one of us is going to eat it.

A slight curl tickled the corners of his mouth. He moved his hand very slowly and tucked the envelope back in his pocket. "For what it may be worth to you, Mr. Garrett, I told Colonel Wearing you would not accept the money."

I reached into my pocket and carefully dragged out a Lucky. I stabbed the end into my mouth, carefully lit a match, carefully brought the match up, and carefully puffed until the cigarette was burning. I did it very well. I wasn't shaking any more than a palsied wino.

"Why is that?" I asked.

His features softened about a millimeter. "In your own dissipated way, you have a certain integrity. Not many brains, perhaps. But I judge you to be a man who, in the words of my ancestors, rolls his own blanket."

I took a deep drag and managed not to burn myself. "All right. Now that we've done our rain dance, what do you know about Dr. Kintner?"

He lifted an eyebrow. "What do you mean?"

"Look," I said. "I know about Jimmy being in the Army hospital and about the diabetes. That has to be why Kintner was treating him—not for any nervous disorder. But why would Kintner have a key to this apartment?"

He folded his arms and looked at me uncertainly, like someone trying to make up his mind. He brought up a huge hand and rubbed his cheek with it. Finally, he folded his arms again and let a dull sadness settle into his eyes.

"As I'm sure you are aware, Mr. James has needed a great deal of help. He was afraid his father would see his…illness as just another weakness. Dr. Kintner agreed to treat him privately, even outside the office. Mr. James insisted that it be somewhere away from the Colonel, and he had me arrange for this apartment. I gave Dr. Kintner the key."

"Has the Colonel ever asked about Kintner or the treatments?"

He thought about it, then shook his head slowly.

"What about Gabrielle? Does she know?"

He shook his head again. "She does not. What I've told you was a secret, Mr. Garrett."

"It still is," I said. "How long has this been going on?"

"Almost two years. Before that, Mr. James would make monthly visits to a doctor in the East. He had me obtain the insulin for him. He still does." He pursed his lips for a moment without taking his stare off me. "I'm not sure it was the best arrangement. Nor am I sure it would have been better to have the Colonel know."

"So, like your ancestors, you just went along and suffered in silence."

"To a point."

"Yeah," I chuckled. "The point of a knife."

He unfolded his arms and opened his hands. Fingers the size of bananas curled into a position for choking. "Mr. Garrett, if you have an accusation to make—"

"Skip it," I said. "I'm too tired to go waltzing around. Can you look after Jimmy?"

"Naturally," he nodded. "The Colonel is being safely attended. I will remain here with Mr. James and await your arrival with Miss Gabrielle in the morning. You see, Mr. Garrett, as you observed earlier, I am devoted to this family."

He turned and began straightening up the room. After a minute, he gathered up some loose dishes and headed toward the kitchenette. He gave me as much notice as he would a fly on a windowsill. He had answered my questions. He had told me what he wanted me to know—no more. Now he was finished with me. I was dismissed. If I wanted more answers, I could go question a yucca tree. I let myself out.

The drive back to the hotel was like a walk down a long dark corridor. I didn't know if I was being followed. I couldn't have cared less. I was tired. I wanted sleep. I wanted not to know about the Colonel and his money, about Monica and her father, about Delmar and Voss and the jade, about Kintner, about Rosetta. I wanted not to know about the thoughts darting through the shadows in my head—stopping, moving again, always there, always out of reach. I wanted not to know. I wanted sleep.

It was sometime after one in the morning when I got to the hotel. The lights were dimmed, and the night crew was lounging sleepily behind the front desk. They hardly stirred as I crossed the lobby and got into the elevator. I rode up to the fourth floor and walked uneasily up the hall. Even on the padded carpet, the crackling of my shoes sounded like gunshots in the still air.

I went in, tossed my hat and jacket on the chair, and kicked off my shoes. I stripped down to my undershirt and shorts and went over to the sink. I ran some water again and splashed in it again and then looked at my face in the mirror again. It didn't help. I left the sink and went over to the bed. It looked like the best thing to happen to me since the announcement of Repeal. I yawned and pulled back the covers, and then stood still. It was there staring up at me from the pillow, blade polished razor-sharp, green handle carved with a giant bird. I just stood and looked at it. I could almost hear Rudy Delmar laughing. I was looking at the Bird of Death.

Chapter Twenty-Four

The pounding sounded like a jackhammer, rocking the room, shaking the fixtures, and rattling what was left of my brain. It seemed only a minute ago that I had put my head on the pillow. Now, I lay there in the dark and wondered if I could lift my head up again. I pushed hard on the edge of the bed and forced myself upright. Then I swung a pair of legs that felt like cement slabs over the edge of the bed and listened to someone's feet hit the floor. They didn't sound like my feet. They didn't sound like anything that belonged to me. I groaned and looked at my watch. Just after three-thirty. Not my best hour.

The fist hit the door again, and I took the Luger out of the nightstand. I padded over to the door and stood next to it, tottering like a drunken sailor on a rolling deck. Somewhere in the sleepy fog, I decided that Delmar wouldn't arrive with so much fanfare. I held the Luger down at my side, found the knob with my free hand, and yanked the door open. I caught Hector Armendariz in mid-rap.

He stood with his fist suspended in front of me, eyes bulging in their sockets. When he saw me, he stepped back and rubbed his hands together. *"Senor,* I look for you everywhere."

"Okay," I mumbled. "You found me. What gives?"

"Senor, you come queek," he blurted. *"Muy importante.* Very important."

I looked at my watch, not because I needed to know the time. "Do you know what time it is?"

"Por favor, senor. You must hurry."

I let out a long, heavy breath that seemed to take most of my strength with it and stepped aside. "All right. Come on in."

Hector bounded through the door, and I snapped on the light. I stood there in a half-waking stupor and watched him hop around the room. He pranced back and forth a few times and settled uneasily by the end of the bed, edging nervously from side to side.

"Ees bad trouble, *senor. De la patada.* You come queek."

"What trouble?"

"Very bad, *senor.* I explain. But you come. *Pronto.*" I stood there and let out another breath. I wouldn't have thought I had so much air in me.

"Not until I put on my pants," I said.

He nodded and hopped around some more with the eager moves of a cocker spaniel waiting for table scraps. *"Si, senor. Muy pronto."*

I got dressed, and we went downstairs and got into Hector's cab. I sat in the front seat and rubbed a hand over my face. It felt as clean and smooth as a rusted washboard. Hector stamped on the gas, and we tore out of the lot, headed down Mesa, and cruised through town out to the lower valley.

The streets and storefronts flew by in a blur, a montage of dull color and poverty. The cab careened around several corners, then rolled into a run-down residential district and pulled up in front of a grayish adobe house. It was the kind of place that a lot of people settled in when they came north across the border. I pictured it with a couple of rooms, some homespun tapestry, and half a dozen hungry kids.

Hector jumped out of the cab, ran around, opened my door, and began pulling me out by the arm. I stumbled out and shook myself loose.

"Easy does it," I said.

We made the few steps to the house, and Hector opened the door without even breaking stride. We went in.

It had a low ceiling and walls painted a burnt peach color, with brown sackcloth drapes covering the windows, a few weary pieces of furniture, and bare wood floors lying almost naked under a couple of throw rugs. A doorway on the right opened into a meager dining room, and another door just past that in the corner led to what would be a cramped bedroom and the rear of the house. The wall straight ahead was almost hidden behind an

227

oversized black felt painting, the kind that you could find by the hundreds in the Juarez tourist shops. A tall, sleek-looking matador stood poised, his cape at full twirl above the reaching horns of a charging bull. The bull looked bewildered, caught in a futile surge, his horns piercing nothing but air.

To the left of the picture, another sackcloth curtain hung over a doorway. Chattering noises came from behind it. Hector called to someone, and a large brown face with large, comfortable eyes peered at me from around the curtain. The face studied me for a minute, then withdrew, and three little brown urchins dressed in pajamas raced out and disappeared into the hallway. Hector motioned to me and pushed back the curtain, and we stepped into a small, crowded kitchen.

The woman with the large face stood in the middle of the room. Compared to the rest of her, her face looked small. She had wide, fleshy arms and a body shaped like a pumpkin that was swathed in a loose red-and-yellow print dress with enough fabric to make a department store awning.

Hector gave me a sheepish look. "Senor Garrett, thees ees my cousin, Camilla. Her husband, Esteban—he ees not here. He drive thee cab too." He patted a hand against his chest. "Like me."

I took off my hat and tried to smile. "How do you do." Then I turned back to Hector and tried not to think about breaking his neck. "Why did you bring me here?"

He said something to the woman, and she obediently stepped aside. Behind her, in the corner, a young girl sat at a table, nervously fiddling with a coffee cup. She had soft brown skin and dark burning eyes under coal-black hair, and she wore a lowcut magenta dress that fitted her slender figure like a rubber glove. She wasn't someone you'd forget right away. I'd seen her at the hotel. And I'd seen her in the blackmail picture with Rosetta and Jimmy. She looked up at me, then quickly nodded to Hector.

"*Senor,*" he said. "Thees ees Lupe Vasquez. She has bad trouble. *La situacion esta de la patada.* You must help her."

"What trouble?"

He motioned toward the table. "*Por favor, senor.* You seet down."

I shuffled across the kitchen and slumped into a chair opposite the girl.

Hector sat next to me, and Camilla followed and put two more coffee cups full of something dark and steaming on the table. I tried it. It was hot, and it tasted like the bottom of a peat bog. I put the cup back on the table and looked at Lupe.

"All right," I said. "Let's have it."

She glanced furtively at Hector, eyes liquid and frightened. She began in a strained half whisper, squeezing her hands on the edge of the table the way I'd seen Rosetta do at the Parrot. "Eet ees *Senor* Delmar. He ees wanting to kill me."

"Why?"

She shook her head. *"Quien sabe, senor?* Last night I am in thee dressing room at El Cotorra Azul, next to *Senor* Delmar's office. I hear heem talking to that man—*Senor* Voss. He say eet ees to send thee message." She paused. "I am afraid, *senor*. That *hombre—el albino.* He ees very bad—*brujo diabolico.*"

She brought her hands up and rubbed them over her arms as if she felt a chill. I'd seen a lot of that lately.

She went on. "I wait until they leave thee office. Then I sneak out thee window and run into thee downtown. I hide there in thee *mercado* until Hector come and bring me here." Suddenly she reached out and grabbed my wrist and squeezed hard. "Please, *senor*. Hector say you are good man, *muy abasado*—very smart. He say you will help. Don't let them find me, *senor*. *Por favor.*"

"What can I do?"

Now she wrapped both hands around my wrist. *"Por favor, senor.* Please. They have already kill Rosetta."

I watched a single tear trace a line down her cheek and settle into a little cleft by the corner of her mouth. "What else did Delmar say?"

She knitted her forehead into tawny ridges. "Nothing to *Senor* Voss. But there was another man in thee office. He ees already there when I go to thee dressing room. They talk very low, and then thee man leave. Then *Senor* Delmar, he ees *furioso* man—*very* angry. I hear heem throw something against thee wall. That ees when he call for *Senor* Voss. He say to find me and Rosetta and to make us talk. Then he say to kill us." She squeezed both fists hard on the table, nails digging into her palms. Suddenly her voice became shrill. *"Senor,* I know nothing—nada. Why he want to kill me?"

"Take it easy," I said. "A guy like Delmar could have a hundred reasons. Is that all you heard?"

She sighed and glanced at Hector again, then looked down at the table. She brought the words up with a lot of effort, like a sick man getting out of bed. "I hear your name, *senor. Senor* Delmar, he ees *muy loco.* He talk of settling accounts with *el Coronel.* I don't know what he mean." She hesitated. "Then he say after you geeve heem what he want, he kill you too."

I sat back in the chair and watched her. She kept staring down, her hands balled into a tight fist on the edge of the table.

"Yeah," I said *"Muy loco."* I turned to Hector.

"Why not go to the sheriff and ask him for protection?"

Hector made a spitting motion and twisted his mouth into a snarl. "He geeve us nothing, *senor.* To him we are *nada.* We are just…beaners." He swallowed hard, as if the word made him gag.

I let out a long slow breath and tried to clear my head. "Let's back up and try again," I said. "I'm a little slow at this hour. What about the other man with Delmar? Do you know him?"

Her eyes were heavy and moist as she looked up. "No, *senor. No lo conozco.* I see heem sometimes at thee club weeth *Senor* Delmar. But I don't know heem."

"Can you describe him?"

She nodded and held her hand up past her head to show his height "About so. A round man—heavy. And dressed good. Always wearing a dark suit."

"An Anglo?"

"No, *senor. Chicano.* They say he ees *burocrata."*

Hector pulled on my sleeve. "That means he ees with thee government, *senor."*

I nodded and kept looking at the girl. "And you're sure you don't know him?"

Suddenly her features clouded. She put her elbows on the table and placed her hands against her temples. "I hear hees name once. Eet ees Ben…Ben…"

"Benitez?"

Her eyes flashed wide, and she sat up. "*Si*, Benitez."

I felt a cold stab in the pit of my stomach, the way you feel when you bet against the dealer and he turns up the last ace.

"Look," I said. "I don't know if I can help. But you've got to tell me all of it. Not just the part about Delmar."

Lupe stared at me across the table. Her face turned quizzical. "*Si, senor?*"

"I know that you and Rosetta were involved with Jimmy Wearing. And I know that the two of you and the Colonel's redskin—*el piel roja*—set him up for some phony blackmail pictures."

Her hands seemed to jump up by themselves and cover her mouth. She looked wide-eyed, first at Hector, then at me.

"If I'm going to help," I said, "you've got to spill it all."

A dark cream flush crept up the sides of her neck. She looked at me for a long moment, then nodded.

"All right," I nodded back. "Tell me about that night at the hotel."

She brought her hands down slowly and rubbed them together. She placed her words as carefully as a blackjack dealer lays out a hand. "Thee Colonel's man, he say we play thee treek on Jeemy."

"Yeah," I said. "Some trick. How did you get him to the room?"

She stared into her cup. "We tell heem there is a friend upstairs, that we have thee party."

"Did you give him anything to put him out?"

She looked up quickly and shook her head. "Oh no, *senor*. We not do that to Jeemy. "She hesitated again. "Besides, *senor*. He ees always *muy borracho—very* drunk. He come weeth us to thee room and then just fall on thee bed."

"Uh-huh," I said. "Then what?"

She shrugged. "Then Rosetta and me, we get undressed, and thee Colonel's man, he take thee peectures. Then we get dressed again and we leave."

"What else?"

"*Nada, senor*. He pay us and take us to thee lobby, and we wait for thee taxi."

"Did Jimmy wake up?"

She shook her head again. "Oh, no. He ees *muy* borracho"

"Did you see anybody else?"

"No, *senor*." She thought for a minute and then her eyes flashed. "Wait. *Si*." She brightened with a hint of recognition. "Two men in thee hall. Eet ees while the Colonel's man ees paying us. First, I not remember, but I do know one of thee men. He ees thee doctor. I meet heem once weeth Jeemy."

"What about the other man?"

She frowned. *"No lo conozco, senor.* A stranger. He ees tall and *muy pslido*—pale, weeth light hair and thee mustache. *Y muy..."* She blushed again. *"Muy maricon.* You know, like thee woman."

I felt another icy pang in my stomach. I didn't have to be wide awake to know the man she was describing was Willis Ordway. "What were they doing?"

"They fight, *senor.* Loud at first. Then they stop when we come into thee hall."

"Did you hear any of it?"

She shook her head and held her hands palms up over the table. *"Nada.* Thee Indian take us to thee lobby and wait weeth us until Esteban come. While we are there, thee doctor leave too—een very beeg hurry. Then we leave, and thee Indian go back up thee stairs—he say eet ees to take care of Jeemy."

Her eyes fluttered a little, and her voice softened. "I guess we do thees theeng to Jeemy. I guess ees not good treek."

"How did you two get involved with him?"

She sat back and stared off over my head. Her mouth tried to smile. "He come into thee club one night and see us een thee gambling room. He say he ees having thee party and he want us to come. He take us to every place een Juarez—spend *mucho dinero.* Then we go to thee desert and watch thee sunrise." She sat for a minute, enjoying the memory. When it faded, she looked at me. "Afterwards he come back to thee club—two, three times a week. He say he like to have us weeth heem." She shrugged. "He ees very polite and very reech. So, we go."

"Did you ever see him alone? I mean, one at a time?"

"No, *senor*. Always together."

"Did he ever take you to his apartment?"

She shook her head. "No. Always to thee bars and thee nightclubs. Jeemy say he like thee crowds."

"Then where did you...?"

I didn't have-to finish the question. The flush crept up into her cheeks again. "We never deed, *senor*. Jeemy never... I theenk he cannot, because... because of thee war."

I nodded. "'Did Delmar know you were seeing Jimmy?"

"Oh, *si*. He say eet ees good we go with Jeemy." Her eyes clouded and she bit her lip. "But always afterwards he breeng us into hees office. He want to know everytheeng Jeemy say, especially about hees father."

"What did you tell him?"

She shook her head again. *"Nada, senor*. Jeemy never talk about heem. After a while, *Senor* Delmar become angry. Then he say he want us to ask Jeemy about thee Colonel." She cocked her head and let a puzzled look fall into her face. "And about...about thee leetle statues."

"Did you ask?"

"Si. But Jeemy say eet ees not to ask, that they are the ancient evil." She made the sign of the cross. *"Es una cosa diabolica*. We tell *Senor* Delmar, and he become *furioso."* Her eyes filled with remembered pain. "He heet me, with hees feest." She placed her hands flat on the table and searched my face. "Ees eet thee statues, *senor*? Ees that why he...he kill Rosetta? Why he want to kill me?"

"Maybe." I turned to Hector. "Can she stay here tonight?"

He scratched his chin and looked puzzled. *"Si, senor*. But what we do?"

"We don't do anything," I said. "You take me back to the hotel so I can get some sleep. Then you meet me there again in the morning."

"Si, senor." He nodded eagerly. "Then what we do?

"Then we pick up some people and put them on a train. After that we come back and get Lupe so she can go and tell her story to Sanchez."

I could feel the girl tensing across the table. "You'll be all right," I said to her. "Delmar won't try anything until late tomorrow. Sanchez is a good cop. He won't let anything happen to you."

Lupe reached over the table and put her hand on my arm. *"Senor,* how you know *Senor* Delmar will wait?"

I stood up. "Because I'm the one he's after. And he won't be coming for me until tomorrow night."

She took my hand in both of hers. Her eyes gave me a message that didn't need words. *"Gracias, senor."*

"Don't thank me yet."

I walked out of the kitchen and left Lupe wringing her hands on top of the table. Then I ambled across the living room, put my hat on, and let myself out into the dry night air. I wondered how many more would die for the little statues.

Hector chattered something to Camilla, then followed me out. We got into the cab and rode back to the hotel without speaking. Hector seemed to want to say something, but he kept it to himself. Finally, the cab lumbered up to the entrance to the Del Norte. I started to get out, but Hector leaned across the seat and grabbed my arm.

"Senor," he said. "What you say to Lupe about *Senor* Delmar. Ees true? He ees coming for you?"

"Yeah," I said. "It's true."

He inhaled deliberately and pulled himself up tall in the seat and gave me a look of frail determination. He was only five feet and change, but he looked taller—a funny little guy that I couldn't help liking. "I help, *senor.* I come when you say."

"What time does the train leave?"

"Noon, senor."

"Be here at eleven."

I got out of the cab and plodded into the lobby. It was as empty and still as a dead man's house. I rode the elevator up to the fourth floor and made the trek up the hall, moving like a sleepwalker. I turned the key in the lock and then hesitated. The thought hit me that someone could be waiting in the room. But no one was.

234

Morning sounds the same in every hotel. The practiced rustling. The steady building of activity. Morning came through my window a little before nine with the sound of a truck being backed into an alley four floors below. I lay there and listened to the sound of footsteps passing in the hall and tried to measure the size of my headache.

I got up and managed a shower and a halfhearted shave. Then I sat on the bed, cradled the phone in my lap, and dialed Jimmy's apartment. The buzz on the other end barely started when Randolph answered in a voice as untroubled as running water.

"This is Garrett," I said. "How is he?"

"Mr. James is still asleep, sir. Shall I wake him?"

"Not yet. Has anyone called or come poking around?"

"No, sir. No one."

"Good," I said. "Has Jimmy got a suitcase there?"

"Yes, sir."

"Then pack it for him. He's going on a long trip. Let him sleep for a while, then wake him up, wash his face, and get him ready. I'll be there a little before noon."

"As you say, sir." He hung up.

I held the plunger down while I rooted through the phone book for Gabrielle's office number. I dialed it and waited impatiently through half a dozen rings. No answer. I fished around on the nightstand and found the scrap of paper with her home number. I dialed it and waited. Again, no answer. I felt the skin on the backs of my hands twitching as I pushed the plunger once more and dialed the number for Wearing Manor. This time, Monica answered.

"It's Garrett," I said. "I'm looking for Gabrielle."

"She isn't here, Mickey."

"Has she called?"

"No, she hasn't. No one's heard from her. Is anything wrong?"

"Probably nothing. I'll be in touch." I hung up.

The memory of the two men on the elevator darted into my head. I stood up and rubbed my hands over my face, and looked at them. They were shaking.

I strapped on the Luger, climbed into my suit, and beat it downstairs as if the building were on fire. The Buick was waiting in the lot next to a weathered Chevy station wagon with an elderly couple standing beside it arguing over who should drive. I got in the Buick, gunned the engine, and left them there in a shower of gravel, arguing over who should call the cops.

The car rumbled across town fast enough to earn me a hack license, and I let the tires squeal as I pulled up in front of the Kenwood Building. I went in and mashed the elevator button until the doors rolled open. The elevator seemed to take all morning, getting me to the second floor.

When the doors rolled open again, I bolted across the hall and barged into the outer office in time to see Angela preening at the desk. She looked up at me with a sour eye, then went on dabbing a lipstick over her mouth as I walked past her and pushed open the inner office door.

The room was as I had last seen it: papers and briefs piled on the desk, books in place on the shelves, filing cabinets closed. There was no telling when Gabrielle might have been there. I turned and walked back out by the front desk as Angela was finishing her paint job.

"Where is she?" I asked.

The girl casually picked up her appointment book and made a show of looking through it. "Let's see." Finally, she closed the book and gave me a go-to-hell smirk. "You don't seem to have an appointment."

"I said, where is she?" This time, the bark was real.

She folded her arms and kept on smirking at me.

"If you mean Miss Wearing, she's not here."

I put both hands on the desk, leaned toward her, and snarled in her face. "Listen, sister. I'm in no mood for games. So just knock off the fancy-pants act, or your next job will be in Albuquerque."

The smirk slid off her face, and she made a quick gulping sound. "I'm sorry. I didn't mean…"

"Sure," I said. "Did she leave a note?"

"No, she didn't." She reached over by the typewriter, picked up an envelope, and handed it to me. "But I found this when I came in this morning.

Someone slipped it under the door."

I took it in both hands and stood holding it. I felt like kicking a hole in the desk. It was a plain unmarked envelope, sealed, with one word penciled on the front—"Garrett." I tore open the envelope and stood looking at a single sheet of paper with some crude handwriting.

Your girlfriend stays under wraps until after you deliver the jade. Be in your hotel room at five o'clock. Be alone. No cops—otherwise, no dame.

I read the note a second time, then slowly folded up the paper and put it in my pocket.

Angela read the expression on my face. "What is it?"

I started to say something, but the words just lay like sawdust in the back of my throat.

Chapter Twenty-Five

Four people were dead, and I had nothing to show but torn ribs, a hunk of green rock, and a sleepless night. Delmar had been a step ahead of me at every turn. And now he had Gabrielle.

The Buick drove itself through town, drifted up onto Piedras, and eased to a stop in front of Jimmy's apartment. I got out and pushed through the gate, and watched the door open in front of me.

Randolph stood there in his shirt sleeves, eyeing me with mild irritation. "You're early," he said as I stepped through the door.

"Not early enough."

"I beg your pardon?"

"Skip it," I said. "How's Jimmy?"

"Still asleep." He folded his arms and fastened a dark stare on me. "I expected Miss Gabrielle to be with you."

"Something came up at the office, and she'll be tied up all day. We had to change the plans. Can you stay here with Jimmy?"

He stood without moving for most of a minute, then nodded. "I'll have to call the house."

"Of course," I said. "Tell the Colonel you're with me. Tell him I'm looking after Gabrielle and Jimmy." A doleful chuckling noise came up in the back of my throat. "He'll understand."

"Will he?"

I avoided the question and turned away. I walked over and looked into the bedroom. Jimmy was lying on his back under a blanket, arms splayed, breathing in slow, shallow snores. I turned back to the living room.

"Is there anything to drink around here?" I asked.

Randolph looked at me with something just this side of contempt. "Of course not." He nodded toward the bedroom. "For him, it's poison. And I would think it early in the day, even for you."

I looked back toward the bedroom. The shallow breathing continued, a little unsteady, maybe a trace slower and more quiet.

I looked back at Randolph. "I guess you're right. I'll call you this afternoon."

I stepped past him and headed for the door, but he clamped his fingers around my arm with the gentle pressure of a drill press. He held me fast and spoke in a voice that had plunged a couple of octaves.

"It has occurred to me, Mr.Garrett, that I am placing a great deal of trust in you."

I pried his fingers loose and shook my arm to keep the circulation going. "It's occurred to me too." I opened the door and went outside, leaving him standing there.

I couldn't take the chance of being seen driving the Buick around town, so I headed back to the hotel. The lot had thinned out by the time I got there, and I pulled into a space right in front of the main entrance. A tall, somber-looking doorman in a green cap and jacket was standing in front of the porch, waiting to hold something green in his hand. I walked up and tipped my hat to him. "Nice morning."

He gave me a noncommittal glance, then stared out over the parking lot. "Yes, sir."

I reached casually into my pocket and brought out a fin. I folded it over once and then reached out and shook the man's hand, pressing the bill into his palm. As I did, I motioned over my shoulder and invited him to look at the Buick. "Keep an eye on it for me, will you? Can't be too careful with all these Juarez hack drivers around."

He cracked a smile as wide as a garage door and shoved the bill into his pocket. "Yes, sir. That I will, sir."

"Thanks," I said and started up the stairs. He'd look after the Buick, all right. And he'd remember the guy who gave him the five-spot.

239

On my way across the lobby, I waved to the two old gents who had taken up their usual spot in the sitting area. They halted their debate long enough to wave back and then look at each other, wondering who the hell they had just waved at.

The morning crew was behind the desk, rustling papers and arranging keys. I gave them a noisy greeting, laid another five on the counter, and asked to have breakfast sent up to my room. A thin character, with a youngish face and thick brown hair that smelled of Vitalis, took the five and handed me a note. It said simply, "Call Sanchez."

The kid behind the counter licked his lips as I folded the note and put it in my pocket. "Will there be anything else, sir?"

"No," I said. "Tell the boys in the kitchen to snap it up with breakfast."

"Yes, sir." He nodded and followed me with his eyes all the way into the elevator.

The maid was just finishing with my room when I got upstairs. I smiled and handed her one more five, and she walked away, clutching it to her as if she'd just won the daily double.

I took off my hat and coat, slipped out of my shoes, and sat on the bed. Business as usual, just like any other morning. It didn't matter that Gabrielle had been kidnapped by a ruthless gangster. It didn't matter that he was demanding a pair of jade figures and that I only had one of them. It didn't even matter that I might not see another morning. All that mattered was that a guy in Room 417 was giving away pictures of Lincoln.

I picked up the phone and dialed the police station. The usual desk sergeant with the usual tired voice answered. I told him who I was and asked for Deputy Sheriff Sanchez. He told me to wait. Business as usual.

Sanchez came on the line and gave me the usual greeting. "Goddammit, where are you?"

"In bed."

"It better be a hospital bed," he bawled. "What the hell have you been doing? It's not enough that the Saens girl was killed last night. This morning we found Kintner. Were you the one who called in here about him?"

"Just being the Good Samaritan," I said. "Always trying to cooperate with the police."

"Goddammit," he said again. "You collect bodies the way most people pick up lint. I've got a mind to throw your ass in the clink."

"Go ahead. I can use some time off. Weems and Stonebreaker can help you flush out Delmar."

He sighed heavily. "All right, all right. Just get down here."

"Not yet," I said. "I need some time."

"What for?" he barked.

"I'm onto something, but I need time to play it out. Just give me twenty-four hours."

"Don't give me that crap," he yelled. "I want to know what's going on, and I want to know now."

"Listen," I said. "Right now, I'm all you've got. Maybe I can help you get something on Delmar. But you've got to give me time to set it up."

I could hear his fingers squeezing the receiver. He let out a long, slow breath, and his voice became as quiet as snow falling.

"Garrett, my neck is stuck way out on this." He hesitated, and I could almost see the lines deepening around his eyes. "I'll give you until five o'clock."

"Make it six."

He laughed hoarsely. "All right, you son of a bitch. Six."

His voice eased again, but now it held traces of worry. "Hey, Garrett. That crack you made last night about Gabrielle's apartment. What did you mean?"

"Six o'clock," I said and hung up.

Breakfast came, and I poked at it, then put the tray out in the hall. I opened the curtains, stretched out on the bed, and tried adding things up on my fingers again. Delmar was making a desperate play, one that could backfire on him, even blow up in his face. And he wasn't a man to take risks. That meant something was squeezing him. Suddenly, he had a lot to gain or a lot to lose. Either way, I was going to be his pigeon. Even if I could find the other piece of jade, even if I could get both figures to him by tonight, he couldn't afford to let me walk away. There was too much at stake. I was riding into a sucker play, and I knew it. But Delmar had Gabrielle.

I lay there, lit a cigarette, and watched a patch of sunlight slowly slide across the wall.

At eleven sharp, there was a quiet tap, and I opened the door for Hector. He stepped in and stood looking as resolute as an alderman on election day.

"We go thee train, *senor?*"

I shook my head. "No, Hector. The plans have changed. Did you tell anyone in the lobby you were coming up here for me?"

"No, *senor.*"

"Good," I said. "I've made myself popular, and the hotel staff will be expecting me to be up here all day. You go back down and get into your cab. Drive out of the lot and then come around into this alley." I nodded toward the window. "I'll meet you there in five minutes."

"*Si, senor.*" He nodded abruptly and left the room.

I put on my hat and coat, slipped on my shoes, then went over to the dresser. I opened a drawer and took out the .45 that Voss had been careless enough to leave when he visited me at the Desert View Motel. I jerked out the clip and checked it. It was full. I thought Voss might be missing his gun. I thought he might want it back.

I put the "Do not disturb" sign on the doorknob, stuck the gun in my coat, and went down the fire stairs to the back of the hotel. Hector was obediently waiting in the alley. I climbed into the cab and crouched low in the seat.

"Where we go, *senor?*"

"Juarez."

Hector set his jaw and stepped on the gas, and the cab clattered out into heavy traffic. I stayed in a crouch, glancing up occasionally to look for a tail. I didn't see one. Maybe half a dozen Juarez cabs rumbled by as we approached the bridge. But no one paid any attention to them, or to us. I was just another tourist being ferried across the border. So far, so good.

As we crossed the bridge into Juarez, I finally eased up and sat back in the seat. I pointed the way for Hector, and the cab nosed slowly through the crowded streets into the market district in the center of the city.·

It was almost noon, and the peddlers and shopkeepers lined the sidewalks, waving trinkets and signs, and shouting their daily chorus of border-town commerce to the people passing by. Every now and then, a few would stop to examine something—jewelry, tapestry, pottery, even leather boots. At the first sign of interest, there would be a shuffling of feet, some fast talking, and the bargaining would start. It was a scene that had played itself out that way for generations.

We cruised slowly for a couple of blocks until I spotted a little shop just off the corner on a side street with dusty hand-carved onyx and wood statues in the window. Hector swung the cab around and parked, and we went in. As I came through the door, a wizened old man with gray hair and tired eyes came over and made a quick study of my clothes. With an almost toothless smile, he tried to interest me in a *porron*—a hand-blown glass beaker with a long spout. Something for pouring my Scotch. I waved him off, and Hector kept him busy while I looked around.

Under a glass counter at the rear of the shop I found a wood carving of an owl, about ten inches high and as ugly as an old traffic cop. Next to it were two rows of onyx chess pieces, and lying behind them a pair of gray cloth sacks with drawstrings. I asked the man about the owl, and he said I could have it for fifteen bucks. I told him ten, and only if I could have something nice to carry it in, like one of the cloth sacks. He hesitated, rattled off some lingo I didn't get, and made another survey of my suit. Then he pulled out one of the sacks and put the owl in it. I paid him, took the bag, and went outside. Hector followed me, looking as if he'd just seen someone take off all his clothes in the middle of the street.

"*Senor*," he said. "That man. He cheat you."

I grinned at him. "Uh-huh."

"Why you want thee owl?"

"I know somebody who likes birds."

We climbed into the cab, and Hector sat shaking his head. "*No comprende, senor*. Where we go now?"

"Out of town," I said. "Go east, along the river. Find me someplace private."

The cab tiptoed out of the city and then eased onto a flat dusty stretch of road called El Camino Del Rio. We drove through about three miles of sand and mesquite along the parched riverbed, until the road turned southeast into a series of rock formations. Tall jagged boulders, their exposed surfaces worn grayish-white from daily assaults by the desert, stood like sentries at the base of more foothills. This was where the Rockies picked up again and grew into northeastern Mexico.

After another mile, Hector pointed ahead to a bend in the road where a dirt trail fell away to the right and curled behind some rocks. "Thee canyon, *senor.*"

I nodded, and the cab swung around the rocks and ambled slowly into a funnel-shaped canyon that looked as inviting as an empty grave. Even at midday, the jutting formations along the rim hovered over angular shadows. Below them, the sun made a cauldron of the rest of the canyon, searing the rocks and the dirt path along the bottom.

Hector slowed the cab and said, "Thees ees eet, *senor.* Nobody come here."

"I can see why," I said dryly.

About thirty yards up one side of the canyon, I spotted a series of wedge-shaped rocks jutting upwards as if someone had buried part of a picket fence and left the top showing. I told Hector to stop, and I got out, took the bag with the carved owl in it, and made my way carefully up the slope. Behind the pointing rocks I knelt down and scooped out a small hole in the loose sand and gravel, then I took the owl out of the bag and replaced it with Voss's .45. The silencer made the gun too long to fit in the bag, so, I took off the attachment and put it in my pocket. Then I pulled the drawstring tight, planted the bag, and filled in the hole, so that only the string was showing.

As I started down toward the cab, an arid gust of wind muscled through the canyon, stirring up the sand and filling my nostrils with the same tart, uneasy smell of the Santa Anas that blow through LA. Hector stepped out of the cab and looked intently up at the sky above the canyon rim.

"Ayee. Thee desert wind, *senor.* She ees making ready."

"That makes two of us," I said and climbed back into the cab.

Chapter Twenty-Six

I t was early afternoon when we got back to the Del Norte. Hector pulled around on a side street and then edged up into the alley behind the hotel. I got out and leaned on the door.

"Is Lupe all right?" I asked.

"*Si, senor.·* But very afraid. *Que se cagaba de susto.*"

"Then, go home and stay with her," I said. "Wait until late this afternoon, around five. Then take her in to see Sanchez." I tossed the owl on the front seat. "Give him this."

Hector picked up the carving, frowned, and looked at me. "What I tell heem, *senor?*"

"Tell him it's the Bird of Death."

He frowned again, then put the cab in gear and backed out of the alley. I slipped through the back door, climbed the fire stairs, and went up the hall to my room. Nobody hollered at me. The "Do not disturb" sign was still on the door. I left it there and let myself in. The room was untouched.

I dropped my coat and hat on the chair and fished the silencer out of my pocket. I studied it. It was an uncommon device, illegal in most states. And it was used only by professionals. I held it up and looked down the muzzle. I could almost see Voss and Delmar leering at me from the other side. I shivered and dropped it in the drawer of the nightstand.

I picked up the phone, called downstairs, and ordered a bottle. Then I pulled out the Luger, popped the clip, and slipped the cartridge out of the breech. I emptied the clip, slid it back into the handle, and stuck the Luger back under my arm. It felt a little lighter, but not enough to pay attention

245

to. It would take a pro to notice.

A soft rapping on the door told me the bartender was calling. I unstrapped the Luger, put it in the nightstand, and opened the door. A fresh-faced kid in a hotel uniform came in and put a tray with a glass and a bottle of Vat 69 on the dresser.

He looked at me as if he wanted permission to go to the can. "Tommy just came on duty, sir. He said you'd want this brand."

I grinned and reached into my pocket, and handed him a pair of fives. "It's good company on a lonesome day," I said. "Here's one for you and one for Tommy. Tell him thanks, and I'll see him later."

The kid took the money, rolled his eyes, made a short choking sound, and almost fell over the chair on his way out the door. I stood there grinning at nothing: Garrett, the big spender.

I cracked open the bottle and bought myself a drink. It slipped down almost without my knowing it, so I poured another and stretched out on the bed. I lit up a Lucky and nursed the rest of the day with the rest of the pack and the Scotch. I lay there and played with the thought of retirement. Maybe Gabrielle was right. I could do without this racket.

The level in the bottle fell slowly as the minutes drifted into hours. I dozed off a few times, but not enough to call it sleep. Mostly, I watched the same patch of sun climb slowly back up the wall, making the same quiet trip it made every afternoon. It had just reached the ceiling when the phone rang. I didn't need to look at my watch. Five o'clock.

I waited for two more rings and then picked it up. The same crusty voice rattled on the other end. "Okay, Shamus. The boss says to bring the goods down to the club at eight. And be alone."

I took a deep breath and squeezed the receiver. "Nuts to that. Tell your boss I'll be in the canyon just below El Camino Del Rio at eight."

There was a pause. I could hear a hand being placed over the receiver. I waited.

The voice started again. "What the hell are you tryin' ta pull? We got the dame."

"What the hell do I care? I've got the goods, and I'm ready to deal. Tell him to be there at eight with the girl and twenty-five G's. Otherwise, I'll find another buyer." I didn't wait for an answer. I hung up.

I went over to the sink and peeled off my shirt. It was soaking wet. I tossed it on the floor and stood there staring at something ugly in the mirror. The phone rang again, about eight times before giving up. I went over to the bed, poured out some courage, and held up the glass. "Here's to long shots," I said out loud.

I sat on the bed and watched the phone as it rang once more. It was an angry ring, harsh, insistent, demanding to be noticed. It seemed to have a life of its own.

I watched it through several dozen rings in a very long hour. Finally, I picked up the receiver and held it to my ear without speaking. There was a heavy silence, then the familiar raspy voice. "Know who this is?"

"Yeah," I said. "How're you doing with the ladies tonight?"

His voice took on the friendly tone of a knife point. "Cut the smart stuff, wise guy. Just get your ass down here. Your time's up."

Without realizing he couldn't see me, I shook my head. "Uh-uh. You know where I'll be and when. Bring the girl and twenty-five grand. I'll wait ten minutes. If you don't show, then you can read about the jade in the papers."

He yelled at someone near the phone, a torrent of angry words I didn't have to hear to understand. He breathed heavily into the mouthpiece. "The dame means nothin' to you?"

I let him hear a shrug in my voice. "Money from her old man, *if* she's healthy."

He snorted out a nasty laugh. "Playin' both ends, huh." His voice settled into a frosty quiet. "You really got 'em—both pieces?"

"You're wasting my time," I yelled at him.

"All right, all right," he said quickly. "I'll be there. But listen, Garrett. No funny stuff. And no law—not if you want to see your girlfriend above ground again."

The line went dead in my hand.

I cradled the receiver and turned around just in time to watch the door trembling on its hinges from the impact of the fist that was trying to punch

247

a hole in it. I swore under my breath. It wasn't a time for callers. I waited until the door stopped recoiling, then pulled it open a few inches. Sanchez barged into the room, knocking me aside, and slammed the door behind him. He glared at me with the warming manner of a drill sergeant nursing a boil.

"Goddammit, Garrett. What the hell's going on?"

"You're early," I said.

"I'll just bet I am," he said. "Your cab driver friend just brought Lupe Vasquez in…with this." He pulled the owl out of his hip pocket and threw it on the bed. "What the hell were they supposed to do, run interference?"

I grinned at him. "You're better than I thought. Where are they now?"

"Down at the station," he growled. "With Jesse."

"Good. He can show them around the city."

"What he'll do is put her in protective custody, which is where I should have you."

I kept on grinning. "Drink?"

He glared and folded his arms and didn't say anything. I took that for yes. I poured a couple of ounces of the Vat 69 into a glass, handed it to him, and watched him drain it without blinking. He sat on the bed and leaned forward, rolling the glass around in his fingers and staring at it.

"Christ, Garrett," he said. "I've broken rules on this. You're a material witness in a couple of killings, and I've been letting you run loose. You can't just leave me on a string."

"I gave you Lupe."

He sent me a grim smirk. "Yeah, and that's about as good to me as last year's calendar. Short of nabbing Delmar, trying to ice her up here in the street, I can't do a thing. And he's not that stupid."

I didn't say anything.

"There's something else." His voice got quiet. "I can't find Jimmy or Gabrielle. Jimmy's a flake. But I've known Gabrielle a long time, and she wouldn't just disappear. I'm starting to think I should be worried. So, tell me what the hell's going on."

I poured a swig, drank it slowly, and took my time lighting a Lucky.

Sanchez was too smart for anything but the truth. The trick was not to give him the part that really counted. I looked at my watch. Already six-thirty.

"What's been going on is blackmail," I said. "Kintner was putting the bite on rich women by taking naked photos of them in his office. As a payoff, he'd get them to sell him art objects for little more than loose change and a promise to bury the pictures. All strictly legal. Then he'd turn around and sell the objects to Ordway at dealer's rates and pocket the difference."

He folded his arms and kept a steady eye on me. "I might've expected something like that. But what's it got to do with Delmar?"

"I think Kintner was fronting for him. And I think Jack Springer knew it. That's why he was killed."

"How do you know?"

I hesitated and thought about not involving Monica. "From a note and some receipts I found in his desk. The note said 'OK—antiques.' I think 'OK' really meant Ordway and Kintner. Springer had just come back from California, and he had a hotel receipt from Brentwood, not far from Ordway's address. And the morning before he was killed, he had already been poking around Kintner's place. Maybe Kintner saw him and tipped off Delmar."

Sanchez shook his head, frowned, and looked at me uneasily. "I dunno, Garrett. It's pretty damn thin. Knowing Kintner, I wouldn't put it past him. But it's just small potatoes. Why should Delmar even be involved? And if what you say about Kintner being a front is true, then why is he dead?"

"Because he was holding out, keeping some of the art objects and selling them for himself. Maybe Delmar found out and sent Voss after him."

He shook his head again. "That doesn't make sense. Delmar wouldn't have him rubbed out just for a few trinkets."

"No," I agreed. "But he might do it if he thought Kintner was holding back something really valuable. Something that even the Mexican authorities wanted so badly they'd pay a bundle and look the other way for anybody who could fork it over—no matter what it took. Something like the Marina Jade."

Sanchez stood up. His eyes were as wide as saucers. "Are you serious?"

I nodded. "And now that Kintner's dead, Delmar thinks I've got the jade."

"Do you?"

Before I could answer, another fist started bruising the door. Once more, and it would be nothing but kindling. Sanchez watched as I took the familiar stroll over to the door, pulled it open, and stepped aside.

Jimmy Wearing strode in and wrapped a burly hand around my arm. He was clear-eyed, clean-shaven, and not happy. "Look, Garrett," he snarled. "I've been cooped up all day with Randolph. He says you..." He looked over and saw Sanchez, and his face went blank. "What's going on?"

Sanchez scowled at him. "Where have you been? And where's Gabrielle?"

Jimmy started to answer, but I interrupted him. "Listen, kid, I'm afraid I've got some bad news. Your friend Rosetta is dead. She and Dr. Kintner were murdered last night."

He stood blinking, moving his mouth like a marionette without sound. He took an unsteady step toward me, and I took both his arms and guided him down into one of the chairs. As I started to straighten up, he grabbed my shirtsleeve.

"Why?" he whimpered. "Why would anybody want to kill Rosetta? She never hurt anybody."

I shot a glance over at Sanchez. He gave me an impatient scowl and paced over into the corner of the room. I turned back to Jimmy.

"She was running with a bad crowd, kid. Looks like she and the doc tried to mix it up with Rudy Delmar and got in over their heads."

He shook his head slowly, mechanically, like a wind-up toy. His eyes were low, fixed on an empty part of the floor. His voice had that quiet detachment that sometimes precedes shock.

"She's not dead. It's a mistake."

"No mistake," I said. "They're both dead."

His head kept moving from side to side, but his eyes didn't budge. "She can't be dead. She's my friend."

I grabbed him by the lapels and shook him, hard. All I needed now was for him to do another folding act. "Maybe you didn't hear me," I said, "Dr. Kintner's dead too."

He came back out of his reverie and glared at me. "I heard you."

"Delmar may have killed them both. Doesn't that bother you?"

He lifted my hands roughly off his jacket and stood up. "Of course, it does. Only nobody's going to miss Kintner—an old queen with a pipe full of imported hop. But Rosetta was my friend. She and Lupe are the only ones who never let me down." Then, almost as an afterthought: "that is, besides my sister."

I started to say something, but Sanchez broke in. "Garrett, this'll keep. I asked you a question, and I want an answer."

I looked at him. "What question?"

"Quit stalling," he snapped. "First, you tell me you've got an angle. Now you say Delmar pegs you for having the jade. Have you got it?"

I looked over at Jimmy. He had settled back into the chair and begun brooding by himself, as if Sanchez and I had left the room. I looked at my watch again. It was closing in on seven. I walked over to the nightstand.

"I might have a line." I opened the drawer and took out Kintner's notebook. "Take a look at this."

Sanchez came over and took the notebook. He switched on the reading lamp and turned away from me, holding the book in the light. As he began flipping the pages, I eased the Luger out of the drawer, turned it around in my hand, and cracked the butt end across the base of his skull. He fell over quietly and lay face-down on the bed. I felt his neck for a pulse. It was there. He'd wake up later, but he wouldn't like it.

Jimmy jumped out of the chair and stood wide-eyed and gasping as if someone had just rammed a two-by-four into his stomach. "What the hell are you doing? Are you crazy?"

"I've got a date," I snapped. "Where's Randolph?"

"He's down in the lobby, but..."

Without waiting, I picked up the phone. I called down to the desk and told them to send up an Indian.

A strained voice said, "An Indian, sir?"

"That's right," I told him. "Any Indian you happen to find in the lobby."

I hung up and saw Jimmy moving toward the bed. "Jimmy," I said slowly.

"I'm afraid there's more bad news. Gabrielle has been kidnapped."

He froze in his tracks. He brought his fists up, opened them, and stretched the fingers out toward me. They were trembling. "No!"

I nodded. "Delmar's got her—down in Juarez. I'm going there now."

He stood staring at me, a kind of quiet fury simmering behind his eyes. Then suddenly, he raised both fists over his head and yelled, "No!"

He started to yell again, but I stepped toward him and gave him an open-handed crack flush on the jaw. He lowered his hands slowly and just stood blinking.

"Dammit," I said. "You've got to hold yourself together...for her."

He swallowed hard and nodded. He watched while I strapped on the Luger and put on my coat. As I picked up my hat, he exhaled heavily and spoke in a voice as cold and hard as stainless steel. "I'm going with you."

"Uh-uh," I said. "I need you here. You and Randolph have to look after Sanchez. I couldn't tell him about Gabrielle, or he'd have gone storming down there after Delmar and loused things up. And I had to sap him, because I'm running out of time. When he comes around, it'll take the two of you to hold him down. I want you to keep him here until around eight. Then you can fill him in. Once he's got the picture, the three of you can come down to Juarez after me. I'll be in the canyon off El Camino Del Rio." I watched him. He hadn't moved a muscle. "Have you got all that?"

He kept looking at me with the same fixity of expression. "Will she be all right?"

"If she's not, some others won't be either."

I went back to the nightstand and took out the green-handled dagger. I reached down and slipped it into my sock and covered it with the leg of my trousers. Jimmy watched me with an odd sort of fascination.

"What're you going to do with that?" he asked.

"Return it to somebody."

I went into the hall and almost walked into Randolph. He grunted, and I pointed to the room, then ducked into the elevator. It took me five minutes to get the Jade Princess from Tommy. Another five got me into the Buick and out of the lot. It was quarter after seven.

Traffic was light, and I drove easily through town. As I started up the bridge to Juarez, a deep copper sun was dipping toward the mountains west of the city. As the sun moved lower, the wind came up higher and rattled a hail of sand against the car. It was that same hot, dry wind that comes down out of the mountain passes around L.A. late in the season. It makes your hair bristle, and your skin start hopping. And it makes otherwise gentle souls think about mayhem and murder.

Chapter Twenty-Seven

I t was about twenty minutes short of eight when I turned onto El Camino Del Rio. Streaks of dying sunlight flared out over the canyon rim. They splashed against the far wall and trickled down into iridescent patches among the rocks, stopping about thirty yards from where I parked the Buick. On the near side, velvety shadows rolled down in deepening layers, like the tide moving toward shore, quietly consuming the land. I tucked the Jade Princess into my inside coat pocket, stepped outside, and listened to the wind. It moved in an anxious vortex around the canyon floor, then moaned through the rocky opening at the other end and ran out across the desert like a train rumbling into the distance. It seemed to be suggesting it was time to leave. I was inclined to agree.

All at once, the wind died, leaving the canyon empty and still, almost naked. I lit a cigarette, leaned against the car, and tried not to think about where I was. I thought about a frail, scared little man who had walked into my office a lifetime ago. I thought about a long, lonely train ride across the desert. I thought about time, about how it doesn't matter to you until it's almost gone. And I thought about Gabrielle.

I was just finishing my cigarette when the wind whirled through the canyon again, bringing a hard spray of sand and dust, and behind it the dull throbbing of an engine. The limousine moved cautiously around the rocks and rolled up to a stop directly behind the Buick. The doors opened, and Voss climbed out of the front seat. He walked up and stood half a dozen feet from me, arms folded, covering me with a limpid stare. He was followed by a plumpish Mexican in a dark blue suit. It was Julian Benitez. He stood and fidgeted and looked at me as if our paths had never crossed.

Rudy Delmar climbed out one of the rear doors and dragged Gabrielle roughly behind him. She looked tired and frightened, but I didn't see any bruises. She saw me and called out with a mixture of hope and dread.

"Michael!"

"Shut up," Delmar growled at her. He took her by the arm and led her up to the front of the limousine, and growled at her again. "Stay here and be quiet."

Benitez turned abruptly and said something to Delmar. Delmar listened to him and then said, "Look, you said your people don't care how they get the figures, just so they get 'em. Now, clam up."

Delmar moved around Benitez and stood next to Voss. Another gust of wind brought more dust, and Delmar squinted through it with a kind of reptilian sneer. I reached up slowly and pulled down my hat.

"Did you bring the money?" I asked him.

"First things first," he said.

His sneer widened, and he reached out and took hold of Gabrielle's arm. He put his other hand inside his coat pocket and kept it there, suggesting he was packing artillery. Then he nodded to Voss.

A heavy smell of liquor hit me in the face as Voss came over and went through the first part of a punishing frisk. He took the Luger and then felt the bulge in my inside pocket. He pulled out the sack, stepped back, and handed it to Delmar without taking his eyes off me while he hefted the Luger.

Delmar opened the sack and took out the figure. He looked at it, then handed it to Benitez. "This it?"

The Mexican turned the statue over in his hands several times, studying it. Finally, he looked up and nodded eagerly.

Delmar turned back to me. "Okay, smart guy. Where's the other one?"

"It's hidden," I said. "You'll get it when I get the money." I pointed toward Benitez. "What's he doing here?"

"Never mind," he snapped. "Just cough up."

"Uh-uh." I shook my head. "I like to know who I'm doing business with."

He gave me a hard glare that slowly eased into a nasty grin. "All right, since you're so curious. His name's Benitez. He's with the Mexican government. I made a deal with them to get the jade back. Ya see, to them, it's some kinda national treasure. They've been after it for years. And they'll be real grateful to anybody who brings it back. Once I turn over the jade, they make me a citizen with a diplomatic title. That way, I can travel up north all I want. And the Feds can't touch me.".

"Why the rush all of a sudden?"

Delmar snickered and looked at Benitez. The Mexican spoke to me. "There ees opposition, *senor*. Not everyone een Mexico City theenks we should be doing business weeth someone of *Senor* Delmar's...reputation."

I chuckled. "I could have guessed that. You had to conclude the deal before the opposition got too noisy." I shook my head and chuckled again. "Now it all fits. Only, you're going to have your hands full explaining away several murders."

His face turned ashen. "Murders, *senor?*" He swung around and spoke to Delmar. *"Senor,* I deed not theenk..."

Delmar put up a hand and interrupted him. "Don't listen to him. He's just blowin' like the wind."

"That's right," I said. "Like the wind through this canyon, stirring up the dust so you can see what's underneath. Maybe you'd like to know a little something about your future diplomat."

I looked back at Delmar. "Ever since Wearing ran you out of the country, you've been looking for a way to even the score. You already had your hooks in Kintner from the Wallis killing, so you brought him down here. I figure he helped gloss things over at the inquest. You didn't get much from him or his little blackmail racket until he started treating Jimmy Wearing. Then you got interested. Between Kintner and your two club girls, Rosetta and Lupe, you could keep a line on Jimmy—and through him, on the Colonel. What better pipeline could you have than a lush with an ax to grind?"

Delmar folded his arms and began looking bored. "I never cared about Wearing's kid."

"Not for long," I agreed, "because you got lucky. Kintner took a blackmail photo of Monica Wearing. He recognized her as the missing witness from Chicago, and he went to you. Now you really had something. You figured she was working an angle on the old man, and that was something you could use. She could still pin a bribery wrap on you, but only if you went north. And grand juries don't like it when witnesses take a powder, especially in a cop killing. She couldn't be sure there wasn't a warrant out for her. And if she ran, that meant losing her meal ticket. So, you had all you needed to keep her under your thumb."

I paused to be sure it was all sinking in.

"Wearing was getting old. He'd already retired. You could just sit tight until Monica inherited everything. After all, the Colonel wouldn't leave his fortune to Jimmy, and Gabrielle didn't want it. So, by controlling Monica, you could control Wearing's papers. Maybe you could even spread around enough editorial ink to change the right minds and work your way back into the States—your own epitaph for the old man."

Delmar leaned over and spat in the dirt. "This don't mean nothin'. Just dig up the jade."

"Keep your shirt on," I said and motioned toward Benitez. "I'm just getting to the part your friend here is going to like. You let Kintner string Monica along, but then all of a sudden, Jack Springer started nosing around. Somehow, he'd gotten wind of Kintner's little grift, and it wouldn't be long before he connected Kintner to you and then alerted the Colonel. You had to have Springer out of the way. And you couldn't use local talent because that also might get back to the Colonel."

I looked toward Voss. "So, you sent for bright eyes here. It was just bad luck for you that Springer happened to see him on the train and alerted me."

Voss stopped playing with the Luger. He took a step toward me, but Delmar snapped at him. "Not yet, Schizy. Keep a lid on it. You'll get your chance."

Voss stopped grudgingly. He stood, breathing heavily and waving the Luger at me. "That's right," I said. "You don't want to spoil the story. We're just getting to the good part."

I looked back at Delmar. "With Springer suspicious, Kintner started getting edgy. And you couldn't afford to have him rattled. If he got caught and Monica's identity was exposed, the Colonel might divorce her, or she might just blow town. Either way, your whole deal would go down the drain. To make matters worse, a guy named Ordway arrived and met Kintner at the hotel, and that really got you nervous. Kintner might be selling you out. So, as soon as Voss arrived, you sent him to the hotel after Ordway, and the next morning, you had him bump off Jack Springer. Once he'd done that, he was supposed to go and put the hit on Dr. Kintner."

Benitez rubbed his hands together and looked nervously at Delmar. His voice sounded like chalk breaking. *"Senor, ees thees true?"*

Delmar waved a hand in my direction. "Garrett's just blowin' hot air, tryin' to cover for himself. He killed them bums, not me."

I glanced over at Gabrielle. She was looking at me now, more attentive than frightened.

Delmar spat again and glared at me impatiently. "All right, Garrett. What about the jade?"

"That's right," I said. We can't forget the jade. After all, you've made enough mistakes trying to get it."

He snorted and kept glaring.

I went on. "Before Springer died, he must have told Voss about the jade. When you found out what it might be worth, you saw a chance to parlay it for a quick deal with the Mexican authorities. That way, you wouldn't have to wait around while old man Wearing lived out his life. So, you decided to let Kintner live until he could get you the figures. That was your first mistake. Springer's death made Kintner even jumpier. And that's when I started talking to him."

Voss was still waving the Luger and staring at me with the look of a predatory animal. I ignored him and went on talking to Delmar.

"You figured it had to be more than coincidence that I had arrived in town about the same time as Ordway. When I showed up at Kintner's office, you were afraid I'd put pressure on the good doctor and make him spill the beans. So, you had Voss take a pop at me outside the museum. But he couldn't put me away, because Jimmy Wearing was there."

"It's kinda goddamn lucky for you he was," Voss chimed in.

"Yeah. Real lucky," I said. I kept looking at Delmar. "Then you figured that after the shooting, the johns would have me tied up for questioning all night. So, you sent your man here to the motel to make sure Kintner hadn't already given me the jade. That was your second mistake. He annoyed me a little."

Delmar kicked the dirt and snickered just as another gust of wind rippled past. "All right, wise guy. So, how *did* you know Schizy was gonna be at the motel?"

I shrugged. "That part was easy. I saw you putting the squeeze on Kintner in the alley off Verdes Place. Ordway and Springer were both dead. So, I was the only one left who had talked to Kintner and who might know about the jade. At least that's what you thought until I came strolling into El Cotorra Azul and started talking to Rosetta Saens. Trying to buy me off was your way of finding out if I really did have the figures. And when I held out for more money, you were convinced. Then, when I passed out, you had me trailed to Gabrielle's apartment. I wasn't going anywhere for a while, so you sent some boys to rifle my room. Only they came up empty."

He snorted and didn't say anything. I turned up my collar and held up my hand to keep the blowing sand out of my face.

"It must have been about then that *Senor* Benitez here reminded you time was running out. With the heat on, it occurred to you that the girls and I might be in it together, palling around with Jimmy for a blind while we worked a deal with Kintner. That meant one of them had the figures, so you sent Voss out after all three. But even that didn't work. Even with Kintner dead and Rosetta tortured and left to die in an alley by this slack-jawed nut case, you still didn't have the jade. And that was your third mistake, because Lupe disappeared."

Benitez was staring at Delmar now, his mouth hanging open. Delmar just kept looking at me from behind a rising tide of hatred.

"Now, to put it mildly," I went on, "things were getting out of hand. You knew Lupe would find me, and together, we'd skip town. So, you decided on a last-ditch play—you put the snatch on Gabrielle. If I ran out and left her down here, Colonel Wearing would have me run up a flagpole. Well, that's one for you."

I turned to Benitez. "So, what have we got? Blackmail, kidnapping, and murder. How will that rest in Mexico City, *senor?*"

Benitez moved his mouth but didn't speak. He reached out and put a hand on Delmar's arm, but Delmar brushed it away angrily. "Don't listen to him," he rasped. "He's lyin'."

He reached inside his coat and brought out a small automatic. It wasn't the kind that would stop an elephant, but it was more than I wanted to argue with. He pointed it at my stomach.

"Think you're real smart—huh, Garrett? Think you got it all figured out? Well, I didn't do all them killings."

"No?" I said. "Voss didn't break Jack Springer's arms and legs? And he didn't carve Rosetta up with a knife and then strangle her?"

Voss jumped forward and waved the Luger only a foot from my nose. "Just like I'm gonna do ta you." I kept looking at Delmar. "You're not hard to figure. Punks like you never are."

He started to say something, but Benitez grabbed his arm again. "*Senor,* please."·

"Save your breath," I said. "You're in it to stay. He can't let us go now—any of us. We know too much. Once he gets the other figure, it's curtains. Then if your people ask questions, he tells them you got dusted off by some lonesome private dick, one who was just scraping the edge of the law. And if they've got the jade, they won't give a damn."

I must have been the last thing Benitez saw. Delmar brought the barrel of the automatic hard against the side of his head, and Benitez went down in a heap.

Gabrielle made a little yelping sound and threw her hands up over her mouth. She started toward me, but Delmar grabbed her by the arm and pressed the automatic into her side.

"No more funny stuff," he hissed at me. "Let's have it."

I took a step toward him. "What about my dough?'

Delmar twisted up his face and squinted at me. His voice had that straining sound of desperation. "Listen, Garrett. I don't know what your game is here, but…"

"Hold it, boss." Voss stepped over in front of me and held up the Luger again. This time, he pulled out the empty clip, looked at It, and threw it on the ground. "I thought it was too easy," he said. "Lemme look him over again."

He patted me down once more, this time finishing the job. When he got to my sock, he pulled out the knife. Then he straightened up slowly, deliberately, grinning and laughing his empty weasel laugh. "One last trick, huh?"

I started to say something to Delmar, but I never got it out. A bomb exploded somewhere in my head as Voss lashed the barrel of the Luger across my face. I sprawled in the dirt, rolled over, and came up spitting blood. I worked my way up onto all fours and shook my head.

The wind howled past me, carrying Gabrielle's voice. "Michael!"

As I started to get up, Voss planted his foot in my left side, and I went down again. My ribs were screaming, and something warm and wet was oozing under my shirt. I gritted my teeth, rolled over once more, and came into a crouching position on my haunches. It took almost everything I had.

Voss was standing over me now, a snub-nosed revolver resting easily in his hand. Even in my condition, at a guess, I figured it was loaded. Delmar hauled Gabrielle over and stood directly in front of me. The muzzle of his automatic was under her chin, pressing into the soft flesh of her throat. Her eyes held something I had never wanted to see there—terror.

"Get the picture, Shamus?" Delmar said. "Now, hand it over."

"Oh, hell," I groaned and pointed up the side of the canyon. "It's up in those rocks."

"Where?"

"Where you'll never find it," I said. "I'll have to go and bring it down."

Delmar took a step back without releasing Gabrielle. He nodded to Voss. "Go with him, Schizy."

I struggled up on my feet and managed not to fall over. My eyes were watering, and I was light-headed. I wiped a handful of blood off my chin and squinted at Gabrielle.

She swallowed hard. "Michael, don't. He won't kill me."

Delmar laughed. "He knows better, sister. One quick move from him, and you're old news." He turned to me. "Now, get going."

I turned and slowly started up the slope toward the pointed rocks, with Voss trailing behind. The wind was racing now, and the blowing sand tore into my face and neck. I squinted up the slope. I could barely see the rocks.

About halfway there, another heavy gust hit us. I stumbled and then felt the gunman's big hand in the middle of my back. He shoved me forward, and I landed on my face in the sand and gravel. "C'mon, big mouth," he sneered. "It's gonna be a pleasure puttin' you under."

I made the last ten yards on my hands and knees. At the pointed rocks, I stopped and turned and then just sat there facing back down the slope. Delmar had moved around to the front of the Buick, still clutching Gabrielle. They were only dim figures in the blowing sand.

Voss stepped up and kicked me hard in the shin. "C'mon. Quit the stall."

"Give me a break," I said. "I've got to rest."

"Yeah." He laughed. "You're gonna rest, all right."

I kept looking down toward the Buick, measuring the distance. It was a good thirty yards. Not an easy shot, even without the storm. And I'd have to do it on instinct. There wouldn't be time to aim. Maybe Delmar wouldn't hear the shooting. Maybe he'd think it was Voss finishing me off. Maybe not. I figured I'd have a second, possibly two. And there was always the chance I'd hit Gabrielle. I licked my lips. My mouth was as dry as the canyon floor.

"C'mon, c'mon." Voss kicked me again.

I got up and moved behind the rocks, and started poking the gravel. "It's right here. Just let me dig it up."

I eased the bag out of the hole and loosened the drawstring. I put my hand inside and held it up in front of me and felt my fingers slide around the grip of the .45. Then I took a slow breath and heard the click of the revolver above my head.

I looked up and saw Voss holding the snub-nose. The hammer was drawn back, and he was aiming the gun at the middle of my face. He leered at me from behind it. "Here's yours, Garrett."

I fired through the bag and shot him twice in the stomach. He reeled backward, dropping his gun and clutching at his middle with both hands. He looked down in disbelief at the welter of blood that began rushing out through his fingers. Then he rolled his eyes and toppled over like a falling tree. I didn't wait for him to go down.

In just a couple of pulse beats, I had the .45 out of the bag and leveled at Delmar. I had a sensation of squeezing the trigger when it seemed as if lightning hit the canyon rim just above me. There was a brilliant flash and an explosion like a D-Day barrage. I could see a body lifted off its feet and thrown over the hood of the Buick. The other just slumped to the ground.

I ran down through the rocks toward the Buick to see which one I'd shot. Gabrielle was doubled over on the ground in front of the car. Her face was buried in her arms. She was sobbing. I helped her up, and she flung her arms around my neck and kept on sobbing.

"Are you alright?" I asked. "Are you hurt?"

She shook her head and held on to me. I didn't mind.

A shout from behind me caught my attention, and I turned around. A man was standing on the canyon rim, waving his hat back and forth above his head, almost like a semaphore. He disappeared, and in something less than a minute, a blue Ford coupe nosed through the opening at the far end of the canyon, cruised quietly up next to the Buick, and stopped.

Sheriff Stonebreaker got out and walked over to us, waving a pearl-handled Colt with a barrel the size of a shinbone. "You folks all right?" he drawled.

I looked at him dumbly. "I think so."

He walked around to the other side of the Buick and looked down at what used to be Rudy Delmar. Without even a ripple in his expression, he turned and spat out a long stream of tobacco juice. He took a quick look at Benitez, then returned to the front of the car and surveyed me with a faint smile.

"Don't figure he ever knew what hit him," he said. He reached out and took the gun I was still holding. My fingers seemed almost frozen to it.

He slid out the clip and looked into the breech, then looked up, his smile widening a couple of notches.

"Two bullets fired. And they went into him." He nodded up the hill toward where Voss was lying, then spat out another stream of juice. "Guess I got this feller over here." A hint of mirth edged into his muddy eyes. "Pretty cute trick you pulled, feinting Voss with the empty gun and then that knife. Put him off his guard up there in the rocks. I guess he thought he had you cold."

"He almost did," I said. "What the hell are you doing here?"

He reached into his hip pocket and brought out the same metal flask I'd seen in his office. He opened it. Brushed off the top with his palm and handed it to me. It contained some of the best-bonded whiskey I had ever tasted. I took two quick gulps and gave the flask to Gabrielle. She held it in a pair of trembling hands and took a swig that made her cough.

Stonebreaker took the flask from her. "Easy does it, little lady." He tipped his head back and poured a good part of a pint down his gullet. Then he put the cap on returned the flask to his hip pocket, and looked at me.

"Benitez called me from the Parrot. He was there when you talked to Delmar. Once the meeting was arranged, he excused himself, made a quick call, and filled me in on the setup."

"So, you and Benitez were working together?"

He nodded. "Almost as soon as you hit town. You see, the Colonel had worked out a plan with the Mexican government. He agreed to turn over the Marina Jade in return for their help in trapping Delmar, getting him to commit a crime on Mexican soil."

"And I was the bait?"

"Yup." He chuckled. "Ya know, it was kind a fun traillin' you around. Even got in a little target practice at the doc's house, keepin you from walkin' into that lug." He motioned toward Voss again. "Only one thing went wrong." He winked at me. "You were the one who was supposed to be kidnapped."

I was about to tell him what I thought of the Colonel's plan when a couple of squad cars rumbled into the canyon, sirens blaring. A handful of Mexican cops scrambled out of the first car and began attending to Benitez. Behind them, three men got out of the second car. Sanchez and Jimmy rushed over to Gabrielle, with Randolph following at a discreet distance.

After making sure Gabrielle was unhurt, Sanchez looked at Delmar, then went up the hill and inspected Voss. He came back down the hill and spoke to the sheriff.

"Both dead. Now I say we lock up Garrett and throw the key away."

"Isn't this out of your jurisdiction?" I said.

He leaned forward and glowered at me. "I ought to break your goddamn neck."

I reached up and rubbed that same neck. "Why not? It's about the only thing that isn't already broken."

Stonebreaker moved over and stepped in front of Sanchez. "Simmer down, Vic. We can close the book on all these killings now. And Garrett didn't do so bad...for a city feller."

He turned and winked at me again and led Sanchez over to where the Mexican cops were talking with Benitez. The man was on his feet now, jabbering about bad *hombres* and *pistolas*.

I lit a cigarette, listened to the usual long-winded explanations, and looked up at the night sky. The storm was mostly gone, and some high stars were showing. One of them winked at me, as if it knew something I didn't. I wouldn't be surprised.

Without being noticed, I gathered up the Jade Princess and the green-handled knife that had fallen next to the Buick. Then I leaned against the hood of the car and listened to my jaw and my ribs singing a chorus of pain. Finally, Sanchez broke from the crowd and came over to me.

"We're taking Gabrielle and *Senor* Benitez to the hospital," he said. "You'd better come too."

I shook my head. "I'm going back with Randolph and Jimmy. I have to see a man about a statue."

Chapter Twenty-Eight

T he lights were on in Wearing Manor. Against the backdrop of the mountain, the louvered doors in the middle of the balcony looked like the center of a stage with the curtain drawn, waiting for the play to start. As I followed Randolph and Jimmy up the walk, a soft breeze tugged at the jacarandas. It had become a nice night, but I didn't have much feeling for it. I didn't have much feeling left for anything.

We went inside, and Randolph disappeared through one of the doors past the entrance. I followed Jimmy into the main hall. We were greeted by a matronly old woman in a maid's uniform who smiled as we approached.

"Mr. James, Mr. Garrett. You're expected."

I gave her my hat and followed Jimmy up the stairs. Just at the top, he stopped and spoke to me in a grudging whisper.

"The red carpet treatment. He must be pretty high on you now. What are you going to tell him?"

I didn't answer. The door to the office was open. We went in.

Colonel Wearing was sitting behind the desk, wearing a robe and pajamas and grinning like a well-fed cat. Monica was seated to his left, legs crossed, hands folded demurely in her lap. Her purse was on the floor next to her chair. She smiled politely as Jimmy went over and slumped into a chair at the other end of the desk out of the way. I just stood in the middle of the room.

The Colonel rose slowly and offered me a crusty smile. "Well, Mr. Garrett. Despite everything, you've done rather well. Jesse Stonebreaker phoned me from the hospital. He told me everything that happened in the canyon. *Senor*

266

Benitez is going to be fine, and so is Gabrielle. I'm afraid Victor Sanchez is rather upset with you, but I'll handle him." He leaned forward in his chair and wrinkled his forehead. "Jesse says you saved my daughter's life."

"No more than he did."

His smile broke into a four-star grin. "You're too modest."

Monica caught sight of the welt on the side of my face. "Mickey, are you alright?"

"I'm here," I said tersely. "That's enough."

The Colonel motioned across the desk toward one of the empty chairs. "Please, sit down."

"I'll stand," I said. "I only came to return something. Then I'll be running along."

I reached inside my coat and brought out the sack with the Jade Princess. I took out the figure and placed it in the middle of the desk. "There was only one," I said. "But I think you knew that."

He looked hungrily at the little statue for a moment, then looked up at me, a glint of conspiracy showing in his eyes. He sat down, pulled out the deep drawer to his right, and brought out another cloth sack. From this, he took a second statue and placed it on the desk next to the Princess. It was the Jade Prince.

Colonel Wearing leaned back in his chair and sat admiring the figures for a long time. Finally, his voice came out, wrapped in a tone of mystic satisfaction.

"Magnificent, isn't it? The power of the Aztecs? The legend says that destruction waits for anyone who tries to possess these figures and doesn't return them to the proper hands."

"And that's what you had in mind for Rudy Delmar."

He nodded slowly. He spoke, as if to someone far away. "I knew it would happen. His greed and his lust for power would be his downfall. I knew he could not stand against the forces of history."

Suddenly, he came back from his reflections and looked at me sharply, a cunning smile dancing at the corners of his mouth. "You really are quite clever, Mr. Garrett. How would you like to work for me?"

"Doing what?"

He shrugged. "Whatever I need done. I've been looking for a man who can take charge, who is strong and clever. Someone who can think for himself and who can be as ruthless as the situation demands. I know Gabrielle has an interest in you. I'm sure we can make some…arrangement."

I shot a quick look at Jimmy. His gaze wavered between his father and me, and his eyes held a blend of anger and suspicion.

"I don't think so," I said. "I've had enough of your arrangements for one trip."

"But surely an intelligent man like you…"

An intelligent man like me knows better than to hang around here and become just another figure in your collection."

Monica leaned forward in her chair, but she didn't say anything.

The Colonel put up his hand and looked at her calmly. "It's all right, my dear." He turned back to me, his smile becoming just the least bit sour. "Is there something else, Mr. Garrett?"

"Only that you can quit patronizing me," I said. "I'm not all that clever. And no one could be as ruthless as you've been. But I'm just clever enough to have figured most of it out. And the way I see it, history won't last long enough for you and me to wind up on the same side."

"Really," he said acidly.

"That's right," I said. "Let me add it up for you. Four people murdered, a couple more beaten up, and your own daughter hung out as bait for a vicious killer. All of it because of your arrangement."

His features turned suddenly sour. "I'll admit that Gabrielle's abduction was…a miscalculation. But I would never have knowingly put her at risk. And surely you can't blame me for the deaths of those others."

"I blame you for the whole damn business," I snapped. "None of it would have happened except for your arrogance and pride and your insistence on coming out on top."

Monica broke in. "Mickey, please."

Colonel Wearing put up his hand again. "It's all right. Let him go on."

Monica settled back in her chair, folded her hands, and watched him uneasily. He kept looking at me, a little warily now.

"Very well, Mr. Garrett," he said. "You seem to have something on your mind. I suggest that you get on with it."

"It's not much of a story," I said. "Nothing history is apt to care about. It's an all-too-common yarn, full of blood and cunning and the kind of hate that grows between enemies who see each other in the mirror every day. And it's about money and power and people being used."

I stopped and lit a cigarette. The Colonel covered me with an attentive stare while his wife kept watching him. Jimmy didn't watch anybody. He just sat motionless, gazing down at the desk.

"Your Deputy Sheriff Sanchez figured to use me as bait to trap a thug. Since Sanchez couldn't cross the border officially without being invited. I was supposed to poke around for him. Maybe I could uncover something big enough to get Delmar extradited. It wasn't much of a plan, but at least Sanchez was honest enough to tell me about it." I shrugged. "Maybe he shouldn't have because, without knowing it, he almost gave your game away. You were planning to do the same thing. I wasn't your first choice, of course. Maybe if I had been, a couple of lives could have been saved."

I took another drag and watched the Colonel settle uncomfortably in his chair. He seemed to know what was coming. I went on.

"Like a lot of people coming to the end of the string, you decided it was time to square accounts. Only with you, that didn't mean little things like covering debts or seeing that your insurance was paid up. It meant big things, like pride and revenge. And your biggest piece of unfinished business was Rudy Delmar. You'd had it in for him ever since he pulled the trigger on a Chicago policeman. A man named Wallis. I don't know the connection, but I don't figure it was any accident that the story in your paper after the inquest was also written by someone named Wallis."

He nodded again, a hint of resignation in his eyes. "Sidney Wallis was my best friend. We worked together on the paper in Chicago ever since I was a boy. He was honest and incorruptible—a first-class newspaperman. And his son Edward was one of a kind. It was as if he belonged to both Sidney's family and mine. One day, he would have been police chief, and more. But he insisted on working his way up through the ranks. He took it upon himself to try that undercover assignment. When he was killed, I grieved for Edward and for Sidney...and for myself. It was like losing my own son, even more than if..."

For the first time, Jimmy looked up. The two men stared at each other without speaking. Then the Colonel rubbed his tired, brittle hands together and looked away.

"So, you decided to go after Delmar," I said. "You must have been planning it for a long time. My guess is you came to El Paso just because Delmar was roosting across the border. You knew all about Dr. Kintner from the inquest, and when you found out about his little blackmail sideshow, you decided you could use him. So, you hatched a plan to make Delmar think he was pulling a fast one on you, while you were really leading him into a trap. But first, you had to get his attention. That's why you needed Monica."

The Colonel didn't move. But Monica slowly turned and looked at me, her eyes filling with a kind of fearful recognition.

"It was no coincidence that you met her in Kansas City," I said. "You had your people trace her there. You talked her into marrying you and brought her here. Then, after waiting long enough to appear discreet, you sent her to see Kintner. You knew he wouldn't be able to resist a dish like her. And you counted on him to recognize her from Chicago." I nodded toward Monica. "Well, he did."

Monica's mouth fell open. She stared at her husband. "Stanfield, is this true?"

"My dear," he said weakly. "It's true I sought you out. But that doesn't mean I appreciated you any less."

"You appreciated her, all right," I said. "You knew about her father being killed and how she must have felt about Delmar. After she was on Kintner's book, you told her just to get her to play along. Then, knowing that Delmar was behind Kintner, you gave her the Jade Princess to put up at one of the auctions. That was the real bait. And after it was sold, you had Benitez drop a few hints around the Parrot. But somehow, they didn't take, and you suspected Kintner of copping the jade for himself. So, then you decided to use someone else—an also-ran reporter named Jack Springer. You knew he'd be nosy enough to stir things up. And you didn't care if anything happened to him. So, you had Randolph dig up enough at the paper to get him started, and then you had Monica tell him about the jade."

Before Monica could say anything, the Colonel spoke to me. "Mr. Garrett, is this really necessary?"

I took a long, heavy drag on the cigarette and blew the smoke across the desk at him. "You're a newspaperman. Don't you want the whole story? Springer did. But about the time he started snooping around, you began having trouble with Jimmy. No telling what set him off, but his drinking and carrying on were becoming a distraction. So, you cooked up the phony blackmail caper just to create an excuse to get Jimmy out of the way. You could send him to Denver or Boise or some other place out of sight while you dealt with the imaginary blackmailer. Jimmy might even wind up grateful." I couldn't help snickering. "It might have worked, if I hadn't come to town."

"So far," I said, even with a few hitches, you were still in the driver's seat—or so you thought. But there were already things happening that you hadn't counted on. Those little curves that history throws at you, just to remind you who's boss. And the first involved Gabrielle. She thought your wife was stealing your collection, so she tried to protect you by contacting a friend in the antique business. You didn't know it, but she was acquainted with Willis Ordway, the same character who brought me to town. The cops told you about me and that I knew about the jade. That's why Stonebreaker pretended to be so interested in it—to find out how much I knew. You weren't sure how I fit in, so you fed me the blackmail line, hoping to sidetrack me. That lasted about an hour—until Springer was killed."

Monica leaned forward in her chair again. "Mickey, please. I told you Stanfield was very upset over Jack's death."

"I'll bet he was," I said to her. "Because it put a crimp in his plans. He had figured to use Springer as a decoy, making Delmar think the guy had gotten the jade from Kintner. But that fell through when Springer got wasted. So, then he decided to use me. That's when he had Benitez contact Delmar to offer him a deal. And that's when he sent Stonebreaker out on the trail after me to make sure I lasted long enough for Delmar to be set up."

Colonel Wearing slumped in his chair and eyed me with a murky expression. His lips made idling little movements, but he didn't speak.

"You also hadn't expected me to be so smart and get onto Kintner so fast," I said. "You knew it wouldn't take me long to sniff out his connection to Delmar, so you sent Randolph and Monica down to Juarez just in case. After all, it wouldn't do to have me bumped off in Mexico before you could spring your trap."

I reached down and crushed out my cigarette. The Colonel just sat there, as motionless as a hunk of marble. I took a deep breath and plowed ahead.

"Delmar got the idea that I had the jade, just the way you planned. But you couldn't take a chance on my gumming up the works by going down there again. So, after Monica laced my drink and I obligingly passed out, you had Randolph take me to Gabrielle's apartment. Maybe you thought we'd get interested in boy and girl stuff and be willing to leave town together."

The Colonel growled at me. "Perhaps I *have* been wasting my time on you after all. Perhaps it *was* a mistake throwing you and Gabrielle together."

"It was a mistake, all right. But not the way you mean. While you were thinking you could slip us quietly out of the way without Delmar knowing, one of his boys followed us to her apartment. And that hung a sign on Gabrielle. But you didn't know that, so you had Benitez put the pressure on Delmar by reminding him that the Mexico City deal was no good unless he delivered both figures, and quick. That made him desperate, and he sent his gun-poke Voss out after Kintner and Jimmy's girlfriends, thinking we were all in it together. By the next night, two more people were dead."

Jimmy glared at his father and whispered, almost under his breath. "You son of a bitch."

Monica shifted uneasily in her chair as I started again. "When I came here that afternoon and exposed your phony blackmail setup in front of Gabrielle, that shook you. Suddenly, it was all getting out of your reach. I was suspicious of what Monica was doing, and I was refusing to leave town. Delmar was on the prowl now. And you were starting to worry about the curse on the jade figures you'd been playing with. At that point, you had to get your son and daughter out of harm's way. But it was too late. Delmar's men were waiting for Gabrielle.

I reached for another cigarette and then thought better of it. "From there, you can be thankful for Sheriff Stonebreaker's cool head and steady hand. He's a lot more cop than he likes to let on."

Somehow, Colonel Wearing looked smaller now, pale and shriveled, almost as if he had lost a lot of blood. Maybe he had. Nothing bleeds like wounded pride.

"I'll admit to some errors," he muttered grudgingly. "But you're right. Thanks to Jesse, it all ended well."

I let out a long, slow breath. "Did it? I'm not so sure. Because when you get right down to it, you're no different than Rudy Delmar. You're just breathing, and he's not. Maybe you didn't do the actual killing, Colonel. But those people are all dead because of you."

With a considerable effort, the Colonel pulled himself up out of the chair. He stretched himself up with all the dignity he could muster. "Young man, I've suffered your insolence long enough. No important lives were lost. And you've no right to compare me to that vile gangster. History is well rid of him. Now, I'll thank you to leave my house."

"I'm going," I said. "But I've got something to leave with you before I do." I took out the knife and laid it on the desk next to the figures so he could see the carved handle. "Recognize it?"

A slow horror grew in his eyes. "How did you get this?"

"This is what's really bothered you all along, isn't it? I got it the same way as the others—from your curse. I found it in my bed last night. Tonight, I was supposed to be the third victim. I looked at my watch. "Only it's after sunset, and I'm still standing up. I guess your Aztecs took the night off."

The Colonel leaned over and studied the knife with the same morbid curiosity that pulls people to the scene of a traffic accident. He licked his lips and looked at me. His voice sounded like a coffin lid closing. "How did Delmar know about this?"

"He didn't."

"But you said…"

"I said I was supposed to be the *third* victim. Delmar's man killed Springer and Rosetta Saens, all right—but not the others."

He swallowed hard and licked his lips again. "How do you know?"

"Voss was more than a paid killer,"·I said. "He was a sadistic psychopath. He liked to hurt people before he put them away. I think he meant to kill Ordway and probably Kintner. But both times, he found someone had beaten him to the punch."

He started to protest, but I didn't let him.

"When I found Ordway, I'd just gotten into town. And he'd been dead for at least three hours. I couldn't have killed him, because I was on the train with Jack Springer. And Voss couldn't have killed him for the same reason. He was on the same train. As for Kintner, that just wasn't Voss's style. And it would be too coincidental for two different people to stage two different killings using exactly the same ceremonial pattern. Besides, Delmar said he didn't do all the killings. But he'd practically admitted to two of them. So, why wouldn't he admit to the others? It wouldn't make any difference to him—unless the killings were done by someone else."

"Then who? And why?"

"Who, I'll get to," I said. "Why is for one of the oldest of reasons—jealousy. When Kintner went to see Ordway at the hotel, it wasn't just about the jade or the trumped-up auctions. You see, he and Ordway were more than just business associates. They were lovers. They had been that ever since Kintner started going to Brentwood to sell off his loot. Only Kintner was also involved with someone else, someone who couldn't stand being rejected—again." I shook my head. "Ordway and Kintner weren't killed by Delmar or his hired muscle. They were killed by someone Kintner had loved and then given the gate. Someone who called it 'another tender betrayal.'"

I turned to Jimmy. "Want to tell them about it?"

Chapter Twenty-Nine

The air in the office hung like a shroud, making everything appear motionless and unreal. The slightest sound seemed as loud as a gunshot. Monica slowly got out of her chair and stood next to her husband. The two of them gaped at Jimmy. The Colonel leaned forward on the desk. His mouth barely formed the word "No."

Monica said, "You can't be serious."

Jimmy kept sitting, elbows pressed into the arms of the chair, squeezing his hands together. The skin around his lips was milk-white. He looked at me with the painful defiance of a wounded tiger.

"Go to hell," he muttered.

"I wish there were some other way, kid," I said. "Because, in a certain sense, you're as much a victim as anybody. But only in a certain sense."

The Colonel was glaring at me now, his eyes flaming with anger. "Young man, I'll have your license. It's bad enough to intimate that my son was involved with those...people. But to accuse him of murder—"

"Sure, you can take away my license. But you can't take away all the years you spent hammering at Jimmy, berating him, convincing him he could never live up to your expectations. You made him what he is, Colonel. Out of frustration and resentment, he became everything you hated—weak, undisciplined, and irresponsible. After a while, he even took pleasure in it. It was the only way he had of defying you. But even then, he was afraid of having you know the truth. When he came back from the war, he told everyone that he'd been wounded in the Pacific. Only he never left California. He threw a wing-ding and wound up in the Army hospital at Fort

Ord. Some doctor there called it severe emotional trauma and melancholia. He might have said manic-depressive. But the Army diagnosed Jimmy as diabetic, figured that was enough, and sent him home."

I turned to Jimmy. "I figure your drinking was mostly fake. Nobody on insulin could take that much alcohol and not turn up cold as a clam."

Jimmy sat, squeezing the arms of the chair. He ground his teeth and made soft hissing noises through them. I looked back at his father.

"I also figure you knew or at least suspected. Diabetes was one thing, but breakdowns don't happen in the Wearing family—not when you're protecting a place in history. So, when Jimmy started seeing Dr. Kintner, it seemed like a good way of avoiding notoriety, and you just let it ride. But Jimmy and Kintner became friends...and more. Jimmy found what he thought was love and respect. And he was involved in something he knew you'd despise. He may not have known that Kintner was using him to get a foot into El Paso society so he could line up his blackmail victims." I shrugged. "But even if he knew, it didn't matter—that is, until Kintner recognized Monica, and you started your little game with Delmar and the jade."

The Colonel turned and looked at Jimmy, a disdainful curl tugging at his lower lip. "Of course, I knew what happened in California. And if I had thought Kintner was anything more than a blackmailing quack, I'd have had him run out of town." He paused and then shot an angry glance at me." But that doesn't mean my son is a killer, or a..."

"I'm coming to that," I said. "As it happened, Willis Ordway was one of several California dealers Kintner was using to unload his tainted art objects. And when he started going to Brentwood, he and Ordway discovered they had more in common than just an interest in antiques. So Kintner decided to call it quits with Jimmy. Nothing happened until Gabrielle called Ordway and told him about the auctions. Then he contacted Kintner, learned about the jade, and decided to go to El Paso. Being a serious dealer, he was familiar with the curse, and he was truly frightened. Not just for himself—for Kintner, and for his old friend Gabrielle. So, before he left, he came to see me."

I stopped, pulled out a cigarette, and ran a hand over my ribs. They were starting to hurt again. I twirled the cigarette around in my fingers, just to give them something to do.

"By then," I said, "Kintner had told Jimmy they were washed up, and Jimmy had gone over the edge. He felt used and betrayed, and something inside him must have snapped. It wouldn't have taken much for him to learn about the curse just from poking around in here." I motioned toward the crammed bookshelves. "Checking at the museum would be easy. Eugene Dentin told me someone besides Voss, a young man, had been asking about the jade. And you can pick up these toys anywhere."

I pointed to the knife on the desk. "So, Jimmy decided to use your favorite curse as a dodge while he killed Kintner and his boyfriend. Under the circumstances, it wasn't a bad plan. You'd be so lathered up over your angry Aztecs, you'd never think of looking in your own house. And the cops mostly take their orders from you. They wouldn't get suspicious unless you did."

I turned and looked at Jimmy. "It might have worked, kid. Only you got careless with the girls. You told them the jade was an ancient evil."

Jimmy sat rubbing his hands rhythmically over the arms of the chair. The corners of his mouth parted in a humorless smile. I dropped the unlit cigarette in the ashtray and spoke to him.

"The first thing you had to do was find out who Kintner was seeing. So, you tracked him to Ordway's room at the hotel. Finding a pretext to go in there might have taken some time, but then your father's little scheme played right into your hands. That night, when Randolph and the girls were taking the phony blackmail pictures, you pretended to be drunk. Then, while they were in the lobby and Kintner and Ordway were marching around the halls arguing, you went into Ordway's room and planted one of your green calling cards."

The Colonel tried to interrupt, but I held up my hand and kept talking to Jimmy.

"But you were so steamed up, you didn't wait for sundown. You went back there sometime in the early afternoon. Tommy, the bartender, and

277

Gabrielle both saw you. When Ordway heard your name, he knew you were related to Gabrielle, and he just let you in. That's when you killed him. It had to be you who pushed the bellhop away from the door when he was delivering Ordway's lunch.

"Then you went down to Juarez and took your time being seen with Rosetta and Lupe. You even brought them back to the hotel with you, probably expecting Kintner to show up. But Gabrielle spoiled your plans, so you pretended to pass out." I chuckled. "It wasn't bad acting, but you walked into the bar a little too clear-eyed and a little too upright. You hardly had time to pour the champagne before Gabrielle walked in. Then, all of a sudden, you collapsed with a skinful. For someone your size, you folded up just a little too fast."

Jimmy kept staring at me, his smile slowly growing into a sickish grin. Monica moved over next to her husband and took hold of his arm. His eyes were frozen on Jimmy, and his breath was coming shallow and quick, almost in a deathbed rattle. I looked at them all—a fine family. There was nothing to do but keep going.

"You hadn't counted on having me in the picture," I said to Jimmy. "So, you decided to lay off Kintner until you had a handle on what I would do. But then, when we found Springer dead, that gave you a real jolt. I guess it's a little unnerving to find out there's another killer on the loose. So, you went to see Kintner and tried to patch things up. You were just leaving when I arrived."

Jimmy bared his teeth a little but didn't say anything.

"Kintner must have told you no dice," I said. "He was feeling the heat from Delmar, and his only concern was the jade. After the auction and the shooting at the museum, you knew I was suspicious of Kintner and that I was going to see him again. So, later that night you went to his house and waited for him to come home. He wouldn't have been suspicious of you. By then, he might even have been glad to see you. The two of you could have smoked some of his stinkweed. He might even have offered to write you a prescription for some happy pills. Then, while he was sitting at his desk, you cut his throat and left another knife."

Colonel Wearing sank slowly into his chair and shut his eyes. When he opened them again, they had that faraway look of someone in a trap, sensing there's no way out. Jimmy leered at him, then brought his leer around to me.

"You tell it real good," he said in an almost whisper.

"It gets better," I said. "Yesterday afternoon in this office, you were secretly pleased that your father was upset. He was obviously rattled, and he had no thought that you might be involved in anything. But you were also worried, because you didn't know how much I knew or suspected. So, you decided to make sure of me, just in case. Last night, you came to the hotel after me, only you ran into Randolph and Gabrielle. You couldn't kill me then, so you went into your drunk act again and let Randolph drag you upstairs. You were pretty convincing, but you had more liquor on your clothes than on your breath."

He started to say something, but I waved him off. "You pretended to pass out. Then, while the three of us were talking, you hid another knife under the bed covers. Tonight, you left Randolph and came to my room to finish the job. If Sanchez hadn't been there, you might have tried to kill me. I think after I clipped him, you almost did. But that's when I told you about Gabrielle being snatched, maybe the only person left that you really cared anything about. That snapped you out of it, and you let me go."

I turned and spoke to the Colonel. "Funny how things turn out. In a way, I almost owe my life to Rudy Delmar."

The Colonel slowly reached out and put his hands on the edge of the desk. He squeezed them almost hard enough to break the wood. "This is utterly preposterous. You haven't one shred of proof."

"If you mean proof that would stand up in court," I said, "you're right. But how much proof you need depends on whom you're trying to convince. And I'm pretty simple-minded. You don't need much to convince me."

I turned to Jimmy. "When you came stumbling into my room last night with Randolph, you said I was staying in a dead man's room. How did you know that?"

"I...I guess I read it in the paper."

"Uh-uh," I said. "I saw the paper here the morning after Ordway was killed while I was waiting to see your father. There were just a few lines on the back page. They said Ordway was found on the fourth floor of the hotel. They didn't mention the number of the room."

He hesitated. "Then I heard it from Monica."

Monica shook her head slowly. "No, Jimmy. I knew that a man had been killed. But I never knew the room number."

"Gabrielle and I knew the room number," I said, "and a couple on the hotel staff. Naturally, they were told to keep quiet about it. And the cops wouldn't have told anybody else, except maybe your father."

I turned back to the Colonel. "How about it? Did you tell him?"

The Colonel pursed his lips tightly and drummed his fingers on the desk. He didn't answer.

"I didn't think so," I said. I looked at Jimmy again. "Tonight, when I told you that Kintner was dead, you mentioned his pipe and his imported dope. You couldn't have known that he was a smoker of exotic blends, or what he smoked them in, unless you'd been in his inner sanctum. And that's not a place he would have taken patients."

I leaned against the desk and looked at the Colonel. "It's not much," I said. "Just a couple of slips that might be explained. But put them next to the fact that a man who can't drink because it's poison to him, who doesn't keep liquor in his apartment, suddenly starts hitting the bottle, passing out, and then bobbing up the next day as if nothing had happened. Something a diabetic couldn't do unless he was putting on an act. And no one pretends to keep passing out without a good reason. Next, consider the fact that Kintner had a key to Jimmy's apartment, that he went there freely even when Jimmy wasn't around, that he spent more time there than a doctor needs for house calls, and that he trusted Jimmy enough to leave his art objects there before he took them to California."

I stopped, took a breath, and patted my sore ribs; then I went on. "Finally, consider Jimmy's previous breakdown, his frequent presence at the hotel and at Kintner's office, and the fact that he was unaccounted for at the time of the killings. You don't need a sharp guesser to add all that up to motive and opportunity."

I looked at Jimmy once more. "As for means, I think the cops might do a peroxidase test on that Japanese dagger in your apartment. Even if you tried wiping it clean, it could still show traces of blood."

Jimmy lurched out of his chair and almost screamed at me. "No. I took care of that."

I turned and exhaled and looked out the window. "Uh-huh. Too bad, kid. With enough time and enough booze to wash it down, I could almost feel sorry for you."

Colonel Wearing lowered himself slowly back into his chair. He looked at Jimmy. Then he looked at me. His eyes showed that deadpan mixture of fear and anger that borders on hysteria. Yet his voice was like a pane of glass.

"Mr. Garrett, if you mention one word of what has been said here outside this room, I shall have you put in jail."

"I wasn't thinking of it," I said. "My client's still dead. And roasting your son won't do anything for him. I'm satisfied that you know the truth. That squares things with me, and I think it would with Ordway. He wasn't much, but he deserved at least that.

"So now it's your headache, Colonel. You can keep it hushed, maybe send Jimmy to a clinic and wait until he knocks off someone else. Or you can buy an army of lawyers and plead temporary insanity. Who knows? You might get him off. It's been done before. Personally, I don't much care if Jimmy does time or not. But he might prefer that to spending more of his life with you."

The Colonel rolled his eyes and ground his teeth, and then exploded with rage. He shrieked at Jimmy in a shrill, venomous voice. "You worthless bastard. How could you? You've brought disgrace on me and on my name. I disavow you. I disown you. You'll get nothing. I'll remove you from the family, from history. You're dead. Dead. Do you hear? Now get out. Get out of my sight."

He fell back in the chair, wheezing, while Monica went to him and began loosening his robe.

I looked at Jimmy. He just stood flexing his fingers and grinning. He looked at me, but he didn't see me. He didn't see anything anymore. His eyes were glassy, filled with something that the years had brought to a slow boil. He looked around the room, his head swiveling almost mechanically on his neck. A low gurgling sound came from the back of his throat. I edged toward him, but I was too late.

In an instant, Jimmy's hands were around the Colonel's neck. The old man's eyes bulged, and he waved his hands feebly. Monica yelled and grabbed at Jimmy's arm, but he backhanded her across the face and knocked her into the corner. I made it around the desk in time to catch him by the shoulder. I pulled him back and planted one squarely on the side of his jaw. It was a good punch. I could feel it all the way to the back of my neck. Yet, it hardly budged him.

Jimmy grabbed me by the shirt and, in one motion, heaved me over the corner of the desk. I landed on the arm of a chair and crashed to the floor in the middle of the room. I was dazed, almost numb. I reached out and began pulling myself up on the other chair just as Jimmy reached for the knife on the desk. He grabbed it and brought it up high, poised above his father. A laugh that was almost a scream came from somewhere inside him.

"Now," he yelled.

The shots were no more than little pops, three of them, almost like sticks breaking. Jimmy stepped back, still holding the knife, his head making the same swiveling movements. A dark red stain began to grow on the front of his shirt. Gradually, his arm lowered until it was hanging at his side. Almost by itself, the knife fell on the floor. Jimmy staggered back and fell hard into the chair at the end of the desk. He sat looking at his father. He didn't say anything. His eyes fluttered. His mouth moved. Then he died.

I got up slowly and went over next to Monica. She was standing by the desk, staring at Jimmy. The little bone-handled automatic from her purse was in her hand. I took it and felt her trembling. "I had to," she said. "He...He..." She looked at me, pleading. "I had to."

"I know," I said.

Slowly, Colonel Wearing rose from the chair. He looked at Monica and at me and the gun I was holding. He turned and took a couple of steps toward Jimmy. Then he just stood. Tears came silently down his face. Finally, he turned back, and his eyes fell on the jade figures. He picked them up carefully in both hands and stared at them with dazed eyes. Then he brought his hands up over his head, let out a wail, and smashed the figures to bits on top of the desk.

Chapter Thirty

Gabrielle stood at the foot of the stairs in the main hallway of the house the following afternoon. She looked pale and drawn, and she showed signs of missing sleep. But she was still functioning.

"I just can't believe it," she said. "Poor Jimmy. How he must have suffered."

"Try not to remember him that way," I said. "What happened to him was the result of things that started a long time ago, things you had nothing to do with. Don't think about what he became. Think about what he was—the brother who cared about you."

She looked away. "Yes. Thank you."

She let out a long sigh. "I guess I owe Monica an apology. She saved my father's life. She's been up there with him ever since it happened."

She looked up the stairs for a moment toward a small hallway on the side where the Colonel's bedroom was. There was something wistful in her expression. Finally, when she turned back to me, her voice had picked up a sharp edge.

"You didn't have to do what you did. Father didn't have to be put through this. And Jimmy didn't have to die."

"Neither did Ordway," I said. "I didn't make anything happen. I only sped it up."

She sighed again. "Yes, I know. Do you think Willy knew? I mean about the blackmail. Do you think he was in on it?"

I shook my head. "He didn't seem the type. Blackmail isn't for the fainthearted."

"When did you suspect that he was involved with Kintner?"

"I started to get suspicious when I realized that you hadn't told him about the jade or the auction arrangements. No one else in your family or at the museum would have told him. That meant it had to be someone who was attending. Then, when you told me about Ordway—about how he was, I started imagining him and Kintner together. They had the same interests, and they seemed to have the same habits. Once you get an idea like that, you begin to see things that you otherwise wouldn't notice—things like lavender cigarettes and a Brentwood phone number."

"I see." She pressed her hands together and looked down at the floor. "What will you do now?"

I shrugged. "Go back to L.A. and try to earn a living. Sanchez is driving me down to the station."

She looked up quickly, with something that, on a better day, could have been a smile. "I heard what you did to him. I guess you're lucky to be leaving in one piece."

"I guess."

The almost-smile drifted away, and she held me with her eyes. "Michael, I'm terribly confused. I'm grateful that you saved me from those men. And I suppose it's unfair. But I can't help thinking that Jimmy would still be alive if you hadn't come here. With everything that's happened, I just…I don't even know how I feel anymore. Yesterday in the apartment and last night I thought…" She shook her head. "Now I just don't know."

"Don't fret over it," I said. "And don't try to make something out of a couple of kisses and breakfast. In a week, you'll be back defending the peons, and I'll be less than a memory."

She moved close and put a hand on my arm. "Michael, in the canyon, when you kept asking Delmar for the money—that was a trick, wasn't it? I mean, you're really not like that, are you?"

"Try me."

She tried to smile, but she couldn't quite get it out. Almost as a reflex, she stepped back, bit her lip, and took another long look in the direction of the Colonel's bedroom. Then slowly, deliberately, she turned and looked back at me. Her tired blue eyes projected a distant satisfaction. "He needs me now."

Gabrielle turned and started up the stairs. At the top, she gave me a fleeting look back over her shoulder, then disappeared into her father's room. I knew I'd never see her again.

I found Randolph at the front door, holding my hat as if someone had been sick in it. I took it from him and put it on.

"Thanks, chief. Come and see me sometime. We'll tip some firewater."

His cool black eyes seemed to push me away. "I think not." He turned and quietly shut the door in my face.

Sanchez was waiting for me by the front gate. I got into the patrol car, and we drove back down the mountain and through the hot, dusty streets toward the station. We didn't talk. I just sat and stared out the window at the inevitable ball of tumbleweed rolling unconcerned into the distance. People don't affect the desert. It just turns its back and goes its own way, alone and empty.

The train was close to leaving when I boarded. I walked up the aisles past no more than a dozen passengers, but that seemed like too many. I kept walking until I came to a Pullman, where there was nothing but empty seats. I flopped down next to a window and took my hat off, and shut my eyes. The car lurched forward a few times and then fell into a gentle rocking motion as we pulled out of the station and headed west.

I settled back in the seat and tried to remember the quiet atmosphere of Lacy's, where the music was as cool as the drinks. Somehow, I couldn't get it into focus. I sat up and glanced out the window, and took a last lingering look at the desert.

Finally, I thought about Colonel Wearing and about history: Maybe there really was something to the story about the Marina Jade. Maybe there really was a curse after all. Only Ordway knew for sure. And he wouldn't tell.

Acknowledgements

David and to Jennifer and Jon.

About the Author

Richard Blaine first wrote about Michael Garrett in the 1980s. As a part-time author, he also consulted with various companies and helped them produce documentation to enable staff members to understand how to use their computer systems effectively. Subsequently, Blaine went to graduate school and then became a mental health counselor, specializing in trauma and anxiety-based disorders. He had a very busy practice, lasting for twenty-five years, from which he then retired and returned to his earlier love of writing historical detective novels.

Also by Richard Blaine

The Silver Setup — A Michael Garrett Mystery